Dear Shadows

A novel by
MAX EGREMONT

Secker & Warburg
London

First published in England 1986
by Martin Secker & Warburg Limited
54 Poland Street, London W1V 3DF

Copyright © Max Egremont 1986

British Library Cataloguing in Publication Data
Egremont, Max
    Dear shadows.
    I. Title
    823′.914[F]   PR6055.G/

ISBN 0–436–14160–4

Set in 11/12 Linotron Bembo Medium, by Deltatype,
Ellesmere Port
Printed by St Edmundsbury Press
Bury St Edmunds, Suffolk

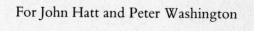

For John Hatt and Peter Washington

I

Some evenings, when I was alone in the flat, I could hear the noise of the young couple on the floor below. She cried and screamed, almost shrieked, as if she was being murdered or at least violently assaulted. At first I thought I could detect the sound of breaking china, the bumps of overturning furniture, a great crash as their double bed gave way.

I say double bed. In fact I had no idea if they possessed a double bed or not because I never went into their flat. Occasionally we would meet on the stairs and I would remember the noise; also the way in which the cries seemed to mix pleasure and pain in a curious variety. Neither he nor she looked especially sensual or odd. She was small, too fat for her tight jeans; he was also small, with dark hair and a beard, rather wiry. We smiled at each other in an embarrassed way.

Christina maintained a separate establishment but it was our custom to spend one or two nights a week together. When she came to me, she would often hear the noise from below as well. It made her laugh. 'I suppose that's what they call passion,' she said.

But what am I saying? Christina has left me; I am alone. I no longer have the right to refer to 'we' – 'we' cannot come to dinner, 'we' are going away to Italy on holiday, 'we' spent a quiet evening at home together. This is over. She has gone off with another man: a person called David from the smart auction house where she has worked for some sixteen years.

I never married Christina. We were together for almost ten years. Now I am fifty, she about thirty-five. Christina. She had become such a familiar presence. Yet perhaps I had been on the verge of ruining her life. She had chosen to stay with me for far too long. I had offered her friendship, someone to be with in the evenings, at weekends and on holidays. Once or twice I had tried to think that this might be transformed into something more, but the illusion had always failed to last.

And what had broken it, what had caused me not to speak the words that – I knew – must have led to marriage? However much I might have told myself that her chief interest was her work I had understood that Christina would certainly have accepted my proposal. I think I had been held back by the notion of the start of a fatal momentum – the irrevocable coming together of our lives into one house, one entity, one name, another family: then an extinction of the past, a deadening of memory.

No. I had hesitated. She had left.

The noise of the couple downstairs made me think of my first wife Laura, of one night in our first home.

She had come in once while I was having a bath. We used to talk about the importance of having a comfortable bathroom, not a great cavern of cold stone and white tiles like the one in her parents' house in the West Country. And it is an important place: a place for thought. Then, as now, I was in the habit of treating myself to long lukewarm baths. I have always tried to work towards a condition in which each thought, each opinion, that I have can exist on its own, in isolation, so that it is nothing to be ashamed of; also to feel that if all these were linked the resulting pattern should produce a portrait of a reasonable man. Sometimes I feel I have, for a moment, achieved this; and such moments occur with greater frequency in the bath than at any other time.

That evening we were going out to dinner, perhaps with my Parkin cousins who have made a name for themselves in the wine trade. It was warm, one of those thick summer nights when London becomes like a tropical city. I was lying in the tub, trying to organise my thoughts, to allow the cool water to calm me. We had only been married a few months. We had not yet moved to Campden Hill and were still more or less camping in a flat in South Kensington near the Victoria and Albert Museum. That flat! It was draughty, dull, papered in varying shades of green and brown; the curtains were thick masses of sensible material that would last for years to depress generations of tenants of the old woman who lived on the next floor and owned the building. The old woman had liked Laura.

I looked up at the ceiling where there was a brown patch, a sign of damp. Overhead was the old woman's drawing-room. Laura used to make silly jokes about incontinence which embarrassed me at parties. The patch was a fixed point around which, I thought, the different portions of my consciousness could come together. Yet this was nonsense. I twisted my body a little in the bath, pleased by the cooling effect of the water, and wondered why rationality seemed to leave me for long, long stretches of time.

Laura. She came in, wearing a light-blue silk dressing gown. Her light-brown hair was long in those days; through the dressing gown her presence seemed to burst into every part of that dingy room. She looked at me, turned away as if shy of what ought to have been a natural encounter: that of husband and wife preparing to go out to dinner with some old, rather dull friends. She stood by the basin, which was at one end of the bath, so that I was confronted with her figure from the side. She opened the small cupboard that had a mirror covering its door and took out a small bottle. She smeared some of the liquid from the bottle on to a piece of cotton wool and began to dab her forehead. 'My face feels as if it's on fire!' she said.

Now, years later, I see that there was no need for her to have come in, no need for her to have forsaken her dressing table with its unruly array of creams, lotions, lipsticks and powders. Even if she had wanted that particular bottle of cooling liquid from the bathroom cupboard, she could have collected it quickly, smiled at me for an instant and gone back to the bedroom to dab or rub or whatever she had wished to do.

3

That evening, however, I was above – or beneath – such thoughts, for she was there, leaning slightly into the mirror, her right hand moving quickly over her cheeks and forehead. My mind – with all its laborious processes of alignment and consolidation – was jolted into the immediacy of her, the proximity of something that went straight to the instincts rather than lingering gently among logical thought or possibilities.

She paused, threw the cotton wool briskly into the lavatory. 'Simon,' she said. 'It's so hot. Why?'

I remember the first time I realised how ill Laura was. It was some four or five years ago. And I saw, from that moment, that she could not be cured by any ordinary treatment or clinical diagnosis. She had decided to give up, to surrender her life.

We had lunch together, to discuss our children. At that stage Angelica was still at university and Edward in the army, on the point of leaving for Northern Ireland. There were various matters outstanding to do with their finances, for both were shortly to come into the money that Bill, Laura's second husband, had made over to them. Bill was away, in Tokyo from what I remember, and had left the documents with his wife.

We had not met for some time so it was a shock when she came into the drawing-room of their Chelsea house wearing dark glasses and limping, a neat, polished stick loose in her right hand. A silent Philippino manservant had greeted me, dressed in a butler's black coat and striped trousers. I was Laura's guest; quickly she offered me a drink while pouring out something for herself.

She was not obviously drunk, yet seemed vague. The drawing-room had few signs of human habitation. The neat formation of the furniture and arrangement of expensive bibelots on the highly polished side tables were lifeless, redolent of an interior decorator's show room. Then Laura caught her stick on the edge of the carpet, stumbled, allowed me to steady her by clasping the bottom part of her arm. We were on our way to the sofa, carrying our drinks, both of which spilled slightly on to the light green fitted carpet to leave dark spreading stains.

First we looked through the documents to do with the children's trusts. Bill had left a typed explanation, each section headed with an underlined sentence. It was beautifully clear. Her hands shook as she handed the papers across to me. That day she was wearing a dark blue suit, a cream silk blouse and a small sapphire brooch pinned at her neck: the clothes of a rich elegant woman. But the dark glasses and the stick told of hidden anxieties, faltering resolve . . .

The house was too hot, even for the London winter. In the small dining-room, at the round table laid for two, the Philippino served us and I was uncomfortable, almost wanting to take off the jacket of my suit. The room was dark, painted a curious mixture of light blue and gold; the net curtains kept the light at bay. I noticed three pictures: overcleaned early nineteenth-century views of harbours and ports, the sails of ships rising above busy quays and low customs houses. And, over the tomato and prawn salad, I asked if her eyes were giving her trouble.

'Oh these?' She touched the dark glasses. 'No, that's simply because I can't bear the glare. It gives me a headache. My eyes aren't too good! But Billy reads to me: all the old favourites – Hardy, Henry Williamson, Hudson.' It seemed grotesque: to hear those names in this place and to imagine Bill stumbling through lyrical evocations of the English countryside. I almost laughed. 'No, my bloody leg's the bore. They say it's gout – but I don't believe them. Billy's found this wonderful new man in Geneva. We're going there next week.'

She was drinking, I could see: either drinking or on drugs of some sort. The loss of the old quickness, the energy, told me that. Words dripped out of her. I asked about Bembridge and the sailing. 'Billy takes us over to France sometimes,' she said in a lacklustre way. 'It's lovely. You must come to see us again, Simon. Bring Christina. What are you up to?'

I saw that she was tired already. I spoke, perhaps too much, in order to relieve her. Williams had just started with us, had just become my boss. So I described the difficulties at work, my doubts as to how I might survive. She knew, of course, that I was still with the same firm, the publishing house that

5

bears my name. 'And George Mason is leaving,' I said. 'You remember George. I've only got Joan to support me now – most of the rest of them are new. But I'll fight for what I believe in!'

'Poor Simon. What a bore!' The sympathy was remote. I wondered if she had heard my words, if she was merely reacting to the whining tone of my voice. 'Do you have to go away much?' The question seemed to have little to do with what I had been saying. 'I was thinking of Christina . . . Billy's always away. Tokyo, Frankfurt, Johannesburg. Then the factory tours in this country: Coventry, Sheffield, Glasgow, Dundee, Cardiff.'

'Does that worry you?' I wanted to know.

'Well, he can't come to any harm. We have weekends together – most weekends. And look what he's given me!' She must be drunk, I decided. Surely to make such a tactless crude remark she must be drunk; and as she attempted a wave of her hand to encompass the small dark room, the silver pheasants on the table, the cut crystal glasses, the harbour views, the graceful sideboard in the style of Chippendale, the white panelled door shutting behind the noiseless Philippino, her body lurched over the side of her chair. Then she coughed harshly, grasped a tumbler of water with both hands and greedily took several gulps.

I tried to ignore what she had become. She was worried. 'Oh God, Simon, can't you do anything about this brute?' she said. 'This Williams!' Some drops of water had fallen on to her blue jacket; the stains glared at me. 'I remember that dear old boy – what's his name? Mason? Such a cuddly old thing, and you worked so well together. Why can't people leave things alone? Why?'

I waited, then mentioned the children. 'Angelica's going through an awkward stage,' she said. 'Sort of anti-establishment, don't you think? Billy says it should go when she has to start work. Edward has taken to the army like a duck to water.'

Was this the same woman? Once she had stood barefoot on the sands. She stumbled on the way to the hall to say goodbye. 'Simon . . .' Her stick stopped a fall; this time I did not have to help. 'We must keep in touch. I do want to know about your

6

work.' We kissed. Her mouth, a smear of pale lipstick, left a stain on my cheek.

My father had enjoyed speaking to us about our forebears. This was one of his passions; he claimed that most Scotsmen were fascinated by the history of their families. His book – in two volumes – on his own can still be found in second-hand bookshops, available at a very low price.

How much hard and boring work he must have put into tracing these ancestors! Apart from the one who came to London and started the publishing company they were neither interesting nor distinguished. My father had a map of the country round Peebles where his brother and sister-in-law still lived in the house that had been built by his grandfather at the end of the last century. To him the place was sacred, the scene of his boyhood, the family home. To me it seemed bleak, unwelcoming, impregnated with the hard existences of the crofters, farmers and ministers of the Kirk who made up the successive branches of our family tree.

'Darling,' Laura used to say, 'don't be too hard on the old boy. It's his life.'

I ought to have been more interested. For somewhere amongst those dour dim figures lie the seeds of my own chaos.

A publisher should not write. It is absurd. But I am not writing. I am merely trying to jot down what has happened to me. It may help to restore some sort of order to my life.

I work in a publishing firm that bears my family's name, although it no longer has any connection with us, apart from the fact that I sit on its board. After the war, my father and his older brother accepted a take-over offer. Now the company is part of the Lindsay Group: a large corporation involved in all sorts of enterprises ranging from motor car components to men's underwear.

I believe that it was a part of the terms of the original merger that members of the family should be given preferential treatment if they applied for jobs with the firm. Certainly I cannot think of any other reason why the management of the time should have taken me on as a trainee. I suppose I thought of myself as a reasonably literate young man. But my qualifications were hardly startling: national service in the army and a second-class honours degree in Modern History.

The firm's office is in a small street in Bloomsbury. My working day begins with a quick breakfast of cereal, coffee and two pieces of toast: then a short walk up Campden Hill to Notting Hill Gate to take the Central Line to Tottenham Court Road. I have a season ticket, so I do not have to wait at the booking office or fiddle with the automatic ticket machines; and if the Underground system grows a little dirtier, a little less reliable, a little more expensive, a little less tolerable with each succeeding year, I am philosophical enough to be able to put up with such a process of relatively gradual decay.

Unlike many others on their way to their offices, I do not bury my head in a newspaper. Indeed if I can get a seat, which I often cannot, I like to observe the other passengers in the carriage. I do not wonder about their lives – as imaginative people are supposed to do – but note their physical appearances, their eccentricities of dress or expression. There is hardly any talk at this hour. If ever a couple – perhaps two friends from the same office – laugh or chatter together, the noise sounds out of place, almost unnatural, in the crammed over-heated train.

Once, some two years ago, while embarking upon this morning journey, I mistook a woman in a white scarf with her back to me at one end of the platform at Notting Hill Gate station for Laura. She seemed to be alone and was looking down the track towards the entrance to the tunnel. I moved towards her, thinking I must speak – just a few words about the children, a few courtesies, even an enquiry about Bill. Then the woman turned. She was pretty, younger than Laura. If I had accosted her – smiling shyly, leaning forward to give my ex-wife a kiss – she would have jumped, put up her hands, perhaps screamed. Yet surely my outward appearance would have saved me: the appearance of a respectable man in a grey suit, who carried an umbrella and an aged brown briefcase, who wore a dark overcoat with a velvet collar that is almost twenty years old.

Sometimes the train stops for a minute or two between stations. The halt irritates me. If it is prolonged, I suffer a hint of anxiety, a momentary vision of forced camaraderie. In an emergency the passengers would begin slowly to establish contact; first to voice previously suppressed fears; to encourage the claustrophobic, the old, the pregnant, the sick and, ultimately, the hysterical; then to search among ourselves for a leader. At last there is a jolt; the train moves on, the routine returns.

From the Tottenham Court Road station I have a walk of about five minutes to my office, which is in a street near the British Museum. This part of London has an air of slight bohemianism: not smart, still holding on to its character despite the ravages of development around Holborn and London University. Although the reverse of bohemian myself, I have grown fond of my place of work.

I walk fast. In winter, if it is cold, I wear a black fur hat. I have taken to this in the last few years after reading an interesting article in the *Sunday Telegraph* about loss of body heat through the head. In winter I also wear a woollen scarf – given to me by Christina one Christmas – and the dark overcoat with the velvet collar that I have mentioned. Generally, at all times of the year, I carry an umbrella.

I walk fast, to take exercise. Decay must be avoided. Once it sets in, there is but a straight downhill path to incapacity, loss of mind, memory, usefulness. Yes, I walk fast, hearing my shoes hit the pavement in an unbroken rhythm that reminds me of army drill. In the street I have noticed that people tend to step to one side before it is necessary for me to change course to avoid them. Possibly I have a look of purpose, of determination; I do not know. Laura used to speak mockingly of my military bearing and I generally hold myself erect. As I am over six feet in height, this might lead others to think of me as a formidable figure. So, walking briskly to my office, armed with a rolled up umbrella and the absolute certainty of my path and destination, I am almost invincible: a proud example of the educated, middle-aged English male.

We must return to the time that I want to describe. Then there was my job. Christina had gone. Laura had left a long time ago. My children – Edward and Angelica – were grown-up. I was cautious but not without hope.

II

I went to stay with Henry Brown at his villa in the south of France. The trip was a business one. Henry is perhaps our most successful author. He is also my responsibility; so when Williams, the new managing director, became worried that Henry's new novel might not be in time for the Christmas market I was dispatched to the villa to go through the typescript.

Henry's first book, *Grasp the Handrail*, is his best. A restrained, naturalistic work, it is based on his childhood and early youth, his relationship with his stiff, unimaginative yet oddly touching father, his mother's slow death of cancer in their large sepulchral Hampstead house. But it was the second novel that brought him into my life when, as a novice, I served as its copy editor. *The Tremendous Sea* still takes me back to a particular time and place: my early married days in that temporary flat in South Kensington.

I had kept my bedside light on, to read through the manuscript into the small hours of the morning with Laura asleep at my side. Had I shown my wife the typewritten pages? I cannot remember. Yet I had thought then of her sleep as a reproach, a silent criticism of my fascination with what I knew to be essentially a piece of trash.

For with *The Tremendous Sea*, Henry discovered that line of florid romance which, when combined with a grandiose prose style and the odd piece of semi-pornographic sex, seemed to delight the public. The novel takes place in Spain, around a group of expatriate English and Americans discovering the south, undergoing a loss of inhibition and intelligence in the sun as they succumb to Mediterranean hedonism. Henry plays it straight. There is no irony, no hint that the metamorphosis experienced by his characters might make them foolish or even dull. *The Tremendous Sea* was followed by similar novels, set in exotic locales which range from the Pacific islands to equatorial Africa. At first I wondered if Henry had focused cynically on an Anglo-Saxon Achilles' heel, if he had ruthlessly exploited this weakness for sunburnt, meridional exoticism that afflicts many who are forced to endure overcast skies and the almost constant threat of rain. Now I think not. Henry Brown's pride in his artistic integrity is, I believe, oddly genuine.

His secretary and companion, Paul, was there to meet me at Nice airport in an expensive German car. Paul, thickly built but with a thin enquiring face, drove fast along the autoroute. It was not far to the villa and on the way we exchanged news, information about our lives, in a desultory but easy manner, before turning up into the hills of a light-brown scrubby landscape dotted with white houses. It was hot. Paul had pushed back the soft roof of the car and the wind blew our hair, rumpled our clothes. I had removed the jacket of my London suit, loosened my tie. He wore a short-sleeved dark blue sports shirt, white slacks, black casual shoes without socks, dark glasses to mask the sun. 'Henry's been counting the days to your visit,' he said, and smiled. The teeth were wonderfully regular and white.

'Why?' Henry could be difficult sometimes: last-minute changes, sudden doubts, fears for his reputation. And he was a hypochondriac, always complaining about his back, stomach, head, throat, liver or bowels. 'Is he sick?'

'It's your memory that's been troubling him. "Ought we to telephone Simon?" he's been saying. He tried not to ask for too much this time.'

I counted the items off on my fingers. 'Five bottles of little liver pills, a small Cheddar, eight jars of Mrs Perkins's Country-Style Marmalade, three medium-sized Mother O'Grady Fruit Cakes with Added Port, four dozen Jumbo spiced pork sausages.'

12

We drove through white gates and up a short drive, and stopped in front of a low pale yellow building with dark green shutters. On the other side of the house to the gravel forecourt there was a large parched garden on two terraces, the second containing a long swimming pool from which you could look down towards the distant glimmer of the bay of what had once been a small fishing port but was now a sprawling development of houses and lumpish apartment blocks. Around Henry there were more villas. He had created the illusion of privacy with small hiding places behind shrubs, hedges or the glistening white wall at one end of the pool. Sometimes he wrote outside, at a small portable table, typing to the sound of the insects and the dim roar of the autoroute. Then he would wear an old panama hat, for he did not like the sun in his face: an old panama hat with an MCC ribbon round its brim.

Inside the temperature was several degrees lower. The house was dark, cool. Luis, the small Portuguese manservant, came to take my case. I followed Paul up to my room which looked out over the terraces towards the sea. The room, painted white like most of the rest of the house's interior, had a narrow single bed and yellow curtains. Against one wall was a tall cupboard of stripped pine; on another hung a cloying impressionistic scene of some fishing boats. Over the bed was a small still-life of tulips in a light-blue flower vase. Henry had once told me that he did not like visitors – 'except you of course, Simon' – because they interrupted his routine. If either Paul or he felt in need of company they went elsewhere: to London, Paris, Rome or New York.

Paul showed me the small adjoining bathroom. Then we went down and, as I watched his hands and arms hang loosely at his side, jerked into sharp movements by his brisk progress, I thought of what these two people had made for themselves, here and in the rest of their lives. It was easy to sneer at Henry, to make fun of his books, to read passages from them aloud in intelligent company to the accompaniment of giggles and guffaws. Sometimes Christina and I had done this together.

But Henry had made fools of us all. I knew the story. One of six children: a dim career at boarding schools and university: two years in a solicitor's office writing *Grasp the Handrail* in the evenings and at weekends: then the gamble of leaving his job

13

with some thirty pounds in the bank, to the disapproval of his father, in order to attempt to establish himself as a professional writer. *The Tremendous Sea* had been written in a boarding house off the Bayswater Road; he once told me that he had not even contemplated its possible failure for that would have meant depression, despair, lassitude, perhaps even suicide. Henry liked to speak of his early struggles, to dramatise his past. At last there had arrived what he liked to call his *annus mirabilis* when, within a few months, it had become evident that *The Tremendous Sea* was going to sell in fabulous numbers and, at a party in Soho, he had met Paul.

Soon the two of them had moved to the villa. Henry's new accountant had recommended a short period of exile, but there were other reasons for their departure, most notably their wish to be away from the Brown family and the memories of a dead life. At the villa a routine had developed. Work began for Henry at eight o'clock sharp and finished in the morning at twelve. After lunch, a short siesta; then back to the workshop from four until eight. He was a machine. Paul looked after the house, the garden, typed Henry's manuscripts, drove his car, accompanied him around the world for publicity tours or trips to research backgrounds for the next novel. They depended upon each other. They were in love.

On the first terrace Paul poured me out a glass of white wine. Both Henry and I come from the English professional classes; his father was a civil servant in the Admiralty, mine a publisher. Perhaps my family had been slightly more prosperous than his, but the styles of our respective childhood homes – the one in St John's Wood, the other in Hampstead – sounded similar. Both had been dominated by silence, by the notion that on the whole the emotions were better left undiscussed, that to probe for definitions or excitement was, on the whole, unwise. It was better to concentrate on day-to-day trivialities, on ordinary problems such as a broken-down electric cooker, the need to burn the leaves at the bottom of the garden, the monstrous and inexplicable bill recently tendered by the local plumber for the unblocking of a drain pipe, the logistics of moving the children by train to Eastbourne for the annual seaside holiday at a house rented by a rich uncle.

And now where was Henry? Happy, stable, free. In love.

14

He had pushed away the past. Meanwhile I was endlessly turning over the same fears in my mind. Should I have minded more about Christina? What were my children really doing? What did they feel for me? Were they so much more attached to Laura and Bill that I had become a mere liability to them, a duty?

Our son Edward: was he happy, fulfilled in his bank in New York? Did his wife find me tedious, pathetic? And our daughter Angelica. There was another difficulty. When I was not with her, I felt worried. I imagined her as a fragile creature. I wondered if I was doing enough to protect the girl. But when we met, I was reminded immediately of her age and intelligence, of her force.

I took a sip of the cold sharp dry wine and turned to Paul. 'Have you booked us into the usual place this evening?' I asked. On every visit I took them both out one night to dinner, at the firm's expense, to a local restaurant that had received a number of stars in the Michelin guide.

'Of course. That was another reason for Henry's agitation. "I do hope Simon won't want any change of plan," he said. Your visits are important to him.' Paul paused and looked out across the terrace. 'Their structure is important. He wants nothing to change. And the last few days have been rather a strain. There've been the first chapters of the new novel. Then, last week, Luis got himself involved in a fight in the bar in the village. The police had to break it up. They wanted a statement from him and as the man hardly speaks any French . . .'

He was interrupted. Almost noiselessly, the small rotund figure of Henry Brown came out through the open door on to the terrace. He was wearing a light blue long-sleeved shirt and khaki slacks; on his feet were a pair of what looked to be old brown leather bedroom slippers. His bald head and smooth gentle face had a healthy tan. He came up to me. He looked pleased. I stooped to greet him for he was a short man. 'My dear Simon,' he said. His voice was high. Sometimes, on the telephone, people mistook him for a woman. 'I'm afraid I have cheated. I've already inspected your luggage, without, I hasten to say, going through any of its more personal contents. I saw the sausages, the cakes, the biscuits, the pills,

15

the marmalade, the cheese. How can we ever thank you enough? And we booked the table, the usual one, beside the balcony. I hope you don't mind. Rather presumptuous of us, perhaps.' Henry suddenly shook my hand. 'Well, old friend,' he said, 'you and I will go to work this afternoon. How long can you stay?'

'I should leave tomorrow.' The day after, there was to be a meeting at the office, presided over by Williams, to discuss plans for next year's list. If I was not there, all sorts of unfortunate decisions might be taken.

'Oh, come on,' said Henry. 'Stay another night. This afternoon and tomorrow morning for work. The rest for pleasure. Say I insisted.' His eyes were bright with mischief. 'Say the typescript needed more work on it than you expected, that I was difficult about changes. Surely my wishes count for something with the powers that be.'

I was surprised, then anxious. Perhaps he had some complicated proposal to make. Perhaps there had been a vast offer from some other publisher, an offer that we could not match and he could not afford to refuse. Yet I thought also that a delay here – at Henry's request – must impress Williams by demonstrating the depth of my intimacy with our most profitable writer. As a director I had to be consulted before any serious changes were made. Let Williams see my real worth, demonstrated by an empty chair. 'It is tempting,' I said. 'May I telephone my excuses tomorrow?'

'That's better.' Henry looked at his watch. 'Luis is a little late,' he remarked to Paul. 'Usually they are so punctual.' He turned to me. 'Our Portuguese,' he explained. 'Paul is so good with them.' As he said this, Luis emerged. The man was almost a dwarf: practically a foot shorter than Henry, with thick black hair and a long luxuriant moustache. The idea of such a figure in a fight was absurd. He looked undamaged, even jaunty, as he announced that lunch was ready.

In the circular white dining-room we sat at a round marble-topped table on which there were some dishes of cold meat, salami, salad, tomatoes, potatoes in oil, another large bottle of white wine, a bowl of peaches and a plate of soft cheeses. Henry, a jug of orange juice at his elbow, was an attentive host, filling my glass, making sure that I had missed

16

nothing of what was on offer. The first meal at the villa generally followed the same ritual. My host wanted to catch up on the London literary gossip, on the latest successes or disasters: also the internal politics of my firm. He listened to my stories of Williams, of the programme of rationalisation, interjecting questions and occasional reminiscences. Paul was silent. At the end, Henry departed for his siesta. 'We shall meet again at half past three,' he said.

Until then I sat with a manuscript in the garden, sheltered from the sun by a large ilex tree. I hardly looked at the typed pages. The gentle cacophony of the insects, the distant hum of the autoroute, the sound from the house of Paul typing Henry's work of the day before: these did not prevent first drowsiness, then sleep. That the manuscript had been sent to me by one of our most reliable readers with an ecstatic report, that it was the first book of compellingly unpleasant short stories by a young man not yet thirty, meant nothing to me then.

Henry and I went to the workshop, a large room with bare white walls and a high bookcase that contained dictionaries, reference books, a complete set of the *Encyclopaedia Britannica* and editions of Henry's novels in the various languages into which they had been translated. Against one wall was a long wooden desk on which, in neat symmetry, rested three or four looseleaf folders, a couple of exercise books and a jar out of which protruded a variety of pencils and pens: evidence of the work in progress. Henry and I sat in two armchairs at the other end of the room, a bright orange and yellow carpet on the floor between us. The workshop had only one window, which provided little light.

Henry's face – calm, almost seraphic, earlier when we had exchanged greetings and talked trivia at lunch – narrowed. Between the eyes, two furrows appeared. The mouth was set.

I made my suggestions: a few cuts, a tidying up of certain sequences, the odd grammatical change. Most of them he quickly accepted. Once or twice I read long passages out to him in order to illustrate one of my points, and wondered, as I had done often in the past, if the glutinous prose or the pomposity of some of the more intense paragraphs might cause us both to lapse into helpless giggles. But Henry was

17

serious. The book, set on the pampas of Argentina, involved the tribulations of a young English-born wife of a much older rancher, her relations with various enigmatic gauchos on the ranch and more sophisticated figures in Buenos Aires. What worried its author at this stage was the possibility that the public might refuse to purchase the work on patriotic grounds. 'You know,' he said, 'the Falklands and all that.' I assured him that his name and reputation would carry the day.

The book was long. After two hours of work, we were three quarters of the way through. Henry suddenly looked up from his copy of the typescript. 'Look, dear boy,' he said, 'we'd better leave something for tomorrow. Would you mind? Then the excuse for your delayed return will be genuine. It would never do to be caught out by the formidable Williams.' I blushed. He had underlined my humiliating position. 'No,' he said, possibly seeing my discomfort, 'that is only a part of the reason. I should rather like, if you don't mind, to finish my quota of words for the day. After all, it's in both our interests that you should have the new book by the middle of next year.'

It was not until the three of us were sitting in the restaurant, at their favourite table beside the balcony, that Henry let loose the true sensation. We had ordered: an elaborate procedure that had involved seeking the advice of the waiter, the intervention of the proprietor (who knew Henry and Paul to be valuable clients, worth cosseting) and a methodical scrutiny of the wine list. The bill would be vast. I tasted the expensive Burgundy. As I put my glass down, Henry said, 'Oh, by the way, did Paul tell you? We had a visit from Laura, Bill and your daughter the other day.'

'Laura?' At first I could not make the connection.

'Yes, Laura.' He laughed, a high-pitched trill. 'You were once married to her. Do you remember?'

'What on earth was she doing here?'

'Only a short trip,' Henry said, 'or so they told us. Bill – it is Bill, isn't it? – had some business in Nice. Something to do with insurance, I believe. He's rather a tycoon, isn't he? I had not seen her since your divorce a long time ago. She telephoned from a Nice hotel. They came for a drink one evening, a Saturday, I think it was. After Bill's business was

18

finished, they stayed on for the weekend. How pretty your daughter has become.'

Angelica had told me nothing. But I had not spoken to her for over a month. 'How long ago was this?'

'The weekend before last.' Paul chipped in with the details. He had a better, more practical memory. 'They'd spent the day water-skiing down at the port. Laura must have remembered our address.'

'You brought her here once or twice in the old days, didn't you?' Henry said. 'I told them about your impending visit. They seemed sorry.'

'Sorry about what?' My voice had a petulant edge.

'That they would miss you. I was fascinated to see Bill.' The first courses arrived, interrupting our conversation. Were they both watching me, to see how I would respond?

'How did you find him?'

Henry laughed. 'Genial,' he said. 'He exudes success, of a sort. A man – I should imagine – who works hard and plays hard. Rather a sporty appearance: the dark blue yachting blazer and so forth. Still fit for his age. A clear shiny skin, sharp eyes, easy movements. No sign of a paunch, unlike some of us.' He patted his stomach.

'They have a house on the Isle of Wight, near Bembridge,' I said inconclusively.

'And a place in London?' Henry asked. 'I suppose they have to be in London all week for his work?'

'Yes. They go to Bembridge at weekends, for the sailing.'

'And the water-skiing, and the tennis and the swimming . . .' Henry looked at Paul, then me, and laughed again. 'I'm afraid that we were quite bowled over by the description of their life. Paul and I talked about it afterwards. Laura has chosen a very different existence to that which I used to think she enjoyed. Wasn't she a student at the Slade when you first met her? She moved in artistic circles from what I remember. Hardly Bembridge. And Simon, I had no idea that she had been ill. Does she always walk with a stick now?'

'Sometimes.' No one was more aware of the contrast than I: the difference between the thin apprehensive young girl – so eager and rash – and the limping gaunt woman.

'She and Bill have never had any children together, have

19

they?'

'No'.

'Was he married before?'

'No.'

'Do Angelica and Edward tolerate him?'

I shrugged my shoulders. Henry and Paul had almost finished their first course. I had scarcely touched my soup. 'It works,' I said.

These two could not know what Bill had done for my children: how he had bought Angelica her flat, Edward his first car, paid for most of their education. Already, now that they were over twenty-one, he had settled lump sums on them, advised them how to invest these to the best advantage. At our last meeting, after dinner in his London house, he had hinted that, if I became tired of publishing, he could find me a position in one of his small subsidiary companies involved with the production of maps and guides.

'We were pleased to see them,' Henry said, 'and, of course, your daughter.' Suddenly he looked towards the middle of the restaurant. 'Oh look,' he said to Paul, 'it's Mrs Rhinegold. Look, Simon.' I saw a large expensively dressed old woman making her way to a table, accompanied by a young nervous-looking man. 'Do you know about Mrs Rhinegold?' And for most of the rest of the evening, as we ate our way through the elaborate food, Henry described the activities of the various exiles from England and America who had houses nearby.

That night I slept well. The Burgundy lulled my thoughts into a companionable state. The next morning I woke late with a slight headache and rushed to get up, to finish the breakfast of coffee and rolls that Luis had brought to my room. In the workshop, Henry was waiting for me, already a little impatient, showing no sign of fatigue.

We began work immediately, pushed forward and were finished in under an hour and a half. There was time to catch the afternoon flight back. Why, I wondered, had he kept me? Was the routine breaking down? Had he begun to crave company? Then, while we were both still in our armchairs, he tapped his copy of the typescript and asked, 'What would Bill think of this?'

'I don't know,' I said.

'Does he read books? Probably he regards them as a waste of time.'

'He likes adventure stories,' I answered. 'Tales of the sea, that sort of thing.' I remembered seeing a Hammond Innes novel on a side table in the drawing-room of the Chelsea house, on top of a large illustrated book on great sailing ships. Once Bill had asked me which authors were published by my firm. He had heard of Henry Brown. 'You must make a packet out of him,' he had said.

Henry tapped the typescript again. 'Isn't this an adventure? It has a strong plot.' He sounded upset. 'Surprises. Twists and turns. I think I keep ahead of the reader.'

'Of course you do.' I hastened to reassure him. 'But it's also a romance. I don't think that Bill has the romantic turn of mind. His feet are firmly on the ground. Except with Laura. He has romantic feelings for her. Almost absurdly so.'

Henry waited a little. 'An intriguing person,' he said. 'Bill, I mean.'

'I suppose so.'

At one time, when Bill and Laura had begun their affair together, when she had first told me about it, the man had fascinated me. I wondered about the magic that had enabled him to steal my wife. Laura had spoken mysteriously of his vitality, of how he seemed to notice her much more than I had ever done. To my mother she had said, 'Simon never compliments me on my clothes. He never says that he thinks I look pretty, or offers any hint of love or affection. It's as if he's scarcely aware of my existence.' Laura had been on the edge of tears, or so my mother had told me later. 'I don't want to hurt anybody,' she had said. 'Not Simon, not you, not the children. But if I don't leave him now, it can only get worse. And the children will suffer more because they'll be older. One must think about the children –'

'What do you feel about him?' Henry asked. Outside, a slight wind was disturbing the trees, rattling the shutters of the villa. 'A measure of contempt?'

At first I could not understand. 'You mean does he treat me in a contemptuous way?' I wondered if I ought to feel insulted.

'No.' Henry looked serious. 'I was thinking of it more from your point of view. Do you feel contempt for his way of life –

his standards, his crudeness?'

'His crudeness?' In a way Henry was right. I comforted myself sometimes with thoughts of their tasteless existence, the dullness of the guests who sat around their dining-room table, the pictures of the sailing ships on the walls.

Henry shifted in his seat. 'When they came here for a drink,' he said, 'and the time came for them to return to Nice to their hotel, I heard him say to Laura and your daughter on the way out "Well, back to old Nickers".'

'Nickers?'

'Nickers. Nice. A little play on words.'

'I see.' That was Bill. 'He adores her,' I said suddenly.

'And she him?' Henry asked sharply. Then he softened. 'I'm sorry. You don't mind talking about all this, do you?'

'I think . . .' I was about to attempt a profound statement, but decided against it. Any attempt at explanation would sound incoherent and confused. 'He adores her,' I repeated. I lapsed into the dead phrases of cliché psychology. 'You must remember Laura's childhood, the uncertainties of her up-bringing. Bill provides support and security, far more than I could. He sees her as a sort of goddess, to be worshipped. He's wonderfully attentive. A rock. Her illness is . . .' I sighed '. . . more psychological, perhaps. These things happen in middle age.'

'And your children?' Henry asked. 'How are they with Bill?'

'They like him. He makes time for them.'

'Aren't you jealous?' Henry asked.

I blushed. 'What on earth about?'

'The time that your children spend with their step-father.'

'He's been wonderful.' This was true. 'Now it's different,' I said quickly. 'Edward is married. Angelica works. But when they were growing up there wasn't much I could offer. The flat in Campden Hill. The cottage. And, just after the divorce, I was alone most of the time. Not much company for a pair of lively adolescents.'

'Edward is in the army. Am I right?' Henry asked.

Suddenly I became frightened. Either Henry was bored, wished to have someone to play with, or there was a deeper reason for this interrogation: a concern for me as a friend, a wish to transmit a message. 'He has left his regiment,' I answered. 'He works in New York for a bank. Why are you so fascinated by my family?'

The wind rose again. Through the small window I could see the top of a hedge shake. Henry seemed not to have heard me. 'When they came here,' he repeated, 'Bill and the girl had been down at the port, water-skiing. I liked your daughter. She is beautiful.' He paused. 'Simon,' he went on. 'Why didn't you marry Christina?'

I put my hand to my head. 'She didn't want that,' I lied.

He stood up. 'Simon,' he said, 'that man is killing her. He's killing Laura.'

'Don't be so bloody ridiculous, Henry.' And the moment passed.

Over lunch, with Paul, we spoke of old friends, of London. Then, in the garden, I read more of my other manuscript, transfixed by the emphatic cold style of this new young man. The stories – with their themes of sexual quirkiness, cruelty, jealousy, the subjugation of women, sadism, the viciousness of the frustrated erotic urge – seemed a return to some sort of brutal reality after Henry's soaring prose. The roles of youth and age had been reversed. The young man was cynical, worldly, suspicious, Henry romantic, determinedly transforming life into a grandiose fairy tale. Each, in his own way, was (I told myself) wrong.

At dinner, my hosts were quiet, courteous but a little distracted. Henry spoke of his poor digestion, of his bad back. That night, in the simple spare bedroom, I slept badly, my heart beating in time to a swiftly moving procession from the past. And in the morning Paul drove me to the airport, speeding along the autoroute as if anxious to end my interruption of their lives, giving me an envelope with a letter in it from Henry which, in my concern with the news about Laura, I left behind on the plane. It contained, or so Paul told me, details of the great man's plans and the dates of his next London visit.

III

The flight arrived at Heathrow in the middle of a wet afternoon.

I took a bus to the Air Terminal, then a taxi to my flat, where I made a cup of tea and sat down in a large grey armchair. The flat looked out on to a quiet street on one side; on the other loomed the light-blue roof of the Commonwealth Institute, without which I would have had a clear view over Holland Park. This was England in the early spring: rain, small signs of incipient leaf on the trees, people hurrying to leave the streets as quickly as possible.

My flat is crammed with books – the tools of my trade – and pictures: my great uncle's small Victorian collection left to me by my father in his will. Some of the pictures are of mythological scenes, occasionally verging on the erotic – nymphs bathing in a pool, a version of Leda and the Swan, chaste maidens bidding farewell to absurdly handsome Arthurian knights; others are narrative or genre paintings, telling a story often with a moral twist. No great or famous artists are represented. There is nothing, for instance, by Waterhouse, Lord Leighton or any of the better-known Pre-Raphaelites.

Three or four years ago Christina had said that there was, to use her words, 'a boom in Victorian paintings'. Excited, pleased for me, she had brought one of the experts from her auction house to look at the collection. He had made a rough valuation and told me that I was sitting on a considerable asset

– 'nothing absolutely first class, if you will forgive me saying so'. Within a year I had sold a large and (as I thought) dull picture of Sir Lancelot and Queen Guinevere. The price had seemed ludicrous The money had bought a dishwashing machine and paid for an overhaul of the cottage's boiler.

So I had discovered the true value of these pictures. It had been Christina who had revealed this and set in motion the first sale. She had obtained for me a generous reduction in the auction house's rate of commission. She had smoothed out one of the wrinkles in my life with her habitual efficiency and tact.

And I had grown fond of her, relieved – almost – to see that her weaknesses could be lovable as well. Her cooking for instance – those disastrous attempts at exotic dishes: chicken in beer, Tandoori pork, a revolting mousse of tinned salmon and gherkins. Perhaps she would poison the brute who had gone off with her. I smiled as my stomach turned in nauseous remembrance.

I did not go to my office until the next morning.

I reached the doorway of the large converted house in Bloomsbury and walked up the two steps into a white hallway with a glass partition on one side, behind which sits the girl who operates the switchboard. She wears spectacles, has reddish hair and is pretty, always smiling: a good introduction to our publishing world. I waved to her, shouted, 'Hello, Janice'; and she returned my cheerful greeting. My office is on the first floor and looks out on to the street. It is the best room in the house, far better than that of the managing director, Williams, who has a slightly larger but noisier and less private place on the ground floor.

My room is quiet, with large windows. The wall opposite the windows has fitted bookshelves from which the often garish covers of books I have edited over the years face out accusingly towards my desk. The desk is at one end of the room. At the other are two reasonably comfortable chairs and a dark green sofa which needs re-covering. Above this is one of the two pictures in the room: a curious abstract study of bright reds, dark greens (they go with the sofa) and black. The

25

other picture, over my desk, is also an abstract, this time apparently of a series of interlocking grey and black wheels with what look like irregular cogs on their rims. I have had this office for ten years. Previously I used what is now the sales manager's room on the second floor. But these two pictures have been with me for almost a quarter of a century. They were bought by Laura and myself after a private view in a gallery in Cork Street during the first year of our marriage. In the Campden Hill drawing-room they had clashed with the Victorian collection, so I moved them here, to my place of work. Then I had thought that I was wonderfully daring, even crazy, to be acting the part of a patron of the arts on an inadequate salary.

My secretary is outside my office, in a small compartment. If I need her, I telephone. She is a fixture in my life, a woman of about fifty – approximately my age – called Mary Wilcox, married to a Mr Wilcox who is assistant manager of a bank in Wandsworth. We understand each other.

That morning, before I had had time to open my briefcase, Mary came into my room. She is small, with a confidential manner that makes her appear to be about to pass on a very important secret. 'John told me to tell him when you arrived,' she said. John is Williams.

I looked at my watch. It had barely turned half past nine. 'You're all very early,' I said.

'John is always here by nine. But he asked me yesterday to say that he would like to speak to you as soon as possible.'

'And have you reported my arrival?' This was too absurd. Was the man now ordering her to spy on me?

'Not yet. I thought I should warn you first.'

I laughed. Williams was several years younger than me, a virtual newcomer to the firm. How ridiculous to be in awe of him. 'What's it all about this time?' I asked. 'You gave him my apologies? Henry kept me another day. There was more work to do on his manuscript than I had expected.'

'I told John,' she said. Mary's small grey eyes softened into a sort of pity.

She had not closed the door of my office. At that moment, I glanced towards it and saw, some seconds before he had a chance to focus his eyes on me, Williams. He was very tall,

26

thin, dark-haired with scarcely a hint of grey, a long face curiously unlined as if he had led a protected innocent life. He looked, in that instant, angry, frustrated. Then, pausing to knock at the open door, he entered, wearing a bright smile. 'Ah, Simon,' he said, 'may I have a few minutes of your time?'

Mary left, quickly. 'John . . .' I began.

'How was our old friend Henry?'

This morning Williams was dressed in black: a loose black suit that hung off his insubstantial frame. He wore spectacles, thin with narrow wire rims. His hair was cut short. The only concession to vanity was a pair of longish side whiskers which ended just above the lobes of his ears. His ascetic appearance had a hint of the fanatic. A Welshman, originally from Cardiff, Williams had worked for ten years in New York before being summoned back across the Atlantic – in exchange for an enormous salary and a share of any profit that he might squeeze out of the company – to 'rationalise' us. His eyes were unyielding. Sometimes I would try to make jokes to him to lighten the atmosphere. Then he laughed, only briefly, as though measuring precisely the usefulness of the time needed for such a response.

'Very well,' I answered. 'I'm sorry that I couldn't . . .'

'The villa must be most attractive at this time of year.'

'It is. It certainly is.' I had another try. 'John, I asked Mary to tell you that the manuscript needed more work on it than I'd originally thought. Henry wanted me to stay . . .'

Williams held up his hand. 'I have never been to Henry Brown's villa,' he said. 'The last time that he was in England, he very kindly suggested that Ilse and I might pay him a visit one day. Perhaps we might take him up on his invitation. Ilse does not like the heat, so we would need to avoid the summer months.'

I imagined the two of them sitting uneasily beside Henry's swimming pool: Williams' long emaciated body, white with bones protruding at awkward angles; Mrs Williams, also thin, only slightly shorter than him but as fair as he was dark, guarding her delicate pale Scandinavian skin against the sun. John and Ilse had met in Stockholm: she an interpreter, he a young executive at a convention of educational publishers. Ilse was as gloomy and impenetrable as a Swedish winter night. 'I was sorry to have to miss yesterday's meeting,' I said, with some force.

'I received your apologies, Simon. I'm preparing a brief summary of some of our conclusions which I will let you have in a day or two. I don't think that you will find anything particularly startling. Of course if you should disagree with any of the suggestions, you have only to let me know. Nothing is definite, yet.' He spoke precisely, each word separate from its predecessor. 'Is Henry Brown's manuscript now ready to be sent to the printer?'

'I want to have a last look, to make sure that there are no loose ends.'

'May I see it?' He smiled politely.

I opened my briefcase, passed across the vast typewritten bulk.

Williams quickly leafed through the thin pages. 'It looks quite remarkably clean,' he said.

Was this a veiled accusation, a hint that he doubted if my extra day at the villa had been necessary? 'I managed to persuade him not to make too many cuts or changes,' I said quickly.

'And that took longer than you had originally thought?' He raised his head, looked down at me. Williams' personal style of management involved a certain amount of psychological warfare.

'Yes,' I replied, again firmly. With Williams, whenever I felt that he was attempting to humiliate me, I tried to remember that I was good at my job, that I had the respect of my authors, that literary agents and other publishers were wont to refer to me as 'one of the best editors in London'.

I take pride in my work. I am patient. I am prepared to spend months, even years, on a manuscript if I feel that it has the makings of a good and unusual book. I enjoy the subtle relationship that exists between an author and his editor. And I work hard. That morning, as on other occasions, I sought courage in this knowledge. I was a professional, worthy of the respect of other professionals. Williams had a shrewd sense of commercial possibility, a nose for a best seller, a good head for figures. I thought in terms of literature, of immortality, of words reaching through to some profound part of the human

28

spirit. Surely the two outlooks were not incompatible. In homage to the first, I was perfectly content to look after Henry Brown.

Williams put the typescript down on my desk. 'I still haven't read it,' he said.

'Would you like to take . . .'

He held up his hand again. 'No,' he said. 'I think I'll wait for the proof. This is quite an occasion, you know: a new work by Henry Brown.'

'An occasion that takes place every year.' I wanted to assert myself.

'A profitable occasion,' said Williams, his eyes like ice.

'Indeed.' We both waited. 'John,' I went on, 'while I was in France, on the aeroplane and in my spare moments at the villa – not that there were many of those – I read rather an exciting collection of short stories, already very highly praised by Myra.'

'Myra?'

'One of our readers.' Really, he had no interest at all in the more serious side of the firm. 'A retired librarian. She lives in Bath.'

'Of course. Please continue. Who is their author?'

'A young man called Docherty. Michael Docherty. He's not entirely unknown. Three of the stories have already been published in various magazines.'

'Where?'

I reached down, extracted Docherty's much thinner manuscript from my briefcase. The information was on the first page. '*The London Magazine*, *Granta* and *Prick*,' I said.

'*Prick*?' A hint of colour entered his yellowy-white cheeks.

'An avant garde publication. It has the support of the Arts Council.'

'I see.' He waited.

'John,' I said, 'I think we should think seriously about this one.' I tried to adopt the sort of precision which I knew Williams liked as I spoke of Docherty's merits. I admitted that the book was not immediately attractive but I enthused about its air of menace, its haunting mixture of the erotic and the sinister. I laughed. 'He lacks tenderness,' I said, 'a common fault among young writers.'

Williams listened, obviously bored. 'How did the book come to us?' he asked wearily.

'Through an agent.'

'Which one?'

'Hermione Salterton.'

'Is she pushing it?'

I did not understand him. 'What do you mean?'

'Does she take it seriously?' He still spoke slowly. A note of condescension had entered his voice. I was a slow pupil. 'A collection of short stories, by an unknown writer. From what you have said, they sound rather obscure as well. Hardly a recipe for profitable publishing.'

'No.' I was determined to argue with him. 'But Docherty is young. He will write more, establish a name for himself, build up a readership. Eventually there should be paperback sales, foreign rights, translations, an American publisher . . .'

'You hope,' interrupted Williams.

'Obviously there is an element of risk,' I said coldly, 'as with most books, especially with quality publishing.'

Quality publishing. But was it right that we should push unwanted, unread books on to a bored public, thrust our ideas of literary excellence forward with the help of the profits made from popular writers like Henry Brown? Why not simply keep the profits, search for more Henrys, satisfy our owners, let readers wallow in what most of them really want? That would be Williams' riposte. What is literature anyway but a series of subjective definitions of excellence? I tried another approach.

'Writers of that kind can make money. Profitable books don't have to be trash.'

'Are you prepared to guarantee that these short stories will not lose money?'

'No.' I searched for inspiration on the clean white blotting pad on my desk. 'But if we take on a young man of Michael Docherty's undoubted talents now, within a few years he will bring not only profit but esteem to the company. He will . . .' (I searched for a telling phrase) 'He will add lustre to our list.'

Williams raised his eyebrows. 'You feel strongly about this, Simon,' he said.

'It's not only my opinion. I sent the manuscript to Myra

30

first. She agrees.'

For a moment he looked uncertain. 'Myra? Oh yes, of course. Myra.' Then he recovered. 'Has George Mason read it?'

George was our senior editor, a man past the age of retirement who still came to the office two or three days a week. He had been with the firm for almost all his professional life and, in his early days, had worked with my father. He had a wonderful memory and talked about 'Tom' Eliot, 'Morgan' Forster, 'Leonard' Woolf, 'Wystan' Auden. I loved George. But he was old, tired and could not be relied upon in a fight with Williams. Now he was more concerned about his cats, the condition of his lame sister who lived at Rye, the torments he suffered at the hands of the gas board when the heating went wrong in his flat.

'No,' I answered. How would George view the stories? He did not like to be thought old fashioned. George, although not old enough to have been a proper participant in those turbulent years, was essentially a man of the 'thirties. Yet he might be drawn to Docherty's surrealist touches, to the force beneath the cold flat prose. He might make comparisons with André Gide or the young Isherwood. In fact the book owed little or nothing to either of these two, but if George liked a work of contemporary fiction he said it reminded him of them. 'I will give him the manuscript if you like.'

'It's not that I don't trust your judgement, Simon,' Williams said with a smile that resembled a toothpaste advertisement. 'But we have to be very careful about what we take on these days. Why not show the book to George?'

'What shall I tell Hermione in the mean time? She rings me up twice a week about it. We've had the blasted thing for over a month, you know.' I was angry.

'Tell her that you are trying to convince your fellow directors of its merits,' Williams said. 'That will keep her quiet.' He smiled again. 'George should be finished with it by next Thursday, in time for our editorial meeting. If he agrees with you and Millicent . . .'

'Myra,' I interjected.

Williams drew his lips together in a tight line of irritation. 'If he agrees with you and Myra,' he went on, 'I don't see how I

31

can stand in your way. Does that sound fair?'

'Would you like to read it?' I asked. I knew what the answer would be. On the whole, Williams did not read books.

'Simon,' he said, 'I only wish I had the time.' He looked at his watch, then told me about the forthcoming conference. His words rushed out; the impatience was unconcealed. Williams wanted us in a hotel at Maidenhead on a Friday evening, for talks with representatives of our 'parent company' that would last for most of Saturday. We would have to surrender a part of a weekend. He stood up. 'It's basically a question of running through the budget for next year and discussing the sort of direction we might take in the future. Quite relaxed. They want the figures and costs brought up to date. I'll be speaking a bit more about it next Thursday. I told the others yesterday. But of course you weren't there.'

Williams left. I picked up the telephone and dialled the office of Joan Fielding, one of my fellow directors. 'Joan,' I said, 'I've just had Taffy in here.' Sometimes we called him that; some of our other nicknames were not so complimentary. 'What happened yesterday?'

Joan, a widow some five years younger than I, had a husky voice, a testimony to years of chain smoking. 'Oh, nothing,' she said. 'We talked vaguely about next year's books and he told us about this meeting at Maidenhead. How was Henry?'

'Very well.' I paused. 'Joan,' I said, 'there's nothing serious afoot, is there?

Joan had suffered. She had married young and had nursed her husband through a lingering death of cancer. First she had looked after their son, then, after he had started school, taken a job as a secretary in the firm. Soon she had risen to her present position. She was intelligent and strong. Williams was courteous, almost deferential, to her. He invited her to parties at his large house in Ealing where Ilse entertained members of London's Scandinavian community to evenings of glög and smorgasbord.

'Not that I know of,' she answered. 'Whatever makes you think that?'

'I'm not sure. Hard to put one's finger on it. Something about his manner. The way he looked at me.'

'Simon,' her voice became a little brusque, 'my outside line is going and I'm expecting a call. Can we talk a little later? I'm sorry. I really don't think you've got anything to worry about. You know my views. This business of reorganisation has been blown up out of all proportion. The figures for the last three months are very good. Williams has rationalised the company's financial practices and structure. The redundancies of a year ago are starting to pay off. I know it was sad to lose Kenneth and Charlie but they both have found niches elsewhere. Look,' Joan said, 'let's talk tactics one day next week. I'll attempt to prove that your fears are groundless.'

The rest of the morning was devoted to work of a routine but important kind. Having been out of the office for three days, I had letters to catch up on and replies to dictate. Mary Wilcox is so adept that I sometimes think it is almost unnecessary for me to speak because she seems capable of receiving my thoughts through some abstruse system of osmosis. She untangles my prose, makes letters and memoranda sound neat and effective. That day I wrote a long letter to Henry, with details of the editorial points on which he and I had agreed. I sent his manuscript up to the production department. I composed a short note to George Mason, telling him of my high opinion of Docherty's stories and that Williams wanted his views.

Then I telephoned Hermione Salterton, the agent, and explained the reason for yet more delay. She sounded fierce, tried to browbeat me, claimed that several other publishers were interested in the book. Did I not know that Michael Docherty had quite a reputation on the strength of the two or three stories that had appeared in certain magazines? 'But you wouldn't know that, Simon,' she said. 'You people are completely out of touch with contemporary writing. All that Welshman thinks about is the balance sheet and satisfying his masters, who don't know a novel from a pair of knickers. I want you to meet Michael. He's remarkable.'

'I'd rather wait until we know if we want him or not.'

Hermione knew that I was soft. She would effect the introduction at a dinner party in her Islington house, embarrass me in front of an audience of carefully chosen guests until it became impossible to avoid some sort of promise to her client. 'All this is most unprofessional,' she said grandly. 'The

33

poor boy is on tenterhooks. George Mason would never have permitted a serious artist to be treated in this way.'

I ignored her. 'Hermione,' I said, 'I am sending the manuscript to George. We will discuss it next week. I'm afraid that I can't give you a decision until then. In the mean time there is really no point in me and Mr Docherty meeting, however remarkable he may be.'

'Don't bully me, Simon.'

'Hermione, please. You and he will simply have to wait. It's a difficult book. Try to see it from our point of view for a change. I want to help this boy. I like his work. I'm on his side.'

'I see this as a test case,' she said brusquely. 'The answer to the question as to whether George Mason and you have finally lost your battle for the company's soul or not. If the decision goes against us, I'll know that you have both sold out to the Welsh garbage merchant.'

'Hermione,' I protested. 'Why must you always think in such simplistic terms?'

'Life is almost always simpler than you think. Goodbye, Simon.'

I put down the receiver. I was too familiar with Hermione's tactics to be fooled by the attempt to portray the matter of Docherty's stories as a potential personal humiliation for myself. Yet there was some truth in what she said. The complexion of the firm was changing. Certain assumptions, obliquely hinted at but all too easy to comprehend, hung over any meeting chaired by Williams. Our parent company, we were constantly told, was very much aware of its responsibility towards its shareholders. We were not a charity. Books were commodities, like biscuits or lawn mowers. We should publish to make money, not make money to publish. Were these points fully understood?

At the end of the morning, I signed the letters that Mary had finished. Then I went alone to my club for lunch. The club is near my office and serves, in its upstairs room – as opposed to the grand dining-room on the ground floor – a fairly cheap quick meal. You sit at a large table, have to take the risk of your neighbour being either unpleasant or aggressively dull, and the sun pours through the large light windows if the weather is good. When I joined the publishing company, at least four of its directors were members of this club, which is noted for its literary connections; now only George Mason and I belong. I believe that George took Williams there shortly after his appointment. Apparently our new master had seemed awkward, a little impatient. He had refused an offer of wine, saying in a slightly truculent way that he drank and ate very little in the middle of the day.

My lunch, if I am alone, is also simple. I drink a glass of lager, order some cold meat or pie, perhaps with some cheese to follow. I like to keep a clear head for the afternoon's work. You see, I am not lazy. Indeed I welcome activity and industry because they occupy my mind, excluding those melancholy thoughts – a mixture of nostalgia and guilt – which can be so troublesome. I find that such moods attack me often in the early afternoon. Then my resistance is at its most sluggish; then manuscripts, the necessary concentration on other people's points at a business meeting, the paraphernalia of work, become an ordeal, as if I am struggling through the humid heat of some luxuriant jungle. Large lunches make this worse.

That day, at the general table in the club, I talked to my neighbour. He was a civil servant: something in the Ministry of Defence, most probably a spy. He spoke of his garden in Essex. The man was ponderous; but he gave me the chance to be silent, to nod occasionally in agreement, to ask questions which ensured that the information continued to flow like thick liquid from a large dark tank. Eventually he changed course, rather slowly, to the subject of East Anglian churches. He planned to retire to Norfolk in order to occupy himself with a detailed study of the ecclesiastical architecture of that county. He remarked upon the wool trade and its effect on local prosperity; did I know about this, he asked? I shook my head. Then he was away again, sprinkling his lecture with dates, the names of obscure medieval dignitaries, statistics of population growth or decline.

The man roused a dormant part of me. East Anglia: a landscape shimmering in the heat. The recollection of a disastrous summer week that Laura and I had spent with the children in a seaside village some twenty years ago.

The sand had intruded everywhere: into the beds, the food, into our clothes, into every external part of me. I thought then that we would never get rid of it, also that Edward and Angelica might never develop further than the querulous weepy stage of that July. I had rented a small house on the advice of a friend who had talked of an idyllic holiday: so unspoiled, so clean, such marvellous bathing, such a wonderful rest, so delightful to be out of London with your wife and children. By the end of the week, we were a divided couple. After a quarrel about my failure to put the bins by the garden gate so that the dust cart could collect them, Laura had revealed that she had begun an affair with another man.

Not in front of the children: a convenient reason for breaking off a row in those days. And the children had been there, standing in the kitchen of that rented house to watch their father and mother shout at each other about unemptied dustbins. When we remembered them, saw their uncomprehending faces, we were silent: then returned to the task of gathering up the sandwiches, the bottle of lemonade, the cake, for the picnic on the beach that they had been promised for that scorching morning. On the sand there was not a sign of wind to relieve the heat; at the back of us, as we faced the calm sea, a haze distorted the houses and church of the village across the marshland. We limped through the rest of the day, oppressed by the dread of an evening alone together.

Later, over the kitchen table, holding a glass of gin in one hand, Laura faced me with the truth. She did not name Bill. Surely I had suspected something, she asked? No: then I realised the extraordinary condition of our life together. In London, she was always arranging parties, trips to the theatre in groups of four or six, nights out in restaurants. I had not really enjoyed all this, yet used to reassure myself that if two people were to live together some compromise was essential. I had tolerated her wish for company in return for her faithfulness. By the sea, she had overturned these dead illusions. Her hand shook slightly, disturbing the liquid in her glass. Her eyes, firmly upon me, flashed when she reached the central point of her story. 'Are you in love with him?' I asked. She raised her head, turned to look out through the windows at the darkness. 'No,' she answered. 'Probably not.'

That night, in the small room with uncomfortable twin beds, across the passage from the children, Laura had slept while I tried to believe that our marriage might be saved. She was remarkable, I thought. It was extraordinary enough that she should have married me. Perhaps she had to be shared. She was after all – or so I believed – a bohemian, almost an artist. I imagined the character and appearance of this other lover. I looked for taste, talent, sensitivity, strength: someone who might quickly brush me and all thoughts of me aside. If I am honest, I looked then for some sort of hero.

'One should have plans for one's old age. Inactivity is fatal.'

At the club, my neighbour – the old civil servant – talked on. He, with his East Anglian churches, his researches into drifts of population, would be happy; that seemed to be the implication. Was he trying to score off me in some way, to demonstrate how effectively he controlled his life compared to what he knew to be my single, slightly chaotic state? We had spoken before at this table. Once I had told him a little about myself: divorced, a publisher, two children, a flat in Campden Hill, a cottage in the country. 'Do you go there every weekend, to the cottage, I mean?' he had asked. I had said no. 'One weekend in three, or every other weekend?' Again I had said no. 'You mean you have no fixed pattern?' He had looked at me as if I were an anarchist, likely to produce a bomb from a pocket of my neat grey suit. I had said no, once more; I went there as much as possible in the summer and in the winter only occasionally, from a curious sense of duty, from a puritanical desire to justify the payment of the rent to my landlord; also to ensure that the pipes should not burst and the roof stay watertight.

'You still have your country place?' It was as if he had caught up with my thoughts.

'Yes.'

He grunted. 'A bolt hole. Should come in handy for retirement. Not that you'll have to think about that for a while. I wouldn't want to live alone in the country. Luckily Ruth is quite dotty about the garden.'

Was he conducting some personal vendetta, a private campaign aimed at my humiliation? Had I offended him, in some forgotten way, at one of our lunches in the past? The man knew that I was essentially alone.

'I go to the cottage on my own sometimes,' I said.

'For long?'

'No.'

He looked at his watch. 'Good God.' He brushed his mouth with his napkin, stood, did up the middle button of his jacket, brushed one hand across his chin and smiled. 'Nice to have seen you. Perhaps I'll send my work on those churches to your firm.' He laughed. 'Don't worry. It's purely for my own interest. As I said, one has to keep oneself occupied. I remember what a burden my old father was after his retirement. Never left us alone. At least my children won't have the same problem with me. Goodbye.'

IV

As I lay in my bath that evening, I could hear the extraordinary sound of the couple below in one of their periodic fits of ecstasy: a series of sighs, great gasps for breath, moans, finally a mighty roar like the climax of some primitive war chant. Then they were quiet. He must have leapt upon her the moment he had returned from work.

One year after Laura went, my father had died. He left some money. The sale of the publishing company after the war had been badly handled and the new owners had paid only a fraction of its true worth. My father would have regarded it as morally wrong to make too much out of his inheritance, to trade in too advantageously what his predecessors had regarded as almost sacred: not only the company itself, but the right to market books under the family name as well.

My brother James is an accountant. Some two years older than I am, he lives near Manchester. I seldom see either James or his wife Angela except at family rituals: deaths, funerals, weddings, events of that sort. We are not close but we understand each other. Indeed it was in some sort of an unspoken alliance that James and I, on the morning after my father's death, had approached the house in St John's Wood where we had both been brought up and our parents had lived since the year of their marriage. We had been met by our mother, already in black. It was a warm day. Her clothes were flimsy and light, old with no cut or style to them. She might, I thought, have been a Greek or Italian peasant condemned to live perpetually in widow's weeds.

We entered the large house in silence, led by my mother past the large porcelain walking stick holder in the hall. Hadn't John Cowper Powys had such an extraordinary conception of the universality of the soul that he used to address his walking sticks as individuals, as if they were part of the great pantheist scheme? When I had read this, I thought of my father – it was several years before his death – and his forest of sticks: how before a walk – perhaps to Lord's cricket ground or Regent's Park – he would stand for a few minutes in front of the holder, giving careful thought to his choice of stick for the day. It was one of the few moments when he had seemed to be pre-occupied entirely with his appearance or comfort: a moment almost of sensuality. The selection of walking sticks had been a luxury; there had been no need, no rational explanation for the purchase over the years of so many varieties – a black-thorn, one with a misshapen handle, another with a crook made from the horn of a goat – no explanation except that of self-indulgence.

The house was dark, despite the brightness of the day outside. This did not surprise me. My early memories were of badly lit passages, bulbs of low wattage dim above the stairs where I had to be careful not to miss the steps, not to tumble on to the dark blue and red Turkey rug that covered the black boards of the floor. One or two pictures – the surprisingly explicit scene by the follower of Waterhouse of water nymphs among lilies, a sombre portrait of my great grandfather by an imitator of Watts – hung in the hall above the staircase. To our right was a black lacquer cabinet – also Victorian – with a large plate in the style of William de Morgan on its top, supported by a wooden stand. Everywhere the colours, once presumably bright, were muted, or subtle as my father used to say when praising a book, a work of art or a human being.

We went upstairs, led by the small figure of my mother. I began to realise that we were to see my father on his deathbed. I felt no sense of pain, not even of anxiety, merely an irritation that this peculiar ritual should be performed in such a characteristically lugubrious fashion. My father was dead. I had loved him. With his death I had hoped, in the midst of my sorrow to see the last of such silent demonstrations of what he believed to be the inevitable series of disappointments, struggles and sufferings that constituted life. In that instant, on the stairs, my temper rising as my mother paused at the top to recover her breath before she led us to the sepulchral bedroom, I saw to my fury that his natural pessimism, his view of the world, its inhabitants and the way that they should make their way in it, would survive in our consciousness, in the memories we had of this house and in the ineradicable influence that he had exerted throughout those fatal years of childhood.

There he was, in their large double bed, his motionless grey face pointed towards the ceiling, his features arranged – presumably by an efficient undertaker – into an expression of incongruous contentment. A thought occurred to me; afterwards I would share it with James. My mother had told us on the telephone that the old man had died in the night. Had she woken in the morning to find him dead or had he expired while she was still awake, perhaps reading or even preparing for bed, arranging her long hair out of its tight bun into the loose tail she preferred for sleeping, perhaps removing her small amount of make-up or emerging from their adjoining bathroom wrapped in the thin silk dressing gown which Laura had given her on the last Christmas day that we had all spent together?

If the last were true, then she had slept the rest of the night beside his corpse – for I noticed that the pillows on her side of the bed were creased and her large-faced watch was still propped up against her reading light. I could follow her line of reasoning. It was too late to bother anyone. One could not call out the doctor at such an unearthly hour or disturb James and Simon. She must wait until the morning; it was wrong to hoist people out of bed in the middle of the night. A dead husband could be equated with a burst pipe, a faulty television set, a window that would not shut, a door that banged in the wind because its lock was broken. In the morning she would ask for help, but not before.

'I love your parents, darling,' Laura had once said to me. 'But they really are quite extraordinary.'

41

To me their behaviour seemed unremarkable, the one part of myself that I knew would not change: a part to which, no matter what might occur elsewhere, I must always be able to return, often in a state of exasperation and anticipated boredom, yet occasionally with relief to a dependable if inarticulate love. Here, beside the deathbed as we stood in silence – awkward, still and tense – the love and inarticulacy came together, then dissolved as my mother started, rather quickly, in that timid voice that seemed to assume that nobody could be the slightest bit interested, to explain the arrangements for the funeral.

It would be at the local church, an establishment with a middle-of-the-road parson who had not offended my father with High Church practices or excess of evangelical enthusiasm. 'I like the choice that the C of E gives you,' the old man had often said, perhaps remembering the more bracing worship of the Kirk of his youth. At the church services, when we had all gone together at Christmas or Easter, my father's tremendous singing of the hymns, his loud affirmation of the responses and the creed, would give to the occasion the air of a revivalist meeting. He may have imagined himself at ease with the muted tones of late twentieth-century Anglicanism, but just as his constant use of the word subtle as a term of praise revealed a wish to admire its virtues rather than actual wholehearted admiration, so the declared liking for the local parson's gentle questioning sermons may also have concealed a secret wish to return to the clear childhood choice between salvation and eternal misery.

'Come to us tonight, mother,' James had said. Then they had not yet moved to Manchester. 'The children are all at home. You must get away from here.'

Her eyes ran away, first to the floor, then to my father's inanimate face, then to the chimney piece on which there stood several photographs in frames – one a large picture of Laura and me and our two children taken the year before she had left me for Bill – then to a small dirty landscape which some expert had once wrongly believed to be the work of Samuel Palmer. My father had inherited the Victorian collection from an unmarried uncle who had written an obscure work on the origins of the Greek myths, travelled a

42

certain amount on the continent and decorated his bachelor chambers with purchases from reliable London dealers. 'Archie had eclectic taste,' my father used to say, glancing at the nymphs cavorting among the lilies, their sexless breasts and creamy white bodies bright against the dark water.

I responded to James' suggestion. 'What a good idea,' I said. I could not offer her the sparse hospitality of my flat.

It was as if we had suggested that my mother accompany us on a brisk walk through a minefield. 'No, no,' she said quickly. 'It's most terribly kind of you to make such an offer, James and' (she glanced at me with a nervous smile) 'you too, dear. But Meg Parker has said that I might go to her for a couple of nights when everything has been sorted out. Until then, I'd rather be here.'

'At least let me sleep in the house tonight,' I volunteered.

She looked hunted, surrounded by enemies. 'Thank you so much, dear,' she answered, still at high speed. 'But Meg is coming round. She said that she'd stay the night as well. People are most awfully kind. Something like this seems to bring out the best in them. Mr Bowles has already been. He saw your father two days ago – and I know what a comfort that was.'

'Mr Bowles?' I asked gently.

'The clergyman, dear. From St Botolph's.'

She had, perhaps unwittingly, made the business not easy but short. I knew that when we left I would feel how unsatisfactory, how frustrating, the morning had been: how neither my brother nor I had been able to voice even a small part of our sympathy, how she had once again driven us away by her humility.

So the death had taken place. He was not yet eighty – but, as my mother would observe depressingly often in the future, it had been a blessing that he had not suffered a long debilitating illness, with all the restrictions which would have been so great a trial for an impatient and previously active man. She had led us down the stairs again. We were certain that she was in a state of numbness; that the removal of my father from her life, which he had dominated and controlled for so long, must be devastating. Yet nothing had been said: nothing beyond the stilted practicalities and the information that Meg Parker – a

43

bossy spinster who was my mother's chief confidante, friend and repository of stories of my father's exasperating demands – was coming to sit with her, to sleep in the spare bedroom after they had sat up late to the accompaniment of Miss Parker's complaints about the rudeness of the attendants in the public library or the unpunctuality of buses and trains.

The great surprise of my father's death was his will. For he left me not only a small amount of money, but the collection of pictures as well.

My father had worked, I suppose, until I was aged about fifteen. I can remember his leaving the house early in the morning every weekday to catch the bus into the centre of London. Then he dressed always in a dark suit, complete with waistcoat, usually a white shirt with a stiff collar, a pair of highly polished black shoes. After he retired and was in the house every day, this uniform was relaxed in favour of a tweed or corduroy jacket and generally grey flannel trousers, usually a white shirt with a soft collar. By this time he had invented a scheme to keep him occupied for the rest of his life: the writing of the history of our family and its involvement with publishing from the early Edinburgh days to the time of the sale.

So idleness was not really a charge that could be thrown at him. There, on the floor and tables of his study, was the evidence to refute it in the form of the firm's old account books and ledgers, the piles of correspondence from authors and printers. Occasionally he would travel to Scotland, always by train, to consult other documents, to check on his ancestors' birth dates and movements around the country, perhaps to visit again the villages where they had lived and the fields they had farmed before an adventurous son had entered the book business in the early years of the last century. For this, he stayed with my uncle and aunt in the draughty house near Peebles. Had he enjoyed these expeditions? Laura used to ask me if he ever enjoyed anything. He had a feeling for the Peebles landscape, for the sense of space and history. He must have liked the silent meals with his brother and sister-in-law, the absence of frippery or fanciness in their lives and household. This was how one ought to live – or so I could imagine him thinking at the end of a damp evening in front of a smoking fire, with no sound except a slight stir of branches in the vast Forestry Commission plantation on the hill at the rear of the sodden garden.

There was the thrill of the research itself. Indeed, he had unearthed so much new information about the firm's pioneering commercial practices, its enlightened treatment of its authors, the fascinating intricacies of the decision to move to London, that my father declared that one volume would not be enough; so he told his old colleagues to bring out the history in two parts, the second a year after the first.

The study was dark; the paper on the walls an intense red, deepening the sombreness of the large clumsily ornate blocks of Victorian bookcases, a cupboard decorated with an elaborately carved floral motif, a great monolith of a desk. On top of the cupboard was a bronze bust of my great grandfather, at one time in the offices of the publishing firm but later given back to the family after they had sold their shares. The flamboyant moustaches and sensual mouth set him apart from his descendants, who had tended to be of a less significant appearance; under his rule the great expansion of the business had begun. My father's face was handsome in a more restrained way; his grey hair short and kept in place with hair oil, the sides of his cheeks shaved clean above the tops of his ears. The bust made its subject look vain and I thought I perceived the occasional link between his grandfather and himself in an irritation if his polished shoes became scuffed, the importance he attached to the freshness of his clothes which led to a constant discarding of old suits, trousers and jackets in favour of new if always traditionally cut replacements.

One morning, in my last year at university, my father set out the options. We were seated in the study, in heavy armchairs on either side of the large fireplace in which he occasionally burned smokeless fuel. The end of the conversation was obvious. I had no money. Either I could sit at home all day under his disapproving eye or go out to the job that he had arranged for me.

My father seemed to consider himself obliged to put several

alternatives. At least he had the sense not to mention the Church, which, a hundred years earlier, would certainly have been among the list of possibilities. The army, that other refuge, also did not figure in his ideas; we had never been a military family. No, he stuck to the professions. Accountancy, banking, the law, the City – these were all paraded before me until finally he reached the point of the interview. He had, he said, been in touch with the old firm to remind them of their promise that members of the family might be given the chance of a job. Was I interested? I said that I was. An interview was set up. I was offered a place as a trainee. My working life had begun.

I am writing this because I want to make clear how much I owe the shape of my life to the old man. He secured my job for me. He left me the collection of pictures. He established the degree of prosperity that allowed me to rent the cottage in the country.

V

When I drive out of London, through its southern suburbs, on to the dual carriageway that cuts through the protected green belt, through the immaculately painted villages and converted farm labourers' cottages, I feel that I am on a voyage of discovery. My brother and I grew up in St John's Wood. As children we used to spend three weeks each August at my uncle's house near Peebles. Holidays there, amid the wild dripping scenery, were not a preparation for the mysteries of English country life.

I had discovered the cottage through Charlie Parkin, my cousin in the wine trade. He had heard that I was looking for somewhere to take my children. He felt sorry for me. He felt also that Laura – whom he had never liked or understood – had behaved badly. Therefore when a friend of his, who was agent to the Erdley family, said that they sometimes rented out some of the cottages on their property, Charlie had mentioned my name.

The agent saw me. He seemed to think that I was a man who could be trusted. Soon a firm of local builders began to turn what was little more than a derelict hulk into a habitable residence. The rent was low; the state of the property and the money that I had had to spend on it dictated this.

The cottage, built in about 1830, lies in a slight dip in the middle of a large wood. Around it, a space of about three or four acres has been cleared, enough for an expanse of grass on which people can sit out when the weather is fine. I chose the

47

place because it is small, easy to lock up and leave. You reach it by driving up a rough track of some two hundred yards that branches off a lane. I had wanted seclusion.

When I had first rented the cottage, Jeremy Erdley's father was still alive. A friendly, bluff figure, he had not married until he was nearly fifty. The woman, some twenty years younger than he, produced one child, a boy, and this trio – old Erdley, his wife and the son Jeremy – had lived in the hideous mansion that is the centre of the estate. Towards the end of his life, after years of almost total lassitude, the old man had discovered a new delight: the opening of the house to the public. Old Erdley had leapt into the fun of it all, turning himself into a sort of universal uncle for the visitors. He signed guide books, led coach parties on personal tours, presided as master of the revels at Tudor-style banquets, even took his turn as driver of the miniature railway which winds through the trees and shrubs of the house's arboretum. 'If this is a democracy,' he would say as he was strapped into a breastplate and armour to do the honours at a display of mediaeval jousting, 'who am I to stand in its way?'

Jeremy Erdley once said he believed that this late burst of showmanship had killed his father. He had also declared – in an uncharacteristic flash of imagination – that, for the old man, the pleasure had made the shortening of his life by a few years worthwhile. I used to feel sorry for Jeremy. He had inherited the place when he was still young, barely into his late twenties. At first he had lived there with his mother, in the shadow of old Erdley's memory, attempting to grapple with the assaults of the tax man, the rise in heating costs and the house's agonizing discomfort. In those days whenever I had seen him – perhaps walking alone through the woods with his labrador, hurrying along the village street towards the estate office with some files under his arm, or self-consciously attempting to imitate the old man dressed as a Victorian stationmaster, besieged by a mob of squealing children on the miniature railway – the boy had looked ill at ease. Then he had taken up with the beautiful Sarah, the girl with whom my daughter Angelica had once shared a flat.

She did not seem to remember me at first when, one hot afternoon, I met them in the wood. Then we had spoken. She asked after Angelica, said that she never saw her now. Their lives had drifted apart. We smiled at each other while Jeremy Erdley stood awkwardly by. I brought the conversation to an end, imagining that they must want to be alone together. Soon they were married. I was not invited to the wedding. Angelica went, and afterwards spoke mockingly of a society occasion, full of falseness and people who wasted their time. Surely, I had asked, the young couple had seemed happy? My daughter had scowled, intimating that she had not had time to notice such things.

I saw very little of the young Erdleys. All the business to do with the cottage and its rent was transacted with the agent. But I had another connection with Jeremy. Edward and he had been at school together, at the institution to which our son had been sent at Laura's wish, whose fees I could never have paid without the help of the boy's step-father. Edward, some four years younger, could vaguely remember Jeremy: a diffident face peering out from behind a hymn book in the school chapel, a thin body buffeted in a House football match as a crowd had roared its disappointment. Edward, too, has little time for such people. Once I was speaking to him about the financial difficulties facing the estate and he had exclaimed, 'Of course they've only got themselves to blame. They didn't diversify. They were handed an asset on a plate and treated it in a totally uncreative way.'

The young couple performed their duties well. After a year of marriage, she gave birth to a son. From time to time Jeremy and Sarah could be seen strolling among the crowds of visitors, usually in fancy dress, often as two characters from the television costume drama of the moment. Invariably she could play the role with dignity. He, especially if called upon to imitate an historical monster or tyrant – perhaps Genghis Khan or Henry VIII – looked less happy, bowed down by the weight of heavy material, uncertain as to how to arrange his sword and buckler, irritated by the itch and heat of the clinging fabric.

Tall, with long legs, she seemed to accentuate her husband's awkwardness. He was tall as well, taller than her, and very thin, as if worry had wrung off every extra ounce of flesh. He had a rebellious lock of hair that fell into his eyes and generally he fiddled with something, crossing and uncrossing his legs, pulling one of his ears or scratching his face. She, on the other hand, either sat or stood still, serving as a firm backdrop, the inanimate support against which he could twitch, fidget or fiddle to his heart's content.

When I had seen her again in that wood, after their marriage, once more walking with Jeremy and his dog, she had surprised me. Sarah had grown up. I had not expected to come upon a sight so close to the ideal. There was nothing particularly exotic about the girl's appearance. She wore jeans, a thick jersey and what looked like one of Jeremy's old tweed jackets, the arms of which hung down over her hands. Without a hat or scarf, her brown hair – cut short – had drifted about her head in the chill winter wind. We met on a path. Around us loomed a stand of tall larches, darkening the midwinter sun. The labrador ran towards me, ahead of his master. The girl, some way behind and holding young Erdley's arm, shouted 'Ned! Ned!' She saw me and quickly withdrew her hand from Jeremy.

At first she seemed a little embarrassed. I tried to put them both at their ease. 'I knew that you had a cottage around here,' Sarah said, perhaps with a hint of reproach.

'You must come and see us.' He uttered the words to enable them to move on. I wondered why, as he said them, she lowered her head as if caught in an act of deceit. I walked away. They went in the other direction, deeper into the wood.

That weekend I had been alone at the cottage. Generally Christina had come with me; if she could not, I usually remained in London. But occasionally I felt the need to escape by myself, to bring manuscripts and catch up with some work. Despite my initial intention, Edward and Angelica rarely stayed there. I did not, and do not, blame them. There was more to do at Bembridge; Bill and Laura could provide a swimming pool, tennis court, sailing boat and the other attractions of July, August and September on the Isle of Wight. In the winter the cottage has even less to offer. The boiler is unreliable and the damp often creeps into the ceilings, floors and fabric of the place, even into the beds. So generally I saw Edward and Angelica in London, after Laura had left me. I took them to cinemas and tea shops, put them on their trains at the beginning of their school terms if their mother was busy, and occasionally had them to stay for a night or two at the beginning of their holidays in the flat in Campden Hill. Then they would speak of Bembridge with hurried excitement, making me understand that I was merely a no-man's-land between school and true freedom.

The cottage had turned out to be for Christina and me. Perhaps you could call it a love nest, or at least a quiet setting for a gentle middle-aged romance. Indeed she had spoken of the place as if she had regarded it at least partly as her home.

VI

One Friday evening in March, the weekend after I had returned from my visit to Henry Brown in the south of France, I sat alone in the cottage. The chintz curtains were drawn in the small sitting room. A wood fire burnt low in the grate. I was in the deep comfortable armchair to the fireplace's right. The white walls were hung with some of the smaller pictures from my great-uncle's collection, mostly of rural scenes, one – more full-blooded than the others – of a pack of foxhounds in full cry. Christina, from the day of her first visit to the cottage, had made suggestions for the place's improvement. I can see her now: her black shoulder-length hair falling away from her sallow cheeks as she reached up to take down the dull view of Winchester Cathedral that I had hung beside the door.

Often I had spoken to her about my children, obsessively covering old ground, repeating anxieties, grasping at the same hopes, encircling the same imponderables. And she had nodded, shown interest, uttered the usual words of comfort. Her courtesy and sympathy had disguised – I thought now – rising impatience and suffocating boredom. That was the trouble; I had never pushed out away from myself enough to be of use as a lasting partner.

Edward we had usually passed over quickly. Even during his time in Northern Ireland, I had not been unduly concerned about Edward, because I had felt that he was too sensible, too level-headed to allow himself to be killed. Of course my feelings were irrational. Yet I had known that Edward would return to offer me advice, to patronize his father, to move ahead under the influence and protection of Bill. Then suddenly he had announced that he was to marry Caroline, whom I had scarcely met. It had been the same with his decision to take the job in New York. The boy had not even vaguely discussed his intentions with me beforehand.

When Edward visits my flat in Campden Hill, he asks – in a way that is still a little military – if I have joined the local residents' association, if he might give me the name of a good plumber he has heard of from some friends of his who live nearby, if it is really wise – or economical – for me to keep the same car for more than five years. Like Williams, Edward sees books as a commodity. Did we have, he once wondered, a computerised method of ordering? Surely it would be possible for every bookshop in the country to have its own small terminal on which an assistant might type out the number of a particular book, transmitting this direct to the publisher's warehouse so that the order could be dispatched that very day. Why, he said, he had recently ordered a book and found the delay of some three weeks while the thing (here his lip had curled slightly) came from the publisher to the bookshop quite ridiculous. No other retailer would tolerate this. In other trades it would mean bankruptcy; no customer would stand for it. The cost of the operation could be funded by some central body contributed to by both publishers and book-sellers. Each warehouse would have a separate code for contact. Edward believed that the Americans were working on such a scheme. As usual this country was light years behind.

Then we would reach Angelica, whom Christina, even Christina, admitted that she found difficult. And Christina was right. Edward was jokey with Christina, proud that he could look upon our liaison with the sympathy of a man of the world; Angelica, on the other hand, had seldom been natural with the woman. Usually she had launched a polite but dull interrogation of the kind adopted by strangers in a railway carriage when the train breaks down. Angelica had not disapproved of Christina, I am sure of that. Nor could she have doubts – at her age, with her knowledge of life – about the morality of our position.

Perhaps the problem had been deeper, I found myself wondering. Perhaps there might be some curious link between father and daughter, some reciprocation of the strong but abstract feeling that I had for her, which could lead to disapproval or even jealousy. More thoughtful than Edward, Angelica could not store her true feelings away behind a bright façade. And there was so much in the world of which my daughter disapproved. She had liked Christina's independence, the fact that she worked hard and successfully. Yet when Angelica had mentioned the snobbish auction house, she had contorted her face, her mouth pressing downward in an angry grimace. I remembered that Laura had been shocked by her, in her university days, when she was a bit of a rebel, when she had flirted with radical politics. I had not minded this, although I knew that I was counted among the infidels in her eyes. The idealism was fine, young, even beautiful. Angelica still saw herself as an enemy of privilege. But now this was coupled with a dislike of decadence, of sentimentalism. Edward and she had previously been divided by his conformity and her rebelliousness. Now they were not far apart.

Angelica was educated, with intellectual tastes. She read books, listened to music and visited art galleries. Once, briefly, she had subscribed to the *Times Literary Supplement*. Angelica, unlike Edward, was interested in my work. I sent her proofs that I had edited and sometimes sought her opinion on manuscripts. And while we had never spoken to each other about what we thought of Bill (I felt it would be dishonourable to try to demean their stepfather in the eyes of my children) I imagined that I could catch occasionally, either from an inflexion of Angelica's voice or her choice of words, a slight mockery.

Christina and I had been through all this too many times. I had prided myself that I knew her well enough to realise when to change the conversational course. The warning signs were a momentary hardening of the voice, a lightning flick of the hand across her forehead, a rapid swinging of one leg to and fro from its position across the other.

Perhaps this talk of other people's families had brought thoughts of her own solitude. Her parents were dead. Her mother had been killed in a car crash when Christina was ten years old, her father, three years before the events that I am attempting to describe, had been felled by a heart attack. He, once a partner in a Bond Street art gallery, had not approved of me, yet had made the best of his daughter's choice. She is an only child.

I liked to think of myself as her rescuer. For, when we first met, Christina had been recovering from a love affair. The man had been about forty then, more or less my age. They had worked in the same building (his field was furniture) and would collide in the passages. The space was cramped, too many people in too few rooms, so they had not been able to avoid seeing each other. I knew how he looked: tall with a lean dilettante's face and body, well-pressed clothes and an air of aesthetic disdain.

Christina had told me about him. He had needed a replacement secretary for two weeks and Christina, at that stage only in her third month with the organisation, had been moved over from the publicity department to fill the gap. At first she had found her new master remote and arrogant: not deliberately unpleasant, more the possessor of a natural impatient discourtesy.

It had always seemed ridiculous to me that, at the end of her first day's work with the man, he should have told her that he had to go for two days and a night later in the week to visit a country house to advise on certain sales that its owner was considering. Christina should come with him, to make notes. She would have to follow her boss around with a pad, ready to take down his observations.

She told me the story. They had driven from London in his fast and flashy car. I thought of her that morning: thin, gawky, her eyes shy as she attempted to answer his questions. He had been pleasant, for the first time, and had spoken respectfully of her father. Then, allowing the conversation to take a more revealing turn, he had described in a light-hearted manner how he had found his way into the auction house after leaving Cambridge with a poor degree. He would not, he admitted, describe himself as a scholar; there were people under him, backroom boys hired specifically for their knowledge (he made the process sound faintly indecent), who filled that role.

No, his job was partly administrative, partly the complex business of making and maintaining contact with potential buyers and sellers – and this was (he said) the purpose of their expedition on that day. Indeed although he had learned a fair amount about his particular field (he had worked at it for almost fifteen years) he would, in all seriousness, describe himself first and foremost as a businessman. On that morning, turning towards her while they were waiting at a set of traffic lights, he had put his hand on her knee.

Coincidences, as I have said, seem absurd. The place that they were driving to that morning was Erdley Castle, then lived in by Jeremy Erdley's mother and father; and here, after displaying his diplomatic talents to their host and hostess, the man had come into Christina's bedroom. She had accepted him, feeling lonely, mystified in the overpowering, ugly and sinister house. Disconcertingly, her tyrant had been transformed into an ally.

The affair had lasted for five or six years. The man passed through various moods. First the suave conqueror of a girl of half his age; then the guilty husband, worried about the deception of his wife and family; then they had reached a sort of plateau on which both were supposedly free to take other partners; finally he became neurotic, obsessed with the vision of Christina as his last contact with youth. The man's home life, or so he told her, was collapsing. His wife, who knew nothing about their relationship, had taken a lover. His oldest son had been sacked from two schools. Christina had long ceased to be his secretary but in the small building she could not escape him. 'At the end,' she had told me, 'he was like a man possessed. He tried to take me to hotel rooms in the lunch hour and hung around waiting for me to leave in the evening. Whenever we managed to snatch a night together, he spent most of it in tears. Once there was even a botched suicide attempt, in his own house, thank God, so the wife had to cope. Then you appeared; Simon the Saviour!'

Christina had tried to analyse the reasons for the man's collapse. She spoke of the male menopause, the dread of growing old, the Peter Pan complex. I, naturally, saw a parallel with my own obsession: the dream of Laura as she once had been. David, the man, had fascinated me. I had

56

pressed for more details until Christina had accused me of prurience. I had wanted to know the exact mechanics of the affair, the hotels he had suggested, the restaurants they had visited together, even the dishes he had chosen. For a moment I had wondered if a new obsession had dawned. Was I in love with Christina? Surely this could be the only explanation for my wish to find out about those vanished days, now as dead as Laura's and mine together. I had hoped that this might be true. And certainly whenever I went to Erdley Castle I used to try to sneak upstairs to see the bedroom and the bed in which – some fifteen years earlier – the man had seduced her young bewildered self.

The room was cold. I threw another log on to the fire, looked down at the manuscript on my lap. I had three books to work on over the weekend: a long, insufferably tedious biography of Palmerston; *Perspiring Freely*, a short study – translated from the original Swedish – of the benefits of setting up a chain of state-aided sauna baths; and the collection of Docherty's short stories.

The stories held the most promise. I could appreciate their power: their ability to conjure up what passed for an air of reality that might make their readers believe – in an oddly self-congratulatory way – that they were at last in touch with a truly contemporary view. This is England: the beastliness, the squalor, the shit. And people wanted to be made uncomfortable! It was a wonderfully indirect absolution of guilt. Docherty, a young man, might serve as a sort of priest. My God!

The telephone rang. I snatched it up, heard myself shout 'Darling!'

But to whom? It was a man's voice. He spoke quickly, apologizing for the short notice, asking me to have lunch tomorrow. He did not give his name.

'Who is it?' I asked.

There was a silence. Was I now the target for a lunatic whose particular mania was the issuing of phantom lunch invitations? Then the words broke through. 'Jeremy Erdley.'

I accepted. At least it would take me away for a few hours.

Later I undressed in the small bedroom on the top floor and climbed into the double bed which Christina had chosen some years ago at a local sale: a large broad bed with a majestic bedstead that she had polished until the brass shone with an almost intrusive brightness. The room was white. Opposite the bed hung an early nineteenth-century landscape in muted shades of green and gold: cattle grazing against a downland background, the sky a soft blue interrupted by two feathery clouds. The picture was perhaps my favourite of those I had inherited from my father. The artist, of an earlier date than most of the collection, had been known as the 'English Claude'. Once a piece of England had looked as still, as solitary and as calm. Then, still clutching the typed pages of his manuscript, I returned to Docherty's story of an old man attacked by a rabid dog on the banks of a canal.

VII

The Erdleys' house was a mansion. Once there had been an almost perfect example of late seventeenth-century architecture on the site: small and restrained. Then, in the middle of the Victorian age, an Erdley had married an heiress, a girl who owned great blocks of Middlesex. He and she had set about rebuilding the ancestral home and had erected a dark gothicised monster for which Ruskin had found words of extravagant praise. Repton's original park had been left; that was fine, but the building activities had merely replaced manageable beauty with unmanageable ugliness.

Soon after the war, before planning laws had become strict or Victorian architecture fashionable, Jeremy Erdley's father had demolished the house's massive wings, leaving only the centre block which – rigid and unforgiving, like some enormous set of castellated civic chambers – had always seemed, even to me, an admirer of the Victorian age, to lack any sort of distinction. Indeed the old man's action had ruined whatever point or grandeur the gothic pile may once have had, although he had succeeded in cutting his heating bills and the cost of maintaining the roof. Young Jeremy, in one of his more lucid moments, had once told me that his father had excused his act of destruction on the grounds that the post-war political climate had been 'revolutionary'. The old man, at that time, had been anxious not only to cut costs but to rid his life of signs of gross ostentation and wealth as well. He had regretted the demolition. The revolution had not taken place and he had decimated this monument to his only distinguished ancestor, the husband of the heiress, once holder of minor office in one of Disraeli's cabinets (it was said that the Prime Minister had muddled his name with someone else's face) and briefly considered for the position of Viceroy of India.

I drove up the drive. On one side lay the planned landscape, carefully planted out with strategic clumps of trees and sculpted into hills, short stretches of plain and an open area of water in the distance where Repton had put an artificial lake. On the other I saw several vehicles on the broad piece of gravel which served as a car park on days when the house was open.

Nearer to the house, people were crossing the drive dragging what looked like an enormous heap of white and red dirty washing. They were followed by others who pulled a trailer that held a number of large drums and containers. I stopped my car. One of the men, with goggles pushed back into his long black hair, raised an arm in a gesture of thanks. I looked towards the car park where other similar objects billowed awkwardly as their owners tried to fold or pack them into a manageable size. Of course. It was the ballooning weekend.

In order to attract the public the Erdleys and their advisers had recently hired a London public relations firm to watch for any trend or craze that might be commercially exploitable. Jeremy had once impressed upon me the major selling points of his product: the house was within easy reach of London; the park was large, flat enough for mechanical events such as veteran car rallies and traction engine displays (several of Repton's original clumps had been cut down in order to accommodate these); the gothicisation of the house enabled it to be referred to as a 'castle' and various basement pantries and still rooms had been transformed into dungeons and torture chambers – complete with imitation racks and treadmills made of fibre glass – to provide what he was pleased to call 'family entertainment'; and on hot summer days the lake was ideal for water-skiing instruction as long as the motor boats took care to avoid the kiddies' pedal-boat marina at its other end and did not frighten the Shetland ponies that were available to give rides to those children who wished to stay on dry land. 'We offer a mixture,' Jeremy Erdley had observed.

'We flatter ourselves that it may be unique.'

I climbed out of the car in front of a massive portico. After the demolition of the two wings this seemed absurdly large for it had been designed for the centre of what had once been a Victorian palace. I turned briefly, heard the noise of a great gust of air or gas and saw that a small group of balloonists had begun to fill their contraption and make it ready for flight.

The wind had a bite. I shivered a little on the gravel before going up the steps to the front door, in through the cold cavern of a hall dominated by a huge equestrian portrait of some eighteenth-century Erdley in the middle of a pack of fox-hounds. A man in black was waiting to guide me. We turned left down a passage, to a door which he opened before announcing my name into what appeared to be a void. Then, in the distance, in the brighter light of the new room, I could see two tall thin figures rising slowly from a sofa.

This was the Erdleys' drawing-room: a vast rectangle with tall bookcases on three sides crammed with leather-bound books, their different shades of brown interrupted occasionally by the dull white of vellum. On the fourth side were the windows, which under almost any other circumstances would seem large but here were incapable of letting in enough light to illuminate the long high interior. At first it seemed as if there was little or no sign of life. Each chair and table existed not in isolation but as part of a grand structure or design; the books appeared so tightly pressed together, so dauntingly a part of the decoration and symmetry of the room, that one might imagine oneself a vandal, a disrupter of order, if tempted to remove any from their shelves. A wood fire crackled in the huge fireplace; there was a slight smokiness in the atmosphere which made my eyes smart. At last I saw evidence of the present, a sign that the house was lived in. On a low table by the fire lay two or three illustrated magazines – one with a photograph of a coyly smiling fashion model in a bright red dress on its cover – and a newspaper irregularly folded, as if recently discarded. Then a girl was alongside me, having risen from the sofa between two of the windows. Behind her, clutching a glass, his eyes already in retreat, stood Jeremy Erdley, the master of the place.

It was his wife who spoke first. 'I'm afraid we got you here

61

at rather short notice,' she said.

I was not sure if I should kiss her or not. I had known the girl for some years. She had shared a flat in London with my daughter. She had been one of Angelica's closest friends. But my whole relationship with the Erdleys, at that stage, was fraught with English complications. They are approximately half my age. They own not only the cottage, but all the land around it as well. They could, if they wished – or so I thought – cut down all the trees, sell the fields to a speculator, seek permission to open a caravan park on my doorstep.

I wished to be friends with the Erdleys not only for these materialistic reasons. I wanted to like them, partly because she was beautiful and he seemed miserable in a way that might (I thought) be susceptible to intelligent sympathy, partly also because of the history of how they have come to be in their position. The accident of this, and the way that the position has changed over the years, intrigues me. Yet whenever we were together there was that English awkwardness of three people trying to please, to say the right thing.

Jeremy Erdley came clumsily up on her left. He caught his thigh on the arm of a straight-backed wooden chair, rattling various small objects – a silver box, a porcelain ash tray, a tiny cup and saucer painted in a dark blue floral pattern – on an occasional table at its side. Jeremy winced. I realised that I was overdressed in my thick tweed jacket, checked shirt and silk tie, and pressed grey flannel trousers. The Erdleys resembled a couple of students. They wore jeans, his newer than her artistically faded blue denim. His light green tweed coat had patches on its elbows and his shirt was open at the neck, despite the chilly air. Her multi-coloured jersey was expensive but casual, obviously hand knitted; her short brown hair stopped just above the collar of what looked like a man's white flannel cricket shirt.

The boy reached me. 'Have a drink?' he said eagerly. 'What can I get you, Sandy?'

'Simon.' His wife corrected him gently.

'Of course. I am so sorry, Simon.' Jeremy's face contorted briefly with embarrassment. His right hand held a quarter full glass of colourless liquid and dissolving cubes of ice.

I walked with him to the far end of the room where a tray of bottles and glasses had been placed on a large round table. Above this were the books, stretching across and upwards to the extremities of the room. I caught a glimpse of some of the titles: Dr Johnson's dictionary, Spenser's *Faerie Queene* (an early edition), Blake's *Book of Job*, a set of Hakluyt's voyages. Often the faint lettering on the spines was impossible to read; and much of the leather looked dull, cracked and unkempt. Presumably the boy knew the value of his library. But perhaps he found its upkeep perplexing: a little too much.

The gin and vodka bottles stood like sentinels on either side of an ice bucket. 'A gin and tonic?' I suggested.

'By all means.' He poured out a generous measure of gin and a small amount of tonic. 'The only way to get through this damned ballooning.'

For one appalling moment, I thought that I might be expected to take part. 'But surely you don't . . . ,' I began.

'Oh yes. I have to be on show. I launch the rally, at half past two. Only a very brief ascent, you understand. Only a brief ascent.' He spoke quickly.

'How many are coming?'

Young Erdley sipped at his drink; then returned the glass to his mouth to take a great gulp of what remained. 'I'm hoping for several thousand,' he said. 'This weather makes it all a bit doubtful of course. Hardly the day for open air sports, although the wind should help to get the balloons up. The trouble is that it might cause them to drift a bit.'

'Several thousand balloons?' It seemed scarcely possible.

He smiled: a gentle awareness of the situation's absurdity.

'Good Lord, no. There should only be about ten or so. I was speaking of the people who come to watch them. But they're not the only attraction. Only a special draw for today. All the other entertainments will be going full blast as well. The model railway, the pony rides, pets' corner, the dungeons, torture chambers, the Mickey Mouse Fun Park. More than enough for most tastes!' Jeremy took hold of one of my arms. I felt his long, thin, bony fingers and their tense grip, through my jacket. 'Just a minute,' he said. 'I must tell you something. Sarah wants to have a word with you afterwards. She's in rather a state about it. I said I'd try to do a little explaining first.' He looked so earnest that I wondered if he might be about to burst into tears. 'I'm afraid she wants to talk business.'

Business? Could it be something to do with the cottage? The rent? Surely that was Erdley's preserve – or perhaps he had given up and handed over control of all his affairs to his wife. 'I'll be happy to try to help,' I said coolly. 'What sort of business?'

'Literary.' I was relieved. Perhaps she had a friend who wrote, or one who wanted a job in publishing. I could make the usual courteous excuses. 'She's written these short stories, you see.' The words rushed out.

'Really? How fascinating.'

'And she wants you to look at them. Not to publish them. Just to look. You and she might have a word after lunch. Alone. She's rather . . .' He was anxious, even desperate, as he sought the right word . . . 'Self-conscious about it all. Rather self-conscious.'

'That's not unusual,' I replied. 'Will she allow me to take her manuscript away?' For a moment I had a vision, brought on by his apologetic description of his wife's wishes, of the two of us going into a smaller more private room to stare at a pile of typewritten pages displayed on a tall stand like one of their pieces of antique classical sculpture. 'I'll need time to read it. I didn't know that she was interested . . .'

Jeremy Erdley cut in. 'No,' he said. He looked solemn. 'She wasn't. Then Orlando was born – our son, you know – and after that she began what she calls "playing around with ideas".' He repeated the words slowly as if they had been extracted from a foreign-language phrase book. 'Playing around with ideas. As I said, she's rather self-conscious about it all. But she wants an expert opinion, and I thought of you. We discussed the business at the beginning of last week and she wanted to see you as quickly as possible. Got very excited. Hence the short notice. I hope you don't mind.'

'Not at all. I always enjoy looking at new work.'

This was a lie. Unsolicited manuscripts were a disruption and rarely of interest. The fear of missing an unknown masterpiece meant that each one had to be read. With friends, the almost inevitable rejection would be difficult, sometimes a source of lasting embarrassment. Yet Sarah Erdley was not a

64

friend. The rejection and few kindly words of discouragement could be expressed with tact. And it would, I told myself, be interesting to learn more about her, to delve into her values and hopes.

Jeremy poured himself another measure of vodka. I noticed that he drank it almost neat, with only a dash of tonic. In repose his face is almost without lines, still thin. Could he be described, in the terms of the cliché, as chinless, I wondered as I watched him edge a little nearer to self-destruction? No, there was a chin. His lips, rather full, pouted as he struggled with the screw top of the tonic water bottle, then relaxed when the gas escaped with a sharp sound. His small blue eyes glinted. They had lost their nervousness, their inclination to run away. Sarah Erdley called to us from the middle of the room. 'What are you up to, Jeremy? If we don't have lunch soon, you'll be late for your ballooning.'

He turned towards her and smiled. He seemed a gentle person, in love with a beautiful girl. 'Lead on,' he said, and the three of us walked out of the large drawing-room back into the long dark passage: then a few yards to a door that had already been opened by the black-coated butler.

This room was smaller, panelled in varnished wood; a massive carved coat of arms – complete with prancing unicorn and what looked like a horse – hung above the high chimney piece. There was no fire and the air was cold. Through the windows at one end I could see the frantic figures of the balloonists preparing for the afternoon's flight.

We stood at the table, which was decorated with two silver wine coolers and a bowl of fruit. Sarah Erdley moved quickly to a chair and put me on her right. Her husband, before sitting down, looked expectantly towards the sideboard.

I have heard young Jeremy talk of his impossible burdens, of the terrible task of preserving his inheritance. In spite of these complaints, the Erdleys lived well. We were waited upon at table. There was a cook who lived in the old servants' quarters in the basement. Their child was looked after by a young nanny. The food, much of it from their own garden, was excellent. There were, of course, penalties to be paid. The house was agonizingly cold in winter, as I had cause to remember from my previous visits. Not even the most efficient central heating system could cope with the variety of draughts, the height of the rooms and the cold-preserving properties of the stone. Then there was the public. From the middle of March until the end of November, the Erdleys were nothing less than a pair of impresarios, as they searched for new ways to attract the crowds.

Sarah Erdley asked, in apparent innocence, 'How is Christina? It is Christina, isn't it?'

I did not blush. 'She's away at the moment,' I answered. This was not the time for long explanations, for a confession of my single state. Then I thought: would there be a chance to see the room upstairs, to put my hand on the mattress of the bed?

'What a pity,' the girl said. 'I wanted to ask her about the Guercino that hangs at the end of the first floor passage. We're thinking of selling it . . .'

And Jeremy, after a gulp at the wine, began to speak of his possessions. It became obvious, amid the talk of values and recent auction prices, that he saw them almost entirely in terms of financial worth. Taxes – either those already paid or the threat of others to come – seemed to govern his life. 'My accountant had told me that the capital gains tax could be rolled over,' he said, discussing some sale that had taken place soon after his father's death, 'but the Inland Revenue were perfectly bloody about it.' I said how sad it was to see the break-up of a great English collection. As her husband's protests slowly subsided, Sarah Erdley turned to me. 'Did Jeremy mention my work to you? I'm afraid we had an ulterior motive in asking you here today. It wasn't just because we thought you might like to see the balloons!'

Her face, leaning across so as to be near to mine, showed diffidence. The words, perhaps prepared, with the joke about the balloons to show that she approached the notion of herself as a writer in a light-hearted way, had not hidden the fact that she minded. I wondered about her secrets. Why had she married Erdley? Had it been greed or material ambition? I remembered her in the flat that she and Angelica used to share: an earnest girl whose looks had not quite come into their own, very young, hovering behind my daughter's self-certainty. Together they had ironed their dresses, spoken of their hopes, their triumphs and disasters. Angelica had been surprised by her marriage, certainly not jealous, but surprised. 'A dark horse' was how she had described her old flat-mate. She must have been equally amazed by the late flowering of the girl's beauty, which again she would claim to spurn.

I wondered: was Sarah Erdley just a silly but beautiful girl on the make, afflicted with the vanity of artistic aspirations? Or was she in love with the man at the top of the table, who had begun to explain his wish, next season, to open a pizza bar as an extension to the tea room? Sarah Erdley's mouth was open. Her blue eyes looked down. As she picked up her knife and fork, her hands shook. Beauty such as hers was impossible to treat in a way that was cool and rational. The girl's face was a revelation of religious suffering. And why? All for the worry of how best to make public the private whims of a bored imagination.

For the wrong reasons, I would try to help her. 'I'd like to take the work away with me if I may,' I said.

'Of course,' she said. She raised her eyes. 'You must tell me the truth. I mean, what you really think.'

'I'm afraid that this is a difficult time for fiction,' I said.

'Who else do you look after?' she asked.

I mentioned two young novelists. She had heard of neither of them. Then I threw in the name of Henry Brown.

'Henry Brown . . .' Jeremy began.

'Oh yes,' his wife said, firmly. She smiled. 'He must be very popular.' She knew enough, had studied the literary pages of the Sunday supplements with the necessary diligence, to look down on Henry. 'A real work horse.'

I thought I could not let her get away with this. I remembered my first meeting with Henry, our lunch in the pub, the gamble that he had taken in giving up his job to write, the leap into the unknown. What could someone like Sarah Erdley know of such things? The girl's beauty began to work against her. So much admiration and attention must have been lavished upon this mocking young face: so much in return for a mere half smile, an entry into a room, a half-baked opinion sweetly expressed, the chance of stirring her interest. It was a long way from Henry: an elderly man worried about his weight and his liver, sticking determinedly to his thousand words a day. Without these words, without their success, he would be bankrupt, holed up in a London lodging house and hawking his hypochondria around the crammed waiting rooms of the National Health Service. I must have looked angry for she blushed. I relented and said only, 'Yes, his production is wonderfully regular.'

'I write very slowly.' Probably she thought that this was the way that it should be.

'Which authors do you admire?'

'Jane Austen. Henry James.' The names came quickly.

'Jane Austen, Henry James . . .' Jeremy began again.

I interrupted. 'What about contemporary novelists?'

She put her hand up to push her short hair back from her forehead. 'I don't read many. Perhaps I should. But there seems to be so much to catch up on from the past.'

'Do you have much time to read?'

'I try to make time,' Sarah Erdley said a little petulantly. 'But it's not easy. Jeremy has put me in charge of the gift shop, the tea room and the handicraft emporium. I do all the ordering, you know.'

'All the ordering. Every bloody scrap of it,' Jeremy interjected.

'And is that interesting?' I asked.

She shrugged her narrow shoulders. 'I try to make the best of it. One has a certain feeling of achievement. Our turnover increases each year.'

'It's a triumph. One of our great successes,' her husband shouted, the vodka and wine suddenly producing a rush of good cheer. 'Those Woodland Creatures Tea-Sets go like smoke. As for the jars of Old-Fashioned Chutney . . .'

One side of her small mouth descended. 'Don't forget that you have to start the rally,' she said sharply. He cursed, muttered something about having lost his watch. The marriage, I decided, was an uneven match. She was bored by him. Had she come to hate this place as well, this cold hideous sepulchre of a house?

After lunch, Jeremy left. Sarah Erdley and I sat in the drawing room. She took the straight-backed chair to one side of the sofa but almost immediately leapt to her feet again and ran towards the window. 'There he goes!' she shouted. 'Aloft at last!'

I rushed to her. Over the park a balloon was drifting slowly away, still near enough to the ground for us to be able to see – in its basket – a large man in a heavy blue jersey and the grinning figure of Jeremy Erdley dressed in a dark red cape fringed with white fur dotted with black. On his head he wore some sort of crown – with its rim again covered in white fur – out of which sprouted pieces of gold metal surmounted by small white balls. A gust of wind took the balloon sharply away from the front of the house. The movement was brisk enough to tip young Erdley's curious headgear over his brow, then down until it covered both his eyes. He raised his hands quickly to try to push it up. He seemed to be struggling. He stumbled towards the edge of the basket, leaned out in what looked to me to be a most unwise way, still straining to dislodge the crown. Clearly the boy could see nothing; his companion in the balloon seized him in a rough embrace and pulled him back towards the basket's centre with such force that the crown fell off the top of Jeremy Erdley's head. The man then let him go and, in a lightning movement, reached to catch the absurd object before it could plummet into the silent crowd below.

I looked at the girl. She had gone white. 'Is this some sort of tableau?' I asked.

The two people in the balloon clutched each other again, as if engaged in a complex Latin American dance routine. The large man tried to put the crown back on to Jeremy Erdley's head with one hand while his other arm clasped the boy to his breast. The wind had blown Erdley's hair to one side in a light-brown mass. He turned towards us – the other man was now holding the crown above his head in the gesture of an ancient coronation ritual – and I noticed that his eyes were once again covered, this time by long strands of hair. He waved his arms, caught the big man's cheek with one of them; whereupon the big man appeared to retaliate by cramming the crown down on the top of Erdley's forehead and ungainly hair. There was a rush of gas, the balloon went higher, out of sight to our left.

Sarah Erdley had her hands over her face. 'My God!' She exclaimed.

'I think they're safe,' I said softly.

She sighed. 'It was Jeremy's idea. He said it would interest the public.'

'For him to go up in a balloon?'

'Yes. Wearing peer's robes and a coronet.'

'Who was that with him?' I asked.

'A local enthusiast.'

We looked out of the window again, to see the balloon come back to earth. It landed slowly, hit the ground with a slight bump. By now the sun had come out and as the two travellers disembarked the metal of Jeremy Erdley's coronet flashed and glinted. The crowd applauded. Erdley managed a nervous smile while his companion gave an exuberant wave. 'Yes,' said Sarah, 'they're safe now.' And I understood from the way that she looked at the thin stooping figure, from her affectionate smile as the back of his red robe trailed across the wet grass behind him, as the coronet once again tipped over his forehead, that her anxiety was real enough.

'He could have fallen out of that basket,' I said inanely. 'There was a moment of real danger.' I watched for the reaction of the boy's wife.

She had recovered. 'Ballooning is a dangerous sport,' she said. 'I don't feel I could ever do it. Once you're married, with children, you become much more frightened about that sort of thing. For instance I used to do the most fantastically daring things when Angelica and I went skiing together, in those parties of friends. But now I'm much more cautious. It makes Jeremy rather exasperated.'

It was the first time that day that she had mentioned our daughter. 'That reminds me,' I said, taking the opportunity. 'Angelica sends you her love. I spoke to her last week.' This was not true.

The girl smiled indulgently. 'How is she?' she asked. 'Our paths never seem to cross these days. But as I'm down here most of the time and she's in London, that's not surprising. What is she up to?'

'Still working.' I almost added: in common with most of the rest of us.

'How brave: I do hope they're kind to her at the . . .' The girl seemed lost.

70

I moved in to help. 'The Elephant and Castle,' I said. 'She's a civil servant.' And suddenly I wished that our daughter was with me in that bleak drawing-room. Angelica could always sweep aside my fantasies, those foolish stirrings of romance. 'She works damned hard,' I declared with an unexpected vehemence.

The girl blushed. 'I only wanted to find out . . .' she began. Then she stopped and started again. 'You brought them both up yourself, didn't you? Edward and Angelica, I mean. Forgive me for asking.' She could see that I was annoyed. 'After their mother left . . .'

'No. They went with her. Surely Angelica must have told you that. Laura re-married. She and her husband have a house at Bembridge, Isle of Wight.'

Sarah Erdley bit her lip. 'I know,' she said. 'I once stayed there, before we were married.'

'With Jeremy?'

'No. But he was a friend of Edward's – from school.'

'So you met Bill?' I asked. 'He's a wonderful host.'

'I don't think . . .'

'Bill is my wife's second husband.' I said, with a reassuring smile. And there was no awkwardness in my voice. 'But my wife is ill at the moment . . .'

'I am sorry.'

I looked towards the window and saw, against a grey sky, three balloons floating away from the house.

'Will your husband have to spend the whole afternoon out there?' I asked.

Sarah Erdley sighed. 'Jeremy? Oh yes, most of it.' she said. 'I'll join him towards the end. There's a prizegiving ceremony, to be held in the refreshment tent if it rains.' She patted her jeans. 'I shall have to get into something a bit more respectable.'

I thought then that I could see the enforced tedium of much of their life. I wondered about her education: probably a series of fashionable boarding schools, perhaps nine or ten months in Paris or Switzerland, then entry into the aristocratic marriage stakes in London where, according to the standards of that world, she had performed well. In a way, it was pathetic. 'I really must go,' I said, and stood up.

Sarah Erdley stood as well. 'Oh dear,' she said. 'Please promise to come again. We're here the whole time.' Her voice veered up into what could have been a cry for help. 'How often are you down?'

'Most weekends,' I answered. 'Sometimes I lend the place in the middle of the week or if I go away, mostly to writers trying to finish something.'

'Which writers?'

I mentioned a few names. 'Once Henry Brown came for a week, with his friend Paul. Their house in the south of France was being re-wired. He needed somewhere quiet to work. It was an absolute disaster. They had bad luck with the weather. It rained virtually every day. And Henry had brought all the wrong clothes, or so Paul told me later. He forgot about the English summer and came prepared for Mediterranean temperatures. I think they were both relieved when the end of the week came.'

We were still standing in the centre of the large room. I noticed that Sarah Erdley's face had the barest hint of lines around her eyes, evidence of her smile. 'I suppose that writers find it impossible to work in some places – if the atmosphere is wrong, I mean,' she said tentatively.

'Where do you write?' I asked.

Her eyes shied away. 'In the bedroom,' she replied.

'Does Jeremy read your work?'

'He has seen some of it,' Sarah Erdley replied. She fiddled vaguely with a strand of her hair. 'I must give you the stories.'

'Is your husband an exacting critic?' I asked, and smiled to put her at her ease.

'He . . . well, he . . .' She hesitated, looked towards the window. The afternoon had deteriorated into rain. There were now no balloons in sight; small clusters of figures stood in sodden groups on the bright green turf of the park. 'He's too busy really to be able to give them enough of his time. He likes some more than others, often those that I'm least satisfied with. Anyway . . .' She walked over to the ornate desk in a far corner of the room, opened its middle drawer, took out a hard-covered light blue binder and brought this across to me. 'I had it typed by an agency in London, which was rather expensive, but I read somewhere that a tidy manuscript is essential, if you want publishers to take you at all seriously. I also read that short stories are notoriously difficult to sell. So I expect I haven't got much of a chance. But I'd love to have your opinion.' Now she was gushing. 'If you'd like me to collect it from your office when you've finished – or perhaps you might think that we should have a talk about some other ideas I've had, for novels and plays.' She laughed nervously. 'I'm afraid I could become a regular literary production line!'

'Hard work is what counts,' I said briskly.

My comment jarred. Sarah Erdley looked angry. I saw the spoilt petulance. In that instant, I was against this foolish child. I looked at my watch, patted the binder, gave a thinner smile. 'We'll be in touch. And thank you for lunch.'

And in the hall, beside the front door, she leaned over to kiss me goodbye.

VIII

I want to set out the history of Laura's behaviour towards me, or a part of that history. I want to see if there are patterns that I should have noticed earlier. I want to try to understand how we came to live apart.

Bill and Laura married soon after our divorce, then began to build up their life together. First came the house in Chelsea: later the villa at Bembridge, convenient for sailing, good for the children.

At that stage I scarcely knew the man. During the divorce, he had remained in the background. For this I know that I should be grateful.

For some time I had cherished Laura's avowal, made during the summer week by the sea in Suffolk, that she was not in love with him. Not even as that year passed, as it had slowly become obvious that our marriage was doomed, had she said anything that could point to a change in this. Some evenings she went out, but would always return. We had ceased to share a room; she could leave the flat at any time without disturbing me. But she chose to stay in, retreating to our old double bed early to read or have a late bath, leaving me to listen alone to the news on the wireless while our children slept.

This was the way that Bill had wanted it, she had told me later. 'He's a sensitive man,' she said. 'You may not believe this but it's true. Throughout that time he was thinking of you, putting himself in your position, imagining what would hurt the most. He wanted to protect you.'

74

Laura chose a good moment to announce that she wanted a divorce. It was in January, a night of cold rain. I returned late from the office. The pavements shone in the dark; the street lamps fought a persistent haze.

But I knew the man. I knew his name, his profession and a little part of his history. I knew of their first meeting, in the spring, under a year before she was to ask for an end to our marriage.

They met at a cocktail party, given by my Parkin cousins who have done so well for themselves in the wine trade. Bill had been there as a valued customer: a tall, thick-set, courteous bald man a year or two older than I.

Charlie Parkin introduced us to him. We spoke for a few minutes, words of complete banality, difficult to hear above the noise of voices in the crammed low room. I saw, across the crowd, my old friend Robin, Laura's cousin in the Foreign Office. 'Robin's here,' I said to her. 'Over there, beside the front door.' And Bill had let out a low cry for help. 'You're the only people Charlie has introduced me to! Please . . .' He laughed quickly after saying this, a snort that had not quite removed the desperate look in his eyes. 'I must see Robin,' I said to Laura. 'I want to meet his wife. You stay.'

So they talked together for the next hour and, on our way home, Laura said, 'What a strange man. I think he must be a little mad. Do you know, he believes that higher education is almost entirely a waste of time?'

I want to get the order of dissolution clear in my mind. In August she told me that the affair had begun. In September, I found a letter in the drawer of her dressing table and knew the identity of her lover.

Someone else, someone outside the tight circle of Laura's adultery, took pleasure from all this. The day after my discovery of the letter, Henry Brown and I had lunch together. Henry was on one of his periodic visits to London. His manner was accommodating. I have this notion that Henry has the perception and imagination of a great writer: the sort of man I would want to have as a counsellor and friend. So, in the expensive fish restaurant around the corner from my office, I told him everything.

At first he looked solemn. 'You have the letter?' he asked. I passed across the sheet of light blue writing paper with a Mayfair address at the top. The message read: 'We won! It must have been you. Until tomorrow . . . All my love. B.'

Henry was cold. He wanted the precise details: physical, geographical, words spoken, the atmosphere prevalent at certain moments in our marriage. 'Do you still sleep together? Was your love life satisfactory before she took up with this man? Where did they meet? How and when might they arrange to see each other? When did she first tell you? Is she still content to cook your dinner? Does the au pair know?' I was honest with him. 'We'll go to this address this afternoon,' he said, in a state of excitement. 'Find out the fellow's name. You must want to know, Simon, for God's sake! Waiter! Will you order us a taxi?'

The flat was in a large block off Park Lane, near Marble Arch. Henry insisted on paying for the taxi. We walked into the hall, along the short passage, then turned right to be faced by three lift doors and a porter who was reading a newspaper. Henry had the letter. He opened it again, looked at the address and asked, 'Who lives in flat number 15a?' The porter, dressed in a blue uniform with gold edges to the lapels of his jacket, put his newspaper down. He was small, fat, his grey hair well greased, old enough (I thought) to be on the verge of retirement. I remember his look of courteous obstruction. 'Can I take a message, sir?' he asked. Henry repeated his question; then, in front of us lift doors opened to allow someone out. I recognised Bill and realised that this was her lover.

He was wearing a dark suit and a white shirt. His face and the top of his head were brown. He had an aura of good health, the fluid movements of confident precision, of freedom. Suddenly, as he looked at the porter, waved and walked quickly towards the door to the street, I saw what made him different and exciting. He had a sense of immediacy, of the importance of the present. His mind was full of that moment, of each step forward, each turn of the passage. 'That's your man,' the porter said, and slyly gave us his name.

'So where does that leave you?' Henry asked as we left the building. 'Will you fight him?' Yes, I thought, by God I will. I

76

will turn Laura into a bloody battlefield, touch every ounce of guilt and shame. 'You know the man?' Henry was quick with his interrogation. 'A strange-looking individual. Tall, I suppose. In reasonable trim. But hardly the stuff of romance. More like a provincial bank manager.' I spoke of our earlier meeting at the Parkins'. 'Ah,' Henry said. Already his mind was racing ahead. 'Now here's your plan. Say nothing to Laura at the moment. Allow them time together. Indeed see that they have as much of each other as possible.' He paused. 'How old is your wife?' he asked. 'Thirty-four,' I said, 'a year younger than I am.' 'Hardly a mid-life crisis then,' Henry remarked. 'No. But that's more the sort of thing that men go in for, I think, don't you? Stupid irrational love affairs in middle age in order to prove something or other to themselves. Women tend to be more sensible. More guarded.' Then I snapped at him, as a taxi came to the kerb. How useful it was, I said coldly, to have a friend who understood feminine psychology, who had such a wealth of first-hand experience to draw on in that field.

We entered the taxi. I leaned forward to give my office address without asking Henry if he wanted to be dropped somewhere else. He seemed unmoved. 'Of course you're upset, Simon,' he said. 'It's a blow to so many things. To a man's pride. To his whole conception of himself. But can it really have come as such a surprise to you? Look back with an enquiring eye. I'm prepared to bet there was ample evidence that trouble was brewing.' He sat on the edge of his seat: small, eager, anxious to miss not a moment of the drama. His face, strangely ageless (did he undergo treatment, even occasional surgery?), preserved the pretence of solemnity, although the small eyes sparkled.

The taxi stopped in the Oxford Street traffic. There was no escape. 'I'm going to tell you something that you may not like,' Henry went on. 'I never thought the two of you well suited.' I looked at him, thought for an instance of violence. 'I'll tell you why,' he said. 'She's too unpredictable. Now that wouldn't matter to some men. But you need a calm presence at your side. So do I, my dear Simon, so do I. Hence Paul. He is my ballast. Now Laura could never be that for you. She and I, of course, have always got on. I would always establish – or do my best to establish – good relations with whomsoever you might choose to marry or set up house with.' At last we were moving again. 'And whatever happens between Laura and you, the work – your work – will continue. If she takes off with that tall bald man, if she stays with you – which I rather hope, for your sake, that she does not – your responsibilities to your firm, to your authors, to the preservation of literary standards and excellence, will go on.'

'And my family?' I asked. 'What about them?'

Angelica and Edward were, at that time, aged ten and eight. Now it seems like another century: before Christina, before the cottage, before Williams, before the emergence of the world of Bill. 'Divided between the two of you, I suppose,' Henry answered. 'Proper legal access will be given of course. Perhaps you could even try to get them absolutely, if you like. After all, she's the guilty party – if one can speak of such matters in terms of guilt and innocence.' He talked as if divorce was an absolute certainty, and of course he was right. The taxi stopped again. 'Now this is where you get off,' Henry said. 'I'll take him on to my hotel. Don't bother about the fare. I can look after that. Save you filling it in on your expenses. You know where I'm staying if you want to get hold of me for any reason – personal or otherwise. I'm out this evening, dining with my agent and a theatrical producer who wants to turn *The Tremendous Sea* into a musical. Did I tell you about that? No? It can only help sales. We might do a new edition, with a more eye-catching cover. Sell it in the foyer of the theatre. Oh, and Simon.' He looked serious. 'I return to Nice by an early flight tomorrow. If you want a rest or holiday or simply a few days out of London we're always there. Be sure to keep in touch.'

I thanked him. In his own way, he meant well.

That evening Laura was standing in the doorway of the kitchen; from the other side came the noise of the children having their supper. 'Simon,' she said, 'can I have a word?' I put my umbrella in the stand, my briefcase on a chair, and followed her.

The bedroom had become her private domain. There she

thought of this interloper, wrote secret declarations to him, planned her next meeting, concocted the lies for her husband and the children. It was a nest of conspiracy and deceit: no longer the place where she and I had celebrated our first few years of marriage. As she turned to face me over the double bed, I nearly asked her if she remembered those days, if they lay crumbling in her mind like monuments of a fallen empire. Beside the bed, on a small table, behind her alarm clock and a pile of books, was the photograph of me, taken – at my mother's instigation – by a professional photographer soon after I had left the army. She must have seen this each night, in the morning when she reached out to silence the alarm, in the evening when she lifted a book from the table to read in bed and later stretched across to turn off the lamp; yet the photograph remained. For a moment this gave me hope.

The curtains were long strips of green, white and red flowers tumbling over each other. The bedroom had been painted white. I had said that, as the other decorating costs had been so much more than we had originally planned, we could not afford the luxury of wallpaper in all the rooms, and white was a safe colour against which any picture or material would not clash. Then there were her pictures: her own work, remnants of her days at art school; and four gaudy splashes by her father. This was before I had inherited the Victorian collection.

We stood by the bed. She seemed worried; her hands twisted a paper clip. Her brown hair was dirty and disordered. She wore a dark blue skirt and a white jersey over a white blouse. Although the day was cold she had no stockings on: just a pair of old black casual shoes on her feet with stained silver buckles. She looked down at her hands, at the contorted metal, then up at me. Her eyes did not flinch. 'Simon,' she said, 'I hear that you've been doing some amateur detective work.'

We had been to the block of flats a few hours ago. It had not crossed my mind that Bill could have transmitted the news so quickly. I had planned a different unveiling of my discovery, later in the evening, with the two of us facing one another in the large armchairs in the drawing-room. 'What on earth do you mean?' I asked roughly.

'Or have you other friends in that building?'

'Which building?'

Her lips were set firm. 'Please,' she said. 'Don't play the idiot.' She named the street, the number and the address of her lover.

'Oh, I see.' I tried to smile.

'I suppose that you thought you wouldn't be recognised. How did you find out? Have you been grubbing about in my bag or in my desk? And who on earth was with you?' She looked down at the floor, then up at me again. The resolve seemed to fade. Her eyes left my face for the wardrobe behind. 'Oh, I know,' she said, with a catch in her voice. 'I can't blame you. Why shouldn't you want to know? People would say that it is your right.'

'I was with Henry Brown,' I said. 'And I found a letter. In the drawer of your dressing table.'

'You and Henry? Why Henry?' She laughed.

It was better not to show anger. 'We were having lunch together. And I was so full of my discovery – the finding of the letter with the address on it – that I might have talked about it to anybody.'

She sat down on the bed, brought her hands together in her lap and looked at the wall. 'Henry encouraged you to go of course,' she said. 'He's such a bloody mischief-maker!' She had lost her temper, perhaps with me, more probably with herself. And she burst into tears.

I sat down beside her and put my hand on her shoulder. 'What stage have you reached now?' I asked. 'What does he want?'

She looked at me again. Her eyes glistened with tears. 'He says that he loves me,' she said, her voice breaking over the syllables. 'He's so insistent, Simon. I don't know what to do. Of course I know the dangers. The damage that I'm doing. I know about the selfishness and the cruelty.'

'Selfishness and cruelty?' I wanted it all to be clear.

'To you. To the children. I've told him all that.'

'And what does he say?'

'He says . . .' She waited for a moment, blew her nose. Then she put away the handkerchief and clasped one of her thumbs in her other hand. 'He says that this is something extraordinary. That we cannot afford to let it die. That any shame, any regret, will be over quickly. That the children will be safe and secure with him – safer and better off than with you. That, as they are mine, he will love them as much as he loves me. That they will become his children.'

'And me?' I asked. 'What position does he plan for me?'

'He says that he can give me a better life,' she went on, as if she had not heard. 'He has nothing against you personally, of course. Nothing at all. It's as if . . .' – she looked anxiously around the room – 'as if he sees you as an innocent bystander, a spectator at an accident so to speak – caught up in all this entirely against your will. He says that it's not your fault that the two of us should have fallen in love . . .'

'The two of you?'

The curtains were still undrawn. The rain fell through the darkness, spattering the large bedroom window. On the other side of the street, I saw, through a lighted window, an old woman, unaware that she could be watched, slide a dress onto a hanger before putting it in a large, tall, dark cupboard. She had a look of satisfaction on her face. 'Are you in love with him?' I asked. Instinctively I began to think ahead. Laura would go. I would be left here, in this expensive flat which was too large for one person. Who would have the children? Then I thought, no. She doesn't really know what she's doing. She doesn't know the real meaning of it all, the consequences of playing around with words like love and selfishness and cruelty. 'Laura,' I said. 'This won't do.' It was a feeble beginning.

She chose to answer my first question. 'Yes,' she said, 'I think it might be the two of us, Simon.' She moved over to her dressing table, opened one of the drawers, took out a small box and brought it across to me before taking off the lid. 'Look,' she said, and there – on a cushion of red plush – lay a string of pearls, a pair of diamond earrings and a bright green emerald ring. 'Have you ever seen anything like them?' She was panting a little, a schoolgirl in search of a shocked response.

'Laura,' I said. 'What are these things?'

And I was shocked: she had achieved this. The shock was caused by a fear that I might never have understood her at all.

81

Had she really – all along – been susceptible to these trinkets? I stopped myself. It could not be so simple, so cheap and awful as that. I picked up the pearls. There were three rows of them, joined together by a diamond clasp. 'When will you wear them?' I asked. 'You have the jewels that your mother gave you when we were married.'

'Granny's old things, you mean?' She looked serious. 'But they're nothing to these. And the pearls are cultured. Look, you can see the difference!' She took the new ones from me. 'See the shine, the texture? Different altogether.'

'Is this why you stay with him?' I asked.

Laura snapped the case shut. 'Simon,' she said. 'For heaven's sake don't make it even more unpleasant . . .'

'Why are you showing these things to me?'

I was standing beside her. She held the case tightly. At least some of my words appeared to have struck home. I realised then that the spontaneous display of the jewels had sprung from her simplicity, a sudden wish to share her pleasure: also her need to replace words with more concrete evidence, a sign of her lack of confidence in her ability to explain. Her hold on the case relaxed as once more she burst into tears. She put one hand up her sleeve to search for her handkerchief and sat down on the bed in a state of what looked to be exhaustion. 'But I can't go,' she said, through great gulping sobs. 'I can't go. It's happened too late. That's what I keep telling Bill. He won't listen. He keeps pushing me.'

It was the first time that she had mentioned his name. I saw this as a landmark. 'What shall we do?' I asked.

Laura looked up at me, through the tears. 'Sometimes,' she said, 'I wish that you could speak to him. I want you to see how impossible it is to argue. I can't even put the opposite point of view. I wish you could hear the way that he talks about us – I mean the two of us together.'

I was angry again. 'Of course I can't see the man,' I snapped. 'Don't be so absurd! What a preposterous notion.'

For a few seconds we were silent. Then she spoke. 'It would have been better if I'd done the cowardly thing, wouldn't it? I mean if I'd run off one morning or afternoon while you were at work and left a note to say that the marriage was over.'

'And taken the children as well?'

'He could find somewhere for us all.'

'I would put the police on to you. I would take out an injunction and drag you through the courts. I can fight you both, Laura.'

'You don't know him, Simon,' she said quietly. 'He won't allow me to do that. He won't allow me to desert in such a desperate and humiliating way. He wants everything to be above board and civilized, a solution that has the consent of all parties. He says that he would hate our new life to begin in an atmosphere of hatred and distrust.'

'What sort of man is this?' I asked. I remembered the long back, the regular quick pace, the short black hair speckled with grey underneath the large bald top of his head. 'Is he married?'

'No', she said. 'Bill has never been married. He says that he's never had the time, until now.'

'And what has kept him so busy?'

'His work.' She spoke quickly of the man's achievement. 'His companies. Everything from motor car components to loo paper and beer. He started from nothing, you know. Absolutely nothing.'

One of our children started to rattle the door from outside, to call for us. 'I don't want you to go, Laura,' I said.

But that evening, after she had put the children to bed, she came into the drawing-room of the flat to say that she was leaving – only for a few hours – to tell the man of our conversation. Then it was only a matter of time.

IX

On the way back to the cottage, the country and the houses of the village were blurred by the pouring rain.

I minded about the way that the countryside was changing, the way that my vision of English rural life was dissolving in front of my eyes. I seemed to have a need to dream of unspoiled landscapes, of a quiet and pleasant land.

By the time I had come to the area, the changes were well under way. One of the three shops in the village had been taken over by an antique dealer; in the window stood a Victorian chest-of-drawers, a large copper warming pan and a bust of Napoleon. Several of the houses, sold before my arrival, had names stuck on their gates and the bright boxes of burglar alarms protruding from their fronts. Then the pace quickened. Jeremy Erdley's father died. Money for taxes and death duties had to be found. More houses were sold. I began to fear for my own position. I knew that the cottage would fetch a good price as a weekend retreat for some affluent city figure who wanted to enjoy the country air.

I wondered about my legal rights. In fact the tenancy made me reasonably secure. Erdley and his agent had to offer the place to me first. Their price would certainly be high, for this was a desirable area – convenient for London although not quite in the commuter belt. But they did not make the approach. My lease was for a certain number of years. Until it ended, the law, or so Christina had discovered from a knowledgeable friend, protected me. If they wanted me to go, the Erdleys would have to buy me out.

So I had remained in the cottage, to watch the changes. Another of the shops in the village closed, to be taken over by the same antique dealer, who seemed to be doing well enough to need two showrooms. Only the general store, which also served as the post office, remained. More houses were sold, more name plates and alarm boxes appeared. On Saturdays there were large estate cars in the High Street, driven by bargain hunters who had come to the antique shops in search of period furniture for their own country residences. Outside the larger houses, grouped picturesquely around the green, Mercedes Benzes, Jaguars and the occasional Porsche awaited their owners. In the pub, which I seldom visited except to buy bottles to take away, large men in chunky cardigans and women in scarves decorated with pictures of horses clutched their gins and tonics and boomed at the mystified landlord.

This, I knew, was progress. Two wishes had coincided: the landowner's wish to raise money and the city dweller's desire for the peace and prestige of country life. I knew also that it was wrong of me to complain, for I was a part of the movement. Before I had come there, the cottage had been the home of one of the Erdleys' woodmen. I had turned the place into a weekend retreat for a London publisher. No, I was as guilty, as out of place as any of those who drove the Jaguars, the Porsches and the station wagons full of antiques. And the past that I wanted to return existed merely in my imagination, a land of dear shadows and colourful illusion.

That next week, I won the battle of Docherty's stories. George Mason read the collection and said that he liked it. He came to an editorial meeting and told us that the author's style reminded him of André Gide or the young Isherwood. I had already secured the support of Joan who had not read the book but was prepared to further what I told her was the cause of 'quality' publishing.

The three of us faced up to Williams. Freddy, the sales director, remained neutral in the middle. The Welshman, however, was as good as his word.

'Simon,' he said with a mirthless grin, 'I capitulate. But if we do this book we must do it well.' He covered his concession with a flurry of instructions. 'I want you to liaise closely with Alison about publicity. Get Jane working on the overseas rights as soon as possible. No, perhaps that should wait till after publication when we can distribute some reviews. Presumably there will be good reviews? Anyway, you seem confident on that point. But we must prepare ourselves. Identify areas of interest, possible markets, key selling points. I want to be kept closely in touch. We can use this book as an argument against elitist criticism that we're not interested in what the snobs call "serious books".' He looked at me sharply. 'I just hope that these stories are as good as you say they are.'

Back in my office, after the meeting, I allowed myself a minute or two of contented contemplation. Then I telephoned Hermione, Docherty's agent. Characteristically the woman attempted to make me feel guilty not only for the delay but even for wanting to read the stories myself before agreeing to take the young man on. Her word on these matters – or so she intimated – ought to be enough. Editors were simply obstacles, placed in her way by a malign fate.

I tried to interrupt. 'Hermione . . . ,' I began.

'Now I hope that you'll cherish Michael,' she continued. 'Treat him properly. Don't allow him to become a mere entry in that Welshman's ledger.'

I pressed on. 'Hermione, I think that Mr Docherty and I should meet now, don't you?'

She sighed. 'You couldn't have chosen a worse time, Simon. Tomorrow is Friday – or perhaps that may have escaped your attention. Next week is hell. Then I go to the farmhouse for my annual "recuperation", as I call it.'

'Oh, dear.' The woman some years ago (before the place had been discovered by the British, or so she claims) had bought and restored a fortified farmhouse in the Dordogne. Once she had showed me photographs of the place, even issued an invitation which I had almost, in a moment of intoxication at the end of a long lunch, been rash enough to accept. 'For how long?'

'A fortnight. But I don't want Michael to have to wait. I

86

want to keep the momentum going.'

Relief surged within me. 'I will be more than happy to meet him on my own,' I said.

'Oh, will you now?' She laughed. 'You promise me that there'll be no monkey business, no precipitate signing of contracts or attempts to make a deal behind my back? With that Welshman in charge anything is possible.' She was particularly annoyed with Williams because he had recently slid out of some expensive arrangement the firm had made before his arrival with one of Hermione's other authors.

'Will you ask Mr Docherty to telephone me?' I said, ignoring the last jibe. I always – or almost always – maintained an outward display of loyalty to my boss.

'If you were really enthusiastic about his work you would ring him yourself.'

'Hermione,' I sighed, 'I thought that I would leave it to you to break the good news to your client, on whose behalf you have worked so indefatigably. Perhaps you might then ask him to get in touch with me in order that we may arrange an early date to meet. I'm up to my eyes in work at the moment.'

'You always are, Simon. You always are.'

Talking to her had exhausted me. I reached across my desk for the biography of Palmerston and prepared to work on its last hundred unedited pages. It was a worthy book, by a professional historian. Other historians would review it well and the sales should more or less cover its costs. Williams saw the work as another sop to his 'elitist' critics. I lifted its great bulk with a feeling of dread, the foreboding of inevitable tedium, of distaste for the thick wedges of pernickety details of moribund treaties and diplomatic alliances. A thought came to me. Dare I destroy the thing, burn it, rip its pages into a thousand pieces and claim that my briefcase had been stolen on the way to work? No. The author would have another copy, a carefully preserved carbon of his inert pompous prose. I remembered how, years ago, I had pushed the idea of this book and told my fellow directors that the man should be given a large advance. I had dwelt on Palmerston's colourful character, his sexual appetite, the drama of his relationship with Queen Victoria. They had heeded me. Williams, at the time of his arrival, had been forced to accept the contract as one already signed, one that it would be foolish to abandon, because here commerce and quality might meet.

Then the manuscript had arrived, its dullness evident from the first paragraph. It was a poor basis on which to fight for books of a higher literary merit and had led to more trouble. On the day that I admitted to Williams that *Palmerston* was not quite the biography that we had hoped for, he smiled and gave me to understand that he would tolerate its failure if I supported the purchase at Frankfurt of the English rights of a Swedish polemic in favour of free sauna treatment, written by a cousin of his wife. To add to my humiliation, the man had given me editorial responsibility for the work, putting me in touch with its original publisher in Stockholm who began to bombard the firm with a series of obtuse requests. 'Simon!' the Swede used to bellow down the telephone. 'Soon I come to England. We do more business. Then you come to Stockholm. I introduce you to some Swedish writers. Yes?'

In the afternoon, to my amazement, the Erdley girl telephoned.

Her voice, soft and charmingly shy, summoned up intimations of the exotic, a hint of renewal. I let her speak. She babbled about her stories. Had I read them? The youthful uncertainty affected me like the promise of adventure. It seemed we were both young together as I laughed, apologised and admitted that I had not had time to look at her work. I would be in touch, I said, as soon as possible. For an instant we were conspirators against the rest of the world.

Replacing the receiver, I recovered my senses and thought that this must be the best moment – the moment of illusion, the dream of sweet possibility. To try to move on would be wrong. Then my mind at once ran off again, into vague fantasies of illicit and impossible pleasure.

That evening, at home, I heard the sound of ecstasy – or agony – coming from the flat below. I went out on to the small landing. For a moment all was quiet. Then the noise began again, a series of grunts rising to a long, impassioned, feminine

88

shriek. I heard the door open, footsteps rush through the hall. There seemed to be several people involved. Voices rose, then fell to a whisper.

Were these the signs of an orgy? I blushed. Clearly there was a whole group of participants. Should I complain? They were disturbing me. It was an absurd contrast to the decorous evenings Christina and I had spent in this building, sipping our drinks, talking precisely to each other about our work, holiday plans or the past. Damn them!

The telephone rang. I ran back into my flat, to the desk beside one of the high windows where I picked up the white receiver. 'Dad?' It was my daughter, Angelica.

'Darling!'

Her voice was eager. 'I thought I'd ring to find out how things were. I haven't seen you for ages. Did you go to France to stay with Henry?'

'Yes. Purely a working trip. Angelica,' I said, 'you never told me that you'd been to Nice.'

'Henry talked about that, did he? It was just a quick jaunt – an excuse for a weekend out of London while Bill did some business. We went water-skiing on the Saturday. The sea was absolutely perishing. It was Mum's idea to look up Henry. Did he mind?' She spoke quickly, still with the same eagerness.

'Not at all.'

'They were awfully sweet.' She laughed. 'We were a bit disappointed because Bill had promised to fly us out there in the new company plane. But it wasn't ready in time so we had to take a boring old British Airways flight instead. How was your visit?'

'Oh, very agreeable,' I said. 'We finished the work. I suppose that neither you nor your mother had seen Henry for years.'

'No. I could hardly remember what he looked like, although I knew his face of course from the photographs in the newspapers and on the back of his books. Then there was that television programme about him last year. What a funny life they lead! Paul is the equivalent of a wife, I suppose,' Angelica said with a quick laugh. 'When we were there, they were bickering about whether to go to a cocktail party or not like a couple of old frustrated spinsters.'

'Henry works very hard,' I said stiffly.

'Oh, we know he does. He told us all about his timetable – how he regulates his day and so forth. But it's such a sedentary existence!'

'It seems to suit them.'

'Of course it does.' Her words rushed on. 'Otherwise they'd be doing something else! But the place does have a creepy atmosphere, you must admit. Those weird servants, the obsessive neatness. A bit like visiting a sanatorium. Totally removed from the real world.'

I thought: the real world of company jets, weekends in Nice, the hiring of motor boats for Mediterranean water-skiing. Surely Angelica should respect what Henry and Paul had made for themselves. 'And what did Bill think?' I asked.

'He thought it was all quite hilarious!'

Suddenly I felt irritated at the thought of them all sniggering about Henry and the life at the villa. There was, I knew, a curious chain in this, a chain of human mockery. Christina and I had laughed at Henry. We had searched for the overblown passages in his novels and revelled in their absurdity. We had laughed at Bill, recounted his vulgar jokes and brash manner-isms, dwelt upon the philistinism of the life that Laura and he had created for themselves. And Bill, Angelica and Laura poked fun at Henry and Paul. Henry shared my feelings about Bill's crudeness. Both my children, I knew, found me ridiculous. But the quest for someone else's weak point sometimes led across a morass of incomprehension, envy, even fear.

'Dad,' she said. 'I haven't seen you for so long. That was what I rang up about. Why don't we have dinner together one evening, just the two of us?'

'That would be lovely.' We agreed on a day of the following week. I named a restaurant. Then she was gone.

X

That weekend I had work to catch up on, so I did not go to the cottage.

The April weather was blustery. On Saturday morning, when I opened the window beside my desk, the wind whipped into the room, flicked the loose sheets of an open manuscript. I shut it out and turned on the reading light.

The night before I had worked late on the Palmerston biography. It was worse than I had expected; and I had sat in front of its vast bulk quite desperate, moved almost to violence. Again, I had thought of the pleasure to be obtained from its destruction, from its disappearance into the dustbin, the incinerator or out of the window where the wind would lift the flimsy pages up over the park, the Commonwealth Institute, the ruins of Holland House, the revolting sand of the dogs' lavatory, the Kensington Motorail depot, the shoddy vastness of Olympia before they reached the suburbs of Barnes, Kingston and the south. On Friday night I had moaned aloud.

Yet I slept well. Indeed I felt satisfied at the way that my professional skills had enlivened the work. On Saturday morning I woke early, to another sensation: the sensation of pleasure at the thought of a day, or rather two days, alone in which I could work and think.

I shaved, then put on an old check shirt, a pair of comfortable grey trousers and a dark blue pullover. In the kitchen, I boiled an egg and made several pieces of toast: a

91

larger breakfast than usual, because I would be having a late and insubstantial lunch. The Italian coffee machine bubbled up on one of the rings of the gas cooker. I laid the kitchen table, placed the egg in its cup, the toast in a wooden rack, poured out the coffee and added cold milk from the fridge. As I sat down and began to hit the egg with a spoon, I felt elated. The biography of Palmerston drifted out of my mind like some huge iceberg viewed from a ship on her way back from the polar seas.

At least some of the morning was to be devoted to reading Sarah Erdley's stories. I wanted to look at these myself rather than send them out to one of our readers as I would have done with most other unsolicited manuscripts. There were two other novels – one by an author we had published in the past, the other the work of a reputable poet. There was an American book by a journalist about CIA duplicity in south-east Asia, offered to us in manuscript by its New York publisher. Finally, and this would delight Williams, there was a short manual on diet and physical fitness, by an Australian nutritionist, complete with illustrations of the human digestive tract and a provisional title of *Eat and be Thankful*.

Sarah Erdley came first. I read fast, saw quickly that her work was as I had suspected: heavy, self-conscious, incapable of rising to any height of imagination or insight. I shocked myself. For I realised – as I sped through the gloomy tales of girls' boarding-school life, the perils of the London season, the loneliness of exile in an establishment near Geneva where young ladies of a certain class went to be 'finished', an awareness of calf love during a walk with a boy in the kitchen garden of a country house, a curious encounter with a tramp in Belgravia – that I was searching for the writer much more than for literary merit.

This infatuation made the stories no more interesting in themselves. In fact I came to see them as obstacles. Henceforth their author and I would always have to break through the clutter of literary ambition. I would reject them, gently of course, emphasising their good points – an occasional sharpness of observation, an ability to catch the nuances of teenage aristocratic conversation, an apposite phrase here and there. I would reject them not just in a cold letter but use their existence to arrange another meeting with her, this time in my office, on my territory. In London, in front of me, in the heart of Bloomsbury – a place of feminine achievement, the country of Virginia Woolf – the girl might begin to flounder, to reach out a hand for help. And I would lie, give encouragement, urge her to write more stories and show them to me in order that we could realise her vision of publication, an esteem different and (she thought) more rewarding than that won by inherited position and looks.

I was excited. This was better, I thought, than if the stories had been remarkable, for talent or genius would have made me wary of her. It was better that the Dochertys of this world should be the creators: not the fragile creatures whose role ought to be to inspire melancholy and romance in others. Yet Docherty, through his stories, might live on through the years, the decades, the centuries – the power of his words triumphing over death: whereas the girl will die, mourned perhaps by her family, friends and children, her country neighbours, and leave, as a memory, a few photographs, perhaps a stylised portrait by a fashionable artist: then a softening echo, a whisper of the past.

What sentimental rubbish! I brought my hand sharply down on to the desk. The crack broke the room's silence. I closed Sarah Erdley's manuscript, scribbled a note on the pad beside me to remind myself to write to the girl next week and suggest that she come to the office. I am a creature of habit and always write down any tasks for the office when they occur to me at home. I opened the American book. I thought briefly of the forthcoming meeting at Maidenhead, to be attended by representatives of our parent company. We were to be on show to these people. Williams would ask each of us to say his or her little piece, to justify our existence; it would be necessary to act up to the audience, to put on a good display, to show that we were an 'outfit' (as Williams called us) that was 'lean and hard'. Suddenly I yearned for the old days, for George Mason's tales of Fitzrovia, the years when we had been left alone to be the sort of company over which my father, uncle, grandfather and great grandfather had presided.

It was typical of Williams that, although I was a director and recognised as the senior editor because (since George Mason had ceased to work full time) I had been there longer than anyone else, he had refused to allow me this title. Indeed, after George's departure – just over a year before the time of which I am writing – Williams had persuaded him to remain on the board. The Welshman informed me that while naturally everyone knew that I was editorial director it would be tactless to make this 'official'; George (dear George as he called the old man) might be offended and the firm needed him too much to risk that. Meekly I had acquiesced, cursed the man to Joan who had told me that one should rise above such petty considerations. After all it did not affect my salary (which had been raised as if I had the new responsibility) or the esteem in which she knew I was held.

Both of us had agreed that George would not have minded; he was not that sort of man. Both of us knew that there was something direly wrong with the chemistry that existed between John Williams and myself. Joan was sorry for me but said that she could not see the trouble. She too found the man essentially unsympathetic, yet coped with him and could admire that quick accountant's brain. And I wanted to strike up the same sort of understanding, but I suspected that I represented in his mind the epitome of everything that he wished to change in the company, perhaps even most of what he thought was wrong with England. Hence the disdain in his eyes whenever we talked; the frequent references to the roughness of the market place, the fact that nobody owed anyone else a living, the awful tradition of British amateurism, the soft idleness of so many people in London compared to their equivalents in New York, the ridiculous barriers of English class consciousness.

Half thinking all this, half attempting to concentrate on the manuscript's tortuous saga of the intelligence war in southeast Asia, I realised that I was behaving in precisely the sort of way that Williams must despise. I looked at my watch. Despite my early start, the morning was almost over. And I was only engaged on the second of the many tasks that I had set for myself. Now Williams and the firm were worrying me. I left the American manuscript and went to the telephone. This too was unprofessional. I should have waited until Monday. I should have been able to put the momentary obsession to one side.

I dialled Joan's home number. She answered almost immediately. 'Joan?' I said. 'It's Simon. I'm sorry. Have I called at a difficult time?'

'No. no,' she said. She spoke in a low voice. 'I've got my parents-in-law here, Jim's mother and father.'

Jim? Of course. Her dead husband. 'Oh, yes. Look, I just wanted . . .'

'And Charlie has brought two friends for lunch.' Charlie? Of course. Her teenage son. 'I was just about to get the dishes out of the oven.'

'Joan . . . I'm so sorry,' I went on. 'I just wanted to talk about this meeting at Maidenhead. I mean, have you any idea what form it's going to take? Oughtn't we to decide how we're going to cope with all these people?' I laughed, trying to sound relaxed. 'You know I think that old Taffy's after me. I've become quite paranoiac about the man!'

'Simon . . .' Her voice suddenly became distant. I heard her say, 'Charlie, show Grandpa the photos of Dieppe. No, not those old ones of Barcelona. He's seen them thousands of times.' She came back to me. 'Simon, I'd love to talk about it now – but I've got all these people here. We'll see each other on Monday.'

'There's never a chance to speak properly at the office.' I almost added: walls have ears.

She paused. 'All right,' she said. 'Why don't we have lunch one day next week?'

'That would look very suspicious. What if we were seen? He'd be sure to think some plot was afoot.'

'He?'

'Taffy.' I uttered the syllables through clenched teeth.

'Simon, really!' Joan laughed. 'You're mad. Who do you think the man is? Stalin?'

'I'm not sure. What about one evening, away from work? Come and have a drink here. It won't take long.'

I thought I detected a slight sigh. 'My diary is at the office,' she said. 'But that's surely something that we can confirm on Monday. Or do you think that he has the whole place wired up so that he can listen to every conversation in the building?'

'I'll ring you.'

'There's really nothing to worry about.'

'I need reassurance!'

She called out again, her voice leaving the receiver. 'No, Charlie! Not the television at this time of day! None of us will be able to hear ourselves speak!' She returned to me. 'Simon, you're impossible. But of course you shall have it. I must go. Please. We'll speak on Monday.'

'Goodbye, Joan.'

I walked back to my desk, to the manuscript. Whole civilian communities had been wiped out in south-east Asia. In Cambodia, Pol Pot had slaughtered hundreds of thousands, perhaps millions, of people. In Viet Nam more bombs had been dropped in one day by the Americans than during the entire course of the Second World War. Now that was suffering for you: real suffering.

Michael Docherty came to my office on Monday.

Before I saw him, I dictated a letter to the Erdley girl. 'Dear Sarah,' I began, then said, 'No, leave that blank. I'll write it myself.' The rest of the note was brief, almost perfunctory. I said that I had read her work. I regretted that we could not publish it but suggested that she should come and see me at the office because there were parts of the stories that I found 'interesting and original'.

As I dictated these words, I wondered if Mary might think them strange. Usually our rejection letters, especially those to authors of unsolicited manuscripts, were courteous but final. Indeed we had a printed form which we sent to entirely unknown figures. I assured myself that this more personal approach could be justified by the fact that the Erdleys were my friends. Yet I felt obliged to say to Mary after I had finished, 'Her husband is my landlord in the country, you know. He owns the cottage.' I smiled and raised my eyebrows. 'Rather embarrassing,' I said. She laughed.

That afternoon, after I had eaten a sandwich at my desk, Michael Docherty appeared. Mary showed the boy in. Aged twenty-three, or so Hermione had told me, he looked older. The short but full black beard gave strength to this impression: also the receding hairline that caused his prominent forehead

96

to seem almost absurdly broad and long. Then there was his size. Not only was Docherty tall – well over six feet – but also large, with a slightly protruding stomach and wide shoulders, big white hands – one of which he reached forward to clasp mine in a tight grip. He was dressed in an old brown corduroy jacket, a pair of dark blue baggy trousers secured by a thin belt, a grey shirt open at the neck and a thin green stained jersey. His small eyes were wary.

Having stood to greet him, I pointed to the chair on the other side of my desk. He sat down, brought his hands together across his stomach and looked at me. The eyes were narrow and dark brown. Docherty waited. He knew that we had agreed to take him on. Probably it did not matter much to him what sort of person I might be: whether I was sympathetic, easy or intrusive as an editor, the possessor of reliable literary judgement, or difficult, demanding, prepared to bully authors into a betrayal of their original purpose. He was confident he could cope.

'I'm glad that we've met at last,' I began.

Docherty inclined his head, as if accepting a declaration of loyalty.

I smiled at him. 'Would you like some coffee? Or tea? It's all disgusting.' I laughed aloud. He managed a brief smirk.

'Tea, please.' Docherty's voice, low and soft, had the remains of a northern accent.

I picked up the telephone and asked Mary to bring in a cup of coffee and a cup of tea. Then I launched into my standard approach with new young authors: a brief speech about how I admired his work, how proud we were to be able to publish him, how I hoped that this might be the start of a satisfactory partnership for us both. Perhaps it may sound a little hackneyed, a little insincere: I do not know. At its end, he said nothing. He turned to accept the cup from Mary who smiled at him. He drank the first sip with an expression of slight disgust. 'Of course,' I continued, 'I know Hermione well. You will find her a doughty defender of your interests.'

'I'm glad to hear that.' He sat still. I wondered if he was using the weapon of silence.

I began again, still determinedly genial. '*The Water Garden* is an interesting title,' I said. 'What made you choose it? Were you thinking of the garden as a symbol of literary variety, as an allegorical device? Writers have seen flowers not only as decorative, as examples of natural aesthetic splendour but also as representatives of the supremely natural states of death and decay. One thinks of Shakespeare and Spenser. Then the link between the garden and love or desire, the physical aspect of growth and reproduction, the erotic dimension. The force of the contrast between a wild landscape and one laid out, or formalised, by man. I see a connection here between the particular and the universal, between an individual's notion of beautiful or ordered natural phenomena and our general vision of the wilderness out of which our ancestors came. In smoothing the contours of a rough piece of land, digging it up into neat flower beds and paths, decorating it with little ponds and carefully sited plants, are we not responding in a way to our fear of chaos, to our original need to organise ourselves against the cruelties and caprices of the natural world? So in the garden we are not only in touch with nature but with our wish to escape from her, our refusal to return to our original state of brutality and frightened ignorance. You are, if I may say so, particularly good at conveying an atmosphere of fear, of the menace that often pervades human relationships – even those of a supposedly intimate and stable kind.' I waited. He was still silent. 'But of course,' I added, 'not all of your stories take place in gardens.'

'No.' said Docherty.

I decided to continue. 'Sublimated Victorian eroticism found the garden – or the metaphor of the garden – an ideal vehicle for its curious form of communication in code. Do you know "Maud" – the verse that begins "There has fallen a splendid tear . . ."?' I recited, deepening my voice and smiling at the same time:

> 'There has fallen a splendid tear
> From the passion flower at the gate.
> She is coming, my dove, my dear;
> She is coming, my life, my fate.

I once heard a recording of Tennyson reading those lines,' I went on. 'One could not doubt – from the extraordinary feeling in his voice – the passion that lay behind them. And there was Meredith of course. Swinburne as well. You remember "Atalanta in Calydon", "The Forsaken Garden", "The Garden of Proserpine"?'

'"The Perfumed Garden",' said Docherty.

I laughed. 'Ah, yes,' I said, '"The Perfumed Garden". A little more explicit than the other works that we have mentioned. An oriental manual of sexual instruction, as I recall.'

'That's it,' said Docherty.

There was another pause. Once more I launched forth. 'Now the story "The Water Garden" – from which you have taken your title – that is the one which tells of an old man's attempts to grow water lilies in a small pond that he has dug at the back of his house, and how the pond comes to be used by a gang of children who see it as a convenient place in which to torture and drown stray cats?'

'Correct,' said Docherty.

'Then one of the children visits the pond alone, falls in, is caught up in the water lilies and cannot get out?'

'Correct,' said Docherty.

'Very good!' I said. 'Very powerful. The contrast between the harmless enthusiasm of the old man for his lilies and the viciousness of the children, both using the pond as an arena in which to act out their different definitions of pleasure. I interpret the pond as a metaphor for the battleground that exists within each one of us where the many varieties of desire and instinct are engaged in a perpetual conflict. Could one see the dead cats as discarded ideals, the paraphernalia of an adult morality spurned by the young, drowned – so to speak – in a pool of natural brutality?'

'If you like,' said Docherty.

There was another pause. 'I find that interpretation eminently satisfactory,' I went on. 'And the action – the torturing and drowning of the cats, then the little boy's own accident – is marvellously done, entirely justifiable from the dramatic point of view.'

Docherty inclined his head again. 'When will you bring the book out?' he asked.

'Probably in the new year,' I answered, leaning forward to

rest my arms on the desk. 'Not too soon after Christmas. Perhaps the end of January or the beginning of February.'

'So it will miss the Christmas market,' Docherty said. A frown appeared on his massive forehead.

'It will miss having to compete with several thousand other books, many of them by established and famous authors, for the reviewers' attentions.' I smiled. 'I'm afraid that we cannot hope for large sales of a first collection of short stories. The most important thing is to get critical attention. You're much more likely to have that after Christmas than before. Anyway, if you'll excuse me for saying so, *The Water Garden* is hardly the sort of thing to tuck into a child's stocking or give to some elderly relation.'

Docherty scowled. 'I suppose you know your own business,' he said.

'I think you'll find that Hermione will agree with me about this.' There was another pause. 'Are you satisfied with the contract?' I asked. 'It gives us an option on your next book, as you've probably noticed . . .'

'The money could have been better!' He moved in his chair and the springs cried out as if in pain.

I raised my hands. 'Oh, I know,' I said. 'And I assure you that if I had more say it would be. But this, alas, is not an easy time – especially for fiction and more especially for short stories.'

'It isn't easy for me.' He seemed angry.

I spoke as gently, as tactfully, as possible. 'May I ask how you get by?'

Docherty's brow contracted. 'I have a job,' he said. 'Supply teaching.'

'Whereabouts?'

He named a district in south London. 'I was thinking of giving it up to concentrate on the writing.'

'Are you married?'

'No.'

I leaned back in my chair, put my elbows on its arms and clasped my hands together so that they made a small barrier between me and this new author. 'Michael,' I said, 'I advise you not to give up your job.' I unclasped my hands, pointed towards the manuscript that lay on the desk. 'To be frank, the

100

financial rewards for this kind of writing are generally poor –
at least to begin with. One can think of exceptions, of young
writers who have had instant success. But they are rare. I'm
sure that your work will be well reviewed and attract a certain
amount of attention. We will certainly do our best to promote
it. But I would not, at this moment, cut yourself off from
other sources of income.' I brought my hands together again.
'Of course,' I said, 'there is always journalism – contributions
to newspapers, periodicals, reviews and the rest. Hermione
tells me that some of your stories have appeared in various
magazines. Perhaps you have contacts in Fleet Street?'

'None.'

'That sort of work is precarious anyway,' I said. 'But I'm
afraid that there is no question of us giving you a larger
advance. My colleagues wouldn't stand for it. Perhaps
Hermione has told you that it wasn't easy for me to get them
to agree to take on what is going to be a hard book to sell.' I
smiled ruefully. 'I'm afraid that profits are what matter to us
now.'

'But don't you own the firm?' Docherty sounded truculent.

I blushed. This must be northern bluntness. 'No,' I said, 'I
do not.'

'But with your name, surely . . . ?'

I interrupted, brusquely. 'My family sold out a long time
ago. Now I am a salaried employee, like everybody else in this
building.' I waited a little. Docherty leaned forward, picked
up his cup and drank the tea noisily. 'To return to what we
were saying about your job,' I said. 'Have you talked it over
with Hermione? Teaching is not a bad profession for a writer.
The holidays are long . . .'

'The money bloody awful!' Docherty almost shouted the
words.

'The rewards of freelance journalism aren't exactly princely
either,' I said quickly. He was large. For a moment I felt
almost frightened. But Mary was outside and would hear the
first splintering of furniture, the crash of violence. I spoke in
what I hoped were measured tones. 'Why not talk to
Hermione? Her advice will be sound.' The thought of the
woman sent a slight shiver through me. She and Docherty
were well matched. 'Meanwhile' – I pointed at the manuscript

101

– 'we have this. Did you bring a coat?'

'No.'

We walked together out of my office, down the stairs to the front door. There we shook hands and I was surprised to find that his grip was softer, more pliable than before. 'Michael,' I said, 'we'll be in touch soon. I'm really delighted.' Docherty, the new author, hurried off without a word.

And I wondered, as I walked back to my room, where it was already time to turn on the lights, if we – or rather I – had made another mistake. The idea of more conversations like the one which had just taken place was not appealing. I sat at my desk. I thought also, and this was more depressing, that the man's work might be merely a series of clever tricks. The different stories were jumbled together in my mind; I would have to re-read them. The dead cats and the lily pond; the soldier returned from Northern Ireland; the man who allows his neighbour to trespass more and more on his goodwill. At first I had believed that Docherty had contrived to mix beauty with squalor, strength with an emphatic and simple prose. This I had thought was the man's chief gift: to be able to convey evil and darkness in a way which proved that they had aesthetic qualities of their own.

Was this right? We were entertained by the immoral, the vicious, by one man's notion of humanity's underside. That was not reprehensible – I thought – as long as the process was then taken a step further: as long as there was a deeper dimension to the boy's work, a wish not only to set up a tableau but to move out of the mud into the clearer waters of moral judgement. Previously I had hoped that there was this solidity at the back of it all. Now, in the aftermath of our meeting, I began to have doubts.

Perhaps the stories, with their sick revelations, sudden outbursts of violence, their triumphs of brutality and dishonesty, were no more than a kind of pornography: a cold delineation of the base and the low to please a slavering public. If I were to put this to their monosyllabic author, what would he say? Probably nothing beyond a grunt or two and a demand for more money. If he chose to defend himself, Docherty might answer that he was merely a chronicler of certain types of human behaviour, of certain human tendencies that would

102

always be there. Under these circumstances, to judge and to condemn was foolish: a waste of words, like answering the obtuse questions of a publisher.

And my first reaction to the stories had revealed that I had the mentality of the sort of person who frequents the parlours, clubs and shops of the pornographers. This made me feel ashamed. My life has been quiet and protected. Even the upheaval of the divorce and Laura's departure had, after the early shock, taken place in an atmosphere of decency and understanding. She had wanted to go; I had let her. There had been no violence, no roughness. My frustration and misery had been kept underground. Now, years later, Bill, Laura and I met on friendly terms. Outwardly we seemed to have found a civilised English solution.

No. My life has been safe. From a protected childhood – in which anything nasty had gone either unspoken or unseen, in which the emotions had lain hidden under a thicket of convention and routine – to a protected middle age the way had been outwardly smooth. Here lay a contradiction. In the abstract I wanted safety, ease in which to pursue my interests: to read more, indulge in a little European travel, make the cottage more habitable. Why then did I linger over the bumps, resurrect them in my mind? My meeting with Laura, our brief life together, our parting: perhaps I am, like the people who buy pornography or visit prostitutes, a mere refugee from dullness, frustration, from the hidden turmoil of my real nature.

I returned to Docherty's stories. For the rest of the afternoon, between incoming telephone calls, I re-read most of them. They were short so the process did not take long. Relieved, I put the manuscript down. Although I had not perceived an extra moral dimension to the work, I thought that I could glimpse, in the chill of the bleak narrative, a sneer of distaste, even of disapproval. Docherty was not a moralist. Neither, I thought, was he a mere exploiter of evil. Surely he was giving his version of the filthy and the wrong in order to say: look, here it is, we mustn't run away but try to understand this enemy within. People wanted this; they wanted to feel in touch with the bad side of what we had become.

XI

I need to describe our daughter.

Angelica's short fair hair frames a sympathetic face but when she speaks this face leaps as she describes an idea or impression. Her chin juts forward a little, away from the rest of her. I used to think that this was symbolic of a questing and independent nature, of a person immune to conquest. It reassured my worries about the fragility of a single girl in late twentieth-century London.

I had a pleasant idea of Angelica: of her prettiness, of her compact figure – slightly above average height, rather dwarfed by both our son Edward and me when we are all together – of the tussle that she must have with a world arrayed against what it pleased me to think of as her innocence. But whenever we met or talked on the telephone, I came up against a different reality. Angelica had grown up.

Angelica and I were to meet for dinner at an Italian restaurant near my flat. The inside is elaborately decorated, with mirrors and pots of cascading plants enlivening the sharp white of the gently arching walls. The proprietor, to create a convivial atmosphere, places the tables too close to each other. There are many features of the establishment that I dislike: the noise, the half-dressed waiters who shriek across the room at each other, the unctuous owner who knows of my literary connections and likes to quote from a poem by D'Annunzio about a walk in a pine forest after the rain. But I know it well. And I would rather take people there than cook them what would undoubtedly be a much more unpleasant meal at my flat.

The evening was warm. I was too hot in my overcoat. The proprietor, exchanging insults by the door with an aged pianist who had not yet begun to play, put on a look of ecstatic welcome as I came in. 'Signor!' I allowed him to help me off with my coat. 'And how is the great world of publishing? You are our ambassador of culture. Have you booked? Yes?' He went over to the desk beside the cloakroom entrance, looked down the list of reservations for the evening. 'For two.' He turned and shouted to one of the waiters. 'Mario! The quiet corner table please!' He gave me a confidential smirk. 'Then you can have a good conversation.'

Angelica was late. I ordered a drink, a glass of mineral water, for I intended to have wine with the meal and did not want to over-indulge. I waited. I felt conspicuous on my own and wished that I had brought an evening paper or magazine on which I might concentrate to the exclusion of other people's pleasure. I looked at my watch. Five minutes went by. I finished the mineral water; its ice was melting in the glass. Ten minutes went by. At last I saw her, waving and smiling as she came across the room, twisting her way through the uneven ranks of tables.

She wore a thick, long, dark blue coat which she had not taken off at the cloakroom. Her fair hair was loose, un-combed. Over her shoulder was a brown bag on a long strap and in one hand she held a black briefcase. She stood beside the table, leaned down to kiss me and said with a sigh, 'I'm so sorry, I had to come straight from work. Poor Dad! I hope you haven't been waiting long.'

A waiter took her coat. Angelica would not let him have the briefcase and placed it by her chair as she sat down opposite me. Her red cardigan covered a white blouse, open at the neck. Her black calf-length skirt was creased; through her dark stockings the flesh of her legs showed in a dim twilight shade, and her face, always pale, seemed taut. The sharpness of her chin and prominent nose accentuated her slightly sunken cheeks and large eyes. Her mouth, with its narrow lips, drew back in a weary smile. 'Have you ordered?' she asked briskly. We looked through the enormous menu cards. She chose quickly: some soup, followed by veal. Having said that I would have the same, I asked the waiter for a bottle of chianti.

'Darling,' I began, 'they're pushing you a bit, aren't they?' I looked at my watch. It was ten minutes past nine. 'Do you often stay this late?'

She put down the menu and rested her hands on the table. They were small, the nails cut back for convenience. I noticed that she wore two rings: one a jagged pattern of gold, the other what looked to be an emerald in a plain setting. 'There's a bit of a panic on at the moment,' she said. 'But it's not unusual for us still to be in the office at ten. Last Tuesday, I didn't get away until after midnight! Luckily it's fascinating, otherwise I think we'd all go mad!' She spoke quickly, in a soft voice.

'I never knew that they set such a cracking pace down at the Elephant and Castle. The taxpayer must be getting his money's worth . . .'

'Elephant and Castle!' Angelica looked at me as if I was mad. 'What do you mean? I left there weeks ago. Hasn't Mum told you?'

'No.'

'Oh, yes. Everything's changed.'

I felt uncomfortable under her scorn. There was a welcome interruption when the waiter brought the wine. As I went through the ritual of tasting it I noticed that he looked at my daughter and smiled slightly to himself. Despite her fatigue and aggressive manner, she remained a young girl. I imagined how short she would be with anyone who made a move that did not have her consent, what a formidable partner she must make in any romance. 'So where are you working now?' I asked, rather timidly.

'In the City. I'll tell you about it.' She took a long swig of wine and made an expression of distaste. 'This is a bit rough, isn't it?'

I laughed. 'It's perfectly drinkable.'

'Not by me!'

I signalled to the waiter. 'Very well. We'll order something else.'

'Dad!' Angelica was almost shouting in her irritation. 'For heaven's sake don't bother. This'll do. It's not worth the wait!'

The soup arrived, a concoction of vegetables and small

stringy noodles. 'Darling,' I began, 'I didn't know that you'd left your job. When did this happen?' I tried to make the question sound reproachful. And I was hurt.

'Last month. I went straight into the new one. Honestly, life's been so hectic. I thought that Mum or Bill might have spoken to you.'

'But it was rather a drastic decision to take, wasn't it?'

'Why? People change jobs the whole time. I know you've worked for the same employer for God knows how many years but . . .' She left the rest unspoken. This was what she thought of me: dull, unadventurous.

'I thought you were doing so well at the Elephant and Castle . . . ,' I began.

'Not well enough, at least as far as I was concerned. And I got fed up with working for the government. I wanted to strike out on my own. I wanted to be allowed more independence, to be free of that frightful bureaucratic control. Also I was ideologically out of sympathy with the civil service. If this country's going to survive at all, it's got to be through private initiative, through individual skills and talent. Not because of any unwieldy set of rules and regulations imposed by some ministry. And I'd rather be up in the front line. What's more, the money's better!'

Through the noise of the restaurant, I heard the distant strains of 'A Nightingale Sang in Berkeley Square' played in a florid arrangement by the old pianist. The music's nostalgic tones, redolent of dances that I had attended in my youth, made me feel sentimental, momentarily cut off from rational thought. I put down my spoon and looked at Angelica. 'Darling,' I said. 'You will be careful, won't you?'

Her spoon, on its way to her mouth with the last dregs of her soup, stopped its ascent somewhere level with her neck. Her eyes, fixed on mine, showed incomprehension. 'Careful!'

'I mean I hope that this City business is reputable.' I had inherited from my father an instinctive distrust of most financial institutions. The old man, or so my mother used to say, would have been much happier if he could have kept his money in a series of chests underneath his bed.

'Reputable? Dad!'

'Well, what sort of things does it go in for?'

There was an interruption, a clattering of dishes and rearrangement of the table as the two waiters brought the next course. Angelica waited until we had been served. Then she said, 'Financial services. Advice about investment. How to make the best use of your money, that kind of thing. It aims to provide a link between embryonic businesses and possible sources of capital.'

'Rather different to the sort of work that you used to do,' I said. There seemed to me to be something more wholesome about a job in the civil service. I would have preferred it for my daughter. I cut into the rubbery veal which slid across the plate.

Angelica ate fast, not wasting time. 'Not entirely,' she said through the food. 'I'm used to controlling budgets, operating within financial guidelines. That ought to come in useful, particularly as they've started me off on the corporate side.'

At least the vegetables – some spinach and a few under-cooked beans – were good. I persevered with the meat, trying to appear intelligent amid my concern for our daughter's future. 'Darling,' I said, 'what is the outfit called?'

She gave a name of which I had never heard. 'It's a small organisation, started about ten years ago. A few bright young men got together, left their original employers and pooled their different types of expertise. They went through a lean time at first and nearly closed down at one stage. Now things are looking up.' Angelica gave me a string of figures, to demonstrate recent results and increase in business. 'And that's only the beginning.'

'Is it a public company? Can one buy shares in it?'

Angelica smiled, tolerantly. At last her eyes were beginning to relax. 'Rather difficult to do that, I'm afraid,' she said. 'The original directors still own a fair amount of the shares. ISS, who moved in last year, have a majority stake. You can, of course, buy shares in ISS.'

'ISS?' During our conversation, I had been steadily drinking the rough chianti. Perhaps the wine had blurred my memory for this was an absurd question to ask.

'Dad!' Angelica's sharpness returned. 'International Services and Systems. Bill's organisation.'

'Oh, yes. Bill's organisation.' I gave up the struggle and

pushed the meat to one side. For a moment, in the restaurant, the talk of the other diners went into a brief lull. The pianist, clear in that instant, tinkled his way through 'My Blue Heaven'. 'So it was his idea that you should move?' I said.

'Not entirely.' Angelica's laugh was free of strain. Apparently she felt that there could be no potential awkwardness in speaking of her step-father to me. I supposed that this was a good sign. 'But I think you could say that he added fuel to the flames, so to speak. I went down to Bembridge one weekend in a state of terminal exhaustion. We spoke about one or two things and he suggested that I should see these people. Two of the directors interviewed me. It was all very friendly. But they made it plain that there could be no question of them taking me on unless they were satisfied that I was absolutely right for the company. They were looking for new people anyway. So you can't really call it favouritism or nepotism or anything like that.' Angelica, in two or three quick cuts and scoops, finished up the food on her plate. Her glass of wine stood almost untouched. She put down her knife and fork in a neat formation, a survival from childhood training. 'So things are rather exciting at the moment. Then there's the new house as well.'

'New house?'

'Dad! For heaven's sake. Don't you remember? I sent you a change of address card?'

'So you did.'

'I want you to come there. I'm going to give a little party soon . . .'

'But Angelica . . . Excuse me asking – but where is it?'

'South of the river. Stockwell Kennington sort of area. Good for public transport to and from the City. Or as good as you can get in London these days.'

'And you have bought this house?'

'With the help of a thumping great mortgage.' And, I thought, the money that had been settled on both of my children by Bill.

The waiter brought the menu cards. Angelica said that she wanted nothing else: just a cup of coffee. I decided to have the same. She refused to allow me to fill her glass, so I poured the rest of the chianti into my own. The coffee came quickly.

'Well, that's all very exciting,' I said. 'A new house, a new job. . . . Will you live alone in Stockwell?' Once she had shared a flat with Sarah Erdley. I wanted to get her to talk about the girl.

Angelica sipped her coffee, undeterred by its scalding heat. 'Good Lord, no,' she said. 'I can't possibly afford to do that. I'll have to take in at least two lodgers.'

'Any thoughts on who . . . ?'

'I don't really mind but I'll have to be careful. I'm going to put in another bathroom, so that we can lead reasonably separate lives.' She thought for a bit. 'Perhaps men are better. Sarah and I used to fight a bit.'

'What about?'

'Oh, this and that.'

For an instant, I wondered what would happen if I asked her in this restaurant, too softly of course for anyone else to hear: have you got a lover, a man who takes you to bed with him? And tell me about all the men who have slept with you in the past. Her self-possession, her confident manner, might collapse and give way to a pathetic confession of loneliness which could draw us back into the sort of relationship that I remembered from years ago. But much more likely would be a quick freeze, perhaps a pretence that she had not heard or understood. I would be forced to retract. Or she might choose to attack, ask me about Christina and laugh and sneer at the thought of her leaving. Instead, I made a feeble joke. 'I hope you find a satisfactory man,' I said, and smiled.

Angelica did not react. 'I'm already looking,' she said. 'I know exactly the sort of person I have in mind. He must be house-trained. He must have regular habits, preferably be out most evenings and have a good paying job. I don't want endless squabbling about the rent.'

'I'm sure that you'll be more than a match for anyone, darling.'

'What do you mean by that?' She looked surprised.

'Just that I can't imagine any lodger ever daring to step out of line if you were his landlady.' I laughed to show that I had meant my remark to be treated as a joke.

'I should hope not! It's my house.'

'Of course it is.'

110

'Well, can you think of any likely candidates, Dad?'

'Me! Good Lord. You mean ageing bachelors in need of a place in which to spend their declining years?'

'No.' Angelica softened a little. 'Young people in your office who might welcome a decent room at a reasonable cost. I'd sacrifice a bit of money if I thought I'd found the right type. I know that publishers aren't exactly over-paid. Anyway, keep your eyes open. My friends all seem to be fixed up. But perhaps it makes more sense to have a lodger whom you don't know too well. Then if you want to get rid of him for some reason or other, there's no awkwardness or friends taking sides or anything like that. But I don't want to advertise.'

'What a busy time you're having,' I said. 'New house, new job. You've been lucky'

'Ah. Do you believe that?' Her smile showed that she did not. 'You make your own luck, you know. To some extent, at least.'

'Perhaps,' I said. I looked around the restaurant, at the mass of people, at a large trolley which held great dishes of fruit, bowls of trifle, flat tarts covered in glazed strawberries and a pile of chocolate profiteroles with the top one split open to reveal an interior of brilliantly white whipped cream. This profusion made me think of money: of its transformation into luxury, good living and bad taste. 'Are Bill's affairs prospering?' I asked.

Angelica lifted her cup to drain the last of her coffee. 'Very much so,' she answered. 'It's almost outrageous. Mum and I have to sit on him hard to make sure that he doesn't get too conceited.'

'Does he talk about his work?'

'A bit. He told me about this job of course. And I ask him how things are going from time to time. Probably I'm the one of us who is most interested. Mum's very dutiful – goes to all the staff parties, dinners with potential clients and customers and the rest when she's well enough. But, as you can imagine, the actual workings of the group are a bit beyond her!' Angelica smiled in a patronising way. Your mother would not want to become too involved, I almost said. Her wish was to be taken care of, to have the delights and security of a rich woman's life. To have to worry about the sources of this

111

would be to destroy a part of its pleasure, which was all about not having to think. And now that your mother is ill, she needs this even more.

'What about Edward?' I asked. 'Surely he must be familiar with high finance by now?'

'Edward?' She spoke his name in an impatient way. 'Oh, Edward's a typical banker. When I rang him in New York he just told me to be careful. To be frank, I wouldn't have expected anything else.'

There was a pause. The pianist had moved into a syncopated arrangement of 'All the Things You Are'. 'So is ISS expanding?' I asked. 'I've never been certain what its main interests are.'

'A complete mixture,' Angelica answered rapidly. 'It's a holding company for a mass of businesses, some small, others not so small. They range from the manufacture of china and glass to financial services and oil. Quite a lot of overseas stuff – but still very much British based. You know Bill's ridiculous sense of patriotism!'

Edward had told me that his step-father had gone mad during the Falklands campaign, ringing up the Ministry of Defence and offering to pay for new ships and helicopters to replace those that had been destroyed. 'And it needs more, does it?' I asked.

'In a sense. But at one fell swoop.'

'How do you mean?'

Angelica waited as if she were calculating and then spoke, this time precisely. 'Bill has got his eye on one or two outfits that are of a similar complexion to ISS: groups, or conglomerates as the Americans call them. If a bid were successful, it would enormously increase the assets of ISS overnight. Of course the idea is ambitious. A battle of that type – between two giants – would cause a terrific stir not only in the City but throughout the international financial community. And it would be a bloody battle. No organisation of the size that Bill is after will surrender without one hell of a fight.'

'Really.' For some reason it distressed me to hear her talk of fights and struggles, to appear to be glorying in what I presumed must be a ruthless and unpleasant operation.

'But, Dad, I think I ought to tell you something.' She

112

looked as though she was discussing a death in the family. 'ISS has got its eye on Lindsay.'

Angelica's face, a moment ago animated with talk of the chase, showed sympathy. I liked this; it was better than its predecessor. And so pleased was I that at first I could not fathom its reason. 'Lindsay?' I asked.

'Dad! The Lindsay group. Your proprietors!'

I must have flushed or turned pale or something because Angelica's look changed to anxiety. I smiled as a cover. This was no time to show weakness. 'How interesting.'

'You must know that they're in trouble.'

'Purely temporary, or so we're told,' I said. 'Merely a little corporate indigestion.' Williams had given this answer when pressed by Joan at one of our meetings.

'Bill thinks it runs deeper than that. Are you upset?'

I was, of course: upset that I did not understand either the financial workings of our owners or Bill's plans for our small company and ultimately for me.

'No,' I said, 'but I'm interested. Has this plan any chance of success?'

'Bill thinks so. They've begun to buy Lindsay shares; discreetly of course. But Lindsay are sure to find out and then it will be all hands to the pumps. The first few weeks are vital.'

Angelica seemed worried, probably wondering if she had made a mistake in confiding in me. Could I be relied upon to keep a secret that had so potentially explosive an effect on my life? Obviously she had noticed my dismay. And her loyalties appeared to be overwhelmingly to the man who had allowed her a lightning glimpse of the workings of high finance: overwhelmingly to Bill. Perhaps I had it in my power, by blabbing to Williams or one of the others – even to Joan or almost anyone in the office – to destroy all the cunning plans of those first few vital weeks.

'But do you mind, Dad?' There was sympathy in her voice, real sympathy. I liked this. 'Even if the bid is successful, you won't have to deal with Bill personally at all. He's too . . .' She paused.

'Grand?'

'No. He simply doesn't operate at that level. He knows nothing about publishing. His interest is the strategy of the

113

whole group. He won't tell you what books to bring out or anything like that! It will be just the same as before, as far as you're concerned. Yet I suppose things could be awkward for both of you. With Mum and everything.'

'All that happened a long time ago.'

We were both silent. When Angelica spoke next, I was scarcely aware of her words. 'Any good stuff coming out in the next few months?'

'Good stuff?'

'Books, Dad. New books from your list.'

I told her about Henry's novel and she laughed. In future Henry's profits might go towards a new yacht for Bill, a daring scheme of redecoration at the Bembridge villa, perhaps a piece of contemporary art that might catch Laura's eye in a Mayfair gallery. Henry, the man I had nurtured. Then I thought of something else. 'Sarah Erdley has written some short stories,' I said.

'Are they good?'

'Not much.'

'And she wants to publish them?' Angelica sounded profoundly bored. 'Is that embarrassing?'

'It's always that much more difficult to turn down a friend.'

'My friend.' Angelica sneaked a quick glance at her watch. She was restless. 'Surely you can just send a polite letter of rejection. The Erdleys can't be so out of touch that they don't realise how difficult it is to get books published in these hard times.'

'That's exactly what I have done.'

'I suppose she's bored,' Angelica said. 'She hasn't got enough to do so she sees herself as a writer. At least it makes the days go past a little quicker. A bit futile really.'

'Her stories are not entirely without promise.'

'Dad!' She wagged her finger at me in a mock gesture of admonition. 'Don't go and fall in love with the girl! You're a bit old for the mid-life crisis, you know.'

I must have blushed for I felt the warmth enter my cheeks. 'There's no danger of that, I can assure you,' I declared.

This time Angelica made no attempt at concealment. She yawned, openly. 'If you'll excuse me,' she said, 'I'm absolutely exhausted. And tomorrow's going to be hell as well. I

114

really must get some sleep.'

'Of course, darling. I am sorry . . .' The waiter hurried across with the bill and I paid in cash: several dirty notes laid out on a plate. We stood up to go, Angelica grasping her briefcase, her handbag hung across her shoulder. In the hall, where the pianist played 'As Time Goes By', we collected our coats and outside, in the cold dry evening, I said, 'Let me drive you back. It will only take a few minutes. And there's so much trouble on the streets these days.'

She brushed the offer aside. 'Good heavens, no. I'll look for a taxi.' We waited, searching the traffic in the main thorough-fare at the end of the street. 'Don't forget,' Angelica said, 'about the lodger, I mean. If a reasonable person should come to mind . . .'

'I won't. I only hope that he or she won't behave like the couple in the flat below me. They make the most extra-ordinary sounds, at all times of the day and night. Ecstasy, I suppose.'

'Good Lord. Are they fucking?' Perhaps I am absurdly old fashioned but the word sounded horrible in her mouth. 'Taxi!' Angelica's shriek made me jump. A taxi, which I had not seen, came up to the kerb. She turned to me. 'Dad,' she said, 'not a word about what I told you. Promise?'

'I promise.'

'And thanks for the dinner. I'll be in touch. You must come to the new house, in darkest Stockwell.'

'I hope you get what you want.'

She kissed me on the end of my chin, climbed into the taxi and was gone.

Joan was talking.

'Simon, you really must pull yourself together about Taffy. All he's trying to do is to improve the place. And he's not a complete illiterate – I don't agree with you there. He's been in publishing all his working life for a start. You've never given him a chance.'

We were in my flat one evening after work. She was sitting on a sofa while I had taken one of the armchairs. Both of us had drinks: a weak whisky and water for me and a glass of tepid white wine for Joan. 'The chemistry is all wrong,' I said. 'Joan, would you be surprised if I told you that Williams and I loathe each other?'

'Simon!'

She went into a long laugh, putting her head back, her eyes closed. Her brown hair was tied up in a knot at the back of her head. She wore a neat red and blue striped dress, clear stockings and black boots that came up just over the calf of her thin legs. Joan was very thin: almost wasting away. Her bones were easily visible in her long hands, her arms and the pale tension of her face.

Joan was a single woman against the world. I knew about her life, the disaster of her dead husband, whom I believed she had loved quite desperately, and the difficulties of bringing up her unprepossessing child alone. Here again, in hours of idle musing, shadows – those dear shadows – threw my thoughts into a twilight trance of pity. On these occasions I would dwell absurdly upon Joan's large brown eyes, on how I could catch a glimpse – when her face was in repose, when she did not know that anyone was looking – of her suffering.

'You may laugh – but it's true,' I said.

'Nonsense!' Joan held her glass out in front of her. The nails of her long fingers were painted a brilliant scarlet. 'You must try to meet him halfway,' she said, in her hoarse voice. 'Don't be so on edge. I noticed it the other day at the editoral meeting. And he let you have your way over those stories by what's-his-name.'

'Docherty,' I said.

'Yet you still glowered at him as if he'd made a mess on the carpet.'

'He only agreed after the book had been sent to George Mason for a second opinion. I took that as a professional slight. Most insulting.'

Joan reached into her black hand bag and came out with a packet of cigarettes. Flourishing a gold lighter, she lit up and blew a light blue cloud into the middle of the room. Then she coughed: a sound of subterranean cataclysm. 'Poor old Taffy,' she said. 'All he wants is a little bit of love.'

'It's not our job to supply him with that.'

'You should see him at those parties in Ealing, after a couple

116

of drinks. He's a different person. Rather touching. Except he does sweat so.'

'Do you know that I've never been inside the house in Ealing once?' I said quickly. 'Not once.'

'Is that one of your great ambitions – to go inside the house in Ealing?'

'Certainly not. But I see the fact that I have not been invited as significant. Highly significant. All the rest of the board have been – and most of the office. Except for me.'

'Shall I try to wangle you an invitation?'

I lost my temper. 'I do not want to go to the man's house,' I shouted. 'That's not what I want at all!'

Joan drew on her cigarette. She did not flinch. 'What do you want, then?' she asked.

'I'm sorry,' I said. 'I'm afraid that the whole business upsets me.'

'With no reason.' Joan paused and blew out another mouthful of smoke. The room was beginning to smell of her strong French cigarettes. 'I agree that Taffy and you are out of sympathy with one another,' she said. 'But this shouldn't worry you. How can I put it?' She raised one hand to her forehead and looked down at the floor for a moment. 'You see, Simon,' she began, 'you're so much a part of the firm. How long have you been there now? Twenty years? Thirty years? A long time, anyway. Everyone knows you. The authors. The booksellers. The agents. The literary editors. And then there's your name. You're founder's kin, after all. If Williams ever got rid of you – which I'm quite sure that he never would – it would be a serious blow to our reputation and stability. People would think that the world was coming to an end!' Joan laughed, a sound that soon gave way to a fit of violent coughing. 'Anyway, Henry Brown would be off like greased lightning. Think how the profits would suffer then! No, Taffy wouldn't even consider such a thing. And there's no need to get upset about not receiving an invitation to the house in Ealing. Sit tight. Keep your head down. These things pass.'

'But Williams is seven or eight years younger than I am,' I protested. 'He'll be there for ever!'

'Will he?' said Joan. 'Oh, I don't think we're nearly a large

117

enough canvas for John. He'll sort us out quickly – a few redundancies, a rapid programme of "rationalisation" as he calls it, one or two more cosmetic changes. Then he'll be off to some larger job. We're just a stepping stone.'

I drank some more whisky and felt a little encouraged. 'You heard that our proprietors are in trouble?' I said. It was surely safe and honourable to speak of Angelica's revelations in general terms.

Joan's forehead erupted into a series of lines and creases. 'I knew that last year's results had been disastrous, through no fault of ours. Some investments in the Far East came unstuck. But the annual report made great play of the fact that this was merely a small hiccup. Taffy was telling me only the other day that the position had already improved.'

'The shares are pretty low.'

'Does that mean much?'

'What happens if someone tries a take-over?' I asked.

Joan frowned again. 'Impossible,' she said. 'The group is too big. Anyway who on earth would have that sort of money?'

'Another organisation of the same type? There are several I can think of.' I smiled knowingly. 'All this is just hearsay of course. But you may have noticed that Lindsay shares, although still low, have risen slightly in the last two or three days – as a result of rumours that a bid is in the offing, or so the City reports in the papers say.'

'But, Simon, would it make any difference to us if the group was taken over? We'd be answerable to different people, I suppose. But that will be Williams's problem: not ours.'

I made no mention of my personal concern about the prospect of working for the man who had made off with my wife. 'What happens if the new people start to dismember the group? They might well have no interest in books or publishing. Then we'll be floated off. A target for any smart alec operator.'

'But we're profitable,' Jean said.

'Just.'

'Enough to be taken seriously. Surely they wouldn't just let us go down the drain!' Joan's voice was incredulous.

'They?'

'Anyone!'

'Why not? It's not as if we had a preservation order slapped on us, like some crumbling historic building.'

Joan sighed and looked at her empty glass. 'You're being frighteningly realistic this evening, Simon,' she said.

'The company is not sacred.' I was relishing my role as a prophet of doom. 'How long have we been going for? A hundred and twenty years? I shouldn't think there'd be much of an outcry if we went under, despite the present fashion for Victoriana.'

Joan laughed. She looked around the room at the pictures. 'You'll be safe whatever happens,' she said. 'You're sitting on a gold mine. All you have to do is to sell a couple of these.'

'Joan,' I said. 'I enjoy my work. I don't want to have to give it up. I even – and this will make you laugh – I even enjoy looking after Henry Brown.'

'Simon,' Joan declared, after another deep draw on her cigarette, 'you're a saint. A veritable saint.'

'No, I'm not. I'm a publisher.'

We were quiet for a moment, as if contemplating this odd comparison. Then Joan, still serious, spoke again. 'You wanted to talk about the Maidenhead meeting,' she said.

'Joan,' I asked, 'will you promise to stick by me if there's any trouble?'

'Now, wait a minute.' She held up her hand with the smoking cigarette between her fingers. 'Wait a minute. What's going to happen? There'll be you, me, Freddy, Stanley and Gerald locked up in a hotel for part of the weekend with Taffy and two or three people from Lindsay's head office.'

'Two or three people . . . ?'

'Their chief executive is coming. And the finance director.'

'Gerald will have to have his wits about him,' I said. Gerald was a sharp youngish accountant, responsible for our financial planning. 'How long do we have to be there?'

'Friday night and the whole of Saturday. We're allowed out after the session ends on Saturday evening.'

'God, what hell!'

'Now, Simon,' Joan said, 'you must pull yourself together. We'll be put through our paces by these people and it's important that no one falters or gives a bad impression. You can do it with your eyes shut – as long as you don't allow your imagination to get the better of you.'

'My imagination?'

She looked stern. 'I mean this nonsense about Williams and the take-over bid.'

'Joan, these are not mere figments of my imagination. I only wish they were. For instance, why hasn't he made me editorial director?' I said, and almost added: and why has he asked you to come to this damned hotel and not let me answer for our section? Freddy of sales was coming alone. So were Gerald and Stanley. I was the only one thought to need someone else's help.

'George Mason is still on the board,' Joan said. 'They didn't want to hurt the old boy.'

'Like hell they didn't.'

'And you are the editorial director, in all but name.'

I hit the elbow of the sofa with my fist. 'They're up to something, you know, they're bloody well up to something! I can sense it.'

'Who are they?'

'The forces of darkness.'

'Simon!' Joan shook her head. 'You're hopelessly paranoiac. And to think that I used to look on you as the epitome of sweet reason.'

'I am. The epitome of sweet reason, that is.'

She looked at me through narrowed eyes. 'You're bloody lucky and I think you're talking rubbish,' she said, suddenly angry. 'All right, so Williams is difficult from time to time. But you're still given complete freedom to publish and commission what you want . . .'

'Am I?' I interrupted. Her anger did not frighten me. 'What about the fuss over those stories by Michael Docherty?'

'Well, what about it? We've taken him on, haven't we? And I think that Williams was quite right to be cautious about that book.'

'Have you read it?' I was sure that she had not.

'Yes.'

'But I thought I had the manuscript . . .'

'Williams had a copy made, after you had sent it to George Mason.'

'How the hell did he get hold of the original?'

'He borrowed it for a few hours when George brought it back to the office to return it to you.'

'But Williams hasn't read it, has he?'

'No,' said Joan. 'But he asked me to. That's why the copy was taken.'

'Why on earth did he want you to read it?' I realise now that the mixture of vehemence and disbelief in my voice must have sounded insulting. It implied that her judgement could be of little or no interest. I saw this search for second, even third opinions as yet another blow to my professional pride.

'He said that he wanted my views.'

'And you gave them to him?'

Joan nodded, a little nervously. 'I did. I was absolutely loyal to you. I said that it was not my sort of book – not something that I personally would take on – but that I was quite happy to support your judgement. In other words, if you were keen, we should go ahead and publish.'

Joan, about five years younger than I, had begun as George Mason's secretary. Then she had looked upon me, or so I had thought, with almost speechless deference. When she had started editorial work – at George's behest – I had helped her, answered her queries, read through manuscripts with her, suggested alterations, insisted that she drop certain pet enthusiasms. I still saw myself as her mentor. She must have shared this feeling; that was why she seemed embarrassed that Williams had gone to her behind my back. 'I see. Very good of you.'

'I would never go against you, Simon, on that sort of thing.'

'George admired those stories.'

'Yes.' Joan paused. 'Poor old George,' she went on. 'All he seems to think about now are those cats. In this last year he's become an old man. You know, I don't believe the old boy reads half the manuscrips that we send him. They lie about in that flat . . .'

'I know he read those stories,' I cut in. 'We had a long talk about them.' This was not strictly true. I had spoken to George briefly on the telephone before the editorial meeting at which Docherty's work was to be discussed. He had told me that the stories reminded him of the young Isherwood and André Gide. He had said that of course he would support so promising a young writer; then there had followed the ritual string of complaints about the gas board, his landlord and the impudent manager of the local off-licence.

Joan's eyes squinted towards the tip of her cigarette as she took another pull. 'Have you met the young man in question?' she asked.

'Docherty? Yes. He came to my office this week. Rather monosyllabic. Shyness, I expect. We had a brief talk.'

'What did he say to you, Simon?' she asked, slightly impatient. 'Oddly enough, although I didn't care for those stories I'd be quite interested to meet the man who wrote them.'

'Why?'

'A certain prurient curiosity, I suppose,' Joan said. 'To see if I could spot any external evidence of their unpleasantness. Any reflection of them in their creator.'

'But they're not all unpleasant.'

'Not all.'

'And it's not gratuitous – the unpleasantness, I mean. Docherty uses it to make a point, to remark on the way that some people live and think now.'

'Does he?' asked Joan. 'It all seemed a bit tendentious to me. What is the point of the pond full of dead cats?'

'Whatever you care to make of it. I have my own ideas.'

'I'm amazed that didn't put George off.'

'Joan,' I shouted, 'the dead cats are not gratuitous!'

'If you say so, Simon.' She waited for a few moments and then said, rather warily, 'What did you tell Mr Docherty?'

I told her my remarks about the book's title, about gardens and their literary connotations, about Shakespeare, Spenser, Tennyson and the rest. 'He seemed quite bowled over,' I said.

Joan looked at me in a mystified way. 'Did you really speak to him like that?'

'Yes. I expressed my feelings. He's writing a novel. We have an option on it.'

'You haven't offered him a vast amount of money, have you?' She sounded genuinely worried.

'Good heavens, no! Taffy wouldn't let me anyway. You

know all that sort of thing has to go through him now.'

Joan looked down at the hem of her dress and pulled it over her crossed knees with a brisk movement. 'Of course we'll act together at Maidenhead,' she said eventually. 'You mustn't worry about these things, Simon.' Then she asked 'How's Christina? It is Christina, isn't it? I like her so much.'

XII

Sarah Erdley received my letter.

She rang me at the office to say that she was going to be in London and wondered if she might come to see me about her work. I had no hesitation in giving the girl lunch. My diary, after all, was empty.

I can remember her clothes exactly. They were smart, evidence that she had dressed up for London. She sat opposite me in the restaurant where we usually take our authors. The proprietor – a shrewd Neapolitan – allows the firm a reduction in charges as long as we guarantee him a large amount of custom. He welcomed me in a quiet manner, preferable to the effusiveness of the Italian who owned the establishment where Angelica and I had been a few evenings before.

The girl took off her black overcoat (it was a chilly day) and whisked her short hair back from her temples. Her white blouse was of plain silk, her skirt the darkest black. In her ears she wore a pair of diamond studs. Her face showed no trace of make-up, although I could see that she had applied small amounts of shadow around her nervous large blue eyes. Sarah Erdley had dark hair, not as dark as Christina's, more a compromise between brown and black. She wore nothing around her neck: not the string of pearls or gold chain or bangle that one might have expected from someone of her class. Apart from a large sapphire glinting out of what I presumed to be her engagement ring, the only ornament in sight was an ungainly jade bracelet that slipped up and down

124

the wrist of her right arm.

Before we had ordered the food, she began to speak, swallowing her words in anxiety.

'I know I've wasted your time,' she said as she leaned forward. The menu card covered one side of her face like half of a set of horse's blinkers. 'I'm so sorry. But I couldn't resist showing the stories to somebody. And' – here she blushed and looked down at the white table cloth – 'I thought there was a sort of connection between us – with the cottage, Angelica, and Jeremy and Edward having been at school together. Jeremy encouraged me, you know. He called it futile – to write stories and not to try to have them published or at least get the opinion of a critic or publisher. Since we opened the house on a more commercial basis, Jeremy has begun to have great respect for what he calls "professionalism". He talks about the age of the amateur being over. Dead and gone.'

Slowly, she calmed down. I was interested to see that the agitation did not spoil her beauty. We spoke about her work. She twisted the sapphire ring around her finger, pushed the jade bracelet sharply back up her arm. 'You mustn't stop writing,' I said at one point. 'Go on. It's the only way to get better . . .'

'You mean that you think there is hope for me?' She smiled. I decided that the excitement was genuine.

'Yes.' And I told her about Henry Brown's life and achievement. 'Have you read *Grasp the Handrail*?' I asked. She had not. It pleased me to use its author as an example. I wished to show that her natural attributes – the looks she had been given at her birth – were not enough. I suppose I was fighting against the carnal wishes of middle age.

'But I don't think I could ever write like he does,' she said, plaintively.

'You don't have to. Unless of course you want to make a lot of money.'

Sarah Erdley coloured a little. 'No,' she said. 'I didn't write those stories with that in mind.'

'What Henry Brown can give you is an example of discipline and determination.' I spoke of the villa, of the rigid routine. 'They go abroad sometimes – he and Paul – to visit his translators or foreign publishers, to give lectures. Occasionally Henry will write a travel article for a huge fee in some glossy magazine. Then they enjoy themselves. They relax, let Henry re-charge his batteries. But the rhythm of life never remains broken for long. They soon return, Paul to his gardening, housekeeping and secretarial duties. Henry to his bare study.'

'And is he happy?' Sarah Erdley asked.

I had, strangely enough, never thought of Henry Brown as happy or unhappy. His life seemed to be so even. 'I hope so,' I said. 'He has Paul.'

'Are they . . . ?' She could not manage the words, either because we did not know each other well enough or were in a public place.

'Lovers?'

The girl smiled, then giggled. 'Yes.'

'Oh, I think they are.'

My brusque tone may have frightened her. She picked at her food while I spoke of Henry's early struggles. At an appropriate interval, she declared, 'He must have made you a fortune over the years,' anxious now to show her appreciation. 'The books certainly have' – she searched for the right word – 'narrative drive? I mean, one can't stop reading, at certain moments anyway.'

'So you do know his books?'

'A little.' Her eyes showed that she was not sure which route to follow. 'They're very good for trains and aeroplanes, don't you think?'

'I am an unrepentant admirer of Henry's,' I said. 'His accomplishments – and those of authors like him – have been unduly deprecated. He tells a story quite brilliantly. He has a remarkable eye for background. Remember the bullfight in *The Tremendous Sea*? Some of his set pieces are terrific. I have never been to Argentina – but after reading his new novel I feel that I know the geography of the pampas intimately. Of course no one could pretend that his characterisation is up to much – but he has his moments even there. Take the old man in *Grasp the Handrail*. That was based on Henry's father.'

'I'll buy *Grasp the Handrail* this afternoon – before I go home,' the girl said eagerly.

'You could do much worse. It's in paperback, so it won't

126

break the bank.'

Sarah Erdley clasped her hands together and then jammed the jade bracelet back up her arm again. 'But Mr . . .'

'Please. You should call me Simon.'

'But what should I do now?'

'You should write some more,' I said.

'And then what? Send them off to another publisher? I don't want to bother you again.'

'No,' I answered. 'You should show them to me. I am interested.'

She looked delighted. 'Really? How terribly kind. I'm so grateful, I really am. I can't tell you how helpful and encouraging this has been . . .'

I knew that the Neapolitan, in addition to the other attractions of his restaurant, had two or three bedrooms upstairs – unpleasant places, it was said (Joan, George Mason and I joked about their existence but had never made use of them), but useful for the quick pleasures of a shameful liaison. How would this girl react if I suddenly proposed that we ought to relax after lunch in one of these? She seemed so anxious to please. Perhaps my suggestion might be received with an awkward assent to what she might presume was an important stage in the development of a relationship between writer and publisher. Later would come the disgust, the remorse. Perhaps those too could be conquered by this eagerness to be literary. And such an ending to the lunch might be, in her imagination, a literary event: the fairy tale life of fiction as against the prosaic journey home to her husband and child.

I shook my head quickly. Such thoughts were wrong. They were disgraceful. Impossible as well. 'No,' I said aloud. 'I want to help. But I don't think you should be too ambitious. Record your impressions of what goes on around you. Write about what you really know. For example, in your first collection, the description of a girl's first day at boarding school is much more effective than the attempted evocation of a working–class family holiday in Torremolinos.'

Sarah Erdley's cheeks reddened again. 'I suppose that I was trying to use my imagination,' she said.

'A creditable aim. But your lack of knowledge of that

particular milieu comes through. Don't be too ambitious, as I said. On the whole it's better to work from experience.'

There was a loud crash from the back of the restaurant, somewhere in the direction of the kitchen door. I turned round. Two waiters had collided with each other. One had spaghetti Bolognese down the front of his white shirt, the other rubbed frantically at his thigh where a shiny mess of ratatouille slid slowly downwards. The Neapolitan rushed towards them, a mirthless smile on his face. 'Now,' I said. 'Look at that. Could you record it, bring out the possibilities of tragedy and farce? Look at them!' The three figures – the waiters and the proprietor – were speaking in vehement low voices, careful not to shout but obviously furious. Suddenly the Neapolitan pushed the waiter with the spaghetti Bolognese on his shirt, withdrew his hand quickly and stared furiously at the mess of tomato, mincemeat and noodles that had stuck to his palm. Then, stiff with tension, the three of them walked to the entrance to the kitchen, and hovered there still quietly quarrelling before, in a sharp movement, they joined together in a tight group to disappear through the large swing doors.

'There,' I said. 'Could you capture that? And look at this room: the green paper with gold tall ships racing across it, the empty chianti bottles tied together at intervals where the walls and ceiling meet, the red plush banquettes and yellow tablecloths, the cream-fringed shades on the lamps. Do you keep a notebook? You should.' As usual, the wine had made me excitable. 'Please tell me,' I said, anxious to make the conversation more personal, 'how are your children?'

'Child,' she said. 'A little boy.'

'And how is he? And your husband – Jeremy?'

'Very well.'

'I am glad.'

'And your family?' the girl asked, still timid.

'My family?' I laughed. 'Good heavens, I have no family.'

'But you have a son and a daughter.'

'Oh, them. They are much as usual. Much as usual.' I spoke briefly of Edward and Angelica's progress. 'She's restless,' I said of my daughter. 'She dislikes the constraints of working for the government so she has a new job. In business.'

128

'I didn't know . . .'

'Oh, yes. And doing well. Unfortunately I can't remember the name of the company. But it's connected with her step-father. He has very extensive interests, you know – in the City and other places.'

'Angelica used to frighten me when we shared a flat,' said Sarah Erdley.

'Frighten you?. Why?'

'She was always so positive.'

'She wants to succeed, that is certainly true.'

'You know, you're very lucky to have two such successful children.'

'I only want them to be happy,' I said. 'That's all.'

Sarah Erdley put down her glass. She had refused my offer of cheese, or pudding or even coffee. Probably she took great care of her appearance; her beauty would be an important part of her vision of herself. It was not, I decided, an unself-conscious business. Yet she seemed naive: almost touchingly so. Or was this merely because she was on unfamiliar ground? What would she be like when she felt that her position was supreme: if she were faced, for instance, by shy floundering admirers, by a person who mounted an uncertain assault?

'And you were once married,' she began, 'is that right? I hope I'm not . . .'

'No, no,' I said, raising my right hand in a gesture of flamboyant reassurance. We had been through all this before. 'I don't mind at all.'

Sarah bit her bottom lip and frowned. 'And the person who comes to stay with you at the cottage . . . ?'

'Oh, you mean Christina?' Should I declare: we used to be lovers? It would have interested me then to have used the word lover, to have thrown out the fact that I was capable – at my age – of having one. I would have watched her for reaction, hoping to arouse a vision of my daring in her mind. In the end, however, I opted for caution and decency – perhaps, I should like to believe now, out of respect for Christina and a wish not to flourish our private life in public. 'She and I are old friends,' I said.

'Just good friends?' The girl was attempting a joke. I looked at her steadily and watched her smile vanish into confusion.

'We have known each other for a long time,' I said. As the wine lifted my spirits again, I wanted suddenly to plunge into a different world. 'My God, the country is beautiful – the English countryside! Don't you agree? Take the woods around the cottage. I can't wait – I mean to get down there again. Next weekend for instance. Without it, my life would crumble!' My voice died away. 'I love those woods.'

The girl jumped slightly, then cast a startled look towards the door.

I had hardly sat down at my desk when the telephone rang. It was Williams, on the internal line. 'Simon?' he said. 'Ah, I've been trying to reach you for the last thirty minutes. Where have you been?'

'At lunch,' I answered. 'Why . . . ?' The time, at a quarter to three, was a little embarrassing. In the old days George Mason and I had often lingered in the club, telling ourselves that we would make up for it by staying late at the office either that evening or the next. Anyway lunches with authors were an important part of the ritual of our trade. 'At lunch,' I repeated, more firmly, 'with an author.'

'Who?'

'A girl called Sarah Erdley.'

'I don't think I recollect her name on our list . . .'

'No, John,' I said quickly, 'she's still very young. She sent me some short stories . . .'

'Not more short stories, Simon. I really don't think the finances can stand yet another collection of short stories by a completely unknown . . .'

'No, no, John.' Again my response was quick. 'I haven't taken the book on. Don't worry. But the writing shows promise. One must always be on the look-out for young talent.'

'Yes.' I thought I heard a brief sigh. 'Simon, I was in New York for most of last week and talked about our forthcoming titles to several publishers, with mixed results. Irving Gruber was interested in the Palmerston biography. And I feel this is an opportunity that we mustn't miss.'

My first reaction was that Irving Gruber – whom I knew

and respected – had gone mad. How could anyone in their senses express an interest in so dull a book? 'Oh, really?' I said.

Williams explained. 'Of course Irving hasn't read it yet. I didn't tell him that you were slightly disappointed in the result. He has this passion for nineteenth-century European history. I think he specialised in it at Harvard – years ago of course but he keeps up with recent research, or so he told me. I said that we would send him a copy of the manuscript as soon as possible. Will you see to that, please?'

'Certainly, John.'

'I'm just working on my presentation for this Maidenhead meeting.'

'Oh, yes.' I wanted, suddenly, to break Angelica's confidence and ask if the group that owned us were really on the run from Bill. No. If Williams were more sympathetic, more dependable in his reactions, I would have spoken. But what if he knew nothing as well, if his superiors had not taken him into their confidences? He would feel threatened, force me to reveal my source.

'I hope that everyone will be well prepared,' he said. In other words he hoped that I would take the necessary trouble. I had every intention of putting on a good show at Maidenhead. Why was the man so habitually insulting?

'I'm sure they will. John . . .'

'Yes?'

'Nothing. I'll send the Palmerston manuscript off to New York this afternoon.'

'It's not too grubby?'

'No. I've made a few cuts.'

'That doesn't matter. It will give Irving the impression that he's receiving a privileged first view of the work. I told him that several other American publishers had expressed an interest.'

'Have they?' What on earth was going on over there – an outburst of collective literary lunacy?

'No.'

'John,' I said, 'what exactly is the point of this meeting at Maidenhead?'

'As I told you, Simon – to satisfy our masters that everything is as it should be.'

131

'I mean, they're not thinking of doing anything drastic, are they?' I spoke quickly, fear speeding the words like water down a smooth long slope.

'Not that I know of.'

'Of course there have been rumours in the office. . . .'

'Ah, yes.' Williams adopted the measured way of speaking that he used when he wanted to make someone feel foolish. 'I seem to remember a nonsensical idea that we were, as a firm, to publish only academic and educational books – get rid of our general list completely. Run it down and keep only the old titles and copyrights which might remain profitable in the future. I wonder who started that one. Perhaps it was Stanley, to remind us yet again – as if we needed reminding! – how very successfully he runs his side of things.'

Stanley was in charge of our academic publishing: that profitable empire built up by my ancestors. A short bouncy man whose friendliness concealed a sharp awareness of his own skill, Stanley presided over a success. Some of his works – Latin primers, Greek lexicons, school textbooks on ancient history – dated back to the days of my grandfather, one to the time of the founder himself. He had shown me a series of letters, dredged up from our archives, between the old man and the Glaswegian professor who compiled what is still one of the standard shorter Latin–English dictionaries. The correspondence revealed a meticulous concern for detail and tough bargaining over contracts. My grandfather had succeeded in persuading the professor to accept less than was usual at that time. As Stanley and I had bent over these yellowing papers, fascinated by the distant battle between two greedy Scotsmen, I had felt certain that he must be thinking what a poor descendant I was of the founding Titans. 'No, no,' I said.

'I was joking,' Williams observed.

'I see.' A resentment stirred within me. What about asking the man why he had shown Docherty's manuscript to Joan as well as to George Mason, without telling me? What about kicking up a little scene to do with trust in the judgement of his editors?

'Anything else, Simon?' Williams asked.

'No.'

Clearly he felt that he should end on a note of geniality. 'I wonder if you're the same as I am,' he said. 'Don't you find that returning to London after New York is a little depressing? What an atmosphere that city has – its wonderful irrepressibility, if you see what I mean!'

'Of course you lived there for some time.'

'I did.'

I thought: why don't you go back if you're so fond of the place? And go back soon. 'You may be right,' I said.

'Perhaps Maidenhead will re-invigorate me.'

'I doubt it.'

'I was joking, Simon.'

'Oh.' I laughed obligingly and he put the receiver down.

In the week of the Maidenhead conference Michael Docherty became my daughter's lodger.

I had gone to one of Hermione's parties, and Hermione, while we were speaking of her client, had said that the poor boy was homeless. His landlord had evicted him because of a quarrel for which the wretched Michael – or Mike as she called him – was not to blame. And I, half-drunk, anxious to please, had mentioned Angelica's spare room in Stockwell. So it had been arranged, Angelica had liked the idea. The man was a stranger but I could, as his publisher, presumably exercise a degree of control. 'At least let me see him,' she had pleaded.

They had met and on the evening after their meeting Angelica had telephoned me at my flat. 'He moves in on Tuesday,' she said.

'Good heavens! Are you sure this is wise?'

'A quiet writer, of regular habits. Just what I wanted. No rowdy parties. He explained that he wants to work in his room most evenings.'

'But what about the rent? Where's that coming from?'

'He has a teaching job.'

'Girlfriend?'

'I didn't ask.'

'Be careful!'

'Dad, please! Anyway, what are his stories like?'

'Interesting. I'll lend you the manuscript.'

'Thanks,' she had said. 'But perhaps when I have more

133

time. And not a word about the other part of our conversation the other evening. Promise?'

'The take-over?'

'That's right. It's strictly confidential. I've heard nothing else, incidentally. I went down to Bembridge at the weekend and Bill was there but I felt I shouldn't badger him about it.'

'Perhaps they've changed their minds.'

'I'll be interested to see if they do.'

'Will you, darling?'

When she spoke of such matters, Angelica's voice took on a harsh mid-Atlantic tone. I didn't like it. But I loved her still. Now I had introduced Michael Docherty into her life. He would be, I decided, a curious contrast to the world of Bill. He might contribute to the continuing process of her education. She was, after all, still young.

XIII

On Friday evening, in the hotel near Maidenhead, as I came down the stairs after my bath, I could hear the sales director Freddy Simpson's voice issuing out from the open door of the bar to the left of the hall. The words wafted up towards me. 'Jim rang from Glasgow yesterday to say that he's had a fantastic run in Scotland with that anthology of football humour . . .'

I entered the bar. Freddy, a fat good-natured man with an orange moustache and a red bald head, called to me. 'Simon! What are you having?' He was with Stanley, who smiled and held out a hand. Gerald, the finance director, was also there: an austere presence in a dark grey suit and thick glasses.

I asked for some whisky. 'Was the football book your idea, Simon?' Freddy asked. 'The reps are simply crazy about it.'

'No. I think John Williams was its originator.'

'Of course he was. I remember him talking about it at one of last year's meetings. The subscriptions have been out of this world. It's gone like bloody hot cakes in the north! Liverpool, Manchester, Sheffield – those sort of places. I was looking through it myself and there are some wonderful things.' Freddy paused and took a gulp of his drink. 'Several good Tottenham jokes which even I didn't know and I've been a Spurs supporter for over thirty years. Have you read it, Simon?'

'I'm afraid not.'

'I didn't think you would have.' He turned to Stanley and

laughed in a way that was not unpleasant. I knew that Freddy thought me a stuck-up snob with a ludicrous passion for the recondite: an intellectual who knew nothing of what most of the country really wanted to read. He was wrong in at least a part of this assessment. I am not, and never have been, an apostle of things of the mind – although I do possess certain tastes that might be described as intellectual. No, my life could be better described as a quest for feeling.

Stanley's smile was avuncular. With his success, his endlessly triumphant growth and profit figures, he could afford to feel at ease. Williams dared not ruffle him. Stanley's knowledge of the academic book market would be welcome anywhere, at almost any price. 'You're wrong, Freddy,' he said. 'Simon is broadening his list. How's the sauna bath book coming along?'

'I still haven't received the final draft from the translator,' I answered. 'Apparently he's having a certain amount of trouble with some of the more obscure Swedish idioms. But I'm afraid I can't claim any credit for that either. It came to us because the author is a cousin of John Williams's wife.' As I spoke the last three words I was aware that a detectably venomous note had entered my voice.

'Sauna baths?' said Freddy Simpson. He turned and winked at Gerald who managed a wan smile in return. 'That's a bit cheeky, isn't it? I wouldn't mind seeing some of the photographs . . .'

'I'm afraid you'll find them rather tame. The book treats the subject from the point of view of health.'

'Ha!' Freddy let out a loud guffaw. 'I've heard that before! I'll bet it's just an excuse for a lot of sexy blonde pin-ups. John's smarter than you think, you know. Wait till the reps get their hands on this one!' He looked down at his empty glass. 'Here! Gerald, it's your turn. Let's keep the party moving, for Christ's sake.'

Gerald ordered us all refills, for which I was grateful. I was in need of some artificial stimulation. With Freddy you always felt that you were about three or four drinks behind. He saw life as a perpetual party, or liked to think he did. In the office sometimes I walked by his room and looked in through the glass partition that separated him from the passage. Generally he would be shouting down the telephone or sprawled back in his chair with his hands clasped behind his head as he regaled some visitor with stories or dictated to his pleasantly shy young secretary. Only two or three times had I seen him alone, his face set in unaccustomed gravity as he read a letter or looked through a sales forecast. At such moments my romantic instinct attributed a deep melancholy to him: an inner silence which almost certainly did not exist.

No, Freddy was at his happiest when surrounded by his reps at a sales conference: a dominant figure in the midst of his underlings, laughing and joking with them but always aware that he was in charge. The reps were in awe of him. Round the conference table they became thoughtful, even shy, opening up only in the evenings after the sessions were over. Then they would drink, noisily. The conferences were held in a different part of the country each time and once big Jim McCallister, our man in Scotland, had done six hundred pounds' worth of damage with the aid of a potted plant in the lounge of a motel near Weston-super-Mare. Freddy had exerted his authority. Big Jim had been warned, threatened with the loss of part of his bonus. The reps spoke of Freddy's anger to this day. He was, beneath the jocularity, a man to be feared.

Now he was shouting again. 'Joan! Over here!' He turned to me. 'The lady's arrived. Now we'll have to behave ourselves.'

Joan was wearing a dark blue dress, fastened around her thin waist by a thick black belt. Her hair was pinned more tightly into the back of her head; only a few strands escaped. Her face – handsome, courteous – leaned forward as she asked for a glass of dry white wine. 'Isn't John down yet?' she said, before reaching into her bag for the usual packet of cigarettes.

'He's working in his room,' said Stanley. 'He may not join us for dinner.'

I felt elated. I could cope with Freddy and the rest of them; Williams was the awkward one, the threat. 'Perhaps he's worried about the morning,' I said. 'I imagine we'll be put through our paces pretty briskly by these people.'

'So you've heard too, have you?' asked Stanley.

'Heard what?'

'The rumours of a take-over, or at least an offer. For the whole group.'

'Well, I didn't . . .'

Joan looked anxiously at Stanley, inhaled on her briskly lit cigarette. 'What do you mean?' she asked.

'Please!' Stanley put up his hands in a gesture of surrender. 'I have no inside information, only the City pages of the *Daily Telegraph* this morning. Didn't anyone else see it?'

'There's something in the *FT* as well,' said Gerald. 'And the shares moved sharply up yesterday. I didn't hear the market report this evening. But it's only the rumour of a bid, as yet.'

'Do they know who the bidder is?' I asked. I felt myself blush. Joan was looking at me, her face set in a frown. I suppose I still hoped that Angelica's story might not be true.

'International Services and Systems,' Gerald answered. 'Or so the *FT* says. A large conglomerate, mostly manufacturing and financial services. A great array of interests. Local newspapers, outboard engines, investment management, electric cookers, building and construction. Quite a bit of stuff abroad. Timber in Africa and Canada, sugar in the Caribbean, oil in the US. Very big.'

'Bigger than Lindsay?' I asked.

'Oh, yes. They were one of the first into the North Sea. Building and servicing the rigs, investing in exploration.'

'Long established?' I asked.

'How do you mean?'

'I mean is it a company with a long history?'

Gerald smiled. He was on familiar ground, away from Freddy's perplexing jokes. 'Been around for ages,' he said, 'but it's only in the last ten years or so that they've really started to take off. As usual most of the success stems from one man. He's been running the show since the early 'sixties. An extraordinary operator.'

No one asked for Bill's name.

They were listening. Joan did not know. She knew of my divorce, of Laura's re-marriage to a tycoon. But nothing of Bill, of his company, of the stupendous level of his success. She had not heard of ISS. Nor had the others. They were outside the rush and ruthlessness of commerce, the reality behind the country's wealth. Like me they were innocents, swimmers on top of a dark sea.

'But, Gerry, old lad,' Freddy began, 'why should these

138

gentlemen suddenly want to break into the tiny world of book publishing?'

'They don't,' Gerald answered. 'In fact I should imagine that is the last thing that they want. It's the Lindsay group that they're after, some parts of which would match up very nicely with their own interests – particularly in manufacturing. Then there are Lindsay's retailing businesses – the newsagents, the DIY stores and the rest. ISS probably see these as ripe for drastic restructuring. They think they can do it. They're a fairly tough bunch.'

'What would happen to us?' I asked.

'Us?' Gerald drained his glass and looked me straight in the face, his eyes dim behind the thick spectacles. 'Oh, we're pretty small beer as far as they're concerned. If the take-over succeeds – and it's by no means certain that it will – ISS may keep us on for a bit, partly to show that they're not just crude asset-strippers. Then, unless we make a startling contribution to their balance sheet, I expect they'll put us up for sale to the highest bidder.'

'And who would buy us?' Freddy asked, his voice robbed of exuberance at last.

'I don't know,' Gerald said. 'Another publisher? Some American? We're too small to exist on our own. Someone might take a stake in the equity and try to keep us going as an independent concern. But that would be difficult. We'd always be at the mercy of a potential take-over, if that person got bored or simply needed some extra cash.'

'But surely they wouldn't let us collapse?' Joan butted in. 'I mean we're one of the oldest . . .'

'Who are they?' Gerald asked scornfully.

'Lindsay, I suppose . . .' Joan looked flustered.

'If Lindsay are taken over by another company, there is nothing they could do, even if they wanted . . .'

'Christ, Gerry,' Freddy said, 'you're making me nervous.'

Gerald shrugged his shoulders. 'It may come to nothing,' he said. 'But one should understand the implications.'

'Have you talked to John Williams about this?' I asked.

'No. And he hasn't mentioned it.'

Joan had turned away from the rest of us. She was waving, smiling and beckoning with one hand. Then I saw – pressing his way politely through one or two other small groups of people – a tall thin figure in a suit of green and grey tweed, a white shirt with a thin dark blue tie spotted with red, a long fresh-looking face pale in the bar's false light. It was Williams. He reached us. 'Well,' he said with a thin smile, 'here we all are, ready for the fray.' He looked around, saw me and passed quickly on to the next person. 'Master of the Revels as usual, Freddy?' He snorted at his own joke.

'What are you drinking, John?' Freddy asked, laughing as well but in a slightly defensive way, a little too quick to follow his leader. 'Come on. You deserve something pretty hefty. I'll bet you've been slaving away up there, trying to undo some of the damage done by the rest of us.'

Williams smiled again. 'Yes,' he said, 'I have been working. A few last-minute calculations, with the aid of your figures, of course, Gerald. I don't think that any of us have much to be ashamed of, at least in terms of the last quarter's results.' The smile widened to a dull beam as he looked at his assembled cohorts. 'Ah, Freddy. Of course, a drink. A small scotch, please. Then I think we might go straight into the dining-room.' He looked at his watch. 'I believe that my secretary made a dinner reservation for half past eight.'

None of us mentioned the rumoured take-over. Of those present, Stanley and Joan had the easiest relationship with Williams. I felt that Stanley said nothing because the future did not worry him. With his reputation he felt entirely secure. Joan, on the other hand, was nervous. But she had decided to wait, perhaps to allow Williams time to relax and unbend.

On the way into dinner, Freddy and I left the others in order to go to the downstairs lavatories next to the hall. We stood self-consciously, three urinals between us, as the wide empty room echoed to the sound of a startling mass flush. 'You know, Simon,' Freddy suddenly said, 'I'm glad you got your way about those short stories by that man with the Irish name.'

'Michael Docherty.'

'That's right. I mean I think it's right that we should still do that sort of book. I backed you up with John, you know. I took your side.'

'Did he show you the manuscript as well?' This was too

much.

'Good grief, no. But he explained it to me and asked me what I thought.'

'Freddy,' I said, 'John Williams has never read the damned thing. How could he explain something of which he was, and is, completely ignorant?'

Freddy fiddled with his trousers, stared at the wall and looked perplexed. Then he turned and walked over to the basins. 'I don't know, Simon,' he said as he washed his hands. 'I just don't know. You've got me there.'

'Anyway,' I said, 'I'm most grateful to you.' I joined him at the row of basins and turned on one of the hot taps. 'We mustn't lose our literary reputation. Don't you agree?' I smiled, put my hands under the flow of scalding water, jumped with the unexpected pain and turned on the cold tap as well.

'You in trouble?' Freddy asked. Now he was standing by the towel dispenser.

'No.' I came across to join him. 'Just the bloody hot water.' I rubbed busily with the towel. 'I think those Docherty stories will go well. The reviewers will be interested. And he's young, a good investment for the future.'

Freddy finished drying his hands and waited for me. 'Simon,' he said, 'now that George Mason has more or less retired, you're our last link with that sort of publishing. Remember the old days with George – the stories at the sales conferences about Morgan Forster, Leonard Woolf, old Uncle Tom Eliot and all? Ha!' Freddy half belched, half laughed. 'What a lovely man George is. People like him oughtn't to be allowed to die. They should be preserved, pickled, stuffed or whatever – with their memories and voices intact, of course, so that they can be living representatives of their type and time. What are we going to do when George goes, Simon? What are we going to do? It'll be like burying a piece of living history, except he'll be dead of course. That'll be a terrible day, won't it? A really terrible day.'

Freddy had probably been drinking in greater volume and at more speed than I had supposed. 'George will last for a few more years yet,' I said as we walked out into the passage. 'He's a tough old bird.'

'While he's still alive,' Freddy declared, his bald head even redder than usual, 'we must never let him go, Simon. George mustn't be allowed to retire. He mustn't be allowed to . . . You and I must see to it.'

The others were already seated at the long table in the middle of the dark, panelled dining-room. As I went to an empty chair at one end, between Stanley and Gerald at the head of the table, I wondered if Freddy's eulogising of George Mason had not been an oblique way of insulting me. I was – as he had said – George's natural successor. Indeed with George's partial retirement I had taken on several of his authors, leaving him with only half a dozen of his old friends and favourites. In fact the loss of George, sad though it would be from the personal point of view, need not be felt strongly by the firm as a whole. He was, as Freddy had remarked, a living monument, a survivor from another era. But he was not indispensable. There was, I felt, an apostolic succession here. George had trained me; I had trained Joan. The tradition no longer depended upon individual mortality.

I banished such thoughts. The point now was to get through the evening. The table placings had fallen to my advantage. Williams was one away from me, the other side of Stanley. Next to him sat Joan, opposite me at the table's other end. On her left was Freddy; beside him Gerald, who was on my right. Williams, talking to Joan (I heard the words 'Ilse finds the winters in London very tame you know – in comparison with Scandinavia'), was not quite out of hearing but far enough off for comfort.

The menus came. Williams, with a natural authority, supervised the ordering. 'Shall we all have the dish of the day? Roast lamb? That will make everything simpler. Quicker,' he declared. 'And to start with? Soup?' I intervened to request a prawn cocktail. Williams' impatient eyes focused on me. It was more expensive, not on the set menu. Flustered, I backed down in favour of the soup, like the rest of them. 'Please, Simon,' Williams said, 'feel free to have whatever you want. I think that the profits will stand it!' He looked at Freddy, an ally in laughter, and they both guffawed together, closely followed by me and the rest of the party. I stuck to the soup.

The wine waiter gave Williams a bulky black folder. The

Welshman glanced through the pages and then at Stanley and me. 'Simon,' he called out. 'Of all of us here, I would say that you were the most likely to be well informed about these matters.' I blushed and forced another smile. It was a shaft of course, aimed with clumsiness but capable of causing a flesh wound. Did he mean that he believed me to be an alcoholic, a heavy drinker who knew his way around thousands of different vintages and vineyards? Or perhaps the implication was subtler, yet almost more unattractive: that I was a pretentious snob who valued such knowledge and expertise to an extent that was ridiculous. Either way I felt affronted as I reached out to accept the list.

'Now we'll know who to blame if our heads are like blocks of concrete in the morning,' said Freddy. Williams and he laughed again.

'Poor Simon,' said Joan.

'I'd trust my life to you,' said Stanley quietly and winked to display his goodwill.

I looked up from the plastic-covered pages. 'Is everyone having the lamb?' I asked. They all nodded. I told the waiter to bring us two bottles of a moderately priced claret, a cru bourgeois from a recent year. When it arrived, I tasted a small amount, said I was satisfied. By then Williams had returned to Joan and was repeating some anecdote about last year's Frankfurt book fair.

Stanley, Gerald and I made an agreeable threesome. We spoke first of Stanley's recent skiing holiday when he had taken his wife and two sons to Austria. 'The boys loved it,' he said. 'They had to be dragged off the slopes.' Gerald too had a story of a family trip, a summer idyll last year on the Devon coast. This stirred the bitter but fascinating pangs of nostalgia; Laura and I in the West Country, shut off from the rest of the world. I asked Gerald for details: the whereabouts of the village where they had rented a cottage, the sort of weather that had prevailed. As he answered, I noticed the warmth with which he described the games of cricket on the beach, the expeditions into the hinterland. At the end, he snapped back into the dry commonsense of a man who seeks statistical evidence before coming to a decision. 'Such trips are generally better in retrospect than reality,' he said. 'One tends to gloss

143

over the rainy days, to laugh about the broken cisterns and uncomfortable beds, to look back with affection on the sly grasping village shopkeeper. Don't you agree?'

Both Stanley and Gerald had a reverence for family life. Younger than I by some five (in the case of Stanley) and perhaps ten (in the case of Gerald) years, they had children small enough to engender protective feelings, to awaken not just sad glimpses of a half forgotten, partly mythical past but an innocent present as well. Edward and Angelica were long past this stage. To recover it, I had to search back, to resurrect a sense of fatherhood buried in their lost childhood. My quest was solitary. They were not interested. And Laura had moved on, far away from those other days.

'Where do you go, Simon?' Stanley was asking.

'Me?'

'Yes. For a holiday.'

They did not know much about my personal life. 'My children are grown up,' I said. 'Family trips are a thing of the past for us now.'

'Have you still got that cottage?' Stanley asked.

'Yes,' I said. 'I still have that cottage.'

'A good escape,' said Stanley.

'Very pleasant it must be,' added Gerald.

Stanley moved to one side as a waitress put a bowl of soup in front of him. 'The odd thing is that the country always makes me nervous,' he said. 'I don't mind the occasional trip, to stay in a hotel in the New Forest or something like that. But nothing more permanent. I suppose it's just not in my blood. Too different.'

'You can never escape entirely,' I said. 'For instance' – I smiled and took a mouthful of the watery vegetable broth – 'my landlord's wife writes.'

'Does she, now?' Stanley made a grimace. 'What sort of things?'

'Short stories.'

'Not more of your short stories, Simon!' Gerald's interjection was good natured.

'No no no,' I assured him. 'They're not publishable.'

'But you're instructing her.' Stanley's voice seemed to have been infected by the leering manner of Freddy. Most of us had

had too much to drink. I had already downed two large glasses of claret. Williams, I noticed, had ostentatiously poured himself out a tumbler of water as well. 'How old is she?'

'Mid twenties,' I said. 'But it shows how difficult it is to get away. Even there I'm a publisher. Not that I mind,' I hastened to add.

Stanley laughed. 'Your name is part of the trouble, Simon,' he said. 'To an educated person it can only mean one thing – that you're most probably connected with this company. And you've got your great-grandfather to thank for that. If he hadn't come down from Scotland and set up shop in Maiden Lane, your anonymity would have been safe. As it is, you're almost a public figure. But that's not too terrible, is it?'

'A bit like having responsibility without power.'

'What do you mean?'

'Well,' I said, 'people often assume that I still have control, or at least a large say, in the way that the company is run.'

'But you do have a large say,' Gerald declared.

'Do I?' I grimaced, pointed a spoon in the direction of John Williams who was still talking to Joan and therefore had his head turned away from me. 'I wonder . . .'

Williams swung his head round. He could not, I realised, have heard; and even if he had the criticism was surely too oblique to be understood. But I flinched. 'Simon,' he called out, loudly so that the rest of the group were silenced. 'Joan and I would like your opinion – as the senior editor – on something that an agent has sent me.'

'Oh, yes?' Surely this was hardly the time or the place. I saw him half turn back to Joan and give what looked like a wink. 'What is that?'

'A cookery book, Simon,' Williams went on, lifting his head so that he could look down at me. 'Of a rather unusual kind.'

'But surely that's more up Joan's street. She handles the kitchen and hobbies list.'

'I think that this involves broader questions of policy,' Williams said. 'Let me tell you its provisional title. The agent has called it *Eating for Love*.'

'Really?'

'Perhaps I should make myself clearer. It deals with the

145

aphrodisiacal qualities of certain dishes as well as the culinary details of how to prepare them.'

I shrugged my shoulders. 'If Joan has confidence in the book, I have no objection . . .'

Freddy started to laugh. 'Cor! When's the proof coming out? Put me down for an early copy!'

'That's not the end of it,' Williams went on. He nodded quickly at the waitress who was bending over him with an offer of vegetables to go with his lamb. 'The book is illustrated.'

'You mean the photographs of oysters, various types of mushrooms and the rest?' I asked.

'And people as well.'

'Doing what?' I had an appalling notion of what might be coming next.

'Eating the food.'

Relieved, I smiled at him. 'It sounds harmless. Is there a market for that sort of thing?'

Williams smiled back. He was enjoying himself. 'The point is, Simon, that the people in the photographs are wearing no clothes.'

'Cor!' Freddy shifted in his chair and grinned at the rest of us. 'Wait till the reps get their hands on this one . . .'

My relief vanished. 'John, you're not serious. We'll be the laughing stock of London!'

'Will we? You mean that it will probably not be reviewed in the *TLS*?'

The blood ran into my cheeks. I was almost shouting. 'I can't imagine anything more bloody stupid than photographs of a lot of naked figures sitting around a kitchen table. It's completely absurd! And revolting as well.' I looked at Joan. 'You can't get us involved in this,' I said to her. She raised her hands in a gesture of resignation.

Williams' voice became quieter, as if he were speaking to a child. 'But the illustrations are not at all like that. In fact they're rather well done. In one sequence, for example, a young couple are shown eating a series of dishes off trays in bed. In another, a party is taking place around a swimming pool – with guests in bathing costumes. There is absolutely no indecency – or overt sexual display whatsoever.'

146

'What about the couple in bed?'

'The photographs are posed so that the food on the trays is shown in considerable detail – close up, so to speak. The figures themselves reveal only parts of their anatomy. The rest is in shadow, or hidden: in other words, left to the reader's imagination. The sheets of course cover the more . . .' – he paused for a moment, frowned and then continued – 'private parts.'

Freddy laughed loudly. I took a sip of wine, looked directly at Williams and spoke in what I hoped was a cool voice. 'Is this another of those Scandinavian productions that your wife so obligingly digs up for us?'

He moved back briskly in his chair as if confronted by a physical challenge. 'Whatever makes you think that?'

By now I did not really mind how the man reacted. 'That book about saunas. The two sound as if they come from the same stable.' Or the same rubbish tip, I almost added. But I thought that a cold reaction would be more effective, would make more of an impression on Stanley, Gerald, Freddy and Joan than a descent into abuse.

'Not at all.' Williams spaced his word out carefully. 'As you know, *Perspiring Freely* is concerned with health and physical fitness. The illustrations bear that out. *Eating for Love* is on an entirely different plane.'

'So it is pornographic?'

'No, Simon. It's fun. A little diversion. A touch of bawdy, you might say. Is there anything wrong with that? We ought to try to keep a sense of humour, you know. People can't be expected to have their heads deep in Dostoyevsky and Proust the whole time.'

'Of course they can't,' I said. 'But this is utterly absurd. How can we be taken seriously if we publish such stuff? And I very much doubt the commercial possibilities. You know how expensive illustrated books are these days . . .'

'We're looking into the possibility of a co-production with the United States, Germany, Italy, France and several other countries – to be printed in Singapore or South Korea. Obviously the text will be in different languages. But there'll be collaboration – sharing of costs, ideas for design and layout – on all sorts of things. The Americans were wild about it

147

when I showed them the synopsis in New York.' He took a mouthful of lamb, chewed for a moment, then looked down at me through his chill brown eyes. 'I know, Simon, how protective you are of the company's reputation. Of course you have every right to be, connected as you are with its founders and having worked with it for so many years – all your publishing life, if I remember rightly. But we should try to see these things in pespective. You and I know, Freddy knows, Joan knows, everyone sitting round this table knows that *Eating for Love* is not great literature.'

'If we want to publish pornography . . .' I began.

'Simon, the book is not pornography. I can guarantee that. Joan and I have seen the photographs. Ask her how she feels.' He turned towards Joan.

She looked embarrassed. She did not meet my eyes but glanced awkwardly at each of the others in turn. 'I think,' she said, 'that we should not be too pompous about these things . . .'

'Have you talked to George Mason about this?' I asked her.

Joan's voice shied upwards as if frightened of its words. 'Briefly,' she said.

'And what did he say?'

'Not much.'

'Has he seen the photographs?' I turned back to Williams. 'If he has, he's certainly one up on me.'

'As a matter of fact, Simon,' Williams said, 'George was in my office yesterday and I did show him some of the photographs – as I will gladly show them to you first thing on Monday morning.'

'Thank you so much, John, but if you would be kind enough to spare me that particular pleasure. . . .'

'George Mason was amused. Amused and tolerant.'

'Old George probably lapped them up,' Freddy interjected. 'No wonder he looked so cheerful when I saw him last night.'

I turned on Freddy in exasperation. 'I very much doubt if George Mason's cheerfulness could ever be ascribed to having seen a photograph of a lot of naked girls eating oysters.'

'Ah,' said Freddy, 'but there are boys as well. Isn't that right, John? Something for everyone.'

I hit the table in anger. 'How appalling!' I turned again to

Williams. 'I suppose that this is our answer to the take-over bid, our contribution to the group's defence! Make money quickly. Get the profits up. Satisfy the shareholders. Who cares about integrity or the firm's good name?' I looked at Stanley and Gerald. Their faces showed the anxiety of men who wanted to remain out of the battle.

'I'm sorry, Simon; I'm afraid I don't quite follow you.' Williams finished the remains of his food. He seemed unperturbed.

'You know perfectly well what I mean.' I glared at Joan. 'And so do you. So do we all.'

Williams placed his knife and fork in a neat formation, wiped his mouth with his napkin and took a sip of water from the tumbler. He looked around the table. 'What is this?' he asked.

Stanley spoke. 'I think that Simon is talking about stories in the newspapers about the rumours of a take-over bid – for our proprietors, that is. And I share his concern. I think we, as the directors of one of the group's subsidiaries, ought to be told what's going on. But perhaps, John, you know nothing about it.'

The last sentence was evidence of Stanley's cunning. It implied that our masters might treat Williams with enough contempt to keep him in the dark about such an important development. Williams, I knew, was vain about these matters. He would rise.

And he did. 'I see that somebody has been reading the *Daily Telegraph*.'

'And the *Financial Times*,' added Gerald.

Williams' face cracked into an approximation of an easy-going smile. The brown eyes, however, remained impassive, even dead, like those of a doll. They rested briefly on me, narrowed in resentment. I drank some more wine, pushed my plate to one side and, to avoid the Welshman's gaze, examined the debris of the meal, the mess of food still uneaten, now cold in front of me. Williams was gathering his forces. We all knew this. A waitress came, removed our plates and raised the possibility of dessert. Freddy asked for some Black Forest gâteau; Gerald and Stanley favoured the fruit salad. They were served from a large trolley with what seemed an interminable slowness. Joan, Williams and I ordered coffee; and he began to speak.

'Stanley is right. I should have mentioned this before. But we knew very little until two days ago and even now there isn't a clear picture of what is going to happen. Let me tell you what I know. The Lindsay group – our proprietors – is the object of a take-over bid. I think one can safely say that this is certain. The organisation trying to gain control is another conglomerate, larger than Lindsay but of a rather different type. It is called ISS – or International Services and Systems. Now Lindsay – and I have the Chairman's personal assurance on this point – is going to fight. I know that the group's profits were down last year and that some of the shareholders were unhappy as a result. But, as this quarter will show, the position has enormously improved. This demonstrates – to my mind conclusively – that Lindsay is perfectly capable of putting its own house in order.'

'What about us?' asked Stanley. 'Let's say that Lindsay lose. Then what happens?'

'I don't think that they will lose,' Williams answered, shaking his head slightly. 'And nor does the Chairman. Once roused, he's a very determined man.'

'But if they do?' I asked.

'Then we will be treated on our merits. There's really not much to fear. Our figures have improved quite dramatically, you know. The decline of the last ten years has been reversed.' This was self-congratulation. He had been with us now for some four years. If changes had taken place, they were his.

'But will these new people want us?' Joan asked. 'What sort of a company is it?'

'ISS? Lean and hard. Hungry, one might say. A little less' – Williams moved his left hand in a slow arc – 'sedate than Lindsay. Possibly less accommodating as far as its subsidiaries are concerned. Less likely to leave them alone. But that need not be a bad thing. It might even be rather stimulating.'

'What about this man?' I suddenly asked.

'Man?' Williams frowned. 'I don't follow Simon.'

'Who runs the show. Who runs . . .' Again the name had gone out of my head.

'ISS?'

150

'Yes.'

'Oh, I see.' Williams did not mention Bill's name. For once his formidable memory seemed to have failed him. 'I didn't know, Simon, that you took such an interest in financial matters.'

'Is he behind the bid?'

Williams smiled again. The lack of sympathy had returned. 'I should imagine so. He is the chief executive of ISS – and a major shareholder as well.'

Joan leaned forward. The smoke poured from her mouth in a great churning cloud. 'John,' she asked, 'are Lindsay going to win?'

'I hope so.'

'Is that all that you can tell us?'

Williams was serious as he turned to her. 'At the moment, Joan, yes.'

'Because if they lose, we're in trouble.'

'Why do you say that?'

'Feminine intuition,' she answered. 'I don't like the sound of these other people.'

'They're too ruthless,' I suddenly blurted out. 'Too . . .' – I searched for the right word – 'too greedy.'

'You're very quiet, Gerald,' Williams observed.

'What is there to say?' he asked. His eyes blinked behind the thick spectacles. 'One can only wait. We may hear something tomorrow.'

Then I saw that Freddy was chuckling to himself, looking down at his empty wine glass. '*Eating for Love*,' he was saying. 'That's rich, that is. Very rich.'

One of the men in the Lindsay group was talking to us in the featureless conference room on the ground floor of the hotel. From my seat on one side of the long wooden table covered with a green baize cloth over which we had spread our papers and folders, our pocket calculators, pencils and pens, I could see out into the garden where the mist was gradually giving way to a bright spring morning.

The message was one of comfort. We would, he said, have seen reports in the newspapers. They, the board, regarded the bidder as wholly unsuitable: worthy of respect of course as a successful concern, but the direction that ISS had chosen to take was very different to that of Lindsay.

'Take you, for instance,' the man said. His voice was level, used to addressing meetings. 'We are proud to have a company with such a historic reputation in the group, a name that is synonymous throughout the English-speaking world with high literary standards and integrity. I know that at one stage the finances were not all that they might have been. Now the results are much more satisfactory. We will be discussing those later. But you are playing a worthwhile and significant part in our operations.' He smiled. 'You are safe with us.'

We moved on to the more commonplace business of the day. Each of us was questioned about his particular responsibilities. During my turn, Joan sat at my elbow but I coped well on my own. There followed a general discussion on the direction that the firm might take. At this stage I wondered if I ought to make a public scene, speak out – especially after the introductory remarks about high literary standards – against the cook book and the treatise on the health-giving properties of sauna baths.

The atmosphere of the meeting stopped me. We had – Freddy, Gerald, Stanley, Joan and I – come together in front of these outsiders: these three softly spoken impersonal men in shapeless dark suits. They were our masters. And as each of us did our bit the others seemed to huddle round him, to wish for his triumph and vindication. Stanley's exposition was languid and unmoved; Gerald's dry and matter-of-fact; Freddy's intelligible and effective, the facetiousness stored away. As for me, I said my piece with a confidence born of some thirty years in the trade. We were united. The irritations and petty rivalries seemed to have vanished. And, from across the table, John Williams watched us with what I thought must be pride.

I said nothing to spoil this, nothing that might disturb Williams' delighted portrayal of us as a happy team. 'Thank you, Gerald. Thank you, Freddy. Thank you, Stanley.' How courteous the Welshman was that morning. 'Simon, tell us a little bit about Henry Brown's new work. I'm sure it would interest our friends . . .'

Our friends or our masters? What did it matter? We were

buoyed up by their faith in us. And I spoke about Henry's plot, his cardboard characters, the ridiculous romance he had fabricated against the background of Argentina. I joked a little and described in slightly mocking tones the way that the hero and heroine meet, the paraphernalia of their grande affaire. Williams intervened to give figures for the size of the print run, the overseas rights, the promotional possibilities. Here was success. Our three interrogators leaned back in their chairs. 'Thank you, Simon,' said Williams. 'Thank you very much.'

I too was pleased. But Williams had not finished. 'I was very glad to hear you speak at the beginning about maintaining literary standards,' he said to one of the dark-suited men. 'We're very much aware of that, aren't we, Simon? We try to do what we can to encourage young talent. And there is one young man of whom we are particularly proud at the moment. Simon, would you please tell our friends about . . .' He paused. Surely he was going to forget the name. But after a quick glance downwards at some notes, it came. 'Michael Docherty.'

For an instant the hypocrisy stunned me. Then Williams' good-natured expression, the expectant faces of the three interrogators and the smile of Stanley opposite brought back the old feeling of delight. I spoke of Docherty's stories, of their qualities, their chilling contempt for sentimentality and cant, their ability to confront the unpleasant realities of human relationships in our numbing contemporary world. The Lindsay directors looked wise and appreciative. As I ended, the one in the middle, who wore a suit of a slightly darker shade than the others (was this perhaps a sign of his seniority?), observed, 'The Chairman will be pleased to hear that you are publishing young writers of talent.' Williams smiled, gave a pessimistic projection of the possible sales of such a book and added, 'But of course we subsidise works of that type with the profits from our other publications. A proper procedure, as I'm sure the Chairman would agree.'

The others nodded. The Chairman, already knighted, was on the board of Covent Garden. He bought modern pictures to decorate the walls of the group's Mayfair headquarters. He sent out New Year messages to his staff headed with quotations from Sophocles, Tennyson, Shakespeare and (once) Montaigne in the original French with a translation provided underneath in smaller type. The Chairman did not like to be thought of as a philistine businessman greedy only for profits and the vulgar trappings of wealth.

Profits. We moved on. Williams and Gerald between them produced evidence of these, not only for the present but the future as well. 'This last year has shown a dramatic improvement,' Williams said, 'and our expectations are that next year will be even better. The policies that we embarked upon' (clearly he meant I to be read for we) 'four years ago are beginning to pay off. And with you we feel secure. You have been good to us.' The three men smiled. They looked satisfied. I laughed inwardly. Cynicism was beginning to reassert itself. I looked out of the window, towards the garden. Then I saw them. Walking towards us across the lawn, laughing: Bill and my daughter Angelica here, a mere few yards away on the other side of a window.

Instinctively I turned away, downwards towards the notes and figures on the papers in front of me. They had been intent upon each other; he had his arm around her shoulder and she stretched up suddenly to kiss his cheek. The glass was between us; they could not see clearly into the conference room unless they came right up to the edge of the window itself. I looked out again. They had turned away to the right towards the path that led to the other side of the building where, I presumed, his car – that hideous, powerful foreign machine – would be parked.

I watched them. Soon they had gone. I almost held up my hand, like a child in school, to announce that our common enemy was among us. Williams talked on, so reasonably. 'I've never felt so confident about the future in every way,' he said.

Lunch. We moved into the dining-room.

I had prepared myself for the awkward encounter, the embarrassed cry of 'Dad!' Bill, in his dark blue blazer, blue and white spotted cravat, light grey flannel trousers and suede shoes (I had marked down his clothes through the window), would be raffishly plausible. 'We stopped for a drink.' (Or

154

would it be coffee at this time of the morning?) 'I'm looking at a boat.' (Surely it would be a boat, at one of those yards on the Thames?) 'We drove down this morning, on our way to the Isle of Wight. What are you up to, Simon? Won't you join us for a bite?'

The onus of an explanation could be thrown back at me, plotting to avoid this man's rapacity. I was sure that I would blush, as if caught in an act of deception. And hovering in the background would be Williams, the Lindsay directors, Gerald (who knew his way around the financial world), Stanley, Freddy and Joan. One of them might recognise that distinctive face from the memory of a photograph in a newspaper. One of them might even come forward and expect to be introduced. Then the whole truth would be out – the truth about my connection with this pirate, a connection given physical reality by the presence of my daughter at his side.

As we stood to leave the conference table, I wished – as on so many occasions in my life – that I had a greater control over my outward expression. Freddy sidled up to me, made some remark about dying for a gin and tonic. I managed only the thinnest of smiles, indeed almost blurted out, 'I've just seen my wife's second husband in the garden here, kissing my daughter. And guess who he is, Freddy? Just have one bloody good guess. Go on.' Instead, I followed the general movement towards the door where John Williams came up to whisper, 'Simon, will you sit next to Ray Carter at lunch? He's the one in the dark grey suit. I know he'll be interested to hear the history of your family's links with the company.'

Bill and Angelica were not in the dining-room. I had an idea. I could remember Bill's repulsive car. As we milled around the chairs of the large table reserved for us, I said to Williams, 'Excuse me. I must just go to . . .' He nodded briskly, as if reluctant to hear the word uttered in public. I walked along the passage. No sign of Bill or Angelica. I went through the hall, out to the car park and stood on the flat tarmac in the sun to check the vehicles lined up in a neat row. It was not there. I returned, visited the lavatories and came back to the dining-room with a sense that a crisis of a sort – an immediate crisis of personal embarrassment and shame – had passed.

155

The others had sat down, leaving a place for me in between the man in the dark grey suit and Freddy. As I acknowledged Mr Ray Carter's welcoming smile, other questions arose in my mind. Had I told Angelica of this meeting? Yes, I was sure that I had. Had I mentioned the date, the time or the place? Of these I was not so certain. If she had known, might their presence that morning have been a deliberate act of defiance, a wish on Bill's part to produce yet further evidence of his power? Once more I, as a small obstacle in his way, felt the heat of his overwhelming acquisitive urge.

Ray Carter was polite. 'It's wonderful that you're still with us,' he said. 'A living link with the past. I know that the Chairman values your presence. Your name is almost a chapter in the history of publishing!' A mere footnote, I assured him: certainly not a chapter. He laughed. 'Well, I don't know,' he said. 'Things must have been rough in those early days, for your ancestors.' Not as rough, I almost declared, as when they were peasant farmers in the Scottish border country, at the mercy of drunken landlords and vile weather. 'But it's rough now, Simon,' he went on. 'In a different way, of course. But we're going to win this one. Don't you worry. We're definitely going to win.'

XIV

Sunday morning.

From my bed I could hear the sound of church bells. Christina would be going to church this morning, most probably to early Communion at eight o'clock. Then she might drive, as she sometimes did on Sundays, to Aylesbury to visit her aged invalid aunt.

The old woman had money, the only significant amount of money of any of Christina's relations. I had, once or twice, joked about the frequency of the visits and the possibility of an ulterior motive. 'What lies behind the façade of words, darling?' I had asked. 'Are they more often a way of disguising truth than a method of its revelation? For instance, you tell me that you are going to see your Aunt Patricia. That is true – as a statement of fact. But how do we interpret it? Your expression, as you declare this, is one of concern – of a person about to engage in an act of selfless charity. One admires you, rejoices that a younger generation still feels a responsibility for its elderly and pathetic relatives. Then we delve deeper, uncover auntie's South African mining connections, the existence of an intriguing little trust based in the Channel Islands, the absence of a direct heir. Could there possibly be some deeper reason, less exalted and noble than the first?'

The tease used to anger Christina. It was unfair. She was a good person: of this I felt certain. And this Sunday she would go, on her own, to the church near her flat in Chelsea and kneel in front of the altar. The thought was oddly touching, the idea of her standing, sitting, kneeling, alone: intent upon the clergyman's words, the prayers and words from the Bible. At the door afterwards the Vicar would shake her hand, pleased to see that this elegant woman in black was a member of his congregation. Occasionally she and I had gone together, to the same church, after we had spent the Saturday night at her flat, and I had bellowed out the hymns. During the sermon, my attention had usually wandered a little, mostly to vague imaginings of what our future might be, to doubts about the rectitude of our life together.

To go to church was a sort of cleansing process, or so Christina claimed. Where else (she asked) could you sit, stand and kneel for sixty minutes in the presence of what surely amounted to a set of just and proper moral ideals? And even if you didn't listen to the words or join in the hymns, psalms and responses, wasn't it also good to be silent, to be out of the world for an hour in this wonderful building in the company of other people who were intent upon self-improvement? Put it like this, she had asked, what harm does it do you? None at all. At the lowest, church was a rest, an interval in your life when you could regain your breath. And the stillness, the sanctified calm, certainly restored something to the mind and the spirit. Would she be saying all this to David? Would he be as moved by it as I had been?

That Sunday I did not go to church. At about half past eight, I shaved, then dressed in a clean shirt, jersey and grey trousers. I walked out for the Sunday papers and returned to make a cup of coffee and three pieces of toast. In the papers, as always, I turned to the literary pages first. No books that were my responsibility were reviewed that day, but I read through the other notices in order to keep in touch. One of our novels, by an author of Joan's as I recall, received an acidic paragraph in the *Observer* and a few pleasant sentences in the *Sunday Telegraph*. I noticed a few words that the publicity department might extract for an advertisement. 'Promising', 'mysterious', 'sensitive', 'unpleasant', 'uninhibited', 'raw'.

I waited until ten o'clock before telephoning Angelica. I felt almost certain that she would not be there. It was this that encouraged me as I dialled the number. Then, to my slight shock, after only half a dozen or so rings, the receiver at the

158

other end was picked up.

'Darling . . .' I began.

'She's out.' The voice was masculine, slightly truculent. 'Who is that speaking?'

'Angelica's father.'

'This is Michael Docherty. Your daughter has gone away for the weekend. She should be back late this evening. Is there anything I can do to help?'

Docherty. The lodger. Of course. 'Good morning, Michael,' I said in a jovial way. 'I'd forgotten that you were living there. Is Angelica treating you well? She's not too demanding a landlady, I hope?' I laughed.

There was a short silence from the other end; then the monosyllabic response. 'No.'

'Well, if you have any trouble, just get in touch with me,' I said. 'I can give you some hints about the best way to deal with her.' I laughed again.

'I'm very happy here,' Docherty said. 'Shall I tell Angelica that you rang?'

'Yes. Please do.'

I imagined that he was perhaps embarrassed to find himself talking not only to his publisher – with whom he should have a formal business relationship – but also to the father of his landlady. Docherty might think that I was worried by the thought of the two of them alone together inside the small house in Stockwell. In fact this did not bother me. No, I had learned to respect my children's independence. And he seemed a curiously sexless figure. I could not imagine him capable of any artful seduction; he was too large, too ungainly. Anyway, the roughness and violence of the stories perhaps showed the frustration of an author who found the first stages of any human contact miserably difficult. Without this, there could be no way through to the mysterious landscape beyond. 'Michael, how's the next one going?'

'The next what?'

'Book.'

'Oh.' The breathing deepened. 'Not too badly.' He waited a few seconds. 'Time is the real problem, you see. I find work very taxing at the moment.' I could not remember what the boy did. Then he gave the answer. 'I've got a temporary post,'

159

he said. 'At a school in Peckham.'

Teaching. I had a vision of Michael Docherty in front of a class of alert sixth formers, releasing the secret theories and expressions of his interior life. To see Docherty at work would be a revelation. I tried again to put the boy at ease. 'I saw Angelica in the distance yesterday morning, at a hotel in Maidenhead, down by the river. You don't know what she's up to this weekend, do you?'

'No. I don't know.'

This was all. I broke into a genial farewell. 'Well, I won't disturb you any more. Have you seen Hermione lately?'

'She writes to me sometimes.'

Weren't the Irish, or those of Irish descent, meant to have been endowed with what was often referred to as 'the gift of the gab', I thought? If so, Docherty was certainly an exception. 'Well, goodbye, Michael,' I said, and that was the end of our talk.

I felt impatient, anxious to be off again in search of the truth. In the hard chair beside the telephone, I sat leafing through my address book. There, on one of the pages densely packed with scribbled numbers, I saw my son Edward's name. Quickly I dialled. The ringing tone seemed strange. Eventually he answered. 'Edward!'

'Dad!' He sound confused. 'Do you know what the time is?'

'Yes. Just after nine o'clock. Why?' Then I remembered. The boy was in New York. 'My God! I'm most terribly sorry . . .'

'Has there been an accident?'

'No, no, no. Edward, I am sorry. I forgot. Did I wake you up?'

'Yes.'

'You don't know where Angelica is, do you? I am sorry . . .'

'Angelica? She must be at Bembridge, surely. Why? Can't you get any answer from there? They may have sailed over to Cherbourg for a day and a night, I suppose. It's one of Mum's favourite trips. Yesterday was her birthday.'

Laura's birthday. Yet what an absurd suggestion. She was not well enough to sail across the Channel. The boy was out of touch. 'Well, can you explain this to me? What were

Angelica and Bill doing yesterday morning – on your mother's birthday – at a hotel in Maidenhead?'

'Where?'

'Maidenhead. Beside the Thames. I saw them. Walking across the lawn.'

Edward was silent. Then he asked, 'Come to think of it, Dad, what were you doing there?'

'A business meeting, with some of the Lindsay people. I looked out of the window and there were Angelica and Bill. By lunch time, when our morning session had ended, they had gone.'

'Most probably they were on their way to the Isle of Wight from London.'

'Through Maidenhead? And why would they stop at a rather mediocre hotel? It's most unlike Bill, who's such a stickler for the best – or what he thinks is the best.' I could not resist this jibe at the man's lack of taste, at his irredeemable vulgarity. 'You know, champagne with everything.'

'Perhaps Bill was trying out another car? I know he's looking for a replacement for the Alfa – something with a bit more "oomph", as he says.'

The excuse was poor. 'I think he was reminding me of his power,' I said, 'of the threat . . .'

'Threat? What threat?'

'The take-over of course. I could end up working for him – if the bid succeeds.'

'Oh that.' Obviously he knew. 'Dad, ISS is a vast public company. Bill is its chief executive. Even if they do get Lindsay, your firm, to be frank, is a very small part of it. I doubt if you'll notice the difference! You'll certainly never have to deal with Bill, or see him any more than you do now. I think you underestimate the size of his operation.'

'And overestimate my own importance?'

'Your own importance in the structure of the group. Of course you're very important in . . .' He stumbled, lost on a remote hillside.

'In what?'

'Well, in publishing in general. Everyone knows that. And there's your name, of course . . .'

'Our name.' It used to irritate, even hurt me sometimes: the

161

way that both he and Angelica seemed to distance themselves from most things connected with my side of the family. Neither of them had any interest in the history of the firm or the achievements of their ancestors. The romance of the arrival of the founder in London, his success in establishing a publishing house in the capital, the brave decision to move south: all this left my children cold. Our forebears were jokes to them, excuses for references to inherited meanness and cracks about the bottles of cheap supermarket whisky that they sometimes found in my flat. 'I don't like to be threatened.'

'Threatened!'

'That's what they were doing, the two of them. "Look out," they were saying, "here we come. And there's no bloody escape." Not very subtle, is it?'

'I'm sorry, Dad, I don't quite follow . . .'

'Bill and Angelica, in that garden. I saw them through the window. They knew that I would. Just at the moment when we were discussing the take-over, I looked out of the window and saw them. Bill knew. He bloody well knew that I was there. He knew that I would see them, through the window.'

Edward was anxious to soothe. 'Dad, I've got an idea. You've always been able to talk to Bill. Why not telephone him next week? Ask if you can have lunch to discuss the bid – if you're so worried about it. And really the Maidenhead theory is pure fantasy.'

'You don't believe me when I say that I saw them both?'

'No, Dad.' Edward was beginning to sound exasperated. It was too early. He wanted to go back to sleep, or return to his wife, Caroline, who thought I was pathetic. And here was his father suffering from a rather boring attack of paranoia. 'I believe that they were there. But I also believe – in fact I know – that their presence had nothing to do with your meeting or the bid or any plot to embarrass or hurt you in any way.'

'Then what were they doing?'

'Look Dad, I don't know. As I said, I expect they were on their way down to the Isle of Wight and stopped off at Maidenhead to have a drink or cup of coffee or whatever. The possibilities are boundless. Why not telephone Angelica tomorrow? Have you got her office number? You know that

162

she's left the Ministry?'

'I have her number. I do know that she has left the civil service.'

'And why not ring Bill as well? It's much better to talk about these things.'

'Is it?' I asked.

Then, with a brisk farewell, our son was gone.

I hate to live in a state of tension. And the best way to defeat an obsession is with a bombardment of a different sort of mental activity.

That Sunday I went first to the *Sunday Telegraph*. I read the front page slowly, paying attention to detail. I tried to conjure up a series of other worlds: bombed-out refugees, industrial conflict, an economic battle between the Treasury and the Bank of England. I turned the pages. The newspaper was stuffed with information, insights into other people's private lives, hints on household management, cooking and health, film criticisms, the theatre and art reviews, the gallery guide: then more politics, loud fatalistic leaders and opinion columns.

This was the world, or the world according to Fleet Street: and the world poured itself slowly into my system as I turned the pages. But he was there. In the financial section, Bill caught up with me again.

The photograph was of his head and shoulders, the head leaning forward in the manner of an expensive but sympathetic medical consultant, dignified, a little forbidding around the thin mouth. The bald head gave off a discreet shine. The photographer had underestimated the glow of the tanned skin, the product of years spent in sailing boats, on water skis or winter sports holidays in the Alps. At least Bill was smiling, and the article written around the photograph would surely provide another reason to feel pleased. It was a eulogy of his managerial talents, his entrepreneurial daring – the daring of a man who had launched 'one of the most significant programmes of business expansion in Europe'.

The journalist analysed the bid. The Lindsay group was described as worthy but tired; its opera-loving Chairman portrayed as too preoccupied with the dignities of office, too much (and the well-worn phrase was used) of the Establishment, too comfortable. Lindsay's component parts were mentioned. We appeared, near the end of the article, 'a publishing company formerly of a traditional and literary kind, now being transformed by new aggressive management'.

This was Bill's world. How finely judged it all was: the share prices, the exact worth of a particular company, the real value of its position in the market, the potential for profit and growth. Such matters, and their attendant risks, must be obsessional. Perhaps this was the reason for the man's odd delight in exuberant pleasures: in the roughness of a Channel gale (once he had told me that he liked 'a bit of a challenge' when sailing), the noisy speed of a motor boat as it dragged a water-skier across the waves, a violent game of tennis on his expensive hard court in the garden of the Bembridge house. Only extreme physical effort could force his work out of his mind.

Christina and I had played tennis with Bill and Laura, on one of our civilised summer trips to the Isle of Wight. I had noticed his contorted face as he threw the ball up for his service, the way his arm beat its way through the air, his glance at an opponent as he exercised one of his quick low returns: a glance of concentrated force. 'He's absurd,' I had told Christina after the game, as we had changed in our room. 'Did you notice on the tennis court – the ruthless determination to win, like a schoolboy? And the way that he tried to pretend that service was in when we all could see it was out by miles?' Christina, taking off her white sports shirt, had laughed. 'Some men are babies,' she had said. 'Complete babies.'

In between these two parts of his life – the fierceness of work and the fierceness of play – lay the territory on which he and I met. Here I found the puzzle of his dullness. When we were talking, I felt myself raised above him and his world, his interests, pleasures, his way of looking at people and ideas. Often I had almost to cover my mouth with one of my hands to disguise a spontaneous giggle at one of his more ignorant remarks, at a coarse gesture or a sentiment that showed

164

grotesque insensitivity and lack of education. Despite all this, I occasionally reminded myself – perhaps when Christina and I had been imitating his heartier mannerisms, his nautical expressions and crudeness – despite all this lofty mockery, he had not only made several million pounds but stolen my wife as well.

Then I understand that I had reason to be grateful to him. Bill never gave any hint that he saw me as one of the defeated. Indeed he would ask me almost deferentially about the latest books or plays, saying how often he regretted that he had not gone to university, once observing how sensible I had been to pursue leisurely interests such as reading and looking at pictures and architecture for they would last me far into old age, long after he had had to give up sailing and skiing because of stiff joints or dulled reflexes.

During one of our visits to Bembridge Bill, knowing of my interest in Victoriana, had even suggested a trip to Osborne. The two of us went, leaving Laura and Christina behind, and as I enthused about the house, its contents, the extraordinary atmosphere and evocation of a dead time, Bill had followed respectfully in my wake. He had fed me with questions, proclaimed his admiration. 'It's so wonderful that it's all survived,' he repeated several times. 'The history, the past. Who keeps it up, Simon? Who pays? Can one make a contribution? I mean, I'd like to help.'

Can one make a contribution? On our return, later in the bedroom, I had relayed this latest Bill absurdity. I told the story this time with no snide inference but from a feeling of affection, an understanding that he was translating Victoria, the Prince Consort and their retreat into terms more easily comprehensible to himself. There was nothing vicious, greedy, even materialistic – or so I had thought then. It was the equivalent of rendering French into English, of breaking a problem down. And, the evening after our excursion, as we had sat outside in four deck chairs, watching Bill as he disappeared into the hut beside the swimming pool in order to adjust the heating system or reduce the level of chlorine, I had looked at Laura and smiled in what I hoped was a gesture of forgiveness for all that she had done to me in the past.

XV

On Monday morning I was a little late in getting on my way.

The alarm clock must have failed, or perhaps I had not set it correctly. I was in a rush on the stairs, taking them two or even three at a time, clutching my briefcase into my side as if it contained a pouch of secret documents, when I saw, huddled beside the front door, the young couple from the flat below. It was another warm morning but they were both wearing overcoats: his a short brown garment, hers longer and dark green in colour. They seemed to be having some trouble. I heard him say, 'Now it's well and truly stuck.'

They raised their heads, saw me and looked terrified and ashamed, as if caught in an act of gross indecency. I thought: is this the moment, might I really ask what does go on? The question could be framed within a friendly but firm complaint about the noise. How could they answer? There would only be more terror, more shame: a petrified silence in the gloom of the front hall which our landlord – a property company based in the Bahamas – had repeatedly refused to redecorate.

I reached the small shrinking figures. The man, whose short black beard seemed to be quivering with anxiety, spoke, his words forced through short irregular breaths. His eyes shied away from me, like a bird when a scarecrow suddenly enters its field of vision. 'The key. The bloody thing's jammed. Jan can't . . .' He stopped, looked for comfort or inspiration at the dirty black and white linoleum of the floor.

'Get it out?' I suggested.

166

He grunted and pointed to the lock where the woman, who was about the same height but broader than her companion, was rattling the key. I had always thought of them as a couple of students. Now I saw that both were in their early thirties, perhaps even older. Her thin spectacles had slipped halfway down her prominent nose. 'Richard,' she began.

'For Christ's sake don't push it too hard or it'll snap and we'll be stuck here till kingdom come!' He gabbled the words in an impatient snarl.

'I'm not!' She wore black trousers, flared over black shoes. She bent over again, her short fair hair tight on top of her head.

'Shall I have a go?' I suggested and put my briefcase down.

Jan, the woman, stepped away from the door. I seized the small metal key, tried a gentle turn, then – as if to take the lock by surprise – suddenly wrenched the key back with all my strength. It worked. The door opened towards us, to reveal the quiet street, a line of parked cars, a policemen wandering along to protect an Arab ambassador's residence two or three blocks up the hill. 'There!' I said.

Jan stared at me. 'Oh, thank you,' she said, 'thank you so very much. I really don't know what we'd have done . . .'

'Most kind,' the man grunted.

And in that moment, with the two of them looking up at me as though I had performed a minor miracle, I felt bold enough to put the question. 'I wonder,' I began, 'I wonder if you would mind if I raised one small matter.'

The woman started to talk hysterically, laughing a little as her words chased each other out. 'You mean about the hall?' she said. 'Oh dear, isn't it terrible? We've written so many times. Of course they only answer every third letter, can you imagine – a company like that, not even bothering to answer, of course we're just dirt as far as they're concerned, rent fodder I call us – and it's worse for Richard because he works from home, you know, so there's no escape, his clients have to come through this mess to see him, it can't do his reputation much good, can it?'

'Have you written as well?' the man asked. His smile was less grateful.

'No,' I answered. 'But it wasn't the hall that I wanted to mention.' I glanced at my watch. I was already late for work.

Damn. 'It was more a question of the noise.'

Jan, the woman, interrupted. 'Richard's in advertising, you know,' she said, still excited. 'You're a publisher, aren't you? Mrs Thomas on the top floor told us.' Mrs Thomas was a pleasant old widow who seldom came to London, preferring to live mostly with her married daughter near Cambridge. 'We must see more of each other. It's silly to live so near – and yet so far.'

'What noise?' asked the man gruffly. They stood before me. I towered over both of them.

'A sort of shouting,' I answered and felt myself blush.

'Shouting!' He looked bewildered. 'Do we shout, Jan? The gentleman says that we shout.'

'Loud voices,' I went on. 'Perhaps it's your television.'

'Television!' Now he sounded angry.

'In the evenings sometimes,' I explained. 'It can be rather loud. I'm sure it must be the television. After all, it couldn't be anything else, could it?' I laughed eagerly.

They knew what I meant, for she looked upset as well, her chatter suddenly reduced to an awkward gaze at the grey stained walls of the hall which she had spent so much time and energy in trying to have re-painted. The edges of his mouth formed a downward arch. 'No,' he said, 'we'll turn it down.'

'That would be kind. I have no wish to be an awkward neighbour but – like you – I do a certain amount of my work from home . . .'

'We'll turn it down,' the man repeated, through clenched teeth. 'Won't we, Jan?'

She smiled at me. He seized her hand. They walked out of the front door and down the hill towards the High Street. From the steps outside the house, I watched as, safely out of my hearing and still holding hands, they talked in an animated way far removed from the studied grimness he had shown to me. They laughed as she reached across to brush something from the collar of his drab brown coat. At the end of the road they turned, saw me still standing but made no sign. Then they scuttled off to the left, huddled once more together, again holding hands, two persons united by the mystery of those haunting cries.

Williams came to the ten o'clock meeting.

The items were routine. Production costs, scheduling of future publications, prospective publicity stunts: business as usual, despite the take-over bid. I flourished a letter that I had just had time to open. It was from Henry. He was coming to England and wished to discuss our plans for the launching of his new book. When I told them this, everyone – Williams, Joan, Freddy, Alison from publicity – was silent, aware of this man's importance.

Afterwards, I went back to my office. I knew that, whatever obstacles were in my way – obstacles of climate, the un-pleasing prospect of my own cooking – I would go to the country that weekend. I had told Sarah Erdley that I would be there. She had written to me, an ingenuous letter, so clear on the page, so regular in its lines and spaces, that I suspected she must have made a fair copy of a previous draft.

Mary had left the letter on my desk that Monday morning, unopened because the girl had put 'personal' on the envelope. The writing was childish: rounded letters, widely spaced words, very different – I remember thinking – to Angelica's brisk angular script. As I opened the envelope, I felt a twinge of embarrassment at catching some despised part of myself engaged in a shameful act.

I fumbled with the thick white sheet of paper and straight-ened it out in my hands. In the top right hand corner, the address was printed in heavy black type that stood up from the page; on the opposite side was a coronet, a tasteless (I thought) reminder of the status of the owner of Erdley. Underneath came the infantile script.

Dear Simon (if I really may!),

It was more than kind of you to have given me lunch the other day. Our talk provided me with much encourage-ment and I have now a much clearer idea of the way that I want my writing to go.

You said that you would like to see some more of my work and that you were going to come down for the week-end. Would you countenance a visit to us some-time either on the Saturday or Sunday? I will telephone

169

your cottage on the Friday evening to find out if this appeals.

I am re-reading 'Emma' and feel very diminished as a consequence.

Yours sincerely
Sarah Erdley

I dropped the paper on the top of my desk. *Emma*. What did a girl like Sarah Erdley really think when she read *Emma*? What was it in the writing that made her feel 'diminished'? Surely Jane Austen could not be her idea of the way that a great writer ought to perform, for I suspected that she had the romantic notion of the writer as a hero, as a personality whose giant form bulged out of his or her work, someone – like Victor Hugo or Tolstoy – to whom a pontificatory role, a willingness to develop overt moral or political themes, went alongside the desire to make public the patterns of their creative imaginations.

But Jane Austen? *Emma*? This was different. Yet so many people admired *Emma*. The book was definitely first division. What are the greatest English novels: a good colour supplement question, one suited to the front page of the review section of one of the quality Sunday newspapers? Oh, the answer – from assorted writers, critics and cultural panjandrums – would come, why such and such, something, another book and, of course, *Emma*. So *Emma* was easy, easy to say that you liked it, that you felt 'diminished' in its presence. No marks really for *Emma*. I smiled. *Emma*! I smiled again. Why not, this weekend, really get the girl working, make her sweat a bit, say that of course nobody's literary education is really complete until he or she has read *Clarissa*, preferably twice? And, after this, a good dose of George Meredith, a wonderful example of Victorian concealment and impenetrable prose.

Ha! I laughed aloud. The telephone rang. It was Mary. 'Shall I come in now?' she asked. Of course. I had said that I would deal with some letters at half past eleven.

She entered, a kindly figure in a dark skirt and brown cardigan. 'Did the meeting go well?' she asked.

I nodded and told her that it had. 'And Henry Brown is

170

coming over.'

'Oh that will be exciting!' Mary was amused by Henry and giggled at his jokes. 'I expect that was why Liz rang about him during your meeting.'

'Liz? Why should she do that?' I was on the alert. Liz was Williams' secretary, a small blonde woman of about thirty-five with a false ingratiating smile. 'What did she want?' Mary stood opposite me, clutching her pad. 'Please. . . . Please sit down.'

She pulled up the other grey office chair so that we were facing each other across the desk. 'Nothing much,' she said, fiddling with the ball point pen that she used to take down my dictation. 'Routine stuff . . .'

'What stuff?'

Mary tried a brisk smile. 'Who Henry's agent is, how many of the novels are still available in hardback, where he stays when he's in London, the number of times a year that you have to go out to Nice . . .'

'But Williams never asked me about this.'

'Just routine, Simon, I'm sure.' But why should she feel that I needed to be reassured?

I leaned forward and put my elbows on top of the desk. 'Mary, I wonder what is really going on around here. You've heard about the take-over bid, I suppose?'

Her mouth twitched. What did Mary tell her husband Bob who worked in the Wandsworth bank? Did they laugh about me together in the evenings? Or did she drive him mad with stories of my brilliance? I was always, and always had been, polite to Mary. She had worked for me now for almost eight years. Before her there had been a girl called Carol; before Carol, Lorraine, who had left to give birth to an illegitimate baby; and before Lorraine, a slow brunette by the name of Diane.

Mary, Carol, Lorraine, Diane: a line that stretched back to the days of my young manhood. Diane and Lorraine had known Laura. They had chatted with her at office parties and the launchings of books. Diane, the dumb Diane, had seen Edward and Angelica as shy little children and commented on their sweetness, the way that they resembled their mother or their father. To all my secretaries I had been courteous: never

171

arrogant or bullying. No, my only signs of displeasure were a curt nod, an abrupt answer, a long sigh. Mary, who valued good manners (how she used to moan about the way that men never gave their seats up to women on the Underground these days!), could have nothing to complain about on that score.

Now she seemed frightened. 'Only what I see in the newspapers. My husband showed me the City pages on Sunday. And there's the office gossip, of course. But I never pay any attention to that.' She plucked a piece of fluff off the arm of her cardigan with a fierce quick action.

'And what does the office gossip report?'

'The usual doom and gloom. That these new people only want us because of the value of the lease on this building. That they'll close down the general publishing side completely and just go in for academic and educational.' She laughed. 'A lot of rubbish, really.'

'And what does Liz say?'

'Liz!' They were friends, I knew that. Often they had lunch together, at the sandwich bar nearby. I suspected that Mary was privy to the secrets of Williams' correspondence and filing cabinet. 'She's as much in the dark as the rest of us . . .'

'I wonder why she wanted that information about Henry Brown.'

'Just routine. Really, I'm sure of it.' Mary had her notepad on her knees, her biro poised. She pulled at her skirt in a gesture of impatience to show that she wished to return to the easier task of taking dictation. 'Probably John didn't want to bother you at the meeting. You would have had to have come back here to get the information. Perhaps he thought it would be simpler to have Liz ring me instead. Perhaps John realised that I would tell you and you'd find out that way. Really there seemed to be nothing secret about it all. Just routine. Liz often wants to know things. John asks her to get information together for some meeting or other.'

'Henry Brown is my author,' I said. 'Enquiries about him ought to be directed through me.'

'Shall I tell Liz that?'

'No.'

I picked up the top letter from the pile on my desk. It was from the author of the Palmerston biography, carping about some of the cuts that I had requested. I started to dictate. 'Dear Cartwright – no, change that to Dear Charles – no, on second thoughts I'll write Dear Charles in myself. Dear Charles, I know how painful it is for a writer to see his work mutilated. But I feel that there are good reasons for the excisions which I have suggested . . .'

I paused for a moment, and thought of the pleasure to be gained from – just once – telling the truth and saying how damned dull this man's stuff really was. Why not turn this letter into one of belated rejection, even of insult? It would have the advantage of driving Mr Cartwright from our doors, determined never to have anything more to do with us. Williams would commend me for my 'toughness', perhaps use the incident as an example of how realistic the firm had become, in tune with the hard conventions of the age. I thought briefly of a few phrases. 'Dear Charles, if you do not agree with my attempts to make your tedious prose marginally more readable, may I suggest that you take both yourself and your manuscript to the nearest lake, fasten the thing to your not inconsiderable stomach – where it should have the same effect as a block of cement – and jump in?'

No. I was a coward. I looked at Mary, smiled grimly and went on, this time aloud. 'I do not think that the cuts detract from the quality or theme of your work but of course I will be delighted to discuss them with you. I am sure that we will be able to work out a solution that is satisfactory to us both, although I must ask you to bear in mind the inevitable effect the length of the book will have on its eventual price, particularly when escalating production costs are taken into account.'

Mary's pen raced over the notebook. In my life as an editor I must have dictated thousands of similar letters. What was there to show for them, what result? Books. Yes. Books, books and still more books. They were my monuments. Like Proust's Bergotte, I would be watched over by them; two by two, three by three, clustered in groups, they must serve as my pall bearers and mourners. Bergotte was a writer. The novelist made no mention of the poor wretch who had edited him, tolerated his tantrums, cut out his split infinitives, toned down the foolish outbursts of self-indulgence, secured him

173

large advances from a reluctant Parisian Williams and insisted that he be given a chance to buy as many cheap copies of his books as he wanted after they had been remaindered. Oh, no. We were the neglected ones. Nobody writes novels about publishers: their moments of delight and their moments of hell. Nobody.

'Nobody!'

I shouted it aloud. Mary took the word down. 'Sorry,' I said. 'Read back the previous sentence, will you? I don't want to hurt Cartwright. Authors are such sensitive people. . . .'

Later, Mary put Hermione through to me.

The woman launched straight in. 'Simon, it's about Michael.'

'Michael?' Who was this?

'Michael Docherty, Simon. You know, you're publishing his book of short stories. *The Water Garden*. Or have you forgotten that already in the midst of these troubled times?'

'Troubled times?'

'The take-over bid, Simon. Or perhaps that has escaped your attention. Perhaps such matters – such mundane matters as who actually owns the company that you work for – do not penetrate the delightful ivory tower of the editorial department. Perhaps it is still fondly imagined that your family exercise a benevolent but distant control: the world of Mr John or Mr Matthew or even Mr Simon. I like to imagine you and your secretary up there, content in your little time warp, out of the Welshman's sight and mind. You know, Simon, I really think I might apply to the Department of the Environment or whatever the place is called now for a preservation order to be slapped on you. Then we might launch an appeal for a small endowment fund in order that you might be handed over to the National Trust as a monument to the past glories of British publishing when it was still an occupation for gentlemen. What fun, Simon! A living piece of history. I think we'll throw George Mason into the deal as well and have you both on show in your office or rig up some sort of club dining room where the public can watch you eat, catch the inflection in your voices as you discuss the wine list with the waiter. Will

174

they choose the Burgundy or the claret today – or perhaps even the amusing little cheap bottle from sunny Spain, certainly not the South African muck because George has his liberal principles to think of? The suspense will be terrific . . .'

'What is the matter with you, Hermione?' I asked. I knew these moods.

'Let me tell you this. While you're carousing in London clubland, swilling down claret and guzzling yourself sick on an inflated expense account, one of your writers is quietly going off his rocker.'

'Docherty?'

'Yes, Docherty. And if you ever want the young man to produce anything else worthwhile both you and I have got to move and move fast.'

'Hermione,' I interrupted, 'it may have escaped your attention but I have already arranged for your precious Michael Docherty to lodge in my daughter's house in Stockwell. There he has a room, a most reasonable landlady – and all within easy travelling distance of his work, which, as I understand it, consists of teaching in a school somewhere in Peckham.'

'Simon, there is no need to be aggressive. Let us at least keep to the essentials of civilised discussion . . .'

'Tell me then, Hermione – as quickly as possible – what is wrong with the boy!'

'He's too overwrought to write,' she said. 'That's what's wrong. He came to see me last week. He tried to explain the trouble but broke down completely in my drawing-room.'

'What is it?'

'What is what?'

'The trouble. The thing that is stopping him from working.'

'A crisis of confidence,' she said. 'Probably some emotional upset as well. He became quite incoherent.'

'Emotional upset?' I thought instinctively of Angelica, of the two of them alone in that house together.

'I don't know, Simon. I'm guessing.'

'But didn't you find out? He's one of your authors . . .'

'For God's sake!' Now she was angry again. 'The boy was in tears on my sofa. In that condition people tell you what they want to tell you. It was hardly the moment to probe, to extract salacious details. Don't be so prurient, Simon!'

'I'm sorry if Mr Docherty is upset,' I said soothingly. 'But I don't quite see . . .'

'Don't see what?'

'What I can do to help, Hermione. Especially if you refuse to tell me what or who is causing the trouble.'

From the other end of the line there came what sounded like a mixture between a cough and a cry of pain. 'Simon! Will you listen? He said a few words about the exhaustion of his work – the teaching and the impossibility of trying to write in the evenings and at weekends. Naturally I tried to calm him. First I suggested that when the school holidays start – which I presume they must do soon – he would get out of London. Go and stay with his parents or something like that to recover and rest. The thought didn't seem to please. Perhaps home life is hell. I don't know. Michael has never spoken about it.'

'Where is home?'

'Somewhere near Liverpool.'

'So what did you think of next?'

'I thought of you. And your cottage which you have so kindly made available to authors in the past. I can imagine no better place for Michael to recover.'

'Did you mention this to him?' I asked.

'No. But I said that I thought he probably needed to leave London for a bit and that I would give the matter some thought.'

'But what about your own establishment, Hermione? Now that really would provide the man with a break. What a wonderful experience . . .'

'And how is he expected to find his way over to France?' Her tone was remorseless.

'Perhaps you might take him.'

'I hardly imagine, Simon, that an energetic but emotionally unstable youth of twenty-five would want to find himself cooped up in a cramped and uncomfortable farmhouse in a foreign country with a woman approximately thirty years older, do you? No, I think we can drop that little notion. Anyway I have guests there this April. The boy should be alone somewhere, only for a week, probably not more. He's

176

an urban creature. Too long a period in the country would drive him crackers, as it does us all. You're only there at weekends, aren't you?'

'Yes.'

'There you are. Lend the place to Michael for a week, perhaps don't go there for one weekend. If you want another book out of him, someone's got to do something to help. And think what the others will say if the much-vaunted first novel never materialises. Think of the superior smiles, the repeated questions about when Michael Docherty is going to fulfil his promise. Another reason for the Welshman to sneer at "literary" publishing. Another reason for the hard men to look down on the effete, over-educated, out of touch, soft, wet . . .'

'Hermione!' I spoke sharply. 'What you are asking is if Michael Docherty can stay in my cottage for a week, is that right?'

'Yes.' The word snapped out. 'Telephone me when you have made up your mind. As soon as possible. Goodbye.'

I felt exhausted, as if drained by some strong purgative. Was it my age? No, I decided. An Olympic athlete would wilt under the assaults of such a fiendish woman. But, as usual, some of her shafts had inflicted pain.

That evening, after work, I met Joan on my way out of the office.

We almost collided in the hall. She was coughing and brought her head down to her hand which, clutching a small white handkerchief, she raised to cover her mouth. Her loosely pinned hair shook, her thin body stiffened in spasms of tension. 'It must be the weather,' she said eventually. 'I haven't been able to stop all day. Where are you off to?'

'Home. And you?'

'Late night shopping. School holidays start next week. I'm hopelessly unprepared as usual.' We walked out into the street together. I was glad to have an overcoat in the chill damp air. 'A good day?' Joan asked.

'Moderate. A bit of Hermione trouble in the afternoon.'

'That old gorgon! What did she want?'

'Help for one of her authors who she says is on the verge of a nervous breakdown.'

'Which one?' Joan asked. She walked in long slow steps at my side, her brown mackintosh rustling slightly.

'Michael Docherty.'

'Him again! Simon, you're becoming obsessed . . .'

'It wasn't me who raised it,' I protested. 'Hermione rang me as if I was responsible – which of course I'm not. She wants the boy to have a complete rest somewhere! She says it's the only way that he'll ever write anything ever again and proposes that I should lend him my cottage for a week.'

'Will you?'

'I don't know.'

'He is rather your pigeon, isn't he?'

'I know that Williams and you don't agree with me about this.'

'But we're more than happy to defer to your judgement.'

We? I did not blame her. Joan could not afford to make an enemy of Williams. And she was good with him. I liked to think of her as an influence, a friend at court who might, by the timely use of the right word or phrase, win a civilised decision from the Welshman. It didn't matter, I told myself, that she supported the aphrodisiac cook book and the sauna bath project. It didn't matter if she could not see the point of Michael Docherty, for I was able to put that down to a lack of education, of literacy, of the self-confident taste needed to appreciate this man's vision. I laughed. 'I hope I won't be shown up as a fool.'

'I'm sure you won't. By the way, we're throwing a small party for Henry. Did John tell you?'

'No.' I blushed. 'What do you mean, Joan?'

She slowed down and turned to look at me. 'He didn't?'

That was it. There was a plot against me. 'He has said nothing to me about it,' I said, my face burning. 'But we only heard this morning that Henry and Paul are coming over. You remember I told you at the meeting . . .'

Joan and I waited beside some lights to cross a busy road. The traffic thundered through the half-dark city. 'Yes,' she said. 'But John had a letter from Henry three or four days ago saying the same thing.'

'Well, why on earth didn't he say so?'

'This morning?'

'Or earlier! After all, I'm responsible for Henry!'

'I thought he had,' Joan said. 'He told me.'

The lights had changed. We walked over to the other side of the street. I leaned forward in order to be sure of catching Joan's words, for today, perhaps in the aftermath of her coughing, she was hunched up, no longer so straight. I wondered, as I had often done, if she was seriously ill, if we took her health too much for granted. Perhaps soon she might collapse and be taken from her flat in the middle of the night in an ambulance summoned by her son. How old was Joan? Young, in her late forties. But look how she treated herself, how she smoked, worked and pushed her way through life. And here was I upset merely because Williams had not shown more concern for my tender feelings.

'John's terribly tied up at the moment, Simon,' she said. 'I'm sure he meant to let you know about Henry. He happened to see me in the passage and told me then, on Tuesday morning I think it was.'

'Does Williams often write to Henry?'

'I've no idea.'

'Why didn't he interrupt me this morning when I said that Henry was coming?'

'Perhaps he didn't want to embarrass you in front of the others. He must have remembered that he hadn't told you about Henry's letter. John's not entirely insensitive. But I've told you that before.'

'So you have.' I suddenly put a question to her. 'Joan, I am safe? You know that, don't you?'

'Safe?' We were within sight of the Underground station. Crowds of people were disappearing down the steps into the troglodyte world below. 'Oh, not that again, Simon, please!'

'You must admit that it doesn't look very good if not only am I not told that Williams has heard that my most important author is coming to London but also receive no hint that we are giving a party for him as well. What sort of a party is it, anyway?'

'A small reception.'

'And who is arranging it?'

'John Williams.'

'And why were you informed and not me? Surely if anyone is . . .'

Joan stopped. 'So that's it,' she said. 'You're jealous.'

'No,' I said loudly, also stopping. We were standing by a newstand festooned with brightly covered magazines of women walking along tropical beaches and pompous looking foreign politicians seated at desks. On a table in front was a pile of evening newspapers for which passers-by made a grab, quickly thrusting some coins into the outstretched grimy hand of an old man. 'Of course I'm not! Don't be so ridiculous, Joan.'

'Well, what's the matter? If you must know, I think John told me because I'm a woman. He wanted advice about the best way to arrange the evening. The feminine touch. After all, Simon, party giving is hardly your department, is it?'

'I have given parties in my time,' I said truculently.

'And organised them yourself?'

'Certainly.'

'When?'

I could produce no convincing answer so shouted at her instead. 'Look, Joan, I'm surprised that you can't see the absurdity of this. It's almost as if that wretched Welshman set out to insult me. First he communicates with one of my authors behind my back, without even having the courtesy to send me copies of his letters to Henry. Then he lays on this party, again without any reference whatsoever to me. How does he know that I'm not busy on the day that he's fixed? I do have a life of my own, you know. I don't just sit around in the evenings doing nothing.'

'It is some time ahead, Simon,' Joan said calmly. 'If you are engaged that evening, I'm sure the date can be changed. The invitations haven't gone out yet . . .'

'When is it?'

'Four weeks from next Tuesday. The day before Henry returns to France.

'How long is he over here for?' I felt ashamed of my need to ask such a question about Henry Brown.

'Three weeks,' Joan answered. 'He arrives the week after next. But surely you've heard more recently than any of us?'

'He didn't say how long he was planning to stay.'

Joan sneaked a look at her watch. 'Simon, I think I must . . .'

But I exploded again. 'It was the same at Maidenhead! Everyone else seemed to know what was going on except for me. Freddy, Stanley, Gerald, you . . . And why was I the only departmental head told to bring down one of my subordinates?'

'Subordinates? Simon, I don't . . .'

'Yes, subordinates, Joan, for Christ's sake. You! You're one of my subordinates. If we didn't have to go on with this fiasco of keeping George Mason on as editorial director, I would be in control. As it is, the whole thing is ridiculously vague. But you – in terms of experience and everything you like to think of, you are my subordinate! And don't think that just because Williams and the powers that be don't choose to tell me the truth about what's going on – the truth about this take-over, this threat to all our jobs, to the integrity and tradition of the company, the company that was founded and built up by my forebears – just because our own people don't choose to tell me, don't think that I'm completely in the dark. You'd be surprised at my sources of information in this matter. And my opinion, although Williams, you and everyone else may think it worthless – my opinion is this: that the other side will win, that we will be taken over, that the group will be dismembered, that our operations will be drastically cut. We're dealing with ruthless people, Joan, people who have no residual sense of morality, people who win! You and I are natural targets, Joan. We're ripe for defeat.'

'Would you include John Williams on a list of "natural targets"?' Joan asked. She seemed unperturbed by my outburst and stepped briskly to one side to avoid a large woman laden with immense packages. 'Is he also "ripe for defeat"?'

The contemptuous way that she quoted my words showed that our old connections, forged over years of working and laughing together, had been broken. Whenever there was a clash between Williams and me, Joan would be with him. If challenged, she would intimate that, in her position, she could not have the luxury of choice or rebellion. Williams was in charge. Ultimately I must appear an irrelevance. This was the story of so much of English life. My ancestors had been the hard men, the mean immigrants from Scotland, the Bills and the John Williams of their time. Now, after a mere hundred and fifty years or so, their descendant was one of the effete, the over-educated and the slow.

'No. But these people are tougher,' I answered.

'Before I go may I make a suggestion?' The crowds parted as they approached the obstacle of two earnest tall people hectoring each other on one side of the busy pavement. 'Are you sleeping well at the moment?' Joan asked. The mockery had gone, to be replaced by what looked like concern.

'Not so badly. Why?'

'You look tired. I remember your complaint about the noise of the people who live underneath you. Some shouting or singing or something. . . . Is it keeping you awake? Have you got a holiday planned?'

'At this time of year?'

'Why not? You'd be going away before the summer rush.'

'Me? Where?'

Joan's expression was one of pity. 'Surely you wouldn't go alone. What about Christina? Wouldn't she come as well?'

'Christina has left me.'

People looked at us as they rushed past. We were an island in the midst of hurrying masses anxious to leave this part of London, to return to their homes and families and their private lives. 'Simon. . . ,' Joan began. She looked agonised, and I thought: my God, she really does mind. Then she drew herself up from her hunched position until she was level with my face and leaned over to kiss me on my right cheek. There was a whiff of cigarette smoke mixed with expensive scent. 'Simon, I had no idea. I'm most terribly sorry.' And she smiled, a look of tolerance, sympathy, warmth and, ultimately, pity. 'Don't worry, we'll protect you. And you will come to Henry's party, won't you? John couldn't cope on his own. You see, we do need you. Please believe that. Goodbye.'

XVI

I drove down in the Ford Escort to the cottage on Friday evening. Not until after seven o'clock had I left the office. I could have gone earlier and taken work home with me to study over the weekend. Something had kept me in my room. I knew what it was: anxiety and shame about what I was going to do.

Damn the traffic! On Hammersmith Bridge I saw the river luminous in the moonlight, brighter and clearer than in the day. At Roehampton I stopped outside the hospital, to allow an ambulance to turn across into the entrance from the other side of the road. Beside the line of stationary cars, their drivers impassive, mere upright shapes in the twilight, glittered the windows of the tower blocks that rose out of the small dip in the land. Here again, as with the Thames, the night brought mystery, even beauty. To live, to see people, under the cover of at least partial darkness might, I thought vaguely, preserve those shadows of my imagination so that I could maintain those quick comforting notions of trust and friendship which invariably dissolve in the harsh glare of day.

She telephoned on Friday night.

I heard the bell as I was carrying my suitcase into the cottage from the car. I dropped the case, left the front door open and ran through to the living room, pausing only to switch on the light.

Sarah Erdley's voice was nervous. 'Do you remember our conversation? You said that you might be able to come and see us this weekend?'

'I remember it well.'

'Let's see. Saturday lunch we've got the veteran car club jamboree. Dinner's out as well – there's a mediaeval banquet at which I have to organise the serving wenches and make certain that ye olde platters of sweetmeats are taken out of the freezer in time. Last week they were only half cooked and a Japanese tourist broke a tooth. Sunday's taken up with the free-fall parachuting. What about tomorrow afternoon? Jeremy is opening an exhibition in the old kitchens but I have nothing until the banquet in the evening. We should be back from the veteran cars by three.'

'What time shall I come?'

'Three fifteen? Better make it half past to be absolutely certain. Just walk straight in. I've got lots of things I want to ask you!'

The next day I boiled myself an egg for breakfast, inspected the cottage and saw that there was a damp patch on the ceiling of the spare bedroom. Then I read the manuscript of a book about a journey through the Himalayas and heated up a tin of tomato soup for lunch. I was here to rest. The business with the Erdley girl was coincidental. It was right that I should take trouble with her, explain the faults in her work and steer her gently away from writing.

I left a good twenty minutes for a journey that usually took ten. The sun was out. The green and brown of the countryside, the red brick and grey stone of the village cottages – built mostly at the start of the nineteenth century by one of Jeremy's ancestors who had been an enthusiast for rural improvement – moulded into the picturesque, the myth of a timeless part of England. Beside the grey bell-tower of the church which dominated the village, I turned left along the road that led to the house. The cottages thinned into ones and twos; a high wall began, to signify the enclosure of a landscaped park. I reached a pair of lodges on either side of a large open archway, a survival from the first half of the eighteenth century. A large notice on the front gate of one of the lodge houses read 'Private. Visitors to Erdley Castle and Fun Park please proceed to the public gate half a mile down the road'.

I turned in, drove through a small plantation of beech trees into the great expanse of the park. In the distance, to my left, I could see an array of tents, parked cars, a crowd of people and hear the clear tones of a loud speaker announcement. The voice was slow. 'Would the owner of the red Marina parked between the beer tent and the toilets please move this car because it is interfering with the efficient working of the toilets.'

The house, vast and grey-green in colour, loomed ahead. I parked on the gravel, walked up the three steps to the front door and the small stairway that led to the enormous hall. Quickly I crossed this, made for the small door on my left and, to my relief, found the familiar long cavernous passage.

Large canvasses, difficult to interpret in the darkness, hung on either side, depicting either battles or the dignity of some Erdley ancestors as he or she posed – for Sir Joshua, Lawrence or one of their imitators – with casual self-confidence, most unlike the habitually worried expression of their descendant. Had they too believed that their life at the house was a struggle, a source not of pleasure or self-delighting arrogance but exhaustion, sleepless nights after frustrating sessions with lawyers, accountants, theatrical costumiers, land agents or car park attendants? No, probably not. Young Jeremy was, in a sense, history's dupe. Few would envy him now, few want to change places in order to live in this ugly cold place, to dread the annual oil bill, to view with horror a drop in the takings from his various frenzied attempts to pander to the public's taste, to exchange the intimacy of private domestic life for the activities of a reluctant impresario.

I turned left beside a grey seascape. A door was ajar; light burst through the crack. This must be the place. I pushed the door. There was a fire lit in the large fireplace. The room seemed empty; then a spluttering sound came from the sofa, the back of which faced me. 'Pookie?' a male voice called out. 'That bloody man Crowther was telling me that they've run out of fairy cakes in the tea-room.'

I coughed.

'Who's that?' the voice called.

The head of Jeremy Erdley appeared from behind the dark

green sofa. His eyes, somewhat glazed, swivelled in desperation as he raised his hand to his unbrushed hair, attempted to sweep some of the long pieces away from his pale forehead (they almost immediately tumbled down again) and stood up. The boy was wearing some sort of mediaeval costume: a bright red doublet with long sleeves. As he stood and turned briefly away from me I noticed that its back was unfastened, the material parting down the length of his spine to reveal a long strip of white bare flesh. The costume ended at the top of his thighs. On his legs he wore a pair of black tights that ended in loose slippers, embroidered with gold thread.

'Where the hell's my crown?' he muttered. He looked about him, ran to an armchair in the far corner of the room and picked up a facsimile of a gold crown. 'Ah!' His eyes, still agitated, came back to me.

'I hope I haven't disturbed anything . . .' I began.

'No no no! Please!' He held up his hand. 'I thought you were Sarah. Just having a bit of a nap.' He pushed the end of the red doublet's sleeve away from his wrist and looked at his watch. 'Thank God you woke me. Only ten minutes before I'm due in the old kitchen to open the exhibition of ancient copper pans and kettles. Sarah said that she'd come and do me up.' He turned his back to me, revealing the bare flesh again.

'What a magnificent costume,' I remarked, wanting to put the youth at his ease.

'You think so? Bloody tight in places, I can tell you. Not quite sure if I've put the cod-piece on properly!' Jeremy Erdley let out a loud bray of laughter, at ease in the cracking of a lavatory joke. 'My Bluff King Hal outfit. Like it?'

'I don't quite see the connection,' I began tentatively.

'With kitchen utensils? Perfectly simple. I hired this two weeks ago to give away the prizes at the finals of the jousting tournament. It doesn't have to be back until next Wednesday. So I thought: why not wear it at the pans and kettles? Cheer them all up a bit. Also one must get value for money in these matters. Cost versus amount of use, you know, and all the rest of it.' Jeremy Erdley frowned. 'By the way, who was Bluff King Hal?'

'Henry VIII.'

'Oh.' He thought for a moment. 'Well, the agency I deal

with described the costume as their Bluff King Hal outfit on the invoice. To be frank, I just wanted something that was vaguely in keeping with the jousting. I had myself announced at the tournament as Bluff King Hal. Did they joust in Henry VIII's time?'

'Perhaps occasionally,' I said. 'But he was much fatter than you. And the style seems to be of an earlier date.'

'Oh. I suppose I ought to have padded myself out – for the jousting, I mean. Too late now. But no one seemed to mind. Do you think I could make a claim?'

'A claim?'

'Yes, to these bloody costumiers. Ask for my money back. The thing shouldn't be called the "Bluff King Hal" outfit if it's not the right date. What sort of period do you think it is?'

'About the time of Agincourt?' I said. 'You can always say that you are Henry V, a rather more heroic monarch in any case.'

'I see.' He frowned again. 'Probably more appropriate for jousting as well. Perhaps it's not so bad after all. And Bluff King Hal could have been thought to refer to an earlier Henry,' He smiled. 'All is not lost.' He looked at his watch. 'I say, Sarah must have fallen asleep or something. Could I possibly ask you to lend a hand? I've got to be in the old kitchens by three thirty. The local paper is sending a photographer. You couldn't do me up, could you? So sorry to ask. But it is rather an emergency.'

Jeremy Erdley turned his back to me and twisted one arm round to point awkwardly to the gap in the costume where his white, slightly light-green-coloured skin was revealed. 'There,' he said.

Reluctantly I went to the other side of the sofa, stood so that I was behind him and looked closely at the coarse red velvet. The doublet seemed to operate on a series of hooks, neatly stitched in so that, once fastened, they were invisible. I began at the bottom, seized the two sides of the divided velvet, pulled them together and fastened a hook.

'Well done!' the boy called out. He turned his head as far as it would go towards me. 'Now the next. I am sorry . . .' I performed the same manoeuvre with the next hook, moved my hands upwards to find its successor but there did not seem

187

to be one. I am not short sighted, yet I knew that a small hook would be difficult to see so I patted the velvet gently with my hand, thinking I might feel the object of my search. Tickled either by these light pats on the small of his back or the itchy texture of the velvet, Jeremy Erdley arched forward and let out a high-pitched giggle. 'What's the trouble?' he asked.

'This hook seems to have come off . . .'

'Damn that costumier!' He reached back suddenly with his right hand, pushed it up towards the bottom of the divide in the doublet and twitched his fingers awkwardly around. 'Here,' he said, 'is there one on the other side?' And as the boy spoke, the hand slipped in between the two sides of velvet and lodged itself, palm outward, fingers caught behind the material, thumb frantically waving. 'I say, I can't get the blasted thing out. Could you. . . ?'

I stopped patting, took hold of the wrist of his trapped hand and, as gently as possible, attempted to ease it upwards, away from the bottom of the divide. 'Ow! Ouch! Oh, Christ!' he called out. 'My bloody arm!'

'I'm only trying to free it . . .'

He leaned forward. I held the boney sides of his ribs in order to prevent him from toppling over: then, unexpectedly, he arched back, almost knocking me off my feet. This forced me to leave go of him and – grabbing at something with which to steady myself – seize the trapped right arm again, accidentally giving it another upward jolt. 'What are you doing? Keep away from my tights or you'll ladder them. . . !'

Behind us, a door opened. 'Jerry!' It was Sarah Erdley's voice. I dropped the elbow and turned round. The girl was standing by the door, her face aghast. She was wearing a pair of jeans and a dark red and blue striped jersey.

'Sarah!' Jeremy Erdley turned and faced me briefly, his cheeks scarlet with exertion, eyes damp with incipient tears. Then he spoke to his wife. 'My hand! Please . . .'

I stood back to allow her to reach him. Sarah Erdley slowly slid his arm out and across, away from the boy's back, and the hand was free. Jeremy rubbed it briskly with the other one, then extended the rubbing to the lower part of his right arm. She rubbed as well, her slight thin hands joining with his. Then she looked at me, bit her bottom lip and said, 'Poor

Jeremy . . .'

Jeremy interrupted. 'We were trying to do this blasted costume up . . .' He looked down at his watch. 'Oh, no! The copper pans! Sarah, for God's sake.' Quickly she went to work, pulling the two sides of the material together, finding the missing hook. The doublet was now complete, its high collar reaching into the recesses of the boy's dark brown hair. 'My crown!' He raced to the chair by one of the windows, seized the crown, returned to give his wife a lightning kiss on the forehead and ran to the door. 'Bluff King Hal!' he shouted, a defiant gesture of bravado, a battle cry as he charged towards the old kitchens. 'Bluff King Hal!'

The door slammed behind him. Sarah Erdley seemed worried. 'I do hope the opening of the kitchen exhibition will go well,' she said. 'Those veteran car people were rather too generous with the whisky. They all have flasks, you see – which they carry in their coats or tucked into the glove pocket of the machine. Each driver offered us a swig. I was careful. I don't much care for the stuff anyway. But Jerry always likes to enter into the spirit of these occasions . . .'

'Literally,' I said and laughed.

'I'm sorry?' Her lips straightened. 'Oh, I see.' She showed no glimmer of a smile.

'His nap will have helped.' I said. 'If one sleeps, the effects of over-indulgence are lessened – although he may now be suffering from a slight headache.' I smiled at her. 'You must be relieved to be able to wear your own clothes for once.'

'Me?' The girl brushed her hands quickly over the dark red and blue striped hand-knitted jersey. 'Oh, I really don't mind the dressing up. My Nell Gwynne outfit arrived this morning, to coincide with the first episode of the television life of Charles II. I'll be wearing it most of this week. Shall we go for a walk?'

'There's nothing you want to show me, of your work, I mean?'

Sarah Erdley blushed. 'I'd rather have a general talk first, if you don't mind. I hope I'm not taking up your time. After all, you came down here to rest . . .'

'Please!' I held up my hand. 'What else would I be doing this afternoon?'

189

First we went out to the hall, where I borrowed a pair of her husband's gumboots. His feet were the same size as mine. Was this an omen? We returned to the drawing-room, Sarah Erdley opened one of the large windows that face out on to the park and we edged our way into the clear afternoon. Some fifty yards out a wooden fence had been erected, to keep the public away from the front of the house. In this fence there was a small wicket gate and four people in mackintoshes – two middle-aged men and two middle-aged women – were staring at a notice pinned to its side. As the girl and I passed them, a woman's voice said, 'I wouldn't fancy the motorcycle scramble – not after all that knights in armour stuff. Would you, Fred?'

Sarah Erdley walked fast, away from the visitors. 'We advertise forthcoming events and try to make people aware of the variety,' she called to me over her shoulder. 'Some return again and again. You ought to see the letters . . .'

I looked across the park at the collection of makeshift tents, the public lavatories, the small wooden stand in the jousting enclosure, the garish booths of the funfair on the opposite bank of the lake. I almost asked, 'Wouldn't it be better to let the place collapse and become a picturesque ruin than to have all this? The house is a monster anyway.'

To our left the ground rose, at first gently and then with an increasing steepness. That afternoon the crowds did not seem to be large: scarcely more, I thought, than about two or three hundred people clustered around the edge of the jousting ring. Beyond them were rows of cars, their paintwork glinting in the light. As we climbed the hill, I looked back and could see two horses, ridden by men in armour, gallop towards each other from the opposite ends of the ring. The men held what appeared to be long lances, stretched out ahead of them, and as the horses converged, as the tips of the lances drew close to their targets, I could not imagine how both, or certainly one, of the combatants would avoid either death or certain injury. But there followed an oddly noiseless contact when both lances hit their opponent's armour, then seemed to bend almost double before the makeshift knights dropped them to the ground and drew up their horses. The crowd clapped deferentially. The knights, on the way out at the far corner of the ring, raised their arms in acknowledgement of the applause; the excitement, brief enough, was over. People began to leave the ring in small groups, the occasional child running after its parents, a young couple holding hands, an old man alone in a tweed cap and a brown overcoat.

I must have been gazing at this for a few seconds, almost oblivious of Sarah Erdley, for she gave me a slight shock when she spoke again. 'The weapons are made of rubber. It's a new system, pioneered here at Erdley. Our rivals are fearfully jealous. You see there are only a certain number of expert knights around – but with rubber lances almost anyone who's a reasonable horseman – or horsewoman – can have a go.' The wind was blowing her short hair on to her forehead so that it formed an anarchic fringe above her thin black eyebrows. We walked on up the hill. 'There's a seat at the top,' she said, in between quick breaths.

We reached the brow, entered a small clump of trees, passed a large green bin marked 'Litter' and emerged to find a wooden bench where the ground began to descend on the other side towards the edge of a wood. She sat down. I followed her example, leaving an area of damp green plank between us. A few figures walked below. No cars were in sight and the outlook – the block of trees ahead, then what seemed to be acres of plantation beyond – gave an illusion of unspoiled empty country.

'Have you written anything else?' I asked.

'I want your advice.' Her face was earnest. 'Do you think that the story about the schoolgirl could be developed into a novel?'

Dimly I remembered the story of which she was speaking: its self-defeating relentless seriousness, its lack of life. There had been gauche, rather embarrassing intimations of the first stirrings of female sexuality, some sort of crush on one of the prefects. She was very beautiful, I decided again; and her look of desperation made me think of a wounded Florentine Venus. 'What sort of childhood did you have?' I asked.

Her mouth was slightly open. Her arms rested on her knees. She leaned forward, out towards the wooded horizon. 'You mean from the point of view of literary material?'

'If you like.'

'Nothing special. We grew up in the Cotswolds. There

were three of us – two older brothers and me.'

'What did your father do?'

'Farming. The hunt.' She laughed rather nervously. 'Not a life of great variety, I'm afraid. He was in the war, of course.'

'But you must be much too young to remember that.'

'I wasn't even born!'

She was possibly over twenty years younger than I. 'How did you meet your husband?'

'Through my brothers, in London. They were friends. His father was still alive at that time. Jerry was working in the City and hating it. The old man died a year later. But we didn't marry until quite a long time afterwards. It's funny, you know, Jerry and I didn't take to each other at all to begin with. I remember saying to Mark – my oldest brother – that I thought he was slightly lacking. First impressions can be so wrong, can't they?'

'You moved straight in here after you were married?'

'Oh, yes. Jerry had great plans. Everything – the Fun Park and all the rest – has been his idea. He said we had to move with the times if the place was to survive. It's become his life, absolutely. Occasionally, like this afternoon, the strain shows a little. You see, he's on a sort of permanent high at the beginning of the season. In May, he'll settle down and become less frenetic. By October, we're both exhausted. Then, after Christmas, he can't wait to have the gates open again and to see the public. I have to think up ways of keeping him amused until the business starts again in April!'

'And you? Do you enjoy it?'

'Oh, yes.' Her voice was defiant.

'Your stories are very private,' I said. 'They show signs of a love of solitude, of a wish for tranquillity.'

'Do they?' She sounded pleased.

'But your life here is hardly compatible with that wish.'

'I know.' She put one hand up and ran it quickly through her hair.

'How do you manage to find time to write?'

'I get up early. We usually have the evenings to ourselves, so I do a little then – if I'm not too tired.' She smiled and looked at the grass. 'Jerry thinks I'm quite mad.'

'Why should he think that?'

192

'Well, I suppose if you don't see the point. . . . He thinks the whole thing is a waste of time.'

Perhaps Jeremy Erdley was not so dim after all. 'But he told me that he liked your work . . .'

'Oh, he always says that. He's very loyal.' She stood. 'Shall we walk to the wood?' We went down the hill. To our right, three children were flying a kite. They ran with it in the air behind them; then stopped, pulled the string and watched as the brilliant orange and white shape soared upwards. 'You were married once, weren't you?' Sarah Erdley asked when we reached the flat terrain again.

'I was.' I thought: not this again. Why does she always ask me this?

She stopped and looked at me in a nervous way. 'I've met Angelica's mother several times.' We began to walk again. 'I suppose you were both very young when you married.'

'We were.'

'Did you meet at university? Was she very clever?'

'No,' I said. 'Laura was an art student. She had no time for the academic life.'

We walked towards the trees, towards the darkness of the wood, and I told her about that lost summer in the West Country. I tried to give some hint of the freedom I had experienced: of the difference between that place, or the atmosphere of that place, and my home with my parents in St John's Wood and our usual summer trips to my paternal uncle in the dark pepper-potted mansion in the Scottish borders.

I gave her the old statistic about the excessive number of suicides in Peebles, tried to explain the deadness of the ritualistic fishing trips, the walks, the endless waiting for pigeons that never came, the reluctant dispensing of thimble-fuls of ancient sherry (bought years ago in some bargain offer from a bankrupt Edinburgh wine merchant), the brooding silences at meals, broken by my father's account of some discovery he had made about our forebears' tribulations under the fifteenth-century system of land tenure or a saga of my uncle's about a fox seen near the Forestry Commission plantation. I tried to explain how Laura had offered an alternative to all that. But when I spoke in such terms, using words like 'alternative', I realised that, as always, I was conveying only a dull picture of what had happened: a version that was a mere shadow of what my feelings had been at the time.

We reached the wood. I came to the end.

'And Christina?' Sarah Erdley asked. 'How did you meet her?'

'In London. Through mutual friends.'

She waited a little. 'I know Angelica's step-father as well. A very energetic person.'

I laughed. 'I may shortly become one of his many thousands of employees.'

'But surely you couldn't work for the man who ran off with your wife!' Her voice rose in shock. 'I'm sorry . . .' She was embarrassed by her outburst.

'I won't have any choice. His organisation is trying to take over the one that owns us.'

'You could leave.'

'And go where?'

'But you must be one of the most experienced people . . .'

'Oh, I am,' I admitted. 'But everyone's cutting down now.'

'What about your authors?' The girl seemed oddly moved by my predicament. 'Couldn't you take them with you? Surely any publisher would kill himself to get Henry Brown on to his books?'

Williams – buoyed up by Bill's millions, if the bid were successful – would offer a fortune to keep Henry away from me were I to leave. And, dependent upon the cash for the preservation of the villa, and the life to which he had become attached, I wondered if Henry would simply go to whoever produced the largest cheque. Under these circumstances, loyalty was an unfair demand to make. Already the signs were there. A party had been arranged, behind my back. Henry loved flattery and attention, even of the most flagrant kind. 'Perhaps,' I answered.

'Surely you couldn't work for the man who ran off with your wife?' she repeated. 'You couldn't put yourself in such a humiliating position. You must loathe him!'

We were walking down the main path of the wood. Tall trees reached up on either side of us, their branches meeting over our heads, the light piercing through. Ahead the path stretched on, disappearing into a darkness at the end where it seemed to turn away to the right. In the wood, the air was colder and I was glad that I had a jersey on under my tweed jacket. Sarah Erdley led the way. 'He's always been perfectly pleasant,' I said.

'But you must bear resentment . . .'

'Why? It all happened so long ago. One ought to be civilised about these matters. One can't bear grudges for ever.'

'Do you ever see her?'

'Oh yes. Christina and I used to stay with them in their house at Bembridge. It's a perfectly amicable relationship. Not that we have a great deal in common.'

Sarah Erdley was quiet for a moment. Then she said, 'I hope you won't mind me asking this – but what do you think about when you're with her? Do you remember the past – the times like that holiday you've just described or other moments when you were both happy together? Or is it all forgotten? I'm sorry. I'm not expressing myself very well. Please . . . if you'd rather not talk about these things . . .'

'I'm surprised that you're so interested.'

'I want to know about marriages!' The words emerged awkwardly, an expression of untreated feeling.

Reason told me to say: you must understand that there is nothing of the past to be reminded of when we are together for they are two different people, the sickly middle-aged woman dressed by her rich husband in expensive jewellery and the young girl of that lost summer. Once again, the shadow was preferable to reality. 'I feel pleased to see her,' I said. 'Interested, as well.'

'Not bitter?'

'No. That is over. Why are you so fascinated?'

She stopped. We had reached the end of the long straight path. 'One never knows what really goes on, does one?' she said. 'Couples seem so united, so happy on the surface while underneath all sorts of tensions and unresolved feelings surge.'

It was a curious outburst and I wondered if the girl had found the words, or a slightly better-expressed version of the ideas behind them, in some novel: certainly not *Emma* but a more intensely expressive work. I stopped beside her. Another thought came to me. Was she attempting to offer some sort of signal, a message that she and Erdley concealed such turmoil? Her eyes lowered before my gaze: the eyelids fluttered, long eyelashes blinking together in quick time. 'At your age, surely, that's far away,' I said.

'Why should you think that?'

'Well, you've only been married for three years, is it?'

'Four. When did your wife leave you? After how many years of marriage?'

I calculated. 'Ten. But that was different.'

'Why?'

'She wanted something else.'

'Don't other people sometimes want that as well?'

Sarah Erdley raised her head. And I saw that if I reached across and kissed the girl now, within six months everything, including my own self-respect, would be lost. Yet I leaned forward, put my hands on her shoulders and pulled her towards me. Slowly she gave way. 'Will you promise to help me?' she asked.

'Yes.'

XVII

'I have a need for something else.'

It was the next day: Sunday afternoon. The girl and I were in another part of the same wood. Overhead the sky was grey and there was a distinct threat of rain. We sat on the long trunk of a fallen tree on the edge of a clearing, the young branches rattling above us in the light wind. Sarah Erdley had driven me a part of the way and we had left her car beside a group of abandoned farm buildings before entering the wood from the other side to the park. We wore waterproof coats: mine a light brown, long mackintosh bought originally to keep out the London showers, hers a shorter, dark green, shabby jacket more suitable for the country.

'I have a need for something else; I'm sure of it,' she repeated. 'That's why I write. Because I need to create a world different to the one in which I move and exist at the moment. Is that disloyal of me, do you think? Does it signify un-happiness?'

'Not necessarily.'

'You know I could never sleep with you.'

I could think of no response which avoided either dis-courtesy to her – by implying that this was not in fact what I wished to do – or evidence of a brutish lust. So I grunted.

'Do you know why?'

Again I grunted.

'Because I love Jerry.' I almost replied to this: well why did you let me kiss you yesterday in this wood? 'You think he's a complete fool, don't you?' the girl went on.

'Not at all. Why should I think that?'

'Most people do. People who don't know him well. They see him in the evening after he's had a few drinks. Or they see one of his fits of physical clumsiness, like that business with the costume. And they think he's a fool, in the same way that his father did.'

I thought, for a second time, well why did you let me kiss you yesterday, in this wood? But I said, 'It would be a fool who did not admire your husband for his efforts to save the house.'

'And he's so sensitive, Simon.' She used my Christian name for the first time. Previously we had called one another nothing. 'Sarah . . .' I began.

She ignored me. 'When we were on our walk yesterday, I suddenly felt an extreme sense of beauty,' she said.

'In this wood?' I asked.

'Yes. Because of the way that the trees arched above us and the light came through their branches in great bright streams. It poured through, didn't it? And we were away from the public, away from what I think of as work – the business of being on show, of always having to be available in case of some crisis with the jousting or the Fun Park or the kitchen utensils exhibition. I lost my head. What we did at that time seemed beautiful as well. It brought us together. But it was only for that moment, Simon. That's all.' She frowned as she studied the mud in front of her green wellington boots. 'And you looked so sad.'

'Me!'

'Yes. I suppose it was partly what you were saying.'

'What I was saying?'

'It seemed so unfair,' she went on. 'After all, publishing has been your life. And now, at your age, to have suddenly to start thinking about a new job. As you said, you won't find it easy. But I have a feeling that you'll overcome these difficulties. I think that you're determined and resilient. The only thing that worries me is that you don't seem to have much belief in yourself . . .'

This was absurd, almost comic. 'Sarah . . .' I began again.

'Have I offended you?' She looked worried and clasped her

198

hands tightly together.

'Won't your husband be expecting you back by now?'

'He's out until the early evening, with a circus proprietor from Winchester. Why? Do you think he might mind us spending so much time together?'

'It had crossed my mind.'

She did not reply to this but said, 'May I ask you something else? Another rather personal question?'

'If you like.'

'Why didn't you marry Christina?'

I thought: should I explode, tell the girl to mind her own business and cut off our relations there and then? But I was not really angry and the memory of the events of the day before were still with me, so I took shelter in ambiguity. 'She had her work,' I said.

'What does she do? I can't remember . . .' Sarah Erdley knocked the palm of one hand gently against her forehead. 'Oh yes, of course. She's been several times to look at the furniture here, hasn't she?'

'And what about yesterday?' I could hold the question back no longer. 'What did that mean? Or was your sensation of beauty purely transitory, gone as quickly as it had come?'

'Yesterday?' Her face cleared into a smile of recognition as the memory floated back into her mind. 'It was lovely of course. But you can't imagine . . . I mean I would hate what happened yesterday to be misunderstood . . .'

'What did happen, as far as you're concerned?'

'Does one always have to be precise?' The reversal of positions had already begun. Now I was the blunderer, the one to be mocked. 'Surely you can see . . .'

'I don't want to sleep with you,' I blurted out.

'Well, that's all right then, isn't it?'

I sighed, brought my hands firmly down on to my knees and then stood up. 'What did you mean when you asked me for help?'

She stood as well and turned towards me with a sympathetic smile. 'Oh, with my writing,' she said.

'I see.'

'But perhaps that's no longer possible, after what's happened?'

'Not necessarily.'

'One could try to be professional about it all,' she said. 'Dispassionate.'

'One could.'

As we walked back through the trees to where she had parked the car, the rain began at last, penetrating the cover of the branches. Neither of us had hats. Sarah Erdley quickened her pace and I followed, our wellington boots (mine borrowed from her husband, whom I was still vaguely intent upon persuading her to betray) squelching and sliding their way across the slippery ground. She called back over her shoulder: 'Bill is very rich, isn't he? Is that what she likes?'

'She?'

'Laura. If I may call her that . . .'

'It provides a security of sorts.' I answered, slightly out of breath. 'Her early life was precarious, from a financial point of view.' And I tried to explain the circumstances of the house by the sea. 'Subsistence farming. Her parents got by. Ducks, geese, chickens, a few cattle. The father called himself an artist.'

'Why spoil your life?' she suddenly said.

'Spoil my life?'

'No. Why should your wife – Laura – allow that sort of thing to govern her life? She might find financial security – but let herself in for something worse.'

'What do you mean?'

'An unhappy marriage.'

I thought that the girl was referring to Laura's decision to marry me. 'She thought I was a way out,' I said. 'She may have felt something stronger. I don't know.'

'I wasn't thinking of that.' We had reached the end of the path, the place where the trees opened out into clear country. The rain had stopped, but the sky was still oppressive with low cloud. 'I meant her present circumstances.'

'She's not unhappy. She's sick.'

'Are you sure?' We both stood by an old stone barn beside which her small green car was parked. 'How often do you see them?'

'Not often. Do you?' I wanted to put Sarah Erdley down.

'No. But about a year ago Edward and Caroline asked us to

dinner, before they went to New York. Bill and your ex-wife were there.'

'And she drank too much.' Laura had a particular penchant for cocktails, made with gin. 'Make me a cockers, Billy,' she used to moan in the early evening. She liked them to be very cold: a small amount of lethal clear liquid in a glass crammed with ice. Bill made them fast, expertly measuring up the portions, twisting or squeezing the lemon, briskly ladling in the ice cubes.

The girl opened the door on the driver's side of the car. 'Are you close to Angelica?' she asked. 'Are you happy that she should be working for Laura's husband? It does seem odd, Simon, don't you think?' In a quick movement, she dipped into the car. I settled myself next to her as she started the engine. 'I want to tell you something. You'll be upset. But I think that you ought to know.' She stared ahead as we turned out of the abandoned farmyard on to a narrow country lane. 'Bill and your daughter – it's not all it should be. They're having an affair.'

Sarah Erdley snatched a glance at me, her eyes alight with a strange mixture of apprehension and zeal. My first reaction was to think that she had dredged up an idiotic notion of black humour from what she was proud to think of as her imagination. Embarrassment, then anger – the raw products of emotion – flared up. 'Do you know what you're saying?'

'I knew you'd be hurt.' Her voice was self-satisfied.

'Look, if this is some sort of prank . . . And you raise it now, quite coolly . . .'

'Not at all. I don't enjoy upsetting people.' She was attempting to soothe. 'But I took it upon myself to let you know. Sooner or later you would have heard, probably in a more indirect and shocking way. Other people talk. The extraordinary thing is that Angelica makes little attempt to hide it.'

'I suppose that you will tell me next that Laura is an accomplice to all this. That she turns a blind eye . . .'

'She doesn't know. Or so I'm told.' Sarah Erdley frowned. 'I'm sorry. I've given rather a false impression. Angelica is certainly not crazily indiscreet. But Bill and she see each other fairly openly, from what I gather. It's often the case, isn't it,

201

that the wife is the last one to find out?'

I thought vaguely of patterns: of Laura meeting her lover, for weeks, months, before I even guessed that anything was wrong. 'I don't believe you,' I said. 'Please let me out. I can walk back . . .'

'Oh, I shouldn't do that. It's miles to your cottage. Anyway, you left your car outside the house.' We were turning into one of the drives that led through the park. 'I am sorry, Simon.'

'Will you thank your husband on my behalf?'

'Whatever for?'

I wanted to say that the girl had betrayed us both: Jeremy Erdley as well as me. By encouraging absurd hopes, she had lured me into the role of an ageing libertine. Now there was the absurdity of this last revelation: this last attempt to get under my skin. 'For his tolerance,' I said, my voice breaking in fury.

'I am sorry – for the way that you must feel.' She stopped on the gravel in front of the ludicrous house. Seconds later we stood facing each other on her side of the car. 'You won't want to see me again. Not for a bit, anyway,' the girl said.

'How tactful of you to say so.' I hoped that my voice had a cold edge.

'Simon . . .'

I began to walk towards my car but turned briefly.

'Simon,' she called out, 'you could stop it. The business with Bill, I mean. It lies in your hands. That's why I told you.' I turned away. As I opened the driver's door of my car, climbed in and started the engine, I did not allow my eyes to return to the girl, although I knew that she was still there on the gravel.

That night I drove back to London, leaving the cottage late to avoid the worst of the Sunday evening traffic. The moon, almost full, lit up a cloudless sky. In the car I turned on the radio. A concert was in progress and I recognised the slow movement of one of those long Mahler symphonies, I think it may have been the fifth. The music reached out: sinuous, enveloping.

I would telephone Edward. And for the next few weeks I would leave the cottage closed. In a fit of irritation, I banged one hand against the steering wheel. Mahler was interminable. I switched off the radio, banished the chords that were rendering my thoughts disjointed and incoherent. This was a time for privacy, for the mapping out of a personal grand design.

XVIII

On Monday morning, at the office, I hoped that my first act was auspicious. It was one of charity.

I telephoned Hermione to tell her that Michael Docherty could borrow my cottage. He came round, within the hour, to collect the keys and stood awkwardly in front of my desk. I told the boy to sit down. He waited for me to speak, and the faint mockery in his eyes almost caused me to cry out, 'Look, first I fixed you up as my daughter's lodger and now I'm supplying you with a rent-free holiday home as well. A little thanks might be in order, a courteous expression of gratitude.'

Then I thought of another question. Docherty had lived in the same house as Angelica for several weeks. Had he seen any to-ing and fro-ing, any nights when the girl did not sleep at home, any odd middle-aged men who slipped in and out of her bedroom at strange hours? Had he been introduced to Bill? I was coming, you see, to take the whole business a little more seriously – still certain, of course, that it was nonsense but keen to be able to hold up in my mind one piece of evidence that would blow the Erdley girl's pathetic imaginings to smithereens.

But I was silent with Docherty on this point. Talk of that kind with so unresponsive a person would be impossible. As he left, clutching the keys, well briefed about the vagaries of the boiler, I felt satisfied. I had performed a good deed. And on top of that, I had another reason to feel pleased, for there, waiting on my desk when I had arrived that morning, had been a deferential note from Williams, apologising for his failure to tell me about the party for Henry Brown.

The omission, he declared, was inexcusable. 'We' (who 'we' were I could not imagine) – 'We all know,' the message ran, 'how much Henry is dependent upon you and how close the two of you have become over the years.' As the day proceeded I brooded on that particular sentence and the pleasure turned to suspicion. Could it be a veiled reference to some supposed intimacy, some faintly indecent connection between Henry and me that might (to a prig like Williams) be thought not only shocking but unprofessional and wrong, a disastrous mixing of emotional and working lives? Was the apology barbed? Were they after me again?

I rang Joan for comfort.

She was calm. 'Simon, he is sorry. If you want to know, I mentioned to him that you had felt excluded. John was horrified. Will you believe me when I say that he is not a monster? And you will come to the party, won't you? John will mind if you don't. And what will Henry think?'

I really didn't know.

A letter arrived at my flat on Tuesday. The writing was neat, the paper thick and at its left hand corner, opposite the heavy black type of the address on the other side, was the by now familiar embossed coronet.

Dear Simon,

I have been thinking about our talks that we had on Saturday and Sunday and feel that I must write in order to make several points clear. When I spoke of certain events that were taking place within your family, I was only thinking of you, Edward and Angelica. You are my friends. That is why I felt you ought to be told what is going on before you hear in a more shocking and upsetting way.

I do not blame you for being angry with me. Wasn't it true that in ancient times they used to execute messengers who brought bad news? Anyway I don't mind because I am thinking, as I said, of your peace of mind and the best method of bringing to an end this unsatisfactory situation.

In case you are interested, I have started to write a new story. This time there are one or two humorous touches and I hope that one day we will be able to discuss it. Having finished 'Emma', I have begun 'Mansfield Park'.

Love from Sarah

The letter was intolerable. But I would fix her. I reached across the desk in my flat, pulled open a drawer and extracted one of the white postcards that I had had printed with my name and address at the top. Now it was my turn to send a message. No dear Sarah or my dear dear Sarah or even dearest Sarah: no form of personal greeting, merely a straight no-nonsense start at the essence of my communication.

I wrote:

I will not be coming to the cottage for a few weeks because of pressure of work. However a young writer called Michael Docherty will be there during that time, finishing a book. I know that he will be most grateful if you can find time to get in touch because life in the country may seem strange to him at first. I have given him your name and address. But he is shy and it would be better if you were the one to make the first contact.

I telephoned Docherty from the office to give him the girl's name. 'But you may be too busy with your novel,' I said. 'She writes herself. Short stories. Nothing published yet. I think you'd get on. And she's beautiful.'

'Oh?'

'And silly.' Then I tried to be encouraging. 'I'm looking forward to seeing some more of your work.'

After a short silence he said 'I'm bloody stuck.'

'That often happens to writers.'

'Not the way it has with me.'

'A change of scene can help.'

'Maybe.' At last the words rushed out. 'Oh, and I must thank you for allowing me to use your house.'

I was pleased. 'I want to help,' I said.

XIX

Robin was the sort of friend I used to have in my student days.

Robin had been at school with me. Then he had done his national service in the navy while I was in the army, before we met once more at the same college in the same university. The son of the Dean of a great northern cathedral, Robin wore spectacles and had wispy golden hair and slightly protruding teeth which he would bare often in a smile of self-delight.

During our second long vacation we went for two weeks on a hitchhiking and train journey around the medieval abbeys of Burgundy. Robin was efficient, accurate in his interpretation of railway timetables, correct in his choice of comfortable but cheap hotels. I was content to follow. My life, I imagined, would be spent among the Robins of this world. Eventually I would marry a feminine equivalent of Robin although – I secretly hoped – not quite so bossy and a little better looking. Together we would have children, take them on camping holidays, go in search of fresh examples of different styles of ecclesiastical architecture. Or she might share my interest in Victorian painting. This would be slightly more daring. Robin did not like looking at pictures. He intimated that, for him, they lacked the grandeur and purity of a great religious building.

The next year Robin asked me if I would accompany him on another trip at the end of our last university term before we both disappeared – as he put it – into the vastness of the world outside the cloisters. Robin had a gift for languages. He hoped to enter the Foreign Office. His father, the Dean, had insisted on his son having a proper holiday that summer.

Robin suggested the West Country. 'Do you know it?' he asked.

I did not. And as we loaded our bicycles on to the train at Paddington, I felt only a slight sensation of dread. Robin had stayed two nights with us in St John's Wood. My father and mother had liked him. Indeed my father had remarked to me as we were leaving the dining-room at the end of the dinner, at which Robin had been particularly talkative (or 'merry' as he liked to call it), what 'good value' my friend was.

It was on the train from Paddington that Robin mentioned the Conway family for the first time. 'By the way,' he said, 'I completely forgot to tell you – how silly of me – that I've got some cousins down in this part of the world. Rather boring, actually– or odd would be a better word, perhaps. But they do live in an extraordinary place, down by the sea. I know it's hardly the weather for bathing at the moment' – he made a brisk gesture towards the compartment's rain-spattered window – 'but the property stands magnificently well. How about it?'

After a hard four days of cycling through bad weather, staying at uncomfortable inns and tolerating the company of my friend, I began to look forward to this promised break in our travels. The night before we were to arrive at the place, Robin gave me a brief description of the family. We would, he intimated, be performing some sort of duty by visiting them, for they saw few people. A year earlier one of their daughters, the younger, had been drowned in the sea. They were left now, in their misery, with only the older girl, whose name Robin could not remember. The Dean, whose relations they were, had told his son that the Conways needed to be cheered up.

'Percy Conway paints,' Robin had told me, with only the faintest contempt. 'Of course that's all very well. But what is the family meant to live off? The house is hers, you know. Left to her by a childless great aunt. Oh, and they – the Conways I mean – go in for a bit of what you might call subsistence farming. The odd cow and calf, hens in the kitchen. Rather an Irish existence, really. As I said, there is something distinctly

208

eccentric about the place. Marjorie presides. Without her the family would collapse. Percy is really good for nothing, a sponger. He sells the odd picture – and odd is the word I can tell you!' Here Robin let out a high-pitched shrieking laugh. 'Mostly of naked women from what I can see. But naked red or purple women – as if they'd had an apoplectic fit or been out in the sun for too long. It used to be said that local girls acted as his models. I don't know if anything untoward took place – but Marjorie would be capable of rising above that sort of thing anyway. You know old Percy must have painted the naked female anatomy several hundred thousand times! Extraordinary.' Robin's face distended into a look of distaste.

'And who buys the pictures?' I had asked.

'I really don't know. Father bought one once – a still life of a vase of lupins. It seemed a fair compromise, he thought. He wanted to help the Conways but one could hardly have one of the nudes on display in the Deanery, could one?'

My first view of the house was in sunlight, on a clear morning with only the vague remains of a heat haze. As a building it was without distinction; removed from its setting, the place would not have deserved a second glance, except as an example of architectural gloom. On the ground floor, the two or three front rooms protruded to form a sort of truncated bungalow. Above them, further inwards, rose the second floor, set back and with small windows that could allow little light into the bedrooms. The house was built of a dull grey stone.

Robin had been right. It stood well, almost at the top of an incline, beneath a small belt of trees planted to provide shelter from the wind that came off the sea. We paused on our bicycles and looked down at the place from another hill where the long drive joined the lane that was the Conways' nearest public road. Ahead of the house, at the bottom of the incline on which the trees had been planted, there were two fields – I can remember the exact number – in which some cattle were standing as if rooted to the ground in the heat: then a light brown strip of sand at the water's edge.

Might one call it a lost domain? I don't know. The property was protected by a semi-circle of high ground that rose above it, and on the remaining side there was the sea. Then, nearer, came the woods that acted as an inner defence: small but close groups of trees a few yards from the house, only cleared at the front where the fields stretched to the beach. Thus from each room on one side of the house there was a clear view out across the waves; on a still night one heard their sound: gentle, even soothing, at such a distance.

I used to talk about it with Laura. She complained that when she had returned from boarding school for the holidays the waves had kept her awake. She said this in our London flat, making a quick irritated gesture with one of her hands. 'Then I got used to them,' she had said. 'I became accustomed again to home.'

The heat of that first day was intense. We arrived at the house uncomfortable after the long ride down the drive. Laura's mother came out, embraced Robin and approached me with a self-conscious smile. As I looked at her tall tired-looking figure – the lines of her face creased into a grimace of a false welcome (I saw immediately that our visit had been dreaded), at her thin arms and legs, at the black dusty skirt and the thin black cardigan that covered a white blouse open at the top to reveal the wrinkled brown flesh of her neck, at the wild grey hair – I remembered that there had been a death in the family: one of her two daughters, recently drowned.

Mr Conway's pictures, with their deep reds and purples, were another reminder of this. Arid offspring of the mind with little trace of feeling or reality, they made me think of those anaemic Victorian nymphs, although the artists' intentions were vastly different. The nudes, the naked women whose portraits were everywhere in that house, were stuck inside their interpreter's hygienic vision. There was nothing Rabelaisian or bawdy about their gigantic shapes, no sly smile of complicity or flirtation on their indistinct faces. Who were they, I wondered, as we carried our knapsacks upstairs, these dead remnants of some life class of pedantic academic exercises in form? I decided that the house was sunk in tragedy.

So, from the very first, my view of the family was coloured by romance. Not even the crash of Marjorie Conway tripping over the carpet in the hall and the sight of her sprawled face downward momentarily stunned and inanimate, on the floor, shocked me out of this. A door to the left opened and the small

210

flimsy shape of her husband emerged to cry out 'Sylvia!' Ignoring us, he leaned over, clasped one of her hands, seized the other shoulder and pulled his wife roughly to her feet.

She apologised to us, to him; even, in what appeared to be a gesture of regret, to the floorboards. Percy Conway grunted, nodded at Robin and disappeared again through the same door. I put down this brusqueness to bohemianism. What a rude man he was! And Marjorie thought of him as a misunderstood genius. Now, occasionally, his pictures come up for sale and there is talk about the influence of the Fauves or a supposed friendship in his youth with Matthew Smith: an attempt to conjure up an interest in this man who chose to lead a recluse's life on what remained of his wife's inheritance.

Sylvia. Laura told me later that he called his wife this from time to time. She did not know its origin, yet there, printed on the frame of one of those great red nudes that hung in the passage outside the dining-room, were the words 'Sylvia 1936'. Laura believed it to be a portrait or life study of her mother at about the time of their marriage. Sylvia, a pet name that was used between them to evoke the past, those events and feelings that had brought them together: a word that was supposed to triumph over present incompatibility and irritation, over displays of selfishness and bad temper.

On my second day, we stood beside the picture and Laura explained. At that time her father had shared a studio in Tite Street and was living on the pittance of a few commissions steered his way by friends. Augustus John had taken an interest in this sharp young man who had recently left art school. The Conways had met at a party in Chelsea, where the arts and society had, at that time, fed off each other. Let me paint you, he had said. You stand so wonderfully well. And your bones are a challenge for any artist. Please let me try. What is your name? Marjorie? Most inappropriate. I shall call you Sylvia. And this was the beginning of the bond.

What a terrible picture it seemed, at least to me. I have no liking for that style, a pathetic derivation of the school of Paris. Laura said simply, 'That was over twenty years ago.' We looked together at the dark red, thin body lying on a brown sofa, one leg raised to prevent indecency. There was no life: just a form, posed as if in a taxidermist's show case. Mr

Conway had seen his wife as an object, much the same as the vase of lupins that the Dean – Robin's father – had bought for one of his spare bedrooms. Sylvia was merely decoration: not even decorative but trapped somewhere between the artist's conception of an appropriate style and his failure to bring a human life to his canvas.

Robin was out, walking with Marjorie Conway. So we – Laura and I – were alone in the passage. She said, 'Do you like it?' And of course I had lied and used the word 'interesting'.

I remember Laura's clothes. A white flannel shirt, with the sleeves rolled up in the heat: a pair of ancient khaki shorts; no shoes on her feet. A child of the woods, I had thought.

'My style is different. Do you want to see?'

We went upstairs, along a white passage that was almost dazzling after the dark panelling on the ground floor. Her bedroom had two small single beds in it, two chests of drawers, two straight-backed cane chairs.

And on one wall, she had painted a large mural, a scene of three oriental figures – small and anonymous in their robes and identical black moustaches – climbing the slope of a green hill. The last man carried a musical instrument, apparently some sort of lute or guitar. Over them, as they made their ascent, flew a brown-coloured bird, its long legs trailing behind, a beak in the manner of a pelican protruding from the front of its head. Above the climbers, further up the slope, the green turned to white to mark the beginning of the snow line and, just before this, were two or three tall fruit-bearing trees of an unidentifiable species growing around a small hut with a curved roof in the oriental style. The colours were bright, garishly so: too loud, too insistent for the small room.

Laura laughed. 'My vision of China. It took about a year to do – on and off. A lot happened in that year. I left school, came back home and decided that it really was going to be worth my while to go to London to the college. They accepted me, which was wonderful. My mother took me up to London again last week, to have another look at the place. She goes up once every two months now, to keep in touch.'

'To keep in touch?'

She had looked at me as if I might be simple. In that look I caught a glimpse of her family's self-absorption, the isolation

of the life that her father had imposed upon them all. 'With
Melissa. My sister.'

'But I thought that . . .'

'She was dead?' Laura had raised her eyebrows.

'Oh, she is.' She pointed at one of the two beds. 'She used to
sleep there.'

'And what does your mother do in London?'

'She visits a woman called Mrs Quinlan. They communi-
cate with the other side.'

'Your mother believes in this?'

She seemed affronted. 'Why, yes. Wouldn't you?

How different it all was. That is what I like to dwell on now:
the differences.

Our first meal together was lunch. It was a revelation of
sorts. The plates and china had been fired by Percy Conway
some years ago when he had briefly played around with a kiln
and a potter's wheel. The style, I see now, was an imitation of
the Omega Workshops: white glazing with painted symbols,
sometimes a poorly drawn fish to remind a guest that he or she
was in a house by the sea. We ate in the kitchen. The rest of the
china was arranged on an enormous dresser which stretched
across one whitewashed wall. Marjorie stood by the iron
range at the beginning of the meal, ladling out spoonfuls from
a cauldron. The food was wholesome: large helpings of stew,
a baked potato each, spinach and other vegetables from the
garden. Percy Conway put a flagon of cider on the table, then
filled our stone mugs.

'Sylvia, why didn't you lay the table outside?' he asked.
'And is boiling stew really suitable for the midday heat of high
summer?' Her eyes had taken fright; her thin lips swiftly
formed an apology.

That morning, as usual, he had been in his studio: a large
shed cut off from the house by a patch of overgrown grass.
And he began to lecture us, after a few brusque questions
about Robin's parents. The theme, from what I remember,
was the iniquity of art dealers. He had received a letter of
rebuff from a gallery in London to his suggestion of a show of
his latest work. The people, he exclaimed, had not even asked
him to call on them. The tone was one of exaggerated
disappointment against a background certainty that his time

213

must come. His brown balding head with longish red hair scraggily hanging off its sides twisted to survey us from his seat, a wooden chair with arms to mark that it was reserved for the head of the household. The voice rolled onwards, delighting in oratory.

'Of course I have written to the proprietor – whom I knew well before the war when he was on the prowl for young artists to fill his stable and tried to woo me with promises of sales and commissions, I refused. He'll remember. That's what happens when you allow underlings to get above themselves, to answer letters personally.' And his wife had nodded briskly, allowing herself only a brief pain-stricken glance down to the smooth surface of the table.

Then Robin spoke. He was very pale. 'I don't feel at all well,' he said desperately. 'Perhaps it's the heat.'

He put his hand up to his head, smiled feebly at Marjorie, stood up and clutched at the table. She left the room with him while the three of us stayed behind. Mr Conway seemed annoyed; he had lost the thread. He said nothing about Robin, muttered a low curse. And why should he have minded?'

The heat was still there in the afternoon. I had been frightened that the image might be broken, that rain might come to force us into the house and make it difficult for me to see Laura alone. She took me outside, down to the shore, back across the fields, pointing out the sights of the place in what became a recital of childhood memories. As children they had been allowed to run wild. Their mother had not been able to cope with the demands of housekeeping, of looking after their father – preparing the large meals that he insisted upon, serving them up with the punctuality which he believed to be so important – and the girls at the same time. So she had sacrificed her wish to watch over their safety.

That was what I wanted to see in Laura: a freedom. As children we had always been controlled, so much so that the control had passed at a certain stage into our own hands and it became second nature to us to hold ourselves back, to suppress. I was delighted, by the heat, the wild country and Laura at my side explaining her private world.

Robin was ill. He went to bed for two and then three days. The Conways did not care what we did. Although Laura was

214

free, I saw that Marjorie loved her secretly, like a dissident writing by candlelight. The household was run around the notion of Percy Conway's art, the mythical greatness of his work. So we were left alone. I imagined the two sisters together: only eighteen months between them, two girls who had shared a room. And I asked Laura, on the second day, about Melissa, mistaking her shy answers, the protestation that she did not mind talking about such matters, for grief.

'We would swim here, and take a short cut back to the house through the wood.' She was calm. And she wanted to know about me. 'You'll be in London when you work for the publishing firm?' she asked. 'I'm coming too you know – to London. I can't wait. I suppose I ought to be rather frightened. But I'm not. Not at all. I'm going to live with my aunt and uncle in Kensington. Tell me honestly, what do you think of the pictures?'

'The pictures?'

'In the house.'

I lied again. 'One can see the development of a style . . .'

'I like the early ones,' she cut in. 'Now he's stuck. Simply turning out the same thing over and over again. It's our life down here, I'm sure of it. He's not advancing or developing at all. And commercially it's a disaster.'

'The drowning must have upset him . . .'

'Did it?' She went quickly on. 'Of course it did. But he works so hard. For very little return. He chose this life, of course.'

'Why?'

'Look.' She pointed at the hill above, the fields, the woods that almost enclosed the house except on the side that looked out to the sea. We were down on the beach. The weather had not changed. 'It is beautiful.'

I should have noticed something. She had no fantasy. The picture on the wall of her bedroom had fooled me. Later she was to say that its theme had come from a poem which her father had read aloud one winter evening. She had been looking for a subject to paint on that bare wall, and the three Chinamen, the mountain, the hut and the fruit trees, the long-legged bird, had seemed a good enough choice. I ought to have noticed too that her mind was full of thoughts of

215

leaving, of jumping out into the world. Already she was tired of discomfort, of the struggle. She wanted, like me, to be free, but from a different cage.

'The house is falling down,' Laura had suddenly said on the beach that afternoon. 'Dry rot or wet rot – I can't remember which. I'm going just in time! There's no money to pay for repairs.'

I almost asked: does he drink? I had another notion, again a part of the romance, of Percy Conway steadily drinking himself to death: a Chekhovian scene of disillusion, gloom and decay. 'Is your father . . . unhappy?'

'Oh yes, I think so. Don't you?' Her answer was brisk. She took her towel and bathing costume from under her arm and held them in front of her with both hands. 'Tell me, is Kensington an exciting part of London?' Before I could reply, she had rushed on. 'I don't know anyone there, apart from my uncle and aunt. Then there are school friends, a few cousins. But I want to meet new people.' She had looked at me in a mischievous way. 'Will you introduce me?'

'Robin will help, I'm sure . . .'

'Oh, Robin.'

And Laura had grimaced, then laughed and pointed up at the cloudless sky. 'We'd better swim before it's too late. You can never depend upon the weather. Change there.' She pointed to a small mound some yards behind us where the sand met the edge of the fields.

She walked a little distance away yet made no effort to hide herself. Because of my reticence, I retired to the place to which she had directed me. Then we walked together down to the sea.

How thin she was at that time. I wondered if she might be suffering from some disease. True, I had noticed this earlier but then it had seemed a part of her casual elegance; the clothes – even such scanty coverings as the loose white flannel shirt and the shapeless khaki shorts – had disguised the rest of her body. She wore a dark blue bathing costume, all in one piece, but even that hung off the sharp corners of her bones. Her hair, cut short, scarcely reached down to the bottom of her neck. Yet her face had a joyful look as we approached the waves.

The tide was out. We had to walk several hundred yards across hard wet sand; the water in the small pools flashed in the sun. Laura plunged ahead, into the calm sea, and broke immediately into a brisk version of the crawl. I followed carefully, surprised that, even in this heat, the water should be so cold, and launched myself out in a stately breast stroke, avoiding the spray of the waves. She splashed away from me. We stayed there only for a few minutes until I saw her run back towards the shore, without looking behind to see if I had chosen to follow, and bury her head in her towel, rub herself in a rush of activity: then stand still in the heat.

I came after her, feeling the sun gradually conquer the cold. 'Stay in longer if you want,' she called out. She was shivering. 'Rub my back,' she said, and held out the towel.

Surprised, I took it. Laura turned away from me. Gently at first I started to apply the towel to her skinny brown shoulders. 'Harder,' she called out, smiling at me as she twisted her head round. 'Come on!' The words came through trembling, slightly purple lips. Her shoulders and back felt so fragile beneath my hands. 'Harder! Harder!'

I stopped. She turned to face me, seized the towel and softened her face into an unconvincing pout, perhaps derived from some memory of a cinema love scene. It was the first self-conscious gesture I had seen her make. Even with my limited knowledge of such matters, I knew that she wanted me to reciprocate, probably again by fulfilling a cinema dream of an instant embrace. Instead I blushed, gave up the towel and watched the pout harden into a glare of disappointment.

'Aren't you freezing?' she asked angrily. I walked away, to the place where I had left my own clothes.

That evening Robin was better, although still in bed. He wanted us to leave the next morning. He had no temperature. As she put a pile of plates in front of her husband and waited for him to carve the roast chicken, Marjorie Conway wondered aloud if he should be allowed to go without seeing a doctor. By then my view of Robin's illness had changed. The scene on the beach had worried me. Yet I knew that I should not be a coward, that to be routed by a seventeen-year-old girl was shameful. Our departure would solve everything. But it would be a retreat, a rush back into captivity.

217

Mr Conway hardly listened to his wife. 'The lad can do what he likes,' he said, and looked towards the big window that faced the sea. 'Really the evening light is magnificent. Subtle of course. You hear a lot about the difficulties of painting in the English light. But look at that! Great men have failed to capture it. Greater men than I.'

Afterwards we sat in the untidy drawing-room, the red and grey curtains open to the dark silver of the incoming tide. On the walls were pictures clustered tightly against each other in crazy symmetry: a mad clash of dark red, purple and dark green with the occasional intervention of a brilliant shade of yellow. Some were still-lifes: of fruit on a kitchen table, flowers, kitchen implements lying beside a chopping board and four enormous circular onions; others repeats of the inevitable women, uneasily reclining on sofas or beds or sitting woodenly on the edge of chairs. It was a pathetic display; there, in that room, lay the history of one man's artistic failure: the romantic concept of a wasted life, the tragedy of experience, promise and effort translated into neglect and bitterness. Epic stuff!

Percy Conway smoked a pipe. He wore a loud check shirt, a grey threadbare jersey, creased light-brown trousers stained darkly with spots of ancient paint, black sandals with a pair of dark woollen socks covering his feet. At first he puffed away in silence. Then suddenly he stood, walked over to the gramophone on a table in one corner of the room and put on a record.

After several loud scratches came the indistinct tones of an orchestra. At first the piece seemed discordant, tuneless; I wondered if something had gone wrong with the machine. Percy Conway sat down again, removed the pipe briefly from his mouth, glared at me and said, 'A little divertissement. I expect you know it?' I must have looked blank, for he smiled triumphantly, pleased to have scored a point over the young. 'Stravinsky.'

I nodded. 'Surprised to hear him in these parts?' he asked. 'We met several times. In Paris, before the war. At one stage I was going to work on some new designs for one of the ballets, I forget which.'

How true was this? Now I see that it had almost certainly

been a lie. Then I saw a line that stretched from his house, from his atmosphere heavy with disappointment, to what I imagined might have been the excitement of a young man smiled upon by the great. The idea was a shadow, passing across my mind. The music jolted and jerked. Marjorie, to judge from the distant sound of the stacking of dishes and running water, was still in the kitchen doing the washing-up.

We listened to the whole piece – I think it was the *Firebird*. At the end, no one spoke. The only sound was that of a mongrel dog wagging its tail, a steady thumping on the floor boards, as if in gratitude. Mr Conway put the record back in its cover. 'We never did work together,' he said. 'An opportunity lost, perhaps. It might have led to other things. But I always wanted to be an artist – not a mere painter of backdrops and sets.' And there on the walls was the evidence of the wisdom or foolishness of that grand design.

Then he had said goodnight. I wondered if he might be going to his studio, but the sound of footsteps on the stairs told us that he had decided to make for his bedroom instead. Marjorie entered briefly. 'Percy?' she called out, peering into the room as if she were short-sighted. Laura looked at her impatiently and said that he had gone up.

She withdrew, to leave us with each other. We talked. Soon we were laughing together about Robin. 'I'll bet he keeps himself most frightfully clean,' Laura said. 'He's probably terribly fussy about the kind of soap he uses. Nothing with too ostentatious a scent. After all, we don't want to be thought well – you know – at all odd, do we? That's not the sort of thing that goes down well in the Deanery.' She was still dressed in the old khaki shorts and the white flannel shirt, covered now with a thick dark blue jersey. Her feet were no longer bare for she had, as a concession either to the evening temperature or an imagined need for an increase in formality, put on some old white plimsolls. 'I say, why are you with him?'

'Why does one choose a particular person as a companion? We feel comfortable in one another's company.'

She blurted out the next few words. 'I'm not an absolute baby, you know!'

'But I never thought . . .'

'This afternoon, on the beach, you treated me like a

219

child . . .' She stretched her legs out, clasped her hands on either side of her head. 'What would you say if I told you that I have a lover?'

Oddly enough I was not embarrassed: merely curious. 'I would be interested to know who he is.'

'Would you really? And why should I tell you?'

'No reason at all.'

'That's right,' she said, with the edge of superiority entering her voice, 'no reason at all.'

'An older man? A friend of your parents?'

'Good heavens, no. No one like that ever comes here.' She saw that she had me intrigued. What would have happened if I had opted for a show of shock or disdain? Might we never have been brought closer together? 'It happened at school. We're only a few miles away from Radley. One of the boys came over at night. We used to meet behind the gym.'

'Used to?'

'Yes. He left at the end of last term, to join the army.' And Laura gave the smile of a conspirator. 'I don't miss him. It wasn't a great passion or anything like that. In fact he wanted to come and see me down here – but I put him off. We hadn't got much in common. It was necessary though, to lose my virginity – although we were both so ignorant! He said that he loved me.'

'And did he?'

'No. It was a game. But the other girls were impressed. I was never much of a success at school. We were so badly taught that the lessons never meant anything, and I could never take games seriously. So this gave me something, at least. I was the only girl there who'd had an experience like that.' She waited for a moment. 'Are you shocked?'

'Why should I be?'

'Robin wouldn't like it. He'd bring his lips together – and raise his eyebrows, like this.' And she did a perfect imitation.

'There are more things in heaven and earth than are dreamt of in Robin's philosophy.'

'I say, I am glad that you came here with him.'

I could not stop thinking about Mr Conway. 'Do you think your father still has hope?' I asked.

'What an extraordinary thing to say!' Laura was annoyed

that the talk had turned away from herself. 'I don't imagine that he thinks beyond the next few days or even hours . . .'

'He speaks to you sometimes . . .'

'He did. He talked to both of us – to Melissa and to me. He would read aloud, in the evening, when we were young. He invented stories about a bear called Hannibal who lived in the garden on the edge of the big clump of beech trees . . .'

I had a picture in my mind: a sentimental idea of her family and the way that she had lived. It was more important, almost more real, to me than the story of the experience behind the gymnasium. On this last evening, I tried to push Laura towards the subject of her past. She wanted to concentrate on the present and, if that was not possible, then the future would do almost as well. So she spoke reluctantly, sparing her words, but I dragged enough out to create an unreal montage of sunlight, the sea on an endless summer afternoon, an absence of tension or regret, a surround of beauty. And all the time she was striving to leave all this, to go to her uncle's house in Kensington, to dive into what she believed to be a wonderful metropolitan world

Her voice was soft. At first she watched me, trying to guess what was afoot. Then she consented to play the game.

She was the first to stand up. We must have talked for several hours. The room was poorly lit, the colours of the pictures dim. We were in the ruins of Percy Conway's dreams. 'I'm exhausted,' she said. 'Do you mind?'

I heard her door snap shut along the passage. I was tired that night and almost asleep when I felt her there, a thin young form beside me, in that narrow single bed. It was like a dawn walk; everything appeared in a new light, almost unrecognisable. I wondered if this could be right. And at the end, before leaving for her own room, she said, 'Will you marry me?' I did not answer. The question passed as if it had been the wordless chatter of an infant. The next morning Robin and I left. I made no mention of what had happened. In the front hall Laura said goodbye, in a friendly but casual way. Mr Conway did not come out of his studio. Only Marjorie was there, worried that our maps might be inaccurate or out of date.

Not for two years did Laura and I meet again, at a party somewhere off the King's Road. She came up and reminded me of her name. Her hair was a little longer, almost down to her shoulders: her face slightly fatter and less brown. And of course she was dressed in London clothes, a dark green dress and black stockings on her thin legs. I was still ready to be drawn into make-believe. Outside my work, which I was just beginning to find interesting, life was commonplace. I was still living at home, in search of a room to rent.

Laura's concerns were, as always, more ordinary but more purposeful. She was bored. The art college was starting to pall; her talent – and she could see this – was not enough. She was poor. She took casual jobs behind the counters of stores or serving in restaurants to help pay the bills. London was not behaving in the way that she wanted. Of course she had friends, fellow students. But it was all so grey, so dependent upon chance and hard work.

We arranged to have dinner. The evening began with jokes about Robin, then I asked about her family. Nothing had changed – oh, except that almost exactly a year ago, she told me, her father had died. Very sad. An incurable disease of the blood. Quick, of course: very quick. Her mother was still clearing the place up. That was taking a long time, with all those paintings! It was necessary to be ruthless; Laura and she had burnt some of the worst ones, rather against Marjorie Conway's will. The fire had blazed merrily, at the place where the rubbish had always been tipped and destroyed. Eventually Marjorie would have move to London and put the house up for sale. It should fetch a fair amount because of its position, and there were the fields as well. Of course the place did need an awful lot doing to it and that would be reflected in the price. Laura smiled at me through the dim light of the Soho restaurant. She had to admit, she said – although she was certain she ought not to think in that way – that she was not looking forward to her mother's arrival. Marjorie Conway would stay with the uncle at first: another person in an overcrowded Kensington house.

The evening came to a chaste ending, simply a farewell kiss in the back of a taxi. We agreed to meet again: then to have lunch together on a spring Saturday when her uncle and aunt had gone away for the weekend to visit some cousins in Kent. We met that morning at an Italian place, the sort of café that

222

was fashionable in those days. Afterwards she offered to show me the house. I remember how poky and dark it seemed, even on that bright day, compared with my memories of her old home, the land that had stretched down to the sea and the sun above the waves. That afternoon we renewed what had begun on my first holiday visit. She did not say at the end, as she had said before, 'will you marry me?' But within a few months it became clear that this was to be the only natural course.

XX

I telephoned Edward at his office in New York.

'Dad!' he answered. 'I was just thinking about you. Have you seen the *Journal* this morning?'

'The *Journal*?'

'Yes, the *Wall Street Journal*. There's a long article about ISS and its designs on Lindsay. Lindsay's shares have put on a spurt. Have you got any? Surely there must be some sort of staff participation scheme . . .'

'Is there? I don't know.'

'Anyway, things are really moving. Bill was over here last week and I tried to draw him on the subject, but you know how discreet he can be. And Angelica rang, over the moon about her new job. She was telling me about the lodger that you've found for her. He sounds rather an odd sort of chap . . .'

'How's your mother? Did you ask?'

His voice dropped. 'A little better. She sat out in the garden all day on Saturday. I think it's really a question of time. Bill takes her in the boat, for short runs. That's what she really enjoys.'

Laura's life now was little different to that of a patient in an expensive sanatorium. Her family was ready with rugs and the right medicine. 'Edward,' I began, then faltered. How could I ask him?

He sounded soothing. 'I hope you're not worried, Dad.'

'Worried?'

'About the take-over.'

'Oh,' I murmured. 'Edward, I must . . .'

He cut in. 'My other line's going. A call I'm expecting from Frankfurt. Look, we must speak soon. Another time, though. This morning's hell, for some reason. The market's going crazy. But it's great to hear from you. ISS's problems are only just beginning, even if they do manage to win. Sorting out Lindsay will be like taking a fork to a heap of runny shit.' I gulped. A Bembridge phrase, no doubt. 'And, Dad, you've nothing to worry about. Absolutely nothing at all. Goodbye!'

I was beginning to realise what a hold Bill had established over my family. And then I understood his true cunning. He and I had spoken about Laura's condition. He had seemed to be taking me into his confidence, unburdening himself on to a person who he had flatteringly concluded would be both understanding and discreet.

'Some women can't accept middle age,' he had declared as we sat together on the terrace at Bembridge while Laura and Angelica were in the gleaming gadget-ridden kitchen preparing the evening meal. And I had sniggered to myself, waiting for the next idiocy, the absurd diagnosis. 'Of course she's sick as well, poor love. But a lot of it's psychological, I'm sure. I've tried to persuade her to see a shrink – not one of these foreign quacks but a very efficient operator who worked wonders on an old business mucker of mine who got a dose of the glooms. But she simply won't hear of it.' Her decline had given him his freedom.

Laura had wanted to have children as soon as possible after our marriage. So Angelica was conceived and born. Then she had wanted another; and eighteen or nineteen months later, Edward was born.

Our flat was small, the noise from the two infants inescapable. Laura did not mind the work, the sleepless nights, the crying and the mess. It was new. 'I am tired,' she said. 'But it's a pleasant sort of tiredness. Rather wonderful, really.'

After Edward's birth, the thrill had begun to wear off and

225

the household slipped into a state of barely controlled chaos. At that stage I was working hard and often brought manuscripts home. Laura began to accuse me of ignoring her, of not being interested in her day or her thoughts. Her perception of herself had changed. She was content with the idea of motherhood, and her painting, the studies at the art college, had been pushed to one side. This was, she decided, worthless compared to the elemental process of procreation. After Edward, her opinions underwent another revolution. Women who lived only for their babies and their homes were killing themselves, losing their minds, already well on the way to atrophy.

The game came to an end: the fun that she had been having as my wife.

XXI

Joan came into my office. 'Simon,' she said, 'I've just realised that no one has shown you this list.'

I looked up from a letter that I was reading, another long communication from the author of the Palmerston biography. 'List?' I frowned at her. 'What list?'

'For the party. For Henry. Don't you remember? We spoke about it.'

'Joan,' I said, 'I haven't even been invited.'

'Now don't be silly, Simon.' She spoke in tones of mock severity. 'You know perfectly well that directors don't have invitations. They just turn up. I sent a memo out with the details of the time and place. Did it never get through to you?'

Then I remembered Williams' letter. I hit my head with my hand. 'I've been so busy lately – with one thing and another . . .'

'Manuscripts piling up?'

'That sort of thing.'

'I know. It can be hell.'

The telephone rang. 'Damn!' I said. Joan stood up to go. I motioned to her to sit down. 'I won't be a minute. It can't be anything very vital.'

It was Henry Brown. 'I've just arrived,' he said, 'and I'm sitting in this depressing hotel wondering what to do. Why don't we have lunch? I want to know all about the plans for the book. Your friend Williams wrote to me about them – but it all sounds rather vague. Apparently a woman called Joan

227

somebody is in charge and if I need to know anything I should get in touch with her . . .'

'Henry,' I began.

'Simon,' he continued at high speed, 'I'd like to hear it all first hand, from you. I'm sure I've met this Joan person and that she's delightful – but you and I know what's really needed on these occasions. You know what I will do and what I don't do, that's the point. I don't mind interviews – either on the television, the radio or in the newspapers. But I won't put up with scurrilous investigations or commentary on my private life with photographs of the house. It's for Paul's sake, really. He hates that sort of thing – and journalists are apt to get the wrong idea and write about him as if he was some sort of parasite or lower form of humanity or something. I won't have it, Simon, and you must tell this Joan as soon as possible. Paul and I are worried. He has stayed behind this time. The Portuguese couple have been playing up again. More fights in the local café. Obviously Luis is a fierce little devil when roused, although he's always been as mild as milk with us. Paul speaks their language quite well now. And they trust him . . .'

I interrupted once more. 'Henry . . .'

'Will you have dinner with me tonight, Simon? I really think this hotel could double for a morgue, you know. Not at all how it used to be. Most of the old staff have gone, though there's still Charles the head porter. And they're building an annexe at the back, so the noise is deafening. Everything is quite topsy-turvy. It's as if the management were blind and deaf. How could they allow so many good people to leave at the same time? And the chef is a Romanian . . .'

I glanced at Joan and put my hand over the receiver. 'Henry,' I whispered. She nodded, looked awkward.

'Well?'

It would be better to see him. 'If you like.'

'Excellent! Come here at about eight. We won't bother to sample the Romanian's wares. There are plenty of other little places in the neighbourhood. I want to hear all the news.'

'I look forward to it.' As I was taking the receiver away from my mouth I noticed that Joan was holding out her hand – not fully extended but reaching forward towards the tele-

228

phone in a slightly apologetic way. I pretended not to notice and put the receiver down. However tiresome and exhausting the man might be, he was my property. 'He sounds a little disturbed.'

'Oh dear. Perhaps I should have told him about the party. I imagine he may be slightly in the dark. John wrote but probably didn't include a copy of the list . . .'

I shook my head briskly. 'No, no,' I insisted, in the patronising tone of a man who speaks from superior know-ledge. 'Henry wouldn't worry about that. There's something else in his mind. I'll find out this evening. Oh, and perhaps I could give him this list.' I took the paper from the other side of the desk.

'That's the original. I'll let you have a copy this afternoon.'

Was this a little gesture on her part, an assertion of some sort? I smiled. 'If you wouldn't mind,' I said. 'There may even be some names that I want to add, although it's a bit late now.'

She did not flinch. 'What will Henry do in London?'

'Well, he's seeing me tonight . . .'

'And after that? What about the weekend? Surely he won't spend it alone in a hotel?' She took a packet of cigarettes from a pocket of her black skirt, extracted one, put it into her mouth and lit up, all in a matter of seconds. 'I mean, if I can do anything . . . The boy will be there but he's going through a quiet stage at the moment. Henry might be amused to come to Sunday lunch. I could even summon up some people to entertain him. Of course I'd need you, Simon.'

Of course. 'How kind of you,' I said. 'Henry has a niece who married a farmer in Shropshire. He usually visits them if he is in this country for any length of time. But I'll pass on your invitation.'

Joan drew on her cigarette, her eyes slightly squinting with the effort. 'To change the subject,' she said, 'I saw Hermione a couple of nights ago and she told me that you were allowing the Irishman to use your cottage for a few days. Apparently he's very grateful . . .'

'Michael Docherty! I should hope so too. If he gets up to any mischief there, I will hold Hermione responsible. The things that that woman forces on one!'

'She was asking me about his book and what we were going

229

to do in the way of publicity.' Joan paused. 'What are we going to do, Simon?'

'That's up to Alison. I've sent her the manuscript.'

'I think Alison might welcome some guidance, perhaps even a meeting with Mr Docherty. Oh, and Alison is worried about the Palmerston biography as well. There's no television series coming up on that period, is there? We could try to promote some sort of a tie-in . . .'

'It's not that kind of book.'

'What kind of book is it?'

I nearly said: excruciatingly, blindingly dull, unutterably tedious. Then I thought that this could only rebound upon me, for the obvious, no doubt unspoken, response was: well, why have you agreed to publish the thing? 'Scholarly.'

'But you said when we commissioned it that Palmerston was sexy.'

'Oh, he was. He had several mistresses. Queen Victoria was rather shocked . . .'

'And the book leaves that out?' Joan asked coldly.

'The author does not dwell on it.'

'John won't like that, Simon. He won't like that at all.'

'Every library in the country will want a copy,' I said desperately. 'The book is a prestige biography, by an acknowledged expert on the period. Surely John must see that to publish a work of this type – although the financial rewards are admittedly not great – enhances the firm's reputation. Or does he want to concentrate entirely on sauna baths and smutty cook books?'

Joan did not answer. She took another pull at her cigarette. 'And what about Mr Docherty?' she asked.

I thought that I should not be rough with her. She had suffered. She was alone. 'What do you think?' I asked.

'You know my views.'

'No, I don't think I do.' I was cold again.

Her face contorted into a look of distaste. 'The stories are so desperately flat, Simon, so gratuitously unpleasant, stuffed with hackneyed Freudianism dressed up as realistic comment on human behaviour. It's all too derivative, too much striving after effect. And the lives that they describe are so pathetically dreary, so unremittingly grey. Then the symbolism is riddled

230

with cliché – tower blocks as phalluses, a boy staring down the tunnel of the London Underground while he waits for a train to take him to his girl friend, a miser remembering childhood constipation as he calculates his riches.' She paused. 'We could try for a press interview, I suppose. Anyway, what are the possible selling points?' Then she relented and laughed. 'You know what John is. I'm surprised that he hasn't asked you these questions already. Or perhaps he has.'

'George Mason likes the stories. He said that they reminded him of the young Christopher Isherwood, with touches of André Gide.'

'Which is how he describes every work of fiction that he feels he ought to like but can't be bothered to read. A most useful old man's device!'

'No, Joan,' I said crossly. 'George studied the manuscript carefully. He even made suggestions for cuts and spotted one or two grammatical errors.' This was a lie. 'So in this case your observations are inaccurate.'

Joan raised her cigarette and took a quick puff. 'I'm sorry, Simon. I seem to have upset you again.'

I raised my eyebrows in a gesture of surprise but said nothing.

'Whenever we see each other now, the meeting seems to end in a row,' she went on. 'I hope you won't mind me saying this – but you're so quick to take offence.'

'You think I should be grateful for the way that you and Williams have seen fit to cut me out of the organisation of this party for Henry?'

'You've told me a thousand times how much you loathe publishing parties . . .'

'Have I?'

'So John and I were anxious not to bother you with the details of this one . . .'

'You might at least have told me the date . . .'

Joan's husky voice took on a pleading note. 'I admit that was an oversight. A serious oversight. But John only decided a fortnight ago that we should give the party – partly because we had no idea before then that Henry was coming over. It was only in response to one of John's letters that Henry told us his plans. And when you got back from Nice you never mentioned them. He told John that he had given you the dates of his English visit then, before you left for the airport.' Her eyes looked down on me as if to say: answer that one, if you can.

I frowned. 'Did he? I can't remember. There was so much to think about, what with the last-minute editorial changes and Williams badgering me to have the manuscript ready for the printer as soon as possible so that we could get the book out before Christmas in order to improve the cash flow to impress our masters who in their turn need to impress their share-holders so that those shareholders will not be tempted to accept the take-over bid. Really, Joan! Sometimes it all seems to me to have very little to do with what I used to think of as publishing.'

'You mean the publishing of your father's, your grand-father's or your great-grandfather's time?' Joan straightened her mouth into an acid smile.

'Not necessarily. Simply the process whereby we think of what will be best for the book and the author as well as for ourselves.'

'So you think that Henry's new novel should come out after Christmas? Simon, I hardly think that would be better for the author. For a start it might cut several thousand pounds off his royalty cheque . . .'

'I did not say that, Joan!' I hit the top of my desk with the palm of my hand so hard that I felt a stab of real pain. She jumped. I went on slowly, in control of myself once more. 'In this case, I believe that we should publish Henry's new novel in October and that the rush is justified. I am not criticising the decision. What I dislike is the thinking that lies behind it, indeed behind virtually everything we do here.'

Joan settled back in her chair. The moment of alarm had passed. She drew again on her cigarette. I found myself wondering what significance Docherty would attach to her constant smoking. He might tie it into a symbolic piece of eroticism, something to do with foreign bodies between the lips or clasped between the fingers. There would follow, at some point in the saga, an explosive and unpleasant sexual encounter, probably with sadistic overtones. I was sure that Hermione had put us on to a winner. 'Simon, there is

232

something the matter, isn't there?' Joan's voice was sympathetic yet sightly exasperated, not unlike the tones one might associate with nurses in mental hospitals.

'No.'

'Don't you want to talk about it?'

'Talk about what?'

The cigarette went up again to those red lips and again descended. 'I know that certain things here do not please you,' Joan said. 'But that is a problem all of us have had to cope with and you're just as adaptable as I am.'

'Am I?'

'Or have you suddenly decided to start fighting for principles in your old age?' She laughed, attempting to strike a light note. 'If so, it's a little late.'

'I intend to try to do what I think is best,' I replied in a pompous tone which I immediately regretted.

'About Christina . . .'

'Yes?'

Joan leaned forward, picked up a pencil that had strayed across from my side of the desk and examined it before looking at me again. 'Perhaps I shouldn't say this, Simon, but why did she leave? Is there someone else? . . .' Her voice trailed away in embarrassment.

I could have made it easy. But I chose to be awkward, to stand on what little dignity I had left. 'I'm sorry, I don't quite understand . . .'

Joan blushed. 'I see that I've annoyed you. I shouldn't have mentioned it. But you and I have known each other and worked together for so long that I thought – perhaps wrongly – that you would accept . . .'

'Accept?'

'Accept that in anything of that nature I could only be thinking about your happiness.'

'I see.'

'You spend too much time alone, Simon,' she said desperately.

Now I took an even loftier line. 'Joan, I hardly think that the office is the place for this sort of discussion – unless of course Williams has sent you to raise the matter in what he regards as the interests of the firm. Is it now company policy that all senior staff should be married, thus advertising the whole-some nature of our operations – a sort of counterblast to the sauna bath and aphrodisiac cookery image? If so, you should also feel a certain urgency. Are you on the prowl, Joan?' My voice dipped into sarcasm. 'But perhaps I shouldn't say this.'

Her face tightened. She reached forward, gathered up the pieces of paper that she had spread out on my desk and put them into a brown file. Then she clasped this to her chest, stood up and looked at me, her eyes firm. 'I'll leave you now,' she said, her voice quavering slightly. 'And I'll see that you get a copy of the guest list as soon as possible.'

It was not necessary for her to duck to get out of my office but I noticed that she did. Probably the movement was involuntary, forced upon her over the years by her unusual height. In it, I saw evidence of frailty, and remorse flooded over me. I remembered from long ago – when she had first started to work for me – her tears late one afternoon as she had talked about her dead husband, his last illness and the difficulties of bringing up a son who had no father. She was a good woman.

'Joan!' I called out. It was too late.

I rang Edward again, at his New York office.

'Edward . . .' I began.

'Dad!' He sounded absurdly cheerful. 'You're being a bit free with the old transatlantic calls, aren't you?'

'I want to ask you something. After you left the army, was it Bill who suggested that you join your bank?'

My son's reply was slow in coming. He wished, I knew, to be thought a meritocrat: one who did not need assistance or influence to succeed. This too was a part of Bill's creed. Once, when Christina and I were dining with Laura and Bill in London, he had, after dinner, when the ladies had left the room, inveighed, slightly under the influence of drink, against what he called 'the old school tie approach' which he claimed was responsible for much that was wrong with England.

Then I had seen the amiability drop, the mouth curl in disdain, the words reveal an inner anger. So why was he doing so much to further the careers of his step-children, I had almost asked? Why had he dangled opportunities of professional advancement even under my nose, offers I had always refused and secretly despised? Now I knew. All the time he was spinning a web around our family: supporting Laura's mother until she had died three or four years ago in a flat off Sloane Square, giving Edward his first chance in the City, attempting first to entrap me into working for him by offering a tremendous salary increase and now by the more expensive manoeuvre of buying the company. My God! Was this it? Was the whole multi-million-pound take-over founded upon one man's infatuation with his step-daughter?

Edward was talking. 'Bill put me in touch with one of the directors, that's all,' he said. 'At least thirty people were after that one traineeship. There were no favours asked for, or granted . . .' He stopped. I realised that I must have let out an exclamation of some sort, perhaps a curse or a wordless cry of pain. 'Sorry, Dad?'

'Oh.' I held the leg of my desk with one hand, as if to steady myself, and began to sweat in the heat of the stuffy office. 'I know that Bill has been a great help to you . . .' I began.

'He's offered advice. Dad, please, forgive me but I'm expecting a call. There it goes – on the other line!'

'Leave it!' I yelled. 'And what has he done for Angelica?'

I heard Edward's voice, now away from the receiver, whispering, 'Put him on hold, will you? This won't take long.' Then he was back with me, speaking slowly, with a soothing patience. 'Dad, again Bill merely pointed out an opportunity. There was a great deal of competition for that job too. She's highly qualified. Remember how well she did in the civil service exam. Her department had a very good opinion of her.'

'How do you know?'

Edward sighed. 'Bill met her boss, at a party given by the government for some Arabs.'

'You know what's happening, Edward, don't you?' I blurted out, raising my voice again in order to smash through his maddening complacency. 'We are all in the process of being acquired. Bought. And at a bargain price as well. People of that type never pay a penny more than is necessary!'

235

'Dad, I don't follow.' Edward was not worried: merely mystified, almost certainly bored. 'Are you upset about the take-over? I don't know if you've seen the *Wall Street Journal* this morning . . .'

'I never see the *Wall Street Journal*!' I was shouting. 'Never! Haven't I told you that before? Will it never sink into your thick head?'

'I understand your anxieties . . .'

'No! I am not talking about the take-over. That does not bother me. Or perhaps I should say that it does bother me but I can do nothing about it. Nothing at all!' My voice dropped, as if I was entering a consecrated building. 'What I may perhaps be allowed some influence over is the way that your step-father chooses to behave to one of my children.'

He chose to misunderstand me. 'You feel that Bill shouldn't have helped us with our careers? Or is it that he has settled money on Angelica and me? Does that upset you?'

'I think you know what I mean.'

'I don't think I do.'

'About Angelica and your step-father.' I waited a little. 'How long has it been going on, Edward?'

'I don't know what you're talking about.'

'I have it on good evidence, Edward.' I spoke gently. I wanted to encourage the boy to be forthcoming. 'Very good evidence.'

'And who has been telling you these absurd stories?'

'Aren't you going to ask me what the stories are? Or perhaps you know already?'

'Very well,' Edward said. 'What are the stories?'

'That their relationship is rather more intimate than it should be. That she is his mistress and has been for some time.'

'Who told you all this? Some ridiculous old cat of a gossip . . .'

'Not at all,' I said. 'Someone of your own generation. Someone who would know.'

'Sarah Erdley,' Edward said.

I was surprised that he should have guessed so quickly. 'You may think that she is rather silly, and I agree. . . ,' I began.

Edward interrupted. 'Dad, I hope you're not going to make a fool of yourself. And I say that only because I would hate to see it happen.'

'What do you mean?'

'Sarah Erdley is a terrible mischief maker. I know that you
see each other in the country and fiddle about with books and
literary talk and things of that sort.' His voice was almost a
sneer. 'She chatters and giggles about it to other people.
Caroline heard indirectly, through a mutual friend who was
over here last week, that the two of you were having an affair.'

'Absolute nonsense!'

'But you do have lunch with her in London and go for long
walks in the country together?'

'She sent me some of her work,' I protested. 'I felt it only
courteous to give the girl a serious explanation of why the stuff
was not good enough to be published.'

'How very civil of you.'

'Anyway, I will not be going to the cottage for a long time,'
I said, determined not to be diverted.

Edward spoke precisely. The line was astonishingly clear.
'You may be interested to know that, in the last day or two,
she has found another soul-mate – or so Caroline's informant
tells her. A gentleman with an Irish name, who has moved
into one of the houses in the village or something.'

'Docherty,' I said. 'Michael Docherty.'

'Possibly. I must admit I wasn't very interested.'

I should have expected this. Docherty was ruthless, and so
was the girl. 'I know him. He writes as well.'

'A literary man,' said Edward, again with a sneer.

'And they are carrying on together already?'

'Oh I don't think that is Miss Sarah's form. Her approach
tends to be more romantic – long walks, exchanges of
confidences, perhaps the occasional peck on the cheek. Then
long telephone calls to her friends in London to have a good
giggle about it all. I rather doubt if your Mr Docherty will
receive a great deal of physical gratification.'

'He can take care of himself,' I declared.

'Poor Jeremy,' Edward said. 'Dad, I don't want to hurry
you, but I have this other call . . .'

'Edward, about Angelica and these rumours . . .'

'Rumours? Surely you don't believe that sort of malicious
gossip, do you?'

'I saw them together only a few days ago – in a hotel near Maidenhead . . .'

'Oh, Dad. You told me that. I said they must have been driving down to Bembridge.'

'Through Maidenhead?'

'It's not far out of their way. And he might have been trying out a new car. I told you that he's looking for a replacement for the Alfa . . .'

'But why should they stop at a hotel – in the middle of the morning?'

'All sorts of reasons. Bill may have wanted to make a telephone call. Angelica may have needed to go to the lavatory. Perhaps he was thinking of buying the place and wanted to look at it without anyone knowing who he was.'

'The establishment is part of a large chain of hotels.'

'Perhaps he was thinking of buying the chain.' Edward sighed once more. 'Dad, I'm going to have to cut you off now. I'm most terribly sorry. But what else can I say?'

In the evening, just after I arrived back at my flat from the office, the couple beneath began their curious ritual of what I presumed to be pleasure. I sat and listened for a moment. The cries seemed at first to be of pain; there was an agonised plaintive edge to them. Then they were transformed into inarticulate demands, a desperate pathetic searching for more.

XXII

I used to tell myself that the great thing about Henry was that he had a sort of crazy wisdom.

This showed itself occasionally in his work, perhaps two or three times in each of the long books. I had learned to recognise these revelations. There is something beautiful – clear and pure – about them, especially in such an incongruous setting. They strike to the heart of some vague apprehension or belief with what one might almost describe as the force of genius.

I know about this, and Henry knows that I know. His readers, those millions of people all over the world, are mostly unaware of it. They buy his books for the adventure, the suspense and the mildly titillating romance. Yet the flashes of vision are reminders that, amid the giggling and the bitchery, the cackling gossip and love of mischief, Henry has reserves of humanity and sympathy: also the insight of an imaginative artist. I suppose this is why I decided to confide in him. I hoped that Henry possessed a soul.

His bronzed round face glowed in the dim light of the French restaurant near his hotel. He wore a baggy, light grey suit, a white shirt and a dark blue pullover to guard against the English chill. For most of the meal I listened to him: to his sagas of the Portuguese couple, how an intermittent stomach ache of Paul's could turn out to be an ulcer brought on by household worries or the irritation of a German neighbour's noisy children. He sought assurances, which I gave, that any

239

ideas about publicity for his latest book would be referred to him for approval first. 'How's the family?' he asked, as the expensive wine was being poured out.

I replied with a smile and a short answer. 'Not too bad.'

Usually, when Henry and I ate in a restaurant together, he would drink at least three quarters of the wine. That night, it was different. I more than kept up with him and halfway through the meal it was necessary to order another bottle. He spoke of air travel, of pains in his back, of his plans for a trip to the United States next year to give a series of talks and television interviews. He seemed satisfied, the repressed tension showing only in his inability to be silent, to down the torrential explanations and self-justification.

Over the coffee, he became reflective, almost lyrical about Paul. 'We had one of our honest talks the other evening Simon,' he said, 'and we've decided to keep the villa. I had been worried that Paul was not really happy there. He's always hankered after Italy, you know, and that expatriate life outside Florence. He says the people are too trashy in the south of France. And of course he has this real interest in Italian Renaissance art.'

I nodded, waiting for my chance. Henry liked to build Paul up. For me this was unnecessary. Paul's good sense, the way that he understood his friend so well, the humour with which he looked upon the more absurd moments of their life together: these were more than enough. He made Henry tolerable by dragging him back from flights of fancy suited to literature but not to this world.

'But he wants to stay where we are now,' Henry went on. 'If anything should happen to me, he'll keep the place on, perhaps rent it out and live there for only a part of the year. One must think ahead. I expect he'll buy a flat in London – somewhere quiet in Bloomsbury perhaps or Regent's Park. He gets all my royalties of course – although I've settled a bit of money on my niece; you know, the one in Shropshire. Paul and I find these talks awfully useful. I don't suppose that you and Laura ever had them, did you?'

'No.'

'And Christina?' His cup was poised half way to his lips. He raised it, drained what was left of the coffee and put the tiny

240

china object down with a slight clatter on the saucer.

'Christina has left me.'

'Of course she has.' He stared into my face. 'And you seemed so well suited. She brought you back to earth, Simon, from time to time – when you were at your most fanciful. I always admired her. She was a professional: competent, alert, punctual and thorough – or so it seemed to me.' He made Christina sound like a dental technician: a brisk girl in a white coat smelling slightly of mouthwash.

'Well, she's gone.'

'Now who was it with? I simply can't remember . . .'

He pronounced the last word precisely.

'A colleague at work.'

'Oh yes, of course, she worked, didn't she?' Henry frowned. He prided himself on his memory and was annoyed when it failed him. 'What sort of a man is he?'

'You can't expect me to be objective in my judgement . . .' I began.

'Did you know him before?'

'A little.'

'And what did you think?'

'Not much.' I poured myself out some more wine, the last of the bottle. 'Smooth. Polished. No edge to him. Profoundly dull, behind the social graces. Patronising.' I paused. 'But a man – or the type of man – who usually gets what he wants.'

'Do you want to kill him?'

The silliness of the question stunned me. 'Kill him?'

'Yes. Is your pride that hurt?'

'Henry, one does not go around killing people.'

'Indeed not. It would be a much less congenial world if one did. But I suppose that, in one's more unrestrained moments, one thinks about it. Only very occasionally of course. Only very occasionally.'

'Henry . . .'

'When a man is humiliated, he wishes to strike back,' Henry went on. He suddenly reached out a small podgy brown hand and clasped my wrist across the table. 'How upsetting, Simon. I thought she was better for you than Laura, whose departure – to tell the truth – I did not particularly regret, although I was fond of her. Indeed I still am – as their visit to the villa this year

241

reminded me.'

'There has been a new development on that front as well,' I said.

'Really. Is she leaving her pet tycoon?'

'No.'

'What is it then? I know she drinks too much. I could see that when they were with me.'

'She does drink. But she is ill. Do you remember her husband?'

'My dear boy! How could I ever forget?'

Henry turned his head and called, 'Waiter!' His voice was imperious. A small man scurried over. 'Two large glasses of Armagnac.' He looked at me again. 'It will help the digestion,' he said. 'Now, where were we? Oh yes, Laura's husband. An interesting example of the contemporary equivalent of a merchant prince. In the fifteenth or sixteenth century he might have been a Doge of Venice, dignified in the robes, forceful in the council chamber, a hard trader and dutiful patron of the arts. Today he has other pastimes: sailing, aeroplanes, water sports. He tells me that he is thinking of buying a chalet in Gstaad. Apparently his – or rather your – family enjoy skiing and it makes sense from the investment point of view. The European economies worry him. But Switzerland, with the Swiss franc, is an oasis of calm and good sense. I listened to all this. You know, there is something creative about such a man. Would it shock you if I said that I rather liked him?'

'No. My daughter was there, wasn't she?'

'Your daughter?' Henry frowned. 'Ah yes. Your daughter. A handsome girl. Remind me of her name.'

'Angelica.'

'Angelica.' He smiled. 'I used to know an Angelica years ago. The child of a woman I once lodged with in Putney.' His eyes glazed over. Then his attention came back to the two of us, at this table in the pretentious over-priced French restaurant. 'I'm sorry, Simon. Indeed I do remember. The lovely Angelica. Rather silent, at least compared to her step-father. She wore a green dress. Fair hair. Am I right?'

'Reddish to fair.'

'Of course. You are fortunate to have such a child. And your boy, how is he doing?'

242

'He works in New York. Henry . . .' I stopped. The words must sound uncomfortable, almost revolting, no matter which ones I used. 'I'm in rather a difficult position.'

'Why?' He was alert. 'Something to do with me?'

'Not directly. In fact not at all – except as a friend.'

'You want my advice?' He raised his hands in a gesture of openness. 'My dear boy, feel free . . .'

And before he had time to finish the sentence, I blurted my message out. 'I've been told by someone who would know that my daughter Angelica and her step-father are having an affair.'

'Well . . .'

'And have been for some time!' My voice rose at the end.

Henry spoke gently. 'If you will forgive me for saying so, I guessed that something of that nature was afoot when they came to visit us.'

'You guessed?'

'Yes.' He lifted one finger and tapped the side of his nose. 'I have an instinct for such things, you see.' His smile was regretful. 'I tried to warn you. Don't you remember?'

'But were they flirting openly?' I was incredulous.

'Oh no. But one gains an impression. The way two people look at each other. The inflexion in their voices when they describe things they've done together. It is' – he frowned – 'a tone of indulgence.'

'But what did they talk about? You say that he bored you with stories about private jets and chalets in Gstaad . . .'

'No, no!' Henry held up his hand again. 'It was not boring. And there was this other dimension. I hadn't seen Laura for a long time. She has changed. How passive she is now, very different to the way that she was when we were all younger. Of course I spotted the drinking. But is that a symptom or a cause? Why does she drink? She scarcely spoke, you know, when they came to the villa. She made the introductions at the beginning, naturally – because neither Paul nor I had met her husband and I hadn't seen your daughter since her schooldays. Then she retreated into the background to allow Bill – it is Bill, isn't it? – to make all the running.'

I laughed, to express irony. 'Remember how, when I last came to the villa, we mocked the limits of his convers-

243

ation . . .'

'You don't take him seriously?'

'Of course I do, in abstract terms. After all, look at his power. And he is trying to take over the company for which I work. Soon he may be my employer, as well as the man who went off with Laura. But when we meet, the seriousness is dissipated by his manner, the idiocy of so much of what he says, by his limitations as a human being.'

'What a snob you are, Simon!' Henry exclaimed with surprising vehemence. 'You despise the man because of his vulgarity and the coarseness of his style. He doesn't read books . . .'

'Really, Henry!' I protested loudly.

'No, essentially it is true. And now see what he has got away with. See how idle your snobbery has made you.' The Armagnac arrived. Henry took a quick gulp and grimaced as he swallowed. 'Laura knows, I should say. She knows and has surrendered. Or perhaps Bill has her so tied up in a cocoon of comfort and money that she does not wish to break it by kicking up a fuss. She always wanted to be rich, didn't she?'

'I was in love with her.'

'And now?'

I gave him the obvious answer. 'Having seen the poor woman recently, you can probably guess.'

He smiled in a feline way. 'Oh, I see. Because she has become a wreck, sodden with gin, unsteady on her feet, her face heavy with disappointment – you no longer feel for her. You are ruthless, Simon. Quite ruthless.' And he let out a high-pitched giggle which made me jump with its unexpected noise.

'She left me.'

'Of course she did.' He waited. I wondered then if he might have an intimation of the way that I still thought of Laura, of how the past could triumph over the reality of a sad limping woman. Did it matter if he knew? But I had always wanted to keep this to myself, to cherish this particular shadow. 'And what are you going to do about it?' he asked.

'That was years ago . . .'

'Simon, I mean your daughter.'

The Armagnac lifted something within me. 'I aim to stop

the whole bloody business,' I declared.

'How?'

'By speaking to the man.'

'To Bill? Have you approached the girl already?'

'No.'

Angelica would manage a steely denial. And wasn't there something appalling and humiliating about discussing such matters with one's child? Bill and I had other subjects to talk about as well: the destruction of my son's and daughter's sensibilities, the attempt to stifle me by seizing my job, the lies that covered the greed and cold calculation. I still believed in the old myth that, left alone, two men could reach through to reserves of common sense and instinctive decency: to an understanding of the shameful and the wrong.

Henry leaned across the table and grasped my hand again. His eyes were bright. 'We must move quickly,' he said.

'We?'

'Yes. Do you think I'm going to desert you at a time like this? What are friends for? Besides, it's in my own interests to help. How are you going to be able to work with all this hanging over your head? I'll need you when this new book of mine is presented to the public. I am not to be fobbed off with Williams or Joan or whatever they call themselves.' He hit the table with one of his small hands, not very hard but enough to produce a sharp tap. 'What are you doing this weekend?'

'Nothing.'

'Right.' Henry shook his head in irritation. 'I was going up to Shropshire to see my niece and her rather dull husband – but that can wait. I will telephone her tomorrow morning. You and I must make a plan. Where do Laura and this man live?'

'In London in the week and the Isle of Wight most weekends, except in the depth of winter.'

'What day is it today?'

'Thursday.'

'Good.' Henry spoke slowly. 'You will telephone Laura tomorrow.' He paused and looked about him. 'You will tell her that you have to be in the Isle of Wight this coming weekend, to visit one of your authors who lives there. You will ask if Bill and she are to be at their house and, if they are, if it will be possible for you to see them on Saturday afternoon.'

245

'And confront him with what I know in front of Laura?' I laughed.

'Good heavens, no.' Henry frowned. 'See the man alone. It should be perfectly possible. After all she's in such a fragile state. You could suggest a walk, or tour of the garden. The essence is speed. And I am coming with you. We leave London on Saturday morning. You need a supporter. Of course you will go to the house alone. Alone and unarmed.'

'Unarmed! Henry, this is all too childish . . .'

'Is it really? Do you want the business to come to a quick conclusion?'

'Of course I do.'

'Then you had better do what I suggest.' Henry was serious. He beckoned to a waiter. 'Now this is on me, Simon,' he said. 'And I want you to have a good night's sleep. I will ring you. You need help!'

The terrible symmetry of one's life. I remembered how, some fifteen or sixteen years ago, Henry and I had followed Bill, traced him to that Mayfair apartment and, for the first time, seen the man who had taken Laura away from me.

Robin had joined the Foreign Office. After a short period in London, he had been sent abroad to Budapest – or was it Prague? While in eastern Europe, he had married a girl who had worked for the British Council. On leave, they had come to a party in London, given by the Parkins. Laura and I were there.

Robin approached me. Of course he was essentially the same: his hair only slightly receding, lines of earnestness developing around his mouth, the voice a little deeper so that his words resonated with a certain authority. 'Still nurturing geniuses?' he asked and gave the old tiresome guffaw through the brilliantly white prominent teeth.

I knew that he had a wife. I wanted to see her; he wanted to see Laura. 'How's my cousin?' he asked. 'So sorry I couldn't make it to the wedding. I was stuck in foreign parts, you know.' The guffaw rang out again. 'Where is she? What have you been doing to her?' And he nudged me, almost spilling my drink. I recognised the studied bonhomie, the determination not to appear unsporting. 'Don't forget that I have a responsibility for her welfare. After all, I introduced the two of you!'

Laura was at the other end of the room. I glimpsed the top of her head. I saw her face relax and then smile in a way that suddenly, for some curious reason, made me believe that she was entirely happy. 'There she is,' I said and, before the smile had faded, he saw her. His look showed appreciation, almost awe. To have married a beautiful woman was clearly a triumph for me.

'Is your wife here?' I asked.

Instinctively I realised that we had embarked upon a crude sort of competition. I knew also that I had won for he seemed cowed, embarrassed. I felt guilty. What if the girl were deformed or disfigured in some appalling way? I felt ashamed, even disgusted. To think that in one's baser moments it was possible to reduce interest in another human being to mere appearances, even to feel pleased that another man's wife was ugly.

Robin took a sip of his drink, as if to steady his nerves. I was determined, in spite of the brief spasm of shame, to see her, perhaps — if possible — to hear her speak. 'Is she here?' I repeated. With his glass still up against his lips and his mouth full of wine, he nodded. He pointed towards the middle of the room. It was impossible, in the scrum of faces and tightly packed bodies, to tell which one he was trying to single out. 'There,' he said eventually, 'with the yellow dress and the bee-hive hair-do.' And I focused upon a large figure, slightly red in the face, with fair hair piled up towards the ceiling. Like Laura she was smiling.

She must have seen her husband. Meeting his eyes, her smile broadened. She had a large mouth with fairly full and what some people would describe as sensual lips. She waved, said something to the two men to whom she had been talking and began to edge her way towards us, preceded by a formidable bust. 'Oh,' Robin murmured to himself, 'Marilyn has decided to come over.'

With her hair reaching upwards, she was almost as tall as

247

me. She looked at Robin impatiently, anxious for him to perform the introduction in order that she might begin to speak. Obligingly he explained who I was, then withdrew his head slightly, as if to allow Marilyn to take the field. And she spoke, in a long gush, about their life in Budapest – or was it Prague? – pausing only occasionally to seek confirmation from Robin. Already, I understood, she had conquered him. 'Are you married?' she asked. I said that I was. Her voice rang with the echo of difficulties overcome, of obstacles pushed to one side. 'But we managed somehow, didn't we, Robin?' He nodded at the floor, looked up at me, averted his eyes and said to a vase on a side table at his elbow, 'We did indeed.'

'Do you ever come to eastern Europe?' she asked. 'Robin, the time . . .' I said that I had dealt with the British Council in connection with an exhibition of some of our books in Warsaw. 'That's near enough. Stop off and see us next time, on your way home. Robin, where did you leave the car?' And they left, after he had muttered something about a dinner party in Hampstead, she striding ahead towards the cold autumn evening.

Alone, I looked across to where Laura had been. She was still in the same place, talking to one man. Now I remember. A tall bald figure, silent, fascinated – or seemingly so – with what she was saying. Afterwards I asked her his name and she feigned ignorance at first, even doubt as to the person I had in mind. I described him: the height, the baldness, the attentive manner. 'But some people are interested in what I say!' she protested. 'Why should that be so surprising?' Who was he? 'Oh, just a businessman,' she had answered, slightly irritated. We were driving home, about to turn out of Queensgate. 'Bill somebody. Why?'

XXIII

On Friday morning I met Joan in the street on the way to the office. It had become cold again. She wore a scarf of plain green wool around her neck and a heavy dark overcoat. I noticed that she carried a small leather briefcase, evidence of work taken to and from her home. She was keen of course; I knew that she was keen.

She called out to me from behind. 'Simon!'

I stopped. To our left, the roar of the traffic in the Tottenham Court Road cut through the icy air. Her face, slightly blue in the cold, came level with mine. That day, I was wearing my fur hat. 'Your friend seems to be having a whale of a time,' she said.

'Henry? I saw him last night . . .'

'No, the short story man. What's his name? Flanigan? O'Rorke? O'Dooley?'

'Michael Docherty. And where on earth did you come across him? He's supposed to be staying in my cottage in the country.'

'Oh, he is. But I saw Hermione last night, at the party to launch that new paperback imprint. She was looking for you. I should watch out.'

'What on earth has happened now?' We turned the corner of the street and almost collided with each other.

'Apparently her beloved Michael rang to tell her that, for the first time in his life, he had discovered love or whatever you want to call it. With a girl whose address you had given

249

him.' She nudged me. 'What have you been up to, Simon? Are you running some sort of a knocking shop on the side?'

'Sarah Erdley?' I asked.

'I can't remember her name. Apparently he talks as if he's obsessed. What's she like?'

'Who?'

'The girl!'

I sighed. 'Silly. Spoilt. And she has literary pretensions as well.'

'She sounds perfect. Good luck to him. And one has to do something in the country, doesn't one? One can't just talk to the trees.'

'He went there to write a novel.'

'John will be relieved,' Joan said. 'With a bit of luck Mr Docherty won't finish it now – with this liaison taking up so much of his energy – and you won't have to shame us into publishing the thing by making us all feel like a bunch of philistines if we don't. Think how much money we'll save! We ought to pay this girl some sort of advance, in instalments of course, on the affair. One hundred pounds now, another in six months and the third in a year, by which time he may have lost his inspiration in favour of more mundane delights and the danger will have passed.'

'Ha bloody ha.'

'Is the girl pretty?'

'Yes.'

'More than pretty?'

'What do you mean, Joan?' We were outside the front door of the office. 'She is attractive. But silly. Quite inordinately so. And she's married, with a young child. Her husband will be most upset. He's a sensitive person who is still very much in love with her.'

Joan looked at me and smiled in a conspiratorial way. 'Do I detect a certain tendresse – on your part, I mean?'

'Most certainly not.' I began to bluster. 'The girl is half my age. The family own the cottage. I am their tenant. Any intimate connection is entirely out of the question . . .'

'Why?' Then she looked serious, but still slightly mocking. 'Oh, I see what you mean. For you and she to have a romance would be contrary to some sort of custom or code of

250

behaviour. Is that right?'

'No, it is not!' Now I was shouting. We were standing by the steps that lead up to the firm's front door.

'Simon! Steady on. It was a joke, that's all. A little joke.'

'So Docherty and Sarah are not having an affair?'

'No! The bit about you and her. As for the rest of it, I have no idea what they're up to. I'm only relaying a piece of gossip from Hermione. No doubt she will want to fill you in on all the details. Anyway, why are you so upset?'

'I am not upset!'

We entered the hall of the building and climbed up the first flight of stairs together in silence. Outside my office door, Joan said, 'Well, we may meet later,' and went on to her own room. I merely grunted.

Mary was waiting, in her small room outside my office. 'Much colder today,' she said. I smiled, a little impatiently, and took off my hat and coat. 'John Williams has rung already. Can you go to his office – but not before eleven? He's busy till then.'

'What the hell's it about this time? I've got three manuscripts outstanding and all sorts of other things. . . . Really!' I hit the side of my leg with my hand in a gesture of irritation.

'I don't know, Simon.' She looked cowed. I realised that I had shouted at someone again. Was I on the verge of losing control?

The telephone rang. Mary picked up the receiver, gave my name and told the caller that she was my secretary. Then she put one hand over the mouthpiece. 'Hermione Salterton.'

'Put her through.'

I ran into my office, sat at my desk and snatched the telephone. The moment that she heard I was on the line, the woman began to speak. 'Simon? Look, it's about Michael. Michael Docherty. The most disastrous thing has happened. He's taken up with some flibbertigibbet of a girl down there and I can't get any sense out of him. Last time I rang he simply hung up on me. Now he doesn't even bother to answer. Really, Simon, what is going on? He spluttered something about a woman. He tells me everything, of course. I'm closer to him than anyone is. But the boy will put his entire literary career in jeopardy . . .'

251

'Hermione,' I said, attempting to remain calm, 'I know nothing at all about it.'

'He says that the girl is a friend of yours. That it was you who introduced him to her. Well, you'd better do something, Simon. And do something fast.'

'Do something?'

'Yes. Speak to the girl. Call her off. If, that is, you don't want to lose one of your most promising young writers.'

'Look, Hermione,' I began, 'I can do nothing. The girl is half my age. I have no influence either with her or with your beloved Michael . . .'

'Simon, the book is to be published after Christmas. It will – you mark my words – receive considerable critical attention. There will be talk of a brilliant literary debut. And what will happen? The writer will have been transformed into an amorous sot, the poodle of some little county tart . . .'

'Hermione . . .'

'Unless of course you move fast enough to prevent this. My guess is that there still may be time. The best way is to approach the woman. You know her. Explain gently that a great career is at stake. The boy must not become embroiled in time-consuming entanglements at least until he has finished his first novel. You, Simon, more than most must surely understand the dedication that literature calls for. If she is at all educated, she will see the point. And I am thinking not only of the boy or even of myself. It will not reflect at all well on your judgement and reputation if *The Water Garden* turns out to be a mere flash in the pan. Short stories are expensive things to publish – especially those by unknown young writers. Williams will be looking for a quick return on his investment, certainly the possibility of a novel to follow in order to capitalise on the first flush of critical esteem. Move quickly, Simon! Move now!' And she put the receiver down with a crack that resounded in my ear.

I sat with my hands clasped together in front of me on the desk. For a few seconds I stared across at the calendar on the wall opposite, illustrated that month with a colour photograph of two seagulls flying above a West Country resort. Mary came in, holding an envelope. 'Joan was here while you

252

were on the telephone. She didn't want to see you but she left this.'

I opened the envelope and Mary left. Joan's writing was large with carefully formed letters: easy to read.

My dear Simon,
    I am sorry. I was both bloody and silly this morning. And at such a difficult time for you. Damn!
    Will you forgive me? We must stick together.
        Love from Joan

For a moment I was close to tears. Embarrassed at myself, although there was no one else in the room, I reached for an object to study or focus my attention on. The nearest appropriate thing happened to be the vast bulk of the Palmerston manuscript. The name of its author blurred in front of my eyes. Why had I ever doubted the decency of my old friend, my former pupil and my one certain supporter left in this building? Why?

XXIV

Angelica and Sarah had shared a flat somewhere off the Fulham Road, north of Stamford Bridge football ground, near the streets where lorries thunder across London. When the windows were open in summer, you could hear the noise of those juggernauts, the crash and roar as their drivers put on a burst of speed. The flat was pleasant enough: small and with a low rent which the two girls divided between themselves. Both of them had private money. Sarah's parents, rich from their Cotswold acres, gave her an allowance; Angelica had the income from the trust made for her by Bill.

He had tried to be sensitive about this and had raised it one evening when we were talking after dinner at his house in Chelsea. He had dressed up his intentions in a clever disguise, playing the pathetic childless husband.

'Laura and I don't seem to be able to manage it together,' he said jocularly.

At first I thought, with surprise, that he was confessing impotence. He reached out a hand and pushed a decanter of port towards me. On the other side of the table two men – our fellow guests – were intent on some private conversation. One of them – stout, his face red against the white of his evening shirt (one always changed for Bill's London dinners) – leaned towards the other, who was thinner, slightly dishevelled, his black tie drooping downwards at its edges. I caught the words 'liquidity', 'under-capitalised', 'hopeless mis-timing of the last rights issue'. Christina, Laura and the ladies had left the

254

gentlemen to their deliberations in the traditional manner.

Bill must have noticed my surprise. 'No, no,' he hastened to say with a smile, 'I mean, to have children. Simon, you are lucky with Angelica and Edward.' He paused, looked at me with what appeared to be wistful unmalicious envy.

I entered the game. The rules had been laid down in those few opening words. 'You see a great deal of them as well.'

'Oh, I know. But Laura and I had hoped . . . You don't mind me telling you all this, do you? Perhaps I'm talking too much. It's rather late and' – he tapped the side of his half empty glass of port – 'one's judgement becomes hazy. Anyway we saw a doctor last week. Apparently the chances of success are very slim. And she is almost at the age when . . .' He raised one hand and smiled again at me, this time in a rueful way. 'There's nothing that can be done.'

'I'm sorry.' A gloating thought rose in mind: even with all your money, nature has beaten you . . . Then it died. I felt ashamed.

'Now I want to do something,' he began. He held a large thick cigar which he lifted, put into his mouth and blew out a cloud of rich blue-grey smoke. Through this, he was watching me. He was not drunk. 'I want to do something,' he repeated. 'But if you don't like it, Simon, I won't. It's entirely up to you. I want' – he raised the cigar again – 'I want to make over some money for Edward and Angelica.' At that time they were fourteen or fifteen or sixteen years old: still at school but already growing away from me. Bill put up a fat finger and wagged it twice. 'You tell me the truth, Simon. I must have your consent. Without it, they get nothing.'

'I don't mind,' I said.

'That's very good of you.' He blew out some more smoke. 'The sums involved are not enormous. I'll let you have copies of the deeds and investment details. Two trusts would seem to be the best way of doing it. Personally I favour professional trustees – a lawyer and an accountant or some such arrangement. They're easier to sack if anything goes wrong.' Bill laughed. He was oddly winning, anxious to make friends. He pushed back his chair and called out to the others, 'Shall we go next door?' He noticed my still full glass of port. 'Take it with you,' he said with a laugh. 'Take it with you,' and, as we

255

walked through to the drawing-room, he started to explain how he bought all his wine direct from a big firm of shippers in Kent.

'What does Bill believe in?' I had asked Christina as we were driving home that evening. 'Money? Power?'

'I expect so. Why?'

'He has only earthly wishes.' The port and the claret from the shippers in Kent had blurred my articulacy. 'Only earthly wishes,' I repeated.

Christina had laughed. 'Does his lack of spirituality upset you?'

I had had to swerve to avoid a pedestrian who had strayed off the pavement. 'Damn!' I turned again to Christina. 'He's giving Edward and Angelica some of his money.'

She seemed to think that there was nothing wrong with such a gesture. Had it been the beginning of a delicate enslavement? Angelica, at the time of the dinner, had been little more than a fat bubbly schoolgirl. Perhaps Bill had decided then that he would want her. I had once heard him say, in the context of some business decision, that forward planning was essential.

A part of the money was used to provide the flat, or at least Angelica's share of the rent. And when, some years later, I called on her there, surprising her once while she was ironing her dress for a party, I believed still that she was what she seemed or what I wanted her to seem: a young girl free, about to discover love. Once the two of them – my daughter and her friend Sarah – had given me tea in the room decorated with Toulouse-Lautrec posters and a print of a Samuel Palmer landscape that I had given her. The friend was shy of me at first; then they had both forgotten their inhibitions as they described the excitement of the dance of the evening before. That was a time, only an hour or two, that I liked to remember. Angelica had none of the brusqueness, the impatience that she was to show later. There was no hint that she thought my life and tastes not only incomprehensible but dull as well. And Sarah, the silly vain child with whom I was to become involved, blushed and hurried her words in the excitement of recollected decent pleasure. Later would come

the knowingness, the capricious discontent of a spoilt woman.
But that afternoon, over the tea cups, the air had been thick
with unshattered illusions.

XXV

Freddy Simpson, the sales director, was sitting in Williams'
room when I arrived. He smiled at me, an open look of
pleasure, as Williams stood up from behind his large brown
desk.

'Simon,' Williams said, 'I felt we ought to have a word.' His
look was more of a leer than a welcome, a ritual baring of his
regular small front teeth. 'I have a project here which might be
right up your street. Freddy and I were discussing it because I
felt I should get his views on the sales potential first. Have you
heard of a philosopher called Wittgenstein?'

'Yes.' Freddy and I were seated together in front of our
master, his desk a wall of authority.

'More than I bloody had!' Freddy let out a guffaw. Williams
frowned at him.

'Well, someone has sent us the synopsis of a possible
biography, or biographical study, I should say . . .'

'It's a big subject,' I began, 'and potentially very difficult . . .'

He continued as if I had not spoken. 'It's hardly the sort of
thing that we'd want to take on, particularly at this time. But
the author approaches the subject in an interesting way. He
calls his work *Wittgenstein in Pictures*.'

I tightened my fists.

'Now I don't know much about the man, but Ilse' –
Williams turned to Freddy and said with a slight smile, 'my
wife – Ilse spent a year on modern philosophy as a part of her

degree course at Gothenburg. I gave her the synopsis to read. To tell the truth, I was about to turn the idea down.' He laughed, put his hands behind his head and leaned back in his chair. 'But she said that there's a BBC 2 series coming on in the autumn about Masters of Modern Thought. Did you know this? And Wittgenstein apparently is among them. So' – Williams raised his right hand, splayed out the fingers and tapped each one with his pencil as he enumerated his points – 'One: we have the interest created by television. Two: we have a text which will be simple and direct, uncluttered with jargon. This will be the editor's responsibility. The man – the author, I mean – should be controllable. He's a philosophy graduate. Young. Works on one of the Fleet Street papers, I can't remember which. Doing this to make a bit on the side. Three: beautiful photographs, with all sorts of fancy shadows and angles, of Vienna and Cambridge. Four: the Americans are already interested. Wittgenstein is international. I've spoken to Bob Klotz in New York. We might even swing a German translation. Five: I want to test those printers in Singapore who claim to be able to undercut the boys in Taiwan by a third. This is a good book to use.' Williams looked at his left hand and frowned. He had run out of fingers. Quickly the right was raised in its place and his pencil transferred. 'Six: there's a terrific potential today for what I call the pop academic book. Thanks partly to television, partly to the Open University, partly to the serious Sunday news-papers, we have a tremendous cultural spread in this country. Think of all those bored housewives, educated for so much more than the washing machine and preparing the kiddies' tea!' Williams let his hands drop on to the desk. '*Wittgenstein in Pictures*,' he said, in a tone that was almost rhapsodic. 'I like it. I like it very much!'

Freddy and I were silent for a few seconds. Then Freddy said, 'I'll try to get those figures that you were talking about, John.'

'Yes!' Williams was still in a messianic mood. The right hand went up again and the left clutched at the pencil. 'I want: one – the number of philosophy graduates leaving the universities each year. Two – the size of the philosophy department at the Open University. Three – the average weekly readership of the three Sunday colour supplements, preferably with a break-down into class types and spending power.' He looked at me. 'This is fabulous magazine material, absolutely fabulous!'

'Who is going to take the photographs?' I asked.

'Ah! Now this is where we really score!' The hands dropped again on to the desk. Williams' eyes were positively alight. 'The author put forward someone whose name I can't remember. Anyway no one will have heard of him. But I did some quick investigating this morning and' – he paused, as if to emphasise the arrival of a climax – 'I've got Nigel Stokes interested!'

'I see.' At first I thought: perhaps it is better to hide one's ignorance on such occasions. I decided to take a risk. 'Who is Nigel Stokes?' I asked.

'Simon!' Williams was shouting, shifting about in his seat with impatience. 'I don't believe it!' He turned to Freddy. 'Sometimes I find it difficult to believe that Simon and I are living in the same country, even in the same century!' Williams looked at me again. 'Do you mean to say that you've never heard of Nigel Stokes?'

'I have not.'

Freddy tried to help. 'He brought out a book of photographs last year, of life and characters in the part of south London where he lives. It did well. There was a piece on Channel 4 about him and his work, called "Camberwell Caprice".'

'Haven't you bought a television yet, Simon?' Williams asked. He looked at Freddy and smiled. 'I think it's safe to do so now, you know. They have perfected the technology so that the box is really quite easy to work and unlikely to blow up in your face.' He let out a great guffaw, obviously pleased with his display of sarcasm and wit.

'Thank you for telling me.'

Freddy tried to help again. 'I don't know much about Nigel Stokes either, John,' he said.

'But you have heard of him.'

'Yes.' Freddy glanced at me. For a moment I thought that he might be going to reach out and clasp my hand. 'But only just.'

'Anyway he's interested, or so his agent tells me. And this is where you come in, Simon. I want you to take charge of this whole project.' A spasm of pain seemed to cross Williams' face and he looked up, away from us. 'Wait a minute,' he said. 'Which is better – *The Pictorial Wittgenstein* or *Wittgenstein in Pictures*?'

'*The Pictorial Wittgenstein* sounds a bit posh,' Freddy said.

'My God!' Williams clutched at his forehead. 'That's something we really don't want! You're right. But the emphasis on the fact that there are lots of pictures – not just old Wittgenstein – that's important. Wouldn't you agree, Simon?'

'Yes,' I said.

'Thank you, Freddy.'

Freddy sat there, looking pleased. He acknowledged what he thought was praise with a slight nod of his head.

'Thank you, Freddy,' Williams repeated.

Freddy nodded again.

'Thank you, Freddy.' And, at last, Freddy saw that the thanks were in fact a way of saying: kindly leave my office and allow me to deal with this contemptible ignoramus on my own. He stood up and walked towards the door, the smile fading from his face. 'Oh, and let me have the results of those enquiries as soon as possible, will you?' Williams called after him. 'Now, Simon.' His thin features pointed across the desk at me, like the rifles of a firing squad. Williams was definitely not a comfortable man. 'The point about the book is this. I want a mixed bag of illustrations. Some old photographs: pictures of Bertrand Russell, Wittgenstein's relations, his Cambridge contemporaries, that sort of thing. Then – if we can get him – Stokes's work, but not separate from the old stuff. Didn't the family have castles or stately homes in Austria or something? We could send Stokes out. The American publishers might pay half.'

Freddy, however, was still hovering beside the door. 'John, just one thought occurred to me,' he said, in a rather nervous way. 'This Wittgenstein, did he have any – you know. . . ?'

'Any what?' Williams was impatient.

'Sort of private life – if you see what I mean?'

Williams looked at me as if to say: you're the one who ought to know. 'No, he did not,' I snapped.

261

'Oh, I see.' Freddy shrugged his shoulders, and gave a wistful smile. 'You can't have everything, I suppose,' he said. 'I was only looking at it from the point of view of the reps. I have to think of my boys, you know, Simon. They need a selling point of some sort. Bookshops can be awfully difficult these days, and what are they going to make of this stuff outside London and a few university towns?'

'We have to make sure that a suitable package is produced,' Williams said. 'Have no fear, Freddy. Simon and I will put our heads together, won't we, Simon? So far as I am concerned the battle will be as good as won if we can get Nigel Stokes to play ball. Thank you, Freddy.' And our intrepid sales director left the room. Williams looked away from me, down at the surface of his desk. 'Dear Freddy,' he muttered. 'What an eye he has for the essentials.' His eyes focused on mine once more. 'Now, Simon, I need your help.' He reached out towards a thin sheaf of papers. 'We have the man's synopsis, plus two sample chapters. We also have his agent saying that three other publishers have expressed interest and unless she has an answer by the middle of next week she will start to talk terms with one of them.'

'The agent is not by any chance . . .' I saw that he was annoyed to be interrupted yet again. But I continued. 'She's not Hermione Salterton, is she?'

'No. A young girl. Clare somebody.'

I was relieved. 'Hermione and I do not always find it easy to understand one another,' I said with a smile.

'Simon, you have to get on with agents,' Williams said in an irritated voice. 'How do you think I feel about the woman? We had her to our house once. She insulted Ilse by trying to tell her that the smorgasbord was not laid out in the traditional Scandinavian way. My wife exercised admirable restraint. But you have to be professional about these things, to try to separate personal dislike from relationships necessary to your job.' This was, I thought, a cunning blow. Also yet again, with the mention of the smorgasbord parties in Ealing, I was reminded that I had never been invited to his home.

'Thank you, John,' I said. 'Hermione and I have worked together on a number of books for the last twenty years or so.' In other words, two can play at the game of camouflaged

262

abuse. Williams had, after all, only returned to British publishing from New York four years ago.

The anger showed in his eyes, but, in common with his wife when her exhibition of smoked fish and cold meats had been criticised, he exercised restraint. 'Good,' he countered crisply. 'All I am trying to say is that it is clearly in the firm's interest that you should continue to do so. But let us return to the matter in hand. Here, as I was saying, is the basis of the book: the synopsis and the sample chapters. I want you to read them as soon as possible and then get in touch with the author. I will speak to the agent today. We can't wait any longer. I'll tell her that we want to publish and that she should state her terms. I'm doing this, Simon, because I know that you will be as impressed as I am.' He smiled. Another insult. He was not even going to bother to seek my opinion before a contract was agreed. 'I know that we ought to take this to an editorial meeting. But I've spoken to Freddy about the sales prospects and now I've spoken to you.'

I nodded. 'I'll read it,' I said.

'Now,' Williams went on, 'we come to my second point. I want to get this out quickly, in time for Christmas if possible. Apparently the rest of the text is almost ready. And if Stokes plays ball we should have the photographs in a matter of months. We can hire a freelance to dig up the contemporary stuff: the pictures of Bertrand Russell, Wittgenstein's family and the rest of it. What about that girl who worked on the Country Customs book last year? Have you got her name and address? Ring her as soon as possible. The two of you can operate together. My word, Simon – I think we may be on to something! There won't be big sales in this country of course – I recognise that. But think of the translation rights, the possibilities of multi-national editions! As I said, Wittgenstein is international! Aren't you excited?'

'I haven't read the sample chapters yet.'

'Ha ha!' Williams laughed, but without humour. 'Cautious as ever. Let me tell you something. Books like this – the excitement of putting them together, of coordinating a well-written text with illuminating photographs, of producing a handsome distinguished volume that people will be proud to have in their living rooms, of setting in motion a really comprehensive and stylish marketing operation – books like this are my kind of publishing!' Williams tilted his chair back, clasped his hands in front of him and looked away from me towards a reproduction of one of the posters that had decorated our stand at the Frankfurt book fair four or five years ago: the first time that we had gone there under his leadership, the time that he had been determined to make – as he had put it – 'One hell of a splash'. 'But, as I said, this project is something of an experiment. We are entering uncharted waters – uncharted at least as far as this firm is concerned. I know we do school books, university study aids and all the rest of it. But the pop academic, Simon! Think of it, the pop academic . . .'

'John,' I cut in, 'I can understand the excitement. But are you really sure that the sales and return on this book are going to make that much difference to us?'

'They won't. I know that.'

'Then forgive me, but why. . . ?

'One must test the waters,' he said.

I laughed. 'Uncharted as they are.' It was not a joke that Williams would be likely to appreciate.

He did not. The look was glacial. 'One must test the waters. If they seem friendly or calm or whatever, then we go in with a really big investment – perhaps a whole series geared to the general reader rather than the student. Wittgenstein is our scout, so to speak. We send him out to see how the land lies.'

The metaphors were becoming confused, as they often did when the man was agitated or enthusiastic. Calm and friendly waters, the lie of the land: his vision encompassed great oceans and continents. Like Bill, I thought, Williams is a modern conquistador. 'And you want me to take charge of this?' I asked.

'Not to take charge, Simon.' Williams smiled again, this time with a hint of knowing secrecy. 'I will be watching over the project very carefully, wanting to be kept in touch at every stage.' Let there be no doubt, the message read, who is to be in charge. 'No, I want you to exercise your talents on both the author and his manuscript. I want you to make this a bloody good book! What else have you got on at the moment?'

'The Palmerston biography . . .' I began.

'Whose biography?' Williams's face crinkled with irritation.

'The life of Palmerston. We've spoken about it several times at editorial meetings.' I prayed that he would not force me to defend this book now.

'Oh yes. Well, shelve Palmerston. He's hardly Christmas material anyway. Has he reached proof stage?'

'No. We're still tinkering with the manuscript.'

'Keep on tinkering, Simon! Keep on tinkering!' He frowned. 'So that's not important. Anything else?'

I mentioned three or four other books on which I was working. And of course there was my strongest card: the latest Henry Brown. 'Then Henry always likes a fair amount of attention,' I said and laughed. Good old Henry. He might save me yet from the 'pop academic'.

'Ah, Henry.' Williams fiddled with the pencil which was now lying on the top of his desk before he looked up at me in a tentative yet serious way. 'I wanted to speak to you about Henry. You say that he likes attention?'

'While a book of his is in the pipeline, yes. He becomes nervous, worried that – when it comes out – his public may not stay with him this time.' I laughed again. I realised that, for perhaps the first time in this conversation, I was speaking from a position of strength. 'One has to play the role of a nurse or comforter, be available at the end of the telephone or even fly out to the villa to listen to the latest catalogue of imaginary fears or slights.'

'Artistic temperament, you mean?' Williams asked.

'You could call it that.'

'It must be rather exhausting for you, Simon.'

I wanted to show my dedication, hard work and selflessness in the cause of my job. I wanted to be appreciated. 'Oh, it is,' I agreed. 'Exhausting, but vital.'

'And time-consuming?'

'Certainly.' I pressed home what I believed to be my advantage. 'One has little time for anything else. That's why I wonder if this Wittgenstein idea, interesting as it is . . .'

'Simon, I want to help you.' Williams was leaning forward. I thought that he resembled an insincere seller of insurance policies. 'With this in mind, I have arranged for Joan to take responsibility for Henry. She will be there for him to talk to

265

whenever he wants.'

The blood rushed to my cheeks. Self-control was important. I checked myself and said merely, 'I see.'

'Of course the arrangement is purely temporary. While you
are working on this new project.'

'Of course.'

'You seem upset, Simon. I thought that you might be
relieved. As you have often admitted, Henry Brown is not the
easiest of persons . . .'

'There's one thing you haven't thought of,' I blurted out.
'Henry won't accept this. He and I have worked together since
he first became a writer. Why, he told me only the other day
that he refuses to have his manuscript dealt with by anyone
else . . .'

'Did he?' said Williams. The look of oily insincerity was still
there. 'When I spoke to Henry, he did not seem to object too
much to the idea of a change.' Williams smiled again. 'Only a
temporary one of course.'

'Henry is one of my closest friends,' I protested.

'Is he? How often do you see him?'

'Every time he comes to England. And I make at least one
journey to the villa a year. Often two. Sometimes more if, as I
said, we are working on one of his books.' I remembered that I
had another potential example of our intimacy. 'For instance
he and I are spending this weekend together.'

For a moment the serenely dishonest smile faltered, then
recovered. 'Well,' he replied, 'you will be able to discuss all
this with him at your leisure.'

'And when did you and he talk about it? I think, John, I
would not be unjustified in accusing you of going behind my
back. In the past all communications between the firm and
Henry have gone through me!'

'We spoke on Tuesday.' Williams was precise. 'I had to talk
to Henry anyway about the party. You may remember that
you told Joan you wanted nothing to do with it and I thought I
should, if only out of courtesy, at least tell him who is coming.
At the same time I raised the question of the plans for his new
book.'

'I wanted nothing more to do with the party because the
whole occasion was thought up without any reference to me

266

whatsoever! It's your party, not mine! And what has the party got to do with a decision – much more important surely from everyone's point of view – to give Henry Brown a new editor?'

'Simon, there is no question of giving Henry Brown a new editor. As I have said to you, the arrangement with Joan is purely temporary . . .'

'Joan!' She had betrayed me.

'Yes. Joan. I felt that she would be able to hold the fort. After all she was trained by you and is used to Henry's idiosyncratic behaviour. And in the meantime there is this Wittgenstein project . . .'

'Wittgenstein!' I saw it all. My voice grew louder. 'What a marvellous excuse! You know, John, I do admire your cunning. Did they teach it to you in New York? You don't really care about this damned Wittgenstein idea. You and I know that its commercial prospects are limited – despite all this talk about colour supplements, translations, foreign sales and the number of philosophy students at the Open University. The book is bound to be expensive, especially if you get this man Stokes or whatever his name is chucking great fee demands and expense account claims all over the place. No! You've got something else in mind, a rather different little scheme. Put me on to Wittgenstein, transfer Henry to Joan – only temporarily at first of course but you're pretty sure that they'll get along well enough for the arrangement to become permanent. Then, hey presto, there simply isn't enough work for me around – especially after Wittgenstein crashes in flames, which he inevitably will, identifying me with a ludicrous failure!'

'Simon!' Williams exclaimed. 'You must be out of your mind!'

'Out of my mind!' I let out an offensive guffaw. 'Yes, I think I must be – not to have seen this coming a long time ago. As far as you're concerned, the quicker I leave this place the better. Not only will you be able to stop paying my salary – I suppose you will simply promote Joan and pay her less because she's a woman – not only will you be able to stop paying my salary and therefore assist the precious cash flow but you will also be rid of that tiresomely argumentative person who does not

267

always greet your plans for our progress with the enthusiasm that they deserve!'

'I take it then that you're not interested in this Wittgenstein project?' Williams' smile had a touch of real humour, lightly mixed with contempt. 'That seems a little – shall we say – prejudiced, especially as you haven't looked at either the sample chapter or the synopsis. After all, as I understand it, the firm used to boast in your grandfather's – or was it your great-grandfather's? – day that every manuscript or suggestion for a book was given serious consideration once it had arrived at this office. "We read everything" – wasn't that an important part of the publicity, something that it was thought might encourage the best as well as the worst authors to come here?' His lips drew in. 'In this case, you may be right. Perhaps I am too sanguine. But surely you ought to do me the courtesy of reading the stuff.'

'I want to ask you something, John. Are you prepared to give me a written assurance that, after this Wittgenstein business is finished, Henry Brown will be taken away from Joan and given back to me?'

'Simon, please.' Williams laid his hands on the desk. He began to shake his head slowly. 'I had no idea that you were so attached to Henry. You're always grumbling about how impossible he can be. And I know that you don't particularly admire his work . . .'

'Then why do you think I have remained his editor for all these years?'

'Because he has made the firm a lot of money.'

'Not at all. Because I think that Henry Brown was once almost a great writer and could become one again!'

'My word, you are devoted to him!' Williams accompanied this with an unpleasant leer.

'What about my assurance?'

'Simon, even to ask for such a thing is absurd. If Henry and you are so close, I imagine he'll be clamouring to return to you anyway. We have told him that the arrangement with Joan is purely temporary.'

'And what does Joan think of it?'

Williams smiled, this time with what looked like real affection. 'Oh, Joan will turn her hand to anything. Now I don't want you to feel that there's any conspiracy here, Simon. You and I have had our differences in the past, little disagreements about changes of emphasis in our list, doubts about some of the other changes I have had to make. Personally I bear no resentment. And to lose you now – someone whose name has been identified with the firm since it was founded, someone who has a reputation not only in British but international publishing as well – would be entirely against both my interests and those of the company. What, for example, would Bob Klotz say?'

'So you won't give me a written assurance?'

Williams' eyes showed impatience. He had said his piece. 'Let me ask you something. Are you refusing to do this Wittgenstein book?'

'You want my resignation, don't you?'

Williams looked at his watch. I noticed that his hand was absolutely steady. 'I cannot see the point in continuing this conversation, Simon,' he said. 'Obviously in your present mood you will accept nothing that I say. In any case I have to go to a meeting at the Lindsay Group's head office for which I will be late if I don't leave within the next five minutes.' My appointment had been cunningly timed. 'Why don't you think about all this over the weekend? You say that you're seeing Henry. He at least should be able to reassure you that there has been no question of anyone going behind your back. Then we will speak again on Monday. I shall be in the office all day.' He stood up. 'I am sorry. The last thing I want, as you know, is any ill feeling.'

XXVI

I rang Henry. We arranged to meet at my flat at half past nine on Saturday morning. He sounded excited. Then I tried to reach Joan. Her assistant answered. 'The poor thing's feeling so awful with a streaming cold and a sore throat that she's gone home. Can I do anything?'

'Will she be at her house?'

'Not quite yet,' the girl said. 'She was going to drop some stuff off with George Mason on the way . . .'

'George Mason!' So he was probably in on the plot as well. They were working on the silly drunken old man. I thought, nevertheless, of his fragility. 'It will kill him if he gets a cold, at his age and in his condition . . .'

'Oh, Joan will be very careful.'

I dialled George Mason's home number. The telephone rang and rang until eventually there came a click of someone picking up the receiver. Whoever it was said nothing, but I could hear the sound of laboured breathing. 'George?' I said. Still no answer. 'George? It's Simon. Have you got Joan with you?'

The breathing softened. Then a high voice, not unlike Henry Brown's, began to recite:

'Pussy cat, pussy cat where have you been?
I've been up to London to visit the Queen.
Pussy cat, pussy cat what did you see there?
Only a little mouse under the stair.'

270

Despite the hour – barely midday – George Mason was drunk. I recognised the signs: the almost soprano pitch of the voice, the transformation of an obsession with cats into a positive mania, the hopelessness that must meet any attempt to have a sensible or coherent conversation. I tried once more. 'George, is Joan there with you?'

The rhyme ceased. And I suddenly felt a desperate over-whelming sense of frustration and anger. 'They're trying to ruin me,' I shouted out. 'The whole damned lot of them! You remember the old days, George – when we worked together, when we discovered Henry, when there was still some decency and integrity in this bloody place!'

The voice began again. 'My dear boy. My dear dear boy. I am so sorry.'

Was there hope I could enlist the support of my old friend? 'George, has Joan been with you this morning?'

'Who?'

'Joan. The tall thin woman. She used to be your secretary. Don't you remember?'

'Oh, her.'

'Has she been with you this morning, George? Is she there now?'

For a few seconds there was silence. Just as I was about to give up, he said 'Nobody here now. Just me and Mr Moggins.'

Mr Moggins? Of course. The cat. 'But has she been with you, George?'

'We don't like strangers.'

'Joan isn't a stranger! You see her every time you come to the office. Has she been with you? If you only knew, George, what they're doing to this company. That bloody Welsh-man . . .'

'Nobody here now, my dear. You must calm down. Everything seems so far away. Far away and such a long time ago. It really is getting better. People tell me that. I'm worried, you know. I believe they're talking about stopping deliveries of milk to one's doorstep. Now that would be most unfair. We depend so much upon our milkman, Mr Moggins and I. And the shops are rather a distance. They won't bring stuff round

271

to you today. I remember – the butcher's boy, the grocer's boy, the boy who brought the papers. All gone! But we'll get by somehow. We always have.'

My heart beat fast that morning. Joan's home number was perpetually engaged. Most probably, I thought, she had gone to bed and left the receiver off. Mary seemed worried about me. Did she know? Had they drawn her into the plot as well? But Mary, I decided, was incapable of treachery. As lunch time approached she began to fuss. Was I going to the club? Should she pop out and get me some sandwiches? Or perhaps I had an engagement that she did not know of? She seemed so comforting, so kindly, as she stood in front of my desk: then hovered in the doorway in order to give me a longer time in which to say that I needed her help in some way or other. 'But you must eat something!' she declared. 'I know that you hardly have any breakfast . . .'

'There's all this.' I pointed at two or three manuscripts that lay before me. 'Not for lunch, I mean. But to be got through. And I'm going to be away for most of the weekend.'

Her look was one of real concern. 'Simon, I don't want to pry – but are you feeling all right?'

'Never better!' She was still hovering. 'Mary, I have these manuscripts. Please!'

She left. At last I was alone. My grip on the arms of my office chair was tight. I had a sensation of barely containable impatience: the wish to have them all in here, the whole lot of them, the mass of enemies, and to speak about the great unmentionables of our lives. In the meantime there were the irritations of delay, the infuriating collection of obstacles that lay across my path.

I seized one of the manuscripts and opened it at the first page. It was the Palmerston biography. The sight of those great blocks of pedantic lifeless prose, the thought of another session with its endlessly self-justifying manner, the constant descents into echoing bathos, its reduction of historical events and characters into ammunition for a series of rancorous pettifogging disputes with rival scholars – all this suddenly made my impatience topple over into furious physical action.

'We have insufficient data to judge the motive power that lay behind such an ultimately personal decision, despite Professor Harbord-Jones's assertions to the contrary.' I picked the mass of paper up, dropped it on the desk again, lifted it once more, turned my chair towards the window behind me and reached upwards to pull the pane of glass open. Then I stood, in order to be able to achieve what I believe is known in cricketing circles as 'a good length'. I transferred the manuscript to my right hand, holding it balanced precariously on my palm where it must have weighed more than any shot ever putted by an Olympic athlete since the first Athenian games, and propelled the great object out through the window into the quiet of gentle Bloomsbury. I did not look after it; I did not care. At least the thing was gone, separated – I hoped – from me for ever. Pleased, I spun the chair round towards the desk again, picked up the receiver and tried Joan's home number once more. Still engaged. So I shouted, at the top of my not inconsiderable voice: 'Mary!'

She stared at me from the door as if frightened to come too close to the bars of some dangerous animal's cage. Perhaps I looked strange, wild. Perhaps my hair had been tousled alarmingly by the effort of flinging the manuscript. Perhaps there was an odd glint in my eyes and a bright flush in my cheeks: I do not know. 'Mary!' I shouted again. I smiled, or attempted a smile, to show that she had nothing to fear. The struggle was a personal one and could be fought only by me; she need not become involved. 'Mary!' The word rang out through the small office. I lowered my voice. 'Mary,' I said, 'I am leaving for the rest of the day. It's easier for me to do this' – I pointed at the heap of manuscripts, now lower by the considerable thickness of the Palmerston biography – 'at home.'

'What shall I say if anyone rings?' Her question was serious. She still looked frightened, anxious to retreat further from the cage. Poor woman! Soon I would explain it all to her. She deserved to know.

'Tell them to call back on Monday.'

'And John Williams?'

'Good heavens! What about him?'

'If he asks to see you, or needs to speak to you urgently?'

She was trying to protect me. We had never spoken of the
difficulties that had arisen between Williams and myself since
he had come to work here. But Mary knew. As I looked at her
and wondered how best to reply, I realised that she was just
about the only person left whom I could trust. Everyone else
had more powerful exterior motives for their connection with
me. Christina had used me simply as a convenience, a sort of
rest home in which she might recover for a few years before
returning to the excitement of the world. To Edward and
Angelica I was merely a tiresome obstruction. The girl Sarah
had been merely amusing herself, dawdling with a silly,
infatuated, elderly literary man. I wanted to believe Henry but
his love of drama made this almost impossible. Williams,
more simply, loathed my guts. Only Mary was safe. Was that
because, as my secretary, she was paid to be? No, surely it was
more than that. There was affection, even respect. She was my
only conquest. 'Tell him the same,' I said.

She looked worried. 'Can I do anything, Simon? Perhaps if I
told John Williams that you're not feeling well?'

'If you like. Have a good weekend.'

I put on my overcoat, gathered up two of the manuscripts
and jammed them into my briefcase. Then I rushed out of the
room and passed Mary without looking at her. I wanted to get
back to the flat as quickly as possible.

In the hall, by the receptionist's window, there was a small
knot of people. I saw a policeman, still in his helmet, towering
above an elderly couple who looked shaken. The policeman
was talking to the receptionist. He leaned down, almost
knocking his helmet off on the top of her window, and I
noticed with a slight shock that he had in his hands the
dishevelled bulk of the Palmerston biography. I did not push
past them; to have done so might have seemed suspicious. I
walked with what I hoped was a casual air and overheard a
question put to the astonished Janice. 'Is this the property of
somebody in this building? If so, can they explain why it
suddenly descended from a very considerable height towards
this lady and gentleman who were walking on the other side of
the street?'

Janice must have looked quickly through the typed pages
covered with scrawled comment and recognised my writing.
She saw me, called out, 'Simon!' The policeman stepped to

one side and looked at the person whom she had identified as being responsible for the projectile. The couple turned as well, the woman's face twitching in the aftermath of what must have been a terrible shock. I was in trouble. The blasted thing might have killed someone. 'I can't stop now, Janice,' I called out. 'I'm already half an hour late' – and I rushed through the doors, conscious that they might be tempted to give chase.

Not until I had reached the end of the street did I dare to look back. But British justice moves slowly. There was nobody pursuing me. At least, on this occasion, I had escaped. And the rain had started, that persistent but faintly warm spring rain. The Palmerston manuscript had been returned. Surely the wet of the gutter or pavement must have damaged it, and several pages might have been borne away by a gust of wind. With gloom, however, I knew that the author must have at least three copies, one of which would immediately be sent to take the place of the damaged original. No one loses anything these days. Then the laborious editorial work – the cuts and the changes – would have to begin all over again, with the author fighting every inch of the way. Damn!

The tube was almost empty. Passengers stood on the escalators in isolation. I was the only one who walked rapidly down. The journey seemed intolerably slow that day. I wanted to be back to have another chance to telephone Joan. And there were plans to be laid for the morning, which was to bring not only the trip to the Isle of Wight – the beginning of the final confrontation with Bill – but also the opportunity to find out exactly what sort of game Henry was allowing Williams to play with him. Wittgenstein in pictures! Nigel Stokes! 'Camberwell Caprice'! Of course the whole episode was an elaborately planned insult. Of course the Wittgenstein book would be a lamentable failure. And who would be responsible? Williams would murmur something to his masters about the excellence of the original conception and how this had been fatally tarnished by incompetent editing and marketing. Perhaps Freddy and I would be asked to leave together. Or perhaps insulted and robbed of responsibility to such a humiliating extent that, in a fit of temper, we would offer our resignations only to have them immediately but regretfully accepted.

And what could I do? Another job – at over fifty – with this disaster behind me? Then there was the embarrassment of my name and the public breaking of the last family connection with a firm that my ancestors had founded. It was odd that I minded about this. On the Underground train, as we rattled out of Oxford Circus station, I could not help thinking of the way that the disruption represented a personal failure on my part: the failure to fight the challenge of the slick, the philistine and the gimmickry of the Williams era.

The train stopped at Bond Street. The doors crashed open. One of the half dozen or so passengers in my carriage got out: a man in an old mackintosh, carrying a battered brown leather folder. Soon we were off again, away from the lights of the station platform into the dark tunnel. Henry Brown, I saw, was the key; the dubious reliability and steadfastness of Henry Brown. For I was going to fight Williams. There was no question of accepting the sort of fate that he and others were conspiring to force upon me. In the dirty carriage, I rubbed my hands together. I had never thought of myself as combative. Now battle was about to be joined on two fronts: at work and on the more awkward circumstances of my private life and history.

I must see Henry this weekend. With him on my side, refusing – as I hoped he would – to leave me and be looked after by anyone else, Williams could do his damnedest. I was irreplaceable. As the doors opened once more for Marble Arch, I felt pleased: partly because I had, in spite of past doubts, convinced myself of Henry's fundamental decency, of the certainty that I, alone with him, could reach through to this. We understood each other; we were friends, allies against the rest of them. Our weaknesses were the cement of years of partnership and success. He could see the beauty of it all, of this I felt confident.

We were off again, rushing towards Lancaster Gate. Wittgenstein, Wittgenstein, Wittgenstein. The wheels rattled in time to the syllables of the name. What an absurd connection it was. The word brutalisation sprang to mind: the brutalisation of the firm that provided my livelihood, the brutalisation of philosophy, the brutalisation of my family and the standards with which I had begun my life. The fight was

276

on. The crash of the doors at Lancaster Gate seemed, in that moment, to echo the imagined sound of sword upon breast plate, of opposing lances splintering in a great cavalry charge: the real thing this time, not just the fake thud of rubber against rubber of those false tournaments at Erdley. No! Queensway came and went. I scarcely glanced at the rubble-strewn station, turned into temporary chaos and filth by the seemingly interminable programme of repair and improvement. The train slowed for Notting Hill Gate and stopped. I leapt off, ran up the escalator and fumbled frantically for my season ticket. The collector, a large West Indian, looked at me, his mouth open in surprise. I ran out into the drizzle and bounded down Campden Hill towards my home.

The key, as always, was stiff. With a jerk of impatience, I turned it and entered the building, and took the stairs two at a time up to my flat on the first floor. In what Christina had been pleased to call my drawing-room, I dropped my case and went straight to the telephone. I dialled Joan's home number, which, by this time, I knew in my head. Again it was engaged, again I slammed the receiver down.

There comes, after great elation, an inevitable sensation of anti-climax. The blood courses no longer, the mind returns slowly to its usual pace. So it was with me. I took off my overcoat, then sat in my armchair, staring at the narrative picture opposite me by a follower of Augustus Egg. It depicted a scene at a railway station and was called 'Embarkation'. Children clustered around the billowing skirts of their angelic-looking mother; a kindly paternal figure consulted his watch while cheerful deferential porters heaved the baggage through the open compartment door inside which gleamed the inviting shiny red leather and golden fittings of brass. It symbolised the dream of mid-Victorian security: the happy family taking advantage of the mechanical triumphs of the age of steam. And, in my deflated mood, I began to wonder: had my great uncle and I participated in a sham notion of the world and through that sham had we derived some sort of dishonestly achieved comfort? He, a lonely bachelor, I, a deserted husband, had chosen to surround ourselves with such curiously idyllic scenes – or pictures where the suffering or misery, the loneliness, had been used as a part of a smug piece

277

of Victorian didacticism, a threat of what would happen to those who did not behave. And could one see, stretching behind these sermonising canvasses, the hardness of our ancestors' Presbyterianism, the gloom of those Peebles childhoods, the Kirk's hovering threat of damnation?

I looked away towards the nymphs. How sexless they were, how profoundly unerotic, simply a passionless interpretation of some ancient myth. Then the grunts and groans began in the flat below, evidence of a more real lust. I clenched my fists, stood, walked two paces towards the door, ready – at that moment – to storm down and deliver a furious protest; realising the futility, the potential for embarrassment and shame, I stopped, tried to soothe myself and went instead to my desk, reached into the briefcase for one of the manuscripts – the work that recommended a new and supposedly unique system of diet – and began to leaf through its pages. The lists of recommended menus – mostly emphasising such delicacies as dried fruit, steamed vegetables, raw onions and various types of nut – reminded me that I had not eaten since breakfast. I was not hungry yet I felt that my body was in need of fuel or, more important, stimulation. A little alcohol was the thing. The bottles were on the tray. I left my desk, poured some whisky into a glass and went through to the kitchen sink in search of water.

The taste at that time of day – the early afternoon – was fairly unpleasant. Nevertheless the whisky seemed to have an almost immediate effect for my brain began, once more, to operate at fever pitch. I seized the telephone, dialled Joan's number; several rings echoed in my ear and I was about to replace the receiver when someone answered. 'Joan?' I asked.

A snort came from the other end. I was in no mood for prevarication. 'Now look here, Joan,' I said, 'I don't know what you and that Welsh bastard are up to – but I regard any attempt to steal Henry Brown as an act of war. As for this preposterous Wittgenstein book, you know perfectly well that it is just an elaborate plot dreamed up by Williams to get me out of the firm. And don't try to pretend that you're not involved in that as well because I know you are. I also know damn well that you're after my job. I'll be honest, Joan, I used to feel sorry for you, I used to want to help – but, my God, the wool has fallen from my eyes now. You've used our sympathy to promote yourself. Oh yes, you've done it very cleverly, with heart-rending stories about domestic difficulties and latch-key children and all the rest; I admit that. But the time has come to stop. To put aside all the play-acting and the deceit, to show yourself in your true colours . . .'

I stopped, out of breath. And almost immediately a string of unspeakably unpleasant obscenities erupted from the telephone wire, uttered in the shrill, vehement, adolescent tones of a half-broken voice. Falsetto alternated with cracked baritone; the words, and their message, were clear enough. If I did not stop insulting his mother, the speaker and various friends – or mates – of his would come to call, not for social reasons but to impress upon me the strength of their feelings on this delicate matter. And I need not think that he did not know who I was; he knew perfectly well and a few moments' research in the London telephone directory would reveal my address. On second thoughts, he continued, they would come anyway, whether I stopped or not. With a noise that almost broke my ear-drum, the youth replaced the receiver, leaving me standing in a state of speechless shock.

Of course. It was the delinquent son. I knew that he had a history of violence. I looked towards the front door. The youth and his mates could easily obtain entry to the house, either by waiting until one of the other inhabitants went out or by breaking the inadequate lock. At least I should be certain that my flat was secure. Quickly I walked the five or six paces and turned the key in both locks. I was safe.

Another drink was needed. Once again the taste was unpleasant but the effect encouraging. I returned to the chair by the telephone, still restless. A thought came to me; naturally I should send for the police if these young hooligans gave trouble. But what stage had the investigation into the matter of the flying Palmerston manuscript reached? Janice had recognised my scribbles and scrawls. Presumably the elderly couple would be able to point to the direction from which the object had come; then, as surely as snow melts in the heat, the window of my office must emerge as the source of the assault. If this had occurred, the police were perhaps on the way already in a car with sirens and flashing lights, determined to stamp on this new outbreak of urban terrorism: the bombarding of innocent civilians with heavy dull historical biographies.

There was still the question of tomorrow. I needed, above all, to be sure of my facts. Angelica, for instance. Was the story that the Erdley girl had told me merely a rumour? I wanted proof. The whisky burned my throat slightly as I swallowed some more. From below came the muffled pants and howls, reminders of crazed youthful passion. I had sat down again, beside the telephone, and picked up my small leather-bound address book that had my initials stamped in gold on the cover: a present from Christina in the early days of our friendship. Impatiently I flipped through the thick pages until the letter E had been reached; then dialled the number of the hideous stately home.

I looked at my watch as the ringing tone began. I had a vague notion of the way that the Erdleys organised their lives. It was the early afternoon. Lunch would be over; he might already be closeted with some publicity adviser or showman in the dark, panelled study, seated behind the huge desk, a symbol of late Victorian imperial pomposity, as they thrashed out a new system of car parking or the plans for some advertising stunt. And she? The telephone rang on. I imagined the harsh bell muffled by the vast distances of that unspeakable house, trailing away into insignificance as it tinkled vainly down the long unheated passages, dying among the varnished beams of the dim high ceilings. Probably she was resting, curled upstairs on a sofa in their bedroom in front of an electric fire, a copy of *Emma* open at her side as she skimmed through the glossy pages of an illustrated fashion magazine.

'Hello?' It was a man's voice. I asked to speak to Sarah Erdley. 'Who is it?' He sounded nervous. I recognised the hesitant manner of Jeremy, the young master. I gave my name. 'She's left me.' The words were slurred. And I realised that, like George Mason, Jeremy Erdley was drunk far too early in the day.

I wondered if he might be in the grip of fantasy. 'Shall I ring again, around tea time?' I asked.

'No.' Jeremy Erdley succeeded in untangling his words. 'You haven't understood. She has left me. Sarah has left me.'

'Left you?'

'Yes. She has gone.'

'I am sorry.' I could think of nothing to add. 'Where to?' I asked.

'Nowhere.' He was breathing deeply at the other end of the line. 'I mean, she hasn't moved out of the house or anything. It's not so simple as that. No. She comes home to spend time with the child every evening. But most nights and a large part of the day, she's away. I think it's the end this time. The end of us together.' I thought I detected a break in his voice. But he recovered. 'I blame that damned publisher.'

Obviously my name had not registered. 'Why?'

'He rents one of the cottages down here and introduces these weird types into the neighbourhood. Sarah has always had a weakness for books – for writers and all that sort of thing. And now this man comes along . . .'

'The publisher?'

'No. The publisher's friend. I can't remember his name. He's writing a book in the cottage. The publisher – Simon somebody – gives Sarah his name, or gives her name to him, I can't remember which. And before you can say Jack Robinson, they're as thick as thieves. Or thicker. They read poetry to each other in the woods. By moonlight. Do you see what I mean?'

I interrupted. 'Jeremy . . .'

'I've only met the fellow once, or is it twice? Rather large. Silent. He has a sort of dumb insolence. Of course I daresay I can manage on my own. But what about the child?'

'Jeremy,' I said, 'I am the publisher, the man who has allowed Michael Docherty to borrow the cottage.'

'Are you indeed?' He did not sound at all surprised. 'Well, you can see what a hole you've landed me in.'

'Will you let me speak to your wife?'

'I told you. She's out. Let me ask you something.' A note of ill-temper had entered his voice, driving out the lugubrious self-pity. 'Let me ask you something. How would you like to have to face the quarter finals of the south-eastern area hang gliding championships alone?'

I felt it was not a position that I was ever likely to find myself in, alone or otherwise. 'I'm really very sorry . . .'

'No. You answer me. How would you like it? Because that is what I shall have to do. Here. Tomorrow afternoon.'

'Jeremy,' I said, 'I would like to talk to Sarah. I may be able to help. Surely you must remember me. Simon, the father of Edward and Angelica. I've had the cottage for years. Your father let it to me. My children are friends of yours and of your wife. Angelica and Sarah shared a flat in London.' I laughed. 'It's a long-standing connection.'

At first he did not reply. I wondered if he might have gone away or fallen off his chair or perhaps even passed out. At last he said, in a much more intense and angry voice, 'Well, you've really landed me in the shit now, haven't you?' The anger grew. 'Yes you bloody well have.' The voice ascended, the emotion pushing it further off course. 'And don't think that I don't know the sort of things your bloody family gets up to. You leave us alone! You come down here – a bloody sponger, a parasite on our backs, always grumbling and complaining about the blasted cottage which we give you for practically nothing. My God, you've got a nerve. One hell of a nerve. And how dare you say that your children are friends of mine! They most certainly are not. I wouldn't have your daughter in the house. She's a whore for a start, with that step-father of hers. Everyone knows, oh yes, but you just stand and watch, don't you? Too yellow to do anything about it. Or is he paying you money – is that it? I think he may be, I think he's got you on the pay roll as well, you damned, dirty, disgusting, oily creep. Well, let me tell you this. If you ever show your face down here again, I'll have you run out of the county. And you can forget the arrangement about the cottage. The lease, the rent, the agreement, everything, is cancelled. The lot! And from now. So get out!'

And he was gone, leaving me holding the telephone receiver. I told myself that I felt sorry for the boy.

XXVII

Henry telephoned, fairly late – although I had lost track of the time by then.

Outside it was dark. I had not drawn the curtains. From below there was silence. I must have drifted off to sleep in my armchair. The sound of the bell woke me with a jolt. My first thought was that Joan's boy and his gang had arrived, as they had promised. I reached down to the grate and seized the poker which lay in front of the false fireplace. At least I would put up a fight. Vague memories of unarmed combat instruction from my national service days coursed through my mind. Did one kick an opponent on the shins? Or was the knee in the groin more effective?

After a few seconds I was calm. It was only the telephone. I rose, somewhat unsteadily, and walked to the desk.

'Are you ready for the morning?' Henry's voice was excited. 'I have a plan. You should not take your car. No. Your mind ought to be entirely occupied with the best way to approach the problems that await us on the Isle of Wight. Therefore I have been in touch with a reputable organisation and hired a neat little motor in which I shall pick you up at approximately half past nine. Does that satisfy you?'

'Henry, I must ask you something. Williams has just told me that Joan is taking over responsibility for your work. I know he wants to prise you away from me . . .'

'*A demain*, my dear. *Au revoir!*'

Damn! My head was starting to hurt.

XXVIII

'I suppose you're very angry with me.'

Henry drove slowly, reluctant to leave traffic lights, coasting along the straight flat roads. Lorries passed us, the faces of their drivers often tense with impatience at the funny looking bald man in a small yellow hired car. This morning the sun had appeared: a watery pale sun. Henry seemed cheery. 'I suppose you're angry with me, Simon,' he repeated.

'Why should I be?'

'About the temporary transfer. To that woman whose name I can never remember.'

'Joan.'

'That's right. Joan. Rather a sad person, I think, don't you? One feels sympathy for her. Surely you don't begrudge her a momentary increase in responsibility?'

'Is that all it is?'

'Whoever told you that anything else had been contemplated?' Henry turned towards me and gave one of his lightning smiles. 'You and I have worked together for so long. Is it twenty years, or perhaps more? Remember the old days with George Mason? We had fun then.' He arranged his face into a severe expression and lowered the pitch of his voice. 'What did the old boy used to say? "An author's words are sacred. But that doesn't mean that I haven't committed sacrilege in my time by crossing out several thousand of them." Ha! The old scamp.' Henry giggled. A van hooted as it passed, dangerously swerving out of the way of the oncoming

284

traffic. Henry returned the hoot. 'The battle has begun,' he said.

'Williams had me rattled,' I began.

'Rattled? Good heavens, why on earth. . . . That bumptious Welshman! But, my dear boy, think of the fearful mess they'd all be in without you. It doesn't bear thinking of. There's your name for a start. In your veins runs the blood of the founder!' At first I thought he might be teasing. But his face was serious as he steered us on to the beginnings of a fast trunk road.

'That means nothing to a man like Williams. Do you know what he wants the firm to be?' I told him about the sauna bath manual and the plans for the aphrodisiac cook book. 'And take this rubbish about Wittgenstein for instance.' I explained the plan for the picture book about the philosopher. 'But the thinking behind that is deeper,' I went on. 'They – or rather Williams – want it to fail. First he wishes to separate me from you. Then saddle me with the responsibility for Wittgenstein. Then spend thousands of pounds on the project. Then watch the thing turn into the most gigantic flop. Then give me the sack! Do you see?'

'Simon, aren't you being a little paranoiac?' Henry turned his head slightly towards me so that I caught a glimpse of his humorous eyes. 'I mean, it is the most tremendously expensive way of getting rid of you. And you've been telling me that Mr Williams is desperate to make money in order to please his masters. To lose a small fortune on a book about a Cambridge philosopher of whom they have probably never heard is a curious way of trying to impress them.'

'But who are our masters now?'

'Those faceless business men in Upper Brook Street.'

'No. Or rather perhaps.' I laughed. 'We're just about to be taken over.'

'Simon,' Henry suddenly asked, 'do you suspect me of duplicity?'

'Should I?'

'What could be your reasons?'

'People tell one things,' I said. 'For example, Williams tells me that you have no objection to being looked after by Joan. That you raised not a murmur of protest. That you told him

285

how sympathetic and efficient you found her . . .'

'The arrangement is temporary. But one must make the best of it,' Henry interrupted.

'Henry . . .' I began.

'You talk about being deserted,' he went on, his voice rising. 'How do you think I felt when you never made an attempt to get in touch with me about this party?'

'The party has nothing to do with me. It was arranged behind my back. There you are,' I said triumphantly. 'That's another example of the sort of game that they're playing.'

He slowed the car down even more and looked at me again. 'Why do you set such store by our connection? I don't understand. Both you and I know that you don't admire my work.'

'That is not true.'

'Now please give me credit for at least a modicum of perception! A series of pot boilers, culminating in this latest one about South America. Hardly literary publishing, is it? Not in the same league as the Irish gentleman whom you are so keen to promote.'

'How on earth do you know about him?'

'Mr Williams. Oh, I stuck up for you, Simon. I said that I was sure that the Irishman would turn out to be a worthwhile investment. Williams seemed less certain. You must show me some of his work.'

I decided to be frank. 'Henry,' I said, 'it's not true to say that I don't admire your books. I do. We must have worked together long enough for you to be able to see that. But there is another aspect of our connection which has become very important to me. You see, you are in a sense my insurance policy. While I look after you – and while you continue to insist that I look after you – neither Williams nor anyone else in the firm can touch me. But leave me – and I am at their mercy. Do you see?'

It was a humiliating performance, or should have been. Had I been told a month or even a week ago that I was going to have to reveal the extent of my dependence upon this odd little man whom I had mocked so often in the past, I would have been horrified. Yet the confession had slipped out easily. Was this because of Henry Brown's essential greatness? The plea, if

286

made to a great artist, should surely bring no sense of shame.

'What am I supposed to say to that?' Henry asked.

'Now you know how dependent I am on your goodwill.'

'Goodwill?'

'Yes. I don't want to call it loyalty.'

'Why ever not? Don't be afraid, Simon. Don't be afraid.'

'Loyalty implies a certain obligation,' I said. 'I should hate to impose that on you, or on anyone.'

'But you expect it. Loyalty, I mean.'

'From my friends, I suppose . . .'

'Ah!' Henry raised one hand from the steering wheel in order to emphasise his point. 'But what about from your lovers? When Christina left, was that disloyalty? When Laura left, was that disloyalty?'

'I wouldn't use the word in that context.'

'Why ever not?'

'You make it sound the equivalent of a life sentence.'

'A life sentence? Oh, come now, Simon! You are hard on yourself.' His fat brown fingers grabbed the upper part of my right arm. 'At any rate, you can be sure of me.'

The trip was crazy, of course.

It fulfilled different needs for both of us. I had to show Williams how close I was to Henry: how he chose to spend one of his rare weekends in England in my company. And for Henry, there was the delightful prospect of observing yet another example of human folly. Yet I was glad to have him with me. I don't think I could have made the journey alone. Once on the island, of course, I would go to the villa without Henry. Bill and I would meet – just the two of us – without Laura or any member of my family. I expected a courteous hearing.

Henry babbled on, about Paul, about their troubles with the Portuguese. 'Simon,' he declared at one point, 'what a relief to be away, only for a few days, of course. It's the Engish climate that makes life impossible here. But would you be shocked if I told you that I still regard this country as my home?'

And with an inward sigh, I remembered Laura's words about him. 'Henry exhausts me, darling,' she had once said.

'He really exhausts me.'

We reached the island in time for lunch. Henry was full of
excitement. 'I want to visit Tennyson's house,' he said, 'and
walk on those wonderful downs. But first things first. We
must eat. Then you should be on your way. You rang them
yesterday?'

'No.' I made up an excuse. 'I thought surprise would be
more effective. They're sure to be there.'

We stopped at a pub in a village near Bembridge. The bar
was crowded, full of men in large heavy cardigans and
laughing women. There was an air of cheeriness; in the
background piped music provided a series of remorselessly
catchy melodies. A pall of cigarette and pipe smoke hung over
the scene. We ordered: two pints of beer, a pork pie for me and
two long sausages for Henry. As we carried our plates and
glasses across to a small empty circular table, pushing our way
through the other customers, I realised that this would be the
first time that I had eaten since breakfast the day before. Yet
the flavourless pie was not welcome, and the smell of Henry's
sausages made me feel slightly sick. Was I ill?

We sat and Henry, having moved his stool so that it was
almost touching mine, suddenly took my hand and placed it
on the front of his jacket in the place where I imagined his heart
might be. 'Feel that,' he said. 'Go on. Feel it!'

Too surprised to protest, I rumpled the surface of the jacket
with my fingers, which closed over the outline of something
hard, with a jagged and irregular shape. 'What on earth. . . !'

'That's right. I thought you might like to know. I generally
have it with me now. Our little Portuguese sold it to us. He
has contacts in Marseilles, I believe. Really the little man is
rather disreputable. But that suits us as well, you know. On
the Côte one meets these curiously violent outbursts of –
passion, if you like. One might use the word machismo. In
many ways it is a more primitive society than that of the
northern races. People are shot, done away with, for the most
meagre reasons. For example – if one forgot to tip the dustman
at Christmas. . . !' Henry raised his hands, the palms facing
towards me and the small neat fingers splaying outwards.

'Don't be so ridiculous,' I said.

'It's true! The Portuguese with his unsavoury reputation acts as the equivalent of a guard dog. Much better than any Alsatian, and more useful as well because he happens to be a hard-working gardener and has a wife who cooks. We have not enquired too closely into his reasons for leaving Portugal. He says that he wished to find more lucrative employment and send francs back to his relations in their village in the north. I doubt the truth of that. My belief is that Luis is on the run.'

'But aren't you breaking the law by harbouring him?'

Henry smiled. 'I am merely an ignorant foreigner,' he said.

'And in the mean time this man supplies you with guns?'

'A gun.' He patted his pocket. 'Would you like to borrow it? This afternoon, an encounter on the doorstep with Laura's husband, the flourishing of the weapon . . .'

'Henry,' I whispered, 'have you gone mad?'

'Oh, don't misunderstand me, my dear. I'm not for one moment suggesting that you use the thing. Anyway the silly little man forgot to pack any ammunition so the chamber – as I believe it is called – is empty. But you might find that if you were to produce the weapon at an apposite moment, old Bill – it is Bill, isn't it? – could become rather more expansive and truthful than might otherwise have been the case. And that's what you're after, isn't it – the truth?'

'I've never heard a more crazy idea.' I sat back, feeling relieved. Henry, in such an excitable mood, might have been capable not only of producing the pistol in the saloon bar but also of letting it off. 'Did you want to give him the perfect excuse for calling the police and getting rid of me?'

Henry lifted his pint glass to his lips and drank about a quarter of it. He let out his breath, smacked his lips in an unattractive way. 'Perhaps,' he said. 'One more thing.' He delved once more into the inside pocket of his jacket. My anxiety returned – but he produced only a scrap of paper. 'Read this.' He passed the letter across.

I unfolded it and saw, from the signature at the bottom, that the sender was Williams.

Dear Henry (it ran)

I was glad to have had the opportunity of a talk with you

289

this morning. I feel sure that you will be happy with Joan. She is one of the best fiction editors in London and I am confident that the two of you will work well together.

We spoke briefly about the future. You will, I am sure, understand that from time to time changes occur in the structure and personnel of a company such as ours. But our determination to publish you successfully and to the mutual advantage of both parties will always be a central part of our operations. I was speaking no more than the truth when I told you the great value that we put on having you on our list. That is why I was pleased to be able to set your mind at rest about the various worries that you had.

Please feel free to contact me personally at any time if you feel that I can help. In the meantime, after the signing of the new contract and guarantees, I look forward to a relation-ship between you and the firm that may transcend the successes of the past.

Yours sincerely
John Williams

'Henry,' I said, 'why are you showing me this letter?'

'Why ever not? I wanted you to know the position.'

'And the position is that you came to the office without telling me, had a secret meeting with Williams and worked out a blue-print for your future riches and my redundancy. That – to judge from what is said here' – I held up the letter with one hand and banged it sharply with the other – 'would appear to be the position.'

'Not quite,' said Henry.

'Look, does it give you pleasure – this business of humili-ating, possibly bankrupting, an old friend by seeing that he loses his job?'

'May I explain what happened?' Henry was amused, which irritated me even more. 'The point is that I insisted in writing into the contract a clause that you must, as long as you are fit to be so – and I am to be the judge of whether you are or not – continue to be my editor. There must be no question of a permanent change, I said – purely a temporary arrangement with this Joan person while you are occupied with the Wittgenstein book to which, it seems, Mr Williams attaches great importance.'

'You had that written into the contract?'

'Yes. As a memorandum of wishes. They could not refuse.' Henry smiled. 'I know the extent of my bargaining powers. And I handled this one myself, without any help from agents or anything. I rather enjoy the tension of a detailed negoti- ation! We went through the clauses one by one. He tried to pull the wool over my eyes and claimed to be under great pressure because of the take-over bid. He wants to get you out, you know, he really does. Oh yes – Joan is his protegée and he says she has such good commercial sense. Apparently he wishes to make her editorial director before the end of this year. Are they. . . ? I wonder. His voice became positively lyrical when he spoke of her and her exceptional ability. And he says she has such confidence and is longing to take on more work, once what they both call "the dead wood" has been cleared away. And he admires her impatience, the way she keeps pushing! Williams and she will run the place – that seems to be the idea.' Henry giggled. 'But I was more than a match for him, I assure you. Remember that I began life as a lawyer. And the man has no charm, so I was unlikely to be seduced by his personality. What a change from dear old George Mason! Of course in those days the business side of things could be left entirely to my agent, a man called Lumley.'

I put my glass down on the small round table, reached across and grabbed the little man's hand. 'Henry,' I said, 'you've just saved my bloody life! And to think that I imagined that you too had turned against me.'

'Anything to help, my dear. Anything at all.'

XXIX

Laura and I had taken a boat trip together.

It was in the early days of our courtship. Briefly, for those six months between our meeting again in London – after the West Country summer – and our wedding, we restored what had happened when Robin had brought me to the Conways' house.

We turned London into a city of romance. The skeleton of this was a series of trips to hidden wonders: to curious chapels, out-of-the-way churches and sets of almshouses, to the lesser-known sights behind the rush of the streets. I was diligent in my researches, learned about the obscure sect that had worshipped here, the great man who had raised his town house there, the extraordinary use to which a set of stables had been put – many times threatened and converted until there was nothing left but an ornamental doorway, a dusty fanlight, one pillar of a set of domineering gates. How receptive she had been! I talked on, the words rushing out, the knowledge gathering itself into clusters of facts which linked to form a great chain of historic truth. All dreams, mere dreams! Or so it seems to me now.

Once, on an unusually warm Saturday, she said, 'I want to go on the river.' So we took a pleasure boat down to Greenwich, with several hundred other people who had had the same idea. I was amused by her contrary demands. First she wanted to stand on deck; then she thought it would be better to sit; then she wanted a drink, only to change her mind and decide that, in the heat, an ice cream would be better. The ice cream made her thirsty so, on third thoughts, a glass of sticky orangeade – a taste that she had retained from her childhood – must be the answer. 'Please get me one!' she implored, her brown face wrinkled into the desperate look of a pathetic urchin of the streets. She saw my amusement, the delight I took in her perversity. And when I returned with the bottle of orangeade with a straw sticking out of its top, having pushed and stood and been abused by other passengers clustered impatiently around an inadequately manned refreshment counter, we laughed together, Laura suddenly clutching me in a giggling embrace. 'Poor Simon. How desperate!' Those were her words.

Greenwich in high summer. Even the trees looked exhausted, their leaves limp in the ponderous humidity. We walked towards the college, across the shimmering expanse of green. Her clothes were sensibly thin – a white plain blouse, a cream skirt, a thin brown belt around her waist – and her short hair bobbed in time to the shaking of her head as she talked, full of what I hoped was more than self-delight. Beside a tree, its branches shielding us from the sun (was it a chestnut or perhaps a plane?), we kissed. I thought ahead, to what I was sure must be the epic of our life – for we both already knew that we would marry each other – of how extraordinary it was that I, in this moment in the middle of the twentieth century, should be so free, so ecstatic. She pulled me closer. 'Now,' she murmured, 'let's do it now.' And I laughed, took my mouth away and caught a glimpse of disdain, of disenchantment or sulky petulance in the look vanishing from her face. 'Coward!' The word was almost bitter. Then she laughed as well. I wonder how she would have reacted if I had sunk with her on to the baking grass. Nothing could have stopped us, except my feeling for convention.

We made the most of the rest of the day. We visited the chapel, the naval museum and studied the great painted ceiling. 'What a sense of theatre!' I remarked. 'Grand – but a little strained. Yet, as decoration, it works.' She nodded, glanced at me and made a reference to some aspect of her studies at the college of art. And the evening came. The best moments were always those of premonition, of anticipated joy. Yet I felt sure we were on the brink of the time of our lives. At last it would be possible to know feeling and beauty, to be a participant in a world one had previously only guessed at and envied.

XXX

'Tell me, did you love the girl?'

Henry was asking me a question. We had finished our food. I was lingering over the remains of my beer, anxious to put off the business until the last possible moment. Henry, I knew, would push me into it when the time came.

I thought instinctively of Laura. 'Yes,' I said. Then I realised that he must be thinking of someone else. 'That is . . .' I began.

'Did you sleep with her often?'

It was Christina. 'Occasionally.'

'The stately home must have been rather odd.'

'Stately home?'

'Where she and her husband live. How did he take to being cuckolded?'

At last I saw that he was referring to the Erdley girl. 'Oh, her,' I said. 'Good heavens, no. I didn't love her.'

'But you slept with her?' Henry let out another of his lightning smiles.

'Never.'

'What were you doing together when she told you all this stuff about Bill and your daughter?'

'Walking in the woods.'

'Is that all? You told me that she is very beautiful. But of course you are a romantic, Simon. And a man of chivalry. No, I can imagine that you were simply walking together.'

'We kissed,' I said, 'but only briefly.'

'I see.' Henry became thoughtful. 'And which one of you was reluctant to take it further? You?'

'She is much younger,' I began.

'And she told you about Angelica and Bill?'

'Yes.'

'The malicious little minx.'

'So you think their affair should have been protected? You think that the man should have been left to do whatever he wanted – with a girl young enough to be his daughter? Is that why you chose to tell me nothing about what you saw when they all came to visit you in the south of France? Is that why?' I was angry. He had let me down after all.

'I had only a hunch, Simon. I think I told you that. Just a question of an exchange of glances, the hint of a conspiratorial laugh. No concrete evidence, as they say. Would it really have been right of me to have agitated you – perhaps unnecessarily – with the result of my intuition, which is by no means infallible? Naturally I mentioned it when you said that you had received more reliable information from another source. Or is that source reliable?' He looked at me, his face alert.

'Angelica and Sarah Erdley were great friends. They used to share a flat together.'

'Oh, I see. Would your daughter have confided in her?'

'At one stage, yes.'

'About so intimate and – one must admit – disgraceful business as an involvement with her step-father?'

'It is possible.'

'There is a curious paradox here,' Henry said. 'You try to seduce one young girl . . .'

'No!' I interrupted.

'You try to seduce one young girl,' he went on, raising his voice to override my protest, 'and she tells you a story about two people who have involved themselves in a similar situation . . .'

'No!'

'A difference being, of course, that in the case of Angelica the seduction seems to have been successful.'

'But Angelica is my daughter!'

'Precisely,' Henry said smoothly. 'And that undoubtedly makes it all most upsetting – or more upsetting than if the girl involved had had no connection with you.'

And Angelica – was she going to be helped by this? Was it fair to her? All I might succeed in doing was to tear apart a carefully stitched pattern of lives. What if there was love between them: between Bill and our daughter, between Laura and Bill, between Laura and Angelica? It was possible. An Oxford philosopher could probably prove that this state was desirable, for all that was missing was a certain strand of knowledge: the knowledge that Bill and Angelica were having an affair. Keep this out and the three of them were contented, satisfied. Bring it in and everyone must start to take up new positions, to show horror and shame.

My God, I thought: what will happen if they are both in love with him? Laura, in her invalid condition, with her laboured breathing, her bad leg, the dark glasses that she wore to stop the sun bringing pain to her fragile eyes: she might still be in love with Bill. And Angelica, so full of the tips and inside information, of the coarse ambitions and toughness of his success and his world – so full of these that whenever we met they poured out of her like rain water from a leaking tank – Angelica too was probably caught.

So it worked, this arrangement. With her illness, Laura was only half a wife – or so Bill could argue. And instead of straying far, instead of involving himself with another woman who would demand more, he took up with her daughter, almost in an educative way. He was careful, he might defend himself by saying, to ensure that there was always a certain distance between them. No ridiculous declarations or promises were allowed; in fact most of the talk was of Laura, of her qualities, her health, the pitiable state in which bad luck had landed her. Under such a smokescreen, in which Bill and Angelica could delude both each other and themselves, another romance had begun. I must break the illusion. But as I walked alone through the small wooden gateway that divided Bill's property off from the road and tramped across the gravel of the short drive towards the red brick front of the large house, I was, at least, honest enough to see that this was an act of selfishness.

I mounted the two steps in front of the heavy black front door and pressed the bell. Almost immediately the door

297

opened, to reveal the tall figure of Bill in light grey slacks, an open-necked yellow shirt and a dark blue jersey. His face, thin and brown, peered out at me. The top of his head, as he leaned forward, was pink. Then I noticed his eyes. Flecked with red, they glistened with the remains of tears. 'Come in,' he said. And he shook my hand, a little limply. 'You were quick.'

We walked together into the hall. I was too surprised to speak. Had Henry telephoned? Had I been followed? He spoke again. 'She died last night.'

'But, Bill,' I began.

'Laura died late last night.' The repetition was slow. He was not looking at me but down at the brown carpet in the hall. I stepped back. My legs touched a tall vase which contained an array of walking sticks. Up against it there rested two tennis rackets, neatly clipped into presses. I looked down, as if to study these remnants of their old life. 'Please come in.'

The drawing-room faced the garden; the sun poured through the large French windows. I remembered the over-cleaned bright seascape of a brig in full sail that took up virtually the whole of one cream-painted wall; the heavy sofas and chairs covered in colourful expensive chintz; then, over the wooden chimney piece, an odd hint of the exotic with the incongruous placing of one of Percy Conway's still-lifes. On the round table to one side of the windows lay the daily papers and some magazines: the pink of the *Financial Times*, a weekly guide for investors, a journal to do with sailing. 'Bill,' I began again.

'Please, Simon.' We were standing together by the windows. I looked out at the flat lawn stretching away to the wire that surrounded the tennis court at its end. 'Let me explain.'

We sat together on the sofa that was nearest to the windows, one of which was open to let in a chilling draught of early spring sea air. Bill clasped his left knee, then relaxed his hands, shifted a little towards me.

He began slowly, keeping his eyes on the pitching ship in the vast picture. 'She was here the whole of yesterday. She had come down on Thursday evening from London, driven by my chauffeur. Did you know that she could no longer drive? That started three or four months ago. She couldn't be trusted

298

in a car. Her eyes, you know.' He paused, frowned and cleared his throat. His voice was deeper than usual. 'Nothing else. Simply her eyes.' I supposed that this was to tell me that the drinking had not worsened towards the end. 'She came down here on Thursday evening. Mrs Miles was there. Tim, the chauffeur, and Mrs Miles saw her into the house. I'm sorry.' He checked himself, brought his left arm sharply on to his knee. 'Mrs Miles is our cook. You wouldn't know that. How could you?'

'Bill . . .'

'No.' He shook his head. 'Let me tell you. They helped her in. The stairs here are a little steep. But she didn't want to go to her room straight away. She asked for a light supper: a poached egg, I think. There was no sign of any trouble. I rang from London and spoke to her at about half past seven. I had to go out to dinner with some Japanese. No.' He shook his head again. 'They were Koreans . . .'

'Bill.' At last he had stopped and turned towards me. He had stopped, I saw, because he was crying. 'Bill,' I repeated, 'where is she? What have you done with her?'

He stood and beckoned to me. I followed him out of the drawing-room, up the wide wooden staircase which Laura had found too steep, and on to the dark first floor. In the bedroom, the curtains were drawn, the sun scarcely piercing the darkness.

Bill turned on the lights. I saw a shape in the large double bed, under the blankets with a white sheet pulled up so as to cover it. This was her room. There were clothes piled on a chair by the dressing table: a blue dress, a black jacket, the smart aftermath of the days in London. Against a wall, to one side of the dressing table, away from the windows, rested a long low bookcase. Instinctively, with the curiosity of a book man, I noticed some of the titles: Hudson, Williamson, several thick anthologies. Bill must have read these to her. Had his voice betrayed a lack of appreciation, a belief that this stuff was a waste of time?

I looked back towards the bed, then once more into the room. There were photographs: three or four stuck underneath the glass on the surface of the dressing table. From where we stood, they were indistinct. In one, someone was

waving; in another a child was perched on a woman's knee.
Then I saw – in a variety of frames, on small side tables, on top
of the cream-coloured chimney piece, marshalled occasionally
in groups and in other places standing alone – other memen-
toes of her past: attempts to preserve a single moment. The
children were the chief subjects: the children and Bill.

This may be all that is left of Laura in a hundred years, I
thought. Her descendants will see the photographs and think:
wasn't she beautiful when she was young, weren't her
children charming? Of course the first marriage ended in
divorce. But what about this man in the open-necked shirt
standing on the deck of a boat grinning with pride and
pleasure? Who was he? Someone will think a little, then
remember. Bill, he or she will say: the second husband. They
had no children together, no lineal descent to perpetuate their
love.

'Everything is in order,' Bill said.

I turned towards him. We were both still, waiting for the
other. 'What will you do?' I asked.

'Everything is in order,' he repeated. 'The doctor has been.
The other people as well. They're coming back this evening.'

I presumed that he meant the undertakers, the men who
were to dispose of the body. 'Where will she be buried?' I
asked.

'Here,' he said. 'She loved this place. Come closer.'

We walked together over to the bed. With a quick move that
startled me Bill jerked at the sheet, which rolled back to reveal
her face. I had forgotten the lines, the disappointed angle of the
mouth. At least the eyes were closed. Someone had swept the
grey hair back away from the forehead and temples so that I
could see the full expanse of her brow. 'Is that peace?' Bill
asked. He replaced the sheet and her face was gone.

'How did you know I was coming?' I asked.

'I told Angelica to give you the news.'

'I had heard nothing.'

'Then why. . . ?'

'Is she on her way down?' I asked.

'Yes, with Edward. He caught the early flight. She's picking
him up at Heathrow.' Bill drew his lips together. He seemed
infinitely sad. 'But I told them to get hold of you. So how did

you know?'

'I didn't.'

Bill's eyes were gentle, oddly tender. 'Simon – the fact that you came, that you arrived this morning without any sort of warning – I mean, could one give it some sort of divine interpretation? I wanted you to be here. After all, you knew her as well as any of us, perhaps even better because you saw her as a child, then as a girl and as a woman. I've always envied you that: the fact that you had an early glimpse of Laura at home, that you knew her father. I never met him. He must have been extraordinary. I'm sure the time will come when he will be appreciated as an artist . . .'

'It won't.'

'Won't it? Oh well, I expect you would know. Please, let's go down.'

On the stairs I thought: I must say it, I must not run away. Then we were back in the drawing room, with the sun and the huge picture of the sailing ship. 'Bill,' I began, 'my presence here is not accidental . . .'

Again we sat beside each other on the sofa. Bill crossed his legs, looked away, dabbed at his eyes with a crumpled white handkerchief. 'I know what you want,' he said, his voice constricted. 'Our bid for your company is worrying you. I'm not surprised.'

'This may not be the time . . .' I had begun to retreat.

He went on, now more definite. 'No, I want to explain myself. I should have spoken to you before, but the truth is, Simon, I find the matter embarrassing. Yet now' – he pointed at the ceiling – 'we must talk because no deception, no misunderstanding, should be allowed to gather around her name. We wanted you to be safe. One day Laura had lunch with you and you told her about your troubles at work. And I said: can't we do something for Simon? After all, to me – and you probably have never realised this – there has always been a . . .' – he stopped, stared at me, then looked away as he searched through his grief for the word – 'a mystique attached to your business and your name. Simon, it's not so much the way the firm is now – but more the whole history, the idea of greatness, of tradition. Do you see? Of course I'm wrong. There had to be toughness, rigid accounting procedures, hard

301

negotiations. But that had dropped away. Only the history remains.' Bill raised his hands. 'There's a sort of purity to it all. I mean, if you knew some of the people that I have to deal with, everyday! Can you see? I'm speaking about contrasts – yet also about what I've missed and would have liked to have known.'

'I don't understand you.'

'No, don't condemn me, or laugh, at least not too quickly!' The tears had given way to an almost manic excitement. 'You see, the take-over is about you. Oh, of course there are commercial considerations as well. And why not? It's potentially a very profitable group. But my idea is also to preserve something: a piece of civilisation, if you like, an entity that can contribute to an educated Englishman's idea of his past. I say past. But that's nonsense. Why shouldn't such standards, such values, survive? One thinks of your line of great writers, your family's connections with Tennyson, Thackeray, George Eliot, Conrad, Wells . . .'

I blushed. 'It's not quite the same today . . .'

'Why not make it so? Why not change the business? I've always been an advocate of constructive change.' Bill smiled. He made a gesture of indulgence with his left hand, gently raising it in the air and then letting it fall again on to his knee. 'We'll write in some terms, when the take-over has gone through. I want you to be editorial director of your company, with complete power to choose whatever books you want to publish. And I don't want you to worry too much about profit or return. Just get the best. You'll know where to find it. Pay well, better than anyone else. And they'll come to you!' He clenched his right fist, shook it at me before allowing the hand to relax. His voice became caught up again in emotion. 'We could have the best in London, in the English-speaking world! The greatest line of writers, think of that! I know, you know, that after death, there can come a resurrection.'

'Bill . . .'

'No, wait. Before you turn me down, before you leave, remember her part in it. I want this. Laura wanted it as well. But – may I be frank with you? – she took a more personal line than I do. Her chief concern was you: your future, your survival in the trade that you know best. Naturally I was sorry

302

for you as well. Of course I was. But I was thinking of the broader aspect. I wanted to preserve something. No, that's not quite right, that's too rigid, too unimaginative if you like, too backward-looking. No, I wanted to restore your company to what it had been. Is that foolish, is that crazy?' Bill's eyes were dry, shining this time with excitement, even passion.

'It may be impossible,' I said.

'Why?' He let out a strange loud laugh. 'If I'm the owner, I can do what I like. If some of my shareholders kick up, I'll simply take the firm out of the group and make it my personal property, which I assure you I can afford to do. And as for the losses, well – as you may imagine – someone in my position can always make good use of those. But I want to talk to you about so many other things, now that it's all over' – he pointed again up at the ceiling – 'before the children arrive. As I said, I see a divine intervention – in your coming today, in the way that you walked up to the house unannounced. You know, if you'd warned me it would have been worse. Then I would have had time to think, to reason with myself, to conclude that this – the first morning without her – was not the right time.'

'I came because I wanted to say something as well . . .' I began.

Bill held up a large hand. 'Simon, let me try to do this. It's terribly important. First there's the whole question of virtue. Do I make myself clear?'

'No.'

'Of course I don't.' He screwed up his face, let the edges of his mouth drop down in a look of desperate concentration. His right hand reached out, beat in time to the syllables of the elusive words. 'I tried to do my utmost to create a climate of virtue, of honesty and decency for my family. This was always to be separate from my work, untainted by what I have sometimes had to do. Not that I have much to be ashamed of compared to some other people! But when you begin in the way that I began, you take advantage of your competitors' weaknesses. You push, push, push the whole time. It's not dishonesty, more a certain ruthlessness, a blindness to certain ideals. But this should – or so I thought – always be set off against a personal or private decency and generosity. You know about my charity work, the way that I give money through the foundation. And I've always done this – even from the beginning. When I had my first success, I started making donations – to hospitals, medical research, then the Playing Fields Association to bring the benefits of sport to the underprivileged . . .'

'I know you've been most generous.' I tried to convey a hint of impatience.

'I've done what I thought was right!' He raised his voice, then it subsided again into the earlier hesitant exploration. 'And all this time I was building up the business. It was a celibate existence, Simon, not unlike that of a monk. I drank nothing, tried to get as much sleep as possible, ignored women. Yet what was I worshipping?'

'Mammon?'

'Perhaps. So I balanced this with what you might describe as a private purity. Then something happened for which I was not prepared. I fell in love with your wife. And stole her from you. I took advantage of your negligence, even of your decency – in the way that I did with those who were in my way in business. I bought Laura.' And he sobbed, once or twice: an ugly coarse sound.

I was embarrassed. 'She went of her own free will,' I said gently.

'Do you think so?' Now he smiled, once more under control. 'I don't think you ever realised how hard I was pushing her. It was an act of robbery, Simon.'

'Couldn't you have settled the score simply by giving another couple of thousand to help battered wives – or perhaps, in this case, husbands?'

He ignored the feeble shaft. 'It was an aberration: an unpleasant descent into private greed and lust and ambition. And I saw what my three strongest feelings really were. Envy, lust and fear. Envy of you for having Laura as your wife. A lust for her, an extraordinary sensation that I had never felt before for anyone. And a fear of the way that these two – envy and lust – might take over my life, might make everything else that I was trying to do impossible because of their all-consuming strength. I hated that, Simon. And I had to have her for that reason; if I had not, I think that the obsession would have killed me.'

304

'And I was in the way?'

'Yes, I suppose you were.' Bill sighed, sank further into the sofa. Outside, the sunlight vanished behind a large grey cloud. The room darkened, its furniture and pictures merging into a sombre series of dull objects 'Then I thought: no, it needn't all be transformed into the coarseness of what I had momentarily shown myself to be. You see I had this vision of you and your business. Your selflessness, for instance. You think of books, of literature, of great writing as something that is above you personally, as a goal that is greater than your own personal needs or material success. They're like a religion to you.'

I interrupted. 'Bill . . .' I wondered if the death had caused him temporarily to lose his senses. Or was all this an elaborate evasion, a subtle way of deceiving me?

'That was what I admired, Simon. I persuaded Laura to leave you.' He sighed again. 'Well, you know what she was like. We should be honest. Like every human being she had weaknesses. She wanted the safety, the security of money. She wanted a little excitement, in the obvious sense of the word. Your life, your job and your increasing dedication to it – the way that you brought your work home with you, the way that you talked to her about poets and novelists she had never heard of, the way that you immersed yourself in it all for a miserable pittance of a salary – this mystified Laura. And I saw one thing immediately, at that party where we first met. I saw that she was bored.'

'What about the children, Bill?' I asked.

'The children?' He smiled. Suddenly he looked exhausted. 'Oh, the children. Well, you know about our little dis-appointment there. Laura and I couldn't . . . That is to say we weren't able to . . .'

I had heard all this before. 'I know, Bill; I know that. You told me some time ago.'

The fatigue gave way to anxiety. His thin lips parted in dismay. 'You said that you didn't mind me setting up the two trust funds: one for Edward, one for Angelica. You didn't mind me making over a proportion of what I had earned in order to give them a reasonable start in life.'

'I don't care about that. What else did you do for Angelica?'

To my surprise, Bill relaxed once more. 'I suppose – if I am truthful with myself – I wanted to make sure that the baseness which lay at the bottom of the way I had lured their mother away from you didn't in any way infect their lives. So I spent as much time with them as possible, lavished attention and money on what I imagined they might enjoy. I tried to get them interested in sport. I bought this house, put in the pool and the tennis court . . .'

'But you've always liked sailing. Bembridge is an ideal base for that.' I wanted to show that I was not quite the innocent he seemed to have in mind. 'This place seems to me to be a fair compromise between their needs and yours.'

He smiled. 'Don't be cynical, Simon. It doesn't suit you. Oh, what you say is partly true. But I wanted to do my best for them. And then what happened? The innocence went. That part of you which I hoped they might have retained – that disinterested working towards an ideal, the dedication to something outside yourself, so to speak, the freedom from everything that has brought me success and riches – that particular part either never existed or it was stifled by my example. See what they have become! Oh, I went on doing my best for them. I helped Edward find a job in a merchant bank after he left the army, I found a niche for Angelica in one of my companies because she said she wanted to go into financial services. But you must see this more than anyone. All those years of being with me – it's rubbed off. And I feel guilty. It's as if they've become tainted with my methods. All your side – the probity, the integrity, the tradition – has gone. And that was what I admired, what I wanted my descendants to be and to have.'

'And what good has it done me?' The cry was straight from the heart, jolted out in spite of myself, in spite of the reserve which I had hoped to maintain with this man. The ridiculous words – or words that seemed ridiculous in the light of the reality of my work and personal position in life – jarred against what I knew to be the truth. Probity, integrity, tradition! They rang out like a requiem for a vanished world, sunk beneath a tidal wave of sauna baths, gimmicky cookery books, brash attempts to turn philosophers into colour supplement heroes. Even my efforts to resurrect them seemed to crumble from within, victims of their own dullness like the

306

Palmerston biography. Docherty, I was left with Docherty: today's answer to the great names of the past. 'Yes,' I muttered, 'there is one man . . .'

Bill seemed not to have heard. 'You're upset, Simon,' he said. 'I can see that. But it can't have come as a complete surprise to you.'

'What?'

'Laura's death, of course.'

'I knew she was ill. But I had no idea it was so serious.'

'Serious!' Bill's voice rose in incredulity. 'Isn't cancer serious enough for you?'

'Cancer!'

'Yes, for heaven's sake, man – she'd had the disease diagnosed at least five years ago. The treatment started immediately. But that can be almost worse. The pain was almost unbearable at times. You can't blame her if she took steps to try to make herself forget. I turned a blind eye. The doctors did their best . . .'

'Why did nobody tell me?' I was angry.

'But, Simon, surely the children must have mentioned it. To be frank I thought they would be the best ones to break the news.'

'They said nothing.'

Bill spoke slowly. 'I tried to be with them as much as possible. Edward went away of course, to New York. At first I was against that. I thought he wasn't quite ready for it, that he should establish himself in the City first, absorb more of what one might call the basics of banking . . .'

'Bill, what about Angelica?'

'Naturally she was very upset. I think perhaps neither of us really appreciated how close she was to her mother. I tried to help as best I could. I wanted to see her properly settled in London, after university. After all, you know the risks for a girl of that age. I spent as much time with her as I could manage. Perhaps – if you will forgive me for saying so – it's easier for a step-father. He can say things that a father cannot, he can establish a dialogue – if you like – that is more frank. And Angelica came to trust me, I think. Then . . .' He threw one hand up again. 'We know what happened. Do you remember how she used to be rather anti-establishment, a little bit of a rebel? She became mixed up in student politics at university, used to speak challengingly to me when she came home. Do you know, Simon, I admired all that? There was an idealism, something beautiful in the vigour and certainty of her youthful dissent. Of course I know all about the history of your family. The Presbyterian tradition, the puritanical streak that Laura used to speak of in your own parents. And I thought: look, it's coming out in Angelica. I didn't mind how much she disapproved of me or what she thought I did or should be doing. Will you believe me when I say that I preferred it to what she has allowed herself to become? And I blame myself. Suddenly the wheel turned. She wanted money, success: the sort of things I could provide. She's hard, Simon, a little hard. You must see that.' Then his face changed, arched into a look of shock and doubt. 'But surely you don't think . . .'

'There is talk, Bill,' I said.

'From who?'

'Her friends. People who have seen you together.'

'And you believe it?'

Before I could answer, there was the sound of a door opening in the hall, followed by footsteps and low voices. I looked at Bill. The surprise in his face changed to a smile; then my two children ran in, Angelica and Edward. Bill and I stood. They went straight to him, grasped his arms or whatever part of him they could reach, kissed his face and held on to his hands. The girl was in tears; Edward and Bill comforted her, speaking softly, their words muffled by heartfelt sympathy. They saw me, turned back to their step-father, stood by him while he explained clearly and concisely what had happened. Edward said, 'Hello, Dad', and Angelica managed a tearful smile. Bill dropped his arms away from them. 'Come upstairs,' he said. And he raised his head so that his pitying eyes were trained on me from above. 'Then we'll talk to your father. He has suffered a loss as well.'

They went out. I looked around the white room, out to the sunlit garden where the branches of the trees moved gently in the soft wind. They were not long. Soon Bill, Angelica, Edward and I were sitting in that Bembridge drawing-room talking about Laura and the past. And I saw what was happening, I saw that Bill was serving as a line across which I could reach my children. He asked questions, smiled in the right places, nudged us towards a loving truthful recollection of the way she had been. This was marvellous. We were happy in our collective memory. So I hoped that he could provide another link, that his great fortune might be used simultaneously to preserve and to create. It was right that he should buy the company, that he should become the keeper of what it pleased him to think of as our ideals. Yet the premise was false; what existed was so different to what he wanted to believe had been or could ever be. Bill would be protecting a chimera, a dear shadow in his mind, a hulk of interest to historians and lovers of nostalgia that had to be sustained by millions brought in from outside.

Angelica kissed me twice. 'The deal should go through next week,' she said. 'You're not frightened, are you?'

'No,' I answered. 'You've all been so kind.'

That evening Henry and I drove back to London. I talked all the way and later in my flat, where he was kind enough to sit with me. 'You're right,' he said. 'The Erdley girl was lying. A spoilt little bitch, out to cause trouble. That's all.'

'She may have believed it. You did.'

'Me?' He giggled. 'That was simply an excess of literary imagination. I always look for drama, you know. For excitement. Writers lead such sedentary lives, don't they? How lucky you are not to be one. And you'll be taken care of as well. Editorial director at last! Aren't you pleased?' And he leaned over to pat me sharply on the knee.

The police were there, in the hall of the house when we came in. Two of them were standing on the stairs. I sighed. The typescript of the Palmerston biography and the direction from which it had descended would be unchallengeable evidence. It would be better to give oneself up. 'Here I am,' I said.

They looked at me, surprised: huge figures, the face of one almost invisible under his helmet, the other a bare-headed anxious youth. The door of the ground floor flat opened and three more policemen emerged carrying round metal containers and spools of film. They were followed by Richard and Jan – the unprepossessing couple – who seemed to be under the escort of a man in civilian dress. The man saw Henry and me, called to the men on the stairs, who went down to be with the couple. Then he approached us: a small dapper figure with meticulously combed short black hair. 'Another pair of customers?' he asked. The cynical smile was faint, a little threatening.

'Customers? My dear . . .' Henry began.

'For the film show?'

'Excuse me, officer,' I said, 'I live upstairs. What's going on?'

'I see.' He looked at me steadily, the smile dead; then decided I was an innocent. 'Well, sir, we've just closed down this little pleasure parlour. I expect you knew nothing about it, but your neighbours were in the entertainment business.'

'Entertainment? What sort of entertainment?'

'Of a rather intimate nature, sir. The sort of thing that appeals to what we might call man's baser instincts. You can get almost anything on video these days. Men, women, girls, boys, baboons, donkeys, parrots . . .'

'Parrots!' Henry let out a shriek.

'Oh yes, sir. Until you've seen this lot you don't realise what protected lives most of us lead. A veritable menagerie . . .'

I interrupted him. 'Could that have been the noise?' I asked.

'Noise?'

'Yes. Noises. Intimate noises.' I looked past the policeman, to the couple who stood – cowed, surly and pathetic – in the hall. 'Is that what it was?' I shouted.

The man – Richard – nodded. I laughed. A radio receiver, held by one of the policemen, crackled with a raucous message. Their leader listened. He frowned and said 'Let's take this lot in. If you'll excuse us. . .'; and they walked out of the building with their captives.

I turned to Henry. 'So it was dirty films,' I said. 'And I thought that someone had discovered true lasting ecstasy!'

He shook his head. 'Simon,' he said, 'you must grow up. There's no such thing. When will you learn? There is no ecstasy. No, I'm wrong. There is ecstasy, for an instant –

occasionally. Then, more important, there is life.' The line might have come from one of his books. 'But you're safe now. That's the important thing: safety.'

'Safety in the present,' I added. 'Here. Now. That's what I need.'

'And that's what you've got, at last. Look, you've had a long day, my dear. Isn't it about time you went to bed?'